"What are the demands?" Bolan asked.

"We're to pull out American support for Israel immediately. The Hezbollah wants us to break off all military and economic aid. And we're supposed to freeze Israeli assets already here." The President sighed and put the paper away.

A tense silence fell over the Stony Man group. Bolan knew each of the individuals was assessing the information in his own way. The demands threw all thoughts of a timetable to the winds. There was no way the U.S. could forfeit relations with Israel in light of the recent developments concerning Iraq and Kuwait.

Yakov Katzenelenbogen spoke in a voice filled with emotion. "Even a slight pullback of military aid as a feint is going to cost. The perceived weakness will only encourage the PLO and Shiite factions to join in the attack begun by the Hezbollah. They will be like vultures gathering for the kill."

"Rest assured, Yakov," the President said, "that I'm not ready to throw in the towel, even as a ploy to buy time."

"How much time do we have?" Bolan asked.

"Seventy-two hours," the President replied. "And the clock is ticking, gentlemen. Once the deadline is past, the hostages will start dying."

DON PENDLETON's

MACK BOLAN®

STONY MAN II

A GOLD EAGLE BOOK FROM
WORLDWIDE®

TORONTO • NEW YORK • LONDON • PARIS
AMSTERDAM • STOCKHOLM • HAMBURG
ATHENS • MILAN • TOKYO • SYDNEY

First edition May 1991

ISBN 0-373-61886-7

Special thanks and acknowledgment to
Mel Odom for his contribution to this work.

STONY MAN II

Printed in U.S.A.

STONY MAN II

CHAPTER ONE

Tel Aviv, Israel

First Day

From his position in the rear section of the military two-and-a-half-ton truck, Mossad agent Lieutenant David Efrat peered through the grimy windshield at the night sky. A pale quarter moon veiled with wispy dark clouds hung over the city. The street was empty, filled only by the noise of the lumbering armored vehicle. A glance at the radio assured him that it was still in working order. The driver and the soldier in the passenger seat were grimly alert, Galil assault rifles canted forward for instant use. Satisfied, Efrat pushed himself against the backrest of his seat, taking care not to meet his prisoner's eyes.

The Israeli agent reached into the pocket of his shirt, pulled out a pack of cigarettes and a lighter and lit up. The flame wavered blue and yellow against his palms. His expelled stream of smoke blew it out before he snapped the lid closed. Unwillingly his gaze traveled to the man on the other side of the truck.

"You fear me, don't you?" The voice was soft, scarcely a whisper above the rumbling of the truck's transmission. The accent was Middle Eastern.

Efrat didn't reply. He took another drag of his cigarette and exhaled a cloud of smoke that gently engulfed the prisoner.

"You don't have to answer me," the soft voice went on. "I can see your answer for myself. Your body speaks out to me."

In the darkness of the covered deuce-and-a-half, Dr. Fahad Rihani didn't look especially frightening. Efrat had fought much bigger men, had killed them, as well. The man was thin to the point of emaciation, making his bald head seem too large for his body. His unkempt beard was as black as coal, yet it seemed light in contrast to his magnetic black gaze.

For a moment Efrat was drawn to his prisoner's stare, feeling that he was standing on the edge of a bottomless abyss, unable to keep from throwing himself in. He tore his gaze away with effort and felt phantom pains of nausea in the pit of his stomach.

Rihani chuckled softly. He shifted, dragging his chains across the metal bench welded into the back of the truck.

Efrat shivered despite himself. The mocking chuckle held more naked threat than the snick of a rifle bolt being drawn back. He dropped his hand to his holstered pistol, but drew no comfort from the familiar feel of the weapon. There was no comfort, either, in the knowledge that Rihani's wrists and ankles were bound by chains. A person couldn't expect to truly bind evil. His mother had told him that when he was a child, and he still believed it. Only God was strong enough to wipe true evil from the lives of men. He resisted the impulse to take out his service automatic and give God a hand only because his superiors had said Rihani was worth more alive than dead, that the man held secrets to aid them against the United States and Russia if it came to that. Efrat didn't think so. The Mossad had been trying to get answers out of the Hezbollah leader since his capture in Beirut in 1983. They had yet to show anything for their efforts.

"Why am I being moved again so soon?" Rihani asked.

Efrat continued with his cigarette, leaving his hand to rest on the butt of his pistol.

"My people are getting closer to finding me, aren't they?"

The Mossad agent said nothing, wishing the cold fingers trailing down his spine would leave him.

"I felt the explosions last night," Rihani said in his dry, whispering voice. "Even in my cell I heard the gunshots."

The truck took a corner. Efrat held his cigarette in his lips while he used his hand to cling to the strap over his head. Rihani seemed to flow with the motion like an eerie, multi-jointed creature wrapped in shadows.

"They won't give up," Rihani said.

Efrat glanced at his watch, counting the minutes until he would be free of his present assignment, swearing to himself that he would get drunk at the first opportunity.

"They'll keep coming until they find me and free me," Rihani went on. "And together we'll keep pushing Israel into the sea."

"That will *never* happen. Never!"

Rihani smiled, a white crescent in the dark matted beard.

Efrat was immediately angry with himself, realizing the Hezbollah leader was only trying to elicit some kind of response. A hot flush crept up his face when he recognized that his present emotional state came from the stories he'd been told about the psychologist rather than a rational fear of the man. Other Mossad agents named Rihani as an expert in mind control. They whispered that Rihani could take a few chemicals, a few hours, the tone of his voice, the power in his eyes, and break most men. In fact, he'd seen tapes himself of men whom Rihani had demolished. The images that came into his mind sickened him, full of broken and twisted things that knew neither God nor country.

"It will happen all too soon," Rihani said.

Before he knew what he was doing, Efrat had his side arm in his hand. The safety snicked off with a sharp, metallic click. The muzzle was unwavering as the Mossad agent trained it between Rihani's eyes.

Cold black fires gazed back at him. There was no fear in Rihani's face, only a dark amusement.

Efrat's arm trembled under the weight of the pistol. Perspiration trickled down his face, and the air in the truck suddenly seemed too thick to breathe. "No," he said in a hoarse voice. "It will never happen. Israel will prevail."

"Kill me, Jew," Rihani taunted.

Efrat felt the involuntary pressure well up in his hand. His finger took up a pound and a half of the two-pound pull, then it stopped. His breath shuddered out. He tasted the salt of perspiration on his lips, then forced himself to speak. "Shut up and leave me alone, or I'll do what should have been done a long time ago."

Rihani smiled and shook his head. His chains rattled with him. "Empty threats." He held up his manacled hands and laughed. The sound was cold and mocking. "You're afraid of me. Even when you have me chained, even peering over the sights of your weapon, you fear me."

Efrat released the trigger, left the safety off and stuffed the pistol into his hip holster. He wiped his face with a handkerchief. The coal of the cigarette was so close to his lip that it burned. He spit the butt out and crushed it under his boot.

"You're correct in being afraid of me," Rihani said. "Perhaps it will even save your life."

Efrat took his walkie-talkie from his belt and keyed it up.

"Provided you can get far enough away from me in time."

"Rover One, this is Control. Come in. Over." Efrat looked away from his prisoner, concentrating on the security net around the truck. Only minutes remained before the transit was completed. His damp shirt clung to his back.

"Control, this is Rover One. Go ahead. Over."

"Security verification only. Condition green. Over."

"Check, Control. Rover One out."

Efrat hit the key again. "Rover Two, report. Over."

"Roger the security verification, Control. Rover Two out."

"Rover Three, report. Over."

"Roger, Control. Condition green. Rover Three out."

Efrat clipped the walkie-talkie back on his belt. He felt naked without an assault rifle, but keeping track of more than one weapon with his prisoner so near was foolish.

"Empty threats," Rihani said, "and insecurities. Your people should have picked someone stronger. How old are you, boy?"

Refusing to be drawn into the conversation, Efrat glanced back up through the dirty windshield. The street was still empty, but somewhere close by, Rovers One, Two and Three would be cruising silently through the night in black sedans.

"I'd wager you haven't seen thirty yet."

Efrat concentrated on the street, trying to ignore both the man's words and the uneasy feeling in the pit of his stomach.

A slight concussion washed over the vehicle, and the driver's head snapped to his left in an effort to track it. Efrat pulled his weapon and stood, keying the walkie-talkie again. "Rover One, this is Control. Report. Over." He was aware of Rihani coiled on the metal bench like an old and leathery snake.

An ancient sedan swept into view from a side street, running with its lights off. As another explosion buffeted the deuce-and-a-half, a half-dozen men swarmed from the sedan, brandishing automatic weapons.

"Control, this is Rover Two. Rover One has been taken out. They've been hit with a LAW warhead. Repeat—Rover One is down. Over."

Efrat tangled his gun hand in a restraining strap as the driver took evasive action. He keyed the walkie-talkie. "Close in. Close in now. Over." He returned the set to his belt, yelling at the other soldier to radio for the away teams. The truck staggered through the street, clipping the front end of the sedan and locking into it. Metal screeched as the sedan was dragged along.

Without warning a third explosion lifted the front end of the vehicle off the ground and slammed it onto its side. Efrat was thrown to the floor. Dazed, he groped for his pistol, then realized it had been torn from him by the restraining strap. Chains rasped along a metal surface. Before he could get away he felt the cold teeth of the links biting into his neck, cutting off his breath. Rihani's strength was unbelievable. He tried to drive his elbows back into the man's rib cage and break the hold, but Rihani's body seemed to be impervious to pain.

More explosions echoed through the area.

Vision blurring, Efrat knew the driver and the soldier in the front seat had been killed instantly. He was aware of the dark shapes crawling in through the driver's window, shoving the torn corpse out of their way. Kicking out with his legs, he managed to hook his fingers into the chain but couldn't get the proper leverage to break the hold. A black sea roared up out of his mind and enveloped him. His neck broke only seconds after his windpipe gave in to the crushing pressure.

CHAPTER TWO

Beirut, Lebanon

First Day—1:38 a.m.

Mack Bolan rode in the passenger seat of the low-slung, bullet-scarred sports car, scanning the war-torn city streets. Ahead, the sedan they pursued made a left turn. Tracking was relatively easy—one of the ruby covers over the taillights had been smashed out, leaving the unmistakable white glare of the bulb.

"They've picked up a friend," Bolan said to the driver.

A flatbed truck skated from a dark alley and fell into place behind the sedan. White smoke belched from the tailpipe as the driver changed gears.

"Do you think they've made us?" Mossad agent Arella Hirschfeld asked in her quiet voice.

"I don't know," Bolan replied, "but we're not going to take any chances." He reached down to the floorboard, sliding his palm over the pair of Uzis tucked away there, grabbed the radio and keyed the mike. "Eagle One."

"Go." The voice belonged to Jack Grimaldi, a longtime friend and fellow soldier in Mack Bolan's everlasting war.

"They're making a party out of it," Bolan told him. "They caught a late hanger-on who might have noticed us, so your team is on deck."

"We're on it, Striker."

Bolan put down the radio and watched as the panel wagon containing Grimaldi and his Mossad counterpart slid smoothly into the traffic behind the sedan and flatbed. He tapped the top of the dashboard with his fingers. "Okay, we're out of here."

Hirschfeld turned right onto a side street.

The Executioner pulled his map case from an inside pocket of his leather bomber jacket, flipped it open, then used a pocket flash to glance at the street map of the area. His previous briefing with the Mossad had added to his store of information concerning ground conditions in Beirut.

"It looks as if your intelligence is on the money," Hirschfeld commented.

"With the source I have it usually is."

"Perhaps you and your partner will earn back the risks we took in getting here tonight." Hirschfeld gazed at him coolly.

The Executioner gave her a wintry smile. "Consider it professional courtesy, lady. We could've come in under our own power and left under the same."

"But you didn't. Instead you arranged for a Mossad team to accompany you here, where—according to your government—we have no need to be."

Bolan called out directions, and the vehicle took a sharp left turn.

"A more suspicious people might think this was all a scheme to discredit us in the eyes of the world."

The warrior dragged his gaze from the bombed-out shells of cube-shaped buildings and stared at her full measure. "I didn't miss the secondary team waiting in the wings tonight when we skipped across the border."

Her laughter was full and honest. "I didn't think you did. I told my superiors it would be risky trying to slip two teams through the border guards while in pursuit of a possible Hezbollah raiding party."

Bolan warmed to the Mossad agent a little, realizing this was her first effort to come clean with him since the infiltration began.

"You have to know my country to understand it," she said, cutting neatly across the street to dash through a gap in upended trash containers. "With the new friendship your country has found with the Russians," Hirschfeld went on, "the feeling in Israel is that you've abandoned us in a precarious position."

"You haven't been abandoned," Bolan replied. He checked his watch and glanced at the map when he saw a street sign that had somehow been left intact. "Go left. Let's try to intercept them for a drive-by and see if we know any of the players in the truck."

Hirschfeld pulled the little car around hard left. Bolan had to brace himself as the vehicle slewed around the corner.

"My orders were to kill you if I felt you were setting me or my team up," the woman said conversationally. She paused at the corner, glancing down at the approaching sedan and flatbed.

"And?"

She smiled at him, but it was thin and filled only with dark humor. "You're still alive." She put her foot to the accelerator, and the vehicle's engine responded smoothly, shoving them out across the traffic.

Leaving the driving in the woman's capable hands, Bolan scanned the occupants of the flatbed with a compact pair of night vision goggles. Pale emerald greens brought the view into flat relief. One of the men was known to him from Hezbollah files Kurtzman had assembled at Stony Man Farm.

"Well?" Hirschfeld prompted.

Bolan put the NVG away as he reached for the radio. "Coman."

Hirschfeld nodded. "Explosives expert."

"Right."

"We're onto something big."

"That's what I was thinking." Bolan keyed the mike. "Eagle One."

"Go."

"Your secondary target has just assumed primary importance."

"Check."

"You've got a confirmed earth-shaker on board."

"Roger. Give me the go and he's history."

"Hold off until we see what their objective is. I'm not sure all the players are in yet."

"On your mark, Striker."

"Understood." Bolan checked the contents of his map case again. The numbers were falling fast now, accelerating to the point of no return. The night was going to go ballistic, and there wasn't a damn thing he could do about it except to try to cut the losses. According to a ghost of intel that had turned up on Stony Man Farm's computers through reliable sources, Hezbollah had picked tonight to attempt a kidnapping raid on American and European citizens in Beirut. Evidently Kurtzman's hard-wired faithful companions were panning out again.

"Striker," Hirschfeld mused.

He turned to her and found her staring at him.

"Somehow," she said, "I find that name more fitting for you than the one on the communiqué from your President."

"Like the man said, 'A rose by any other name...'"

"Oh, you're definitely no rose. Military, yes, but something quite a bit more. I've seen eyes like yours—not the color exactly, but of the same cold intensity—among the more seasoned Mossad pros."

"Comes with a hard life," he said with a gentle smile.

"No." She shook her dark hair. "No, it comes from seeing too much death. I feel for you," Hirschfeld continued. "You've made the struggle—whatever struggle possesses you—your life. You measure its passage in battles, won or lost. There's no thought of your future ever in your mind." She looked away. "Even in Israel it hasn't gotten so bad for most of us that we can't dream of another life. I, myself, am married. My husband is a captain in the army. Soon, perhaps, we hope to have children."

"I wish you well."

"I know. That's why I told you. Sometimes we need to be reminded that something is coming of our efforts."

The radio squawked.

"Go," Bolan said into the mike.

"Course change, Striker."

"Give."

Grimaldi called it.

"He's coming our way," Bolan said. "Back off and run parallel while we pick him up."

Hirschfeld was already making driving adjustments.

"They're yours, Striker."

Consulting the map case, Bolan said, "I know where they're headed." He glanced up in time to see the flatbed and sedan pass by. The woman was on them immediately, riding low behind a ten-year-old Chevy luxury car.

"The Ambassador Hotel," Hirschfeld said.

"Yeah." Bolan flipped open his warbook, dragging a forefinger down the computer printout listings Kurtzman had drawn up for him at Stony Man. He flipped the page, found the Ambassador Hotel and read the names.

"U.S. and British journalists," Hirschfeld said, "American, Soviet and British businessmen all looking to make deals in the Middle East to offset trade relations everywhere else in the world."

"You missed the West Germans," Bolan remarked as he put his warbook away.

"There are only a few, and not really worth holding as hostages yet. Later, perhaps, once the German economic growth has leveled off and spread into other countries more."

Bolan keyed the radio. "Eagle One."

"Go."

"Target confirmation, guy."

"The Ambassador Hotel."

"You called it."

"Damien Gray's staying there, too, Striker. Be a hell of a prize if they can pull it off. Gray's visit to Kuwait was publicized to death in the States, and the public adores him right now. He's the fair-haired reporter who can do no wrong when it comes to exposing government corruption in high places."

Bolan knew either way it went, the investigative reporter was going to have an explosive story to tell, whether it was the kidnap attempt itself, or the fact that it was foiled by a covert force of Americans and Israelis. "On my signal."

"You got it."

The Executioner reached under the seat and came up with an Uzi. He dragged free a web belt with extra clips for the machine pistol and grenades, then cinched it around his waist. Hirschfeld raised her elbows as she drove so that he could hook hers, as well.

The warrior slipped a hand inside his leather jacket and loosened the Detonics .45 Scoremaster in the shoulder holster.

Hirschfeld downshifted, wrapping the engine tightly as she powered around the car in front of her. She shifted back up, quickly closing the distance to the flatbed truck. The wicked snout of an assault rifle poked through the passenger window.

Bolan scooped up the radio. "We're made." He dropped it immediately, cradling the Uzi in his arms.

Responding to Hirschfeld's quick reflexes, the sports car swerved, heeling away from the right side of the truck as a row of bullets chipped into the bomb-pocked street. The muzzle-flash was a continuous blur while staccato thunder rolled across the street.

The Executioner triggered his weapon in even bursts, taking out the double sets of rear tires. The flatbed started wobbling as the rubber came loose. The rear end swung out and clipped the front end of the sports car as Bolan focused on the rear window. The flatbed's greater weight and height lent more power to the impact. The little car shivered as the right headlight shattered and spilled away.

Another burst from the Executioner's Uzi struck sparks from the cab of the flatbed, then the clip ran dry. He rammed a fresh magazine home as the truck driver began a zigzag motion that, with the shredded tires, left the flatbed careening drunkenly.

"Get around him," Bolan directed.

"I'm trying."

Glancing ahead of the flatbed, Bolan saw the sedan speed up and pull away from the truck. He keyed the radio's mike. "Close it in. Now. Let's get these people boxed and neutralized."

The other four Mossad teams responded at once.

Bolan held the mike toward Hirschfeld. "We need that secondary team."

She nodded, then jerked the wheel hard right as the flatbed driver sideswiped the sports car again. Metal ground against metal, sending a shower of sparks flying into Bolan's window. Autofire raked the back of the sports car. Using the Uzi one-handed while Hirschfeld barked orders into the radio, the Executioner tracked a solid stream of 9 mm parabellums into the shooter. The corpse hung halfway out the window until the man next to it shoved it out onto the road.

The flatbed driver pulled hard left, smashing into the sports car and almost pushing it off the street. Unable to make the turn, the truck crashed through a boarded-over plate-glass window of an abandoned building.

Bolan keyed the radio. "Jack."

"We got the mop-up detail here, Striker. Keep going. We'll catch up."

Bolan changed clips again, then rerouted the street map of the area in his mind, calling out directions.

Hirschfeld responded automatically. "You don't think the Hezbollah team will break off after this?"

"No. Where are those backup teams?"

"I don't know. They had orders to stay well back of the action unless I called."

Bolan ran the numbers on the three remaining teams, and none could pick up an intercept course faster than they were. "It looks like it's you and me for the moment."

He placed her Uzi between the bucket seats, then acknowledged the radio.

"We're finished up here," Grimaldi informed him. "We found a rocket launcher with a half-dozen rounds behind the seat."

"Keep moving, Jack."

"A stationary target is a dead target, Striker. I read you loud and clear."

Hirschfeld said, "The Lebanese military will be moving on this now in conjunction with the Syrians." She downshifted, caught a corner with the rear end floating loose, then powered up to make a frantic grab at traction.

"You saying you want you and your team out of this?"

"No, but exfiltration is going to have to be damn quick. When I call it, you go with us, or you and your friend find your own way home."

"Agreed."

The sedan wavered into view as the sports car roared onto the street in front of the hotel. Doors opened and men with automatic weapons leaped from the interior. A helicopter flashed by overhead. An object was jettisoned from the chopper's open cargo bay, then an explosion ripped brick, mortar and glass from the steel skeleton of the hotel and threw it directly into the path of the sports car.

There was no time for Hirschfeld and Bolan to brace themselves for the collision.

CHAPTER THREE

Tel Aviv, Israel

First Day—1:52 a.m.

Feeling the slack length of the Mossad agent's corpse against him, Dr. Fahad Rihani released a pent-up breath and struggled to get out from under the deadweight. He gazed at the shadowy figures approaching him through the smoky haze rising up from the overturned truck. Their manner of dress didn't indicate their nationality, but the weapons in their hands were Israeli.

One of the three shadows froze, then said, "Dr. Rihani. We're with Badr Faisel and are here to free you."

"Here," Rihani called, shoving the corpse from him.

The man reached out a hand and helped him to his feet. "Are you okay?"

"I think so."

"Praise be to God."

"Praise be to God," Rihani echoed. He held up his manacled hands. "Do you have a key to these, brother?"

"No, but I'll make one." The man smiled, a white gleam in a smooth face, and held up a pistol. He knelt to attend to the chains.

Sporadic gunfire sounded on the street. A man cried out in agony, then a lone shot cracked and the moaning vanished.

"Where's your beard?" Rihani asked. The Israeli interrogators had been at him for years, and he still bore the scars of their attempts to break him. Paranoia was only one of the less visible. No Hezbollah man went willingly without his beard. Even with the dead Mossad agent in his arms, he was too aware that this could prove to be yet another Israeli trick to deceive him. Once he truly saw Faisel, then he'd know.

"Sacrificed, brother," the man replied. "But now that you are free, it will be allowed to grow again. Stand steady, please, and may God guide my arm and my eye."

"May it be so," Rihani said, turning his face away from the chains.

The shot sounded unnaturally loud and left him with a temporary deafness. Cordite stung his nostrils. The manacles jerked against his wrist almost painfully. He pulled at the chains and found them to be still secure.

"Stand away, brother," another man ordered.

Rihani looked at the newcomer through eyes slitted against the dust filling the rear of the truck. "Numair?"

"Yes, it's me, Dr. Rihani." Numair grinned, brandishing the fire ax he carried. His Uzi was slung over his shoulder. "Hezbollah has grown from the time you've been taken from us, grown strong and powerful." He stepped closer, hefting the ax expertly.

The first man retreated to the cab of the truck to stand guard. The third man was sheathing his bloody curved knife, staring down in satisfaction at the throat of the guard.

Numair brought the ax crashing down. The chain links sheared with a metallic screech as the head of the ax buried itself in the metal bench.

Rihani tested the links and found them free. "Now the legs, brother."

"As God wills," Numair said. The ax fell twice more, then the chains were no more.

Lightness of being touched Rihani, and he gloried in it, giving himself a moment to drink in his newly acquired freedom. To be truly shorn of his shackles was a thing he hadn't dreamed of in years. He'd only concentrated on survival, to further chip away at the confidence of the Israelis. The Mossad could only guess at the things he knew, couldn't begin to measure the power he could ultimately control given the opportunity. The plan he had set into motion within the Hezbollah years ago could flower again.

"Are you well?" Numair asked.

In the darkness Numair resembled a young and towering jinni born of desert legends Rihani had heard while still a child. "Yes. It took a moment for the reality of this to settle over me. Let's go." He held the ends of his ankle chains in his hands as he stepped over the body of the Mossad agent. Numair climbed out the door, then reached back in and pulled Rihani free with one hand.

The liberated terrorist stood on the wreckage of the vehicle's cab and breathed in deeply. The desert air rolling in from the sea tasted of freedom itself. The myriad stars had never seemed so bright. And the anguish and loss that fueled his need for revenge had never burned so hot.

"Dr. Rihani," Numair said in a gentle voice, "we must go. We were successful in destroying the three Mossad cars guarding this truck, but there will be more. We couldn't have killed them all before they alerted someone."

"I know," Rihani replied. He watched as Numair dropped effortlessly to the ground, then allowed himself to be helped down.

"The tape, brother," Numair said to one of the other men. He used gray duct tape to bind Rihani's chains farther up his arms and legs and allow freer movement. "I wish that there was another way."

"For now," Rihani said, "it's enough." He accepted the dark coveralls he was offered and pulled them on, embarrassed to be seen dressing even like this in front of the other men.

Numair called six men forward, then turned to Rihani. "These men go with God tonight so that you may continue your escape."

The six men dropped to their knees before him, their automatic weapons clenched in their fists.

Wailing sirens sliced the air.

"May God be with you," Rihani said, "and keep you forever in His love." He touched his fingers to his forehead, then to his heart.

Numair clapped his hands, and the men sprang for the three cars in groups of twos. They headed down the street in different directions, yelling and firing their weapons.

Rihani knew they were honestly happy. Not many men knew the precise time they were going to meet their God. He glanced at Numair. "And our escape?"

"On foot, Dr. Rihani, so that we won't draw as much attention. And it's only a short distance."

"Then lead on."

Numair barked an order, and the remaining four men fanned out and vanished into the night. "We're going to the central bus station," the young man said. "God willing, Badr Faisel and the others will be waiting for us."

"May it be so," Rihani said. He took the lead automatically. A street map of Tel Aviv had been burning in his mind for almost a decade. He used conversations, notes, anything that he saw or heard to add to that store of knowledge during his imprisonment. The central bus station was on Levinsky Street, less than two kilometers from their present position. His feet were sore and unshod, but he ignored the pain. Whatever pain he felt now, whatever he had felt, would be returned a thousandfold to the Israelis in only a few short days.

"Wait." Numair stopped, reached inside his coveralls pocket and pulled out a flare gun. Aiming it at the overturned military truck, he pulled the trigger.

The flare streaked from the gun and exploded against the truck. Flames leaped up suddenly, and whooshing noises reached Rihani's ears. An explosion ruptured the truck's gas tanks and shook the vehicle like a terrier shaking a rat. It came to rest on its side again, consumed by fire.

Numair tossed the useless flare gun aside, then wrapped his arm again in the sling of the Uzi. "The alley," he suggested. "It's better to stay away from the main roads."

The sound of a pitched gun battle whipped through the streets.

Producing a square box, Numair touched a toggle switch, and a circular screen flared to green life in his hand. From his quick glance, Rihani assumed the box to be some kind of tracking device. "One of the cars has been stopped," Numair told him. "No, two of them have."

A muffled explosion sounded behind them, echoing eerily through the alley.

"They've completely destroyed one of the vehicles," Numair said. "It'll take them longer to verify, but soon they'll know you didn't escape that way."

His throat dry from anticipation he was unwilling to feel, Rihani slowed down as they neared the entrance of the bus station. The odor of rotting vegetables gave the air a musty sweetness that was almost intolerable. He lifted an arm and breathed through the cloth of his sleeve.

Numair tossed the tracking device into an overflowing trash can. "They've apprehended the last car."

Numair glanced across the unlit street, and Rihani followed his gaze, seeing the dim shadow of a figure standing by the bus station entrance.

Numair pulled a lighter from a pocket and flicked it once. Another shadowy figure advanced on the first, and took the man out. A brief light flared back.

"Come," Numair whispered, waving him across the street. His Uzi was brandished openly now. Whatever remained of resistance or interception would have to be faced down.

Reaching for the last of his flagging strength, Rihani kept pace with the man, skirting the dead security guard who lay outside the gate house. More men, obviously Hezbollah from the unruly shagginess of their beards, moved between the huge buses well away from the main offices.

Fluorescent lights bounced off the white-and-gray enamel sides of the buses. The rumble of diesel engines filled the night, limiting the sirens to occasional peeps. The air was thick with exhaust fumes.

"Here."

Rihani tracked the voice out of the darkness, recognizing it at once. He slid down the side of a large bus to meet the man coming toward him. "Badr."

"Yes, Fahad, it's me." Faisel wrapped his bearlike arms around Rihani and gave him a fierce hug, his eyes glistening with tears. "God take their eyes for what these cursed people have done to you," Faisel said vehemently. "You're withered and almost dead."

"Wrong, my brother. They only succeeded in wearing away everything in me that didn't hate them with enough fierceness to live despite their tortures. I'm purer for the loss of flesh and earthly wants. I live only so that they may die."

"As it ever was, my brother."

"As it ever shall be."

Faisel pushed him up the steps of the nearest bus. "Quickly. We have no time to lose."

Nearly a dozen men sat in the shadows of the bus. Three others followed Faisel up the steps, carrying the body of the gatekeeper. Another corpse sat wide-eyed in the first seat. The body was jacketless, and a small trickle of blood dripped from a bullet hole in one temple.

Numair took a gray jacket from a compatriot, slipped it on and took his seat behind the steering wheel. His big hands slid over the controls, bringing the throbbing diesel engine to sudden life. His Uzi was beside him on the seat.

Rihani sat with Faisel halfway back in the bus. "How did you find me, Brother?"

"Even the Mossad can't keep secrets forever," his old friend replied. "Especially from the Americans, who still trust too much in the strength of their dollar. Just as the Israelis have been hiding you all these long years, we've been searching for you. Though you've been gone, the jihad has progressed. Tonight, while we're effecting your rescue here, more of our brothers are taking American, British and Soviet hostages in different cities, different countries. We've found a loose unity with different factions of the PLO. The Muslim world has changed of late. No longer are all the countries content to sit back and let the Western world pick over our bones. Once I knew you would be returned to us, I put our plans into motion. Others who find out you're once again leading the holy war against the Israelis will come to stand with us.''

The bus lurched toward the gatehouse, then smoothed out as it accelerated. Numair paused at the street, opening the door to allow another man entrance. The vehicle got under way immediately again.

"It isn't the same," Faisel said, "without the KGB. Much has changed since you were taken from us."

"I know of this new friendship between Russia and the United States from my talks with the Israelis," Rihani replied. "I knew this day would come when our Russian supporters would desert us because of their own failing economy. They no longer know of the fires banked by their own heritage. They seek only the power of wealth. They don't see money as a god that will ultimately eat them and suck the marrow from their shattered bones.''

The air brakes hissed, and Numair pulled over to the side of the street. Three cars passed in different directions as two men got out carrying rolled bundles.

Rihani watched in the reflection of a building window as the man on the right unrolled his bundle and spread it across the bus logo. Magnetic strips obviously held it in place. The characters were Hebrew, reading Magic Bus, a special charter line that ran between major cities. The men quickly reboarded, and Numair pushed the bus into gear again.

"In case deception fails, my brother," Faisel said, "we always have these." He slapped the stubby barrel of his Uzi. "You must rest now while you can," he added.

Rihani shook his head, denying himself any thoughts of rest, feeding off the hatred and need for revenge that had kept him alive so long. "No, there's much to be done. Israel's destruction has to begin tonight even as I regain the life they sought to rend from me. Tell me of the hostage gathering.''

CHAPTER FOUR

Beirut, Lebanon

First Day—2:13 a.m.

"Hang on!" Arella Hirschfeld shouted. Bits and pieces of mortar, brick and glass slammed across the hood and windshield of the sports car, then the acceleration of the turbo engine pressed Mack Bolan against the seat. The right rear tire blew, throwing the car into an uncontrolled skid.

The Executioner ground the radio at his feet into a mass of broken plastic and electrical wires rather than leave it behind intact to be used against them. He slid an ear/throat mike system from the pocket of his leather bomber jacket and put it on, pressing the button to bring it to life even as he evacuated the vehicle.

Hirschfeld was on her feet a heartbeat later, her Uzi cradled in her arms.

Bolan blinked up into the descending cloud of dust and smoke. Gaping holes stared through the side of the hotel. Fires burned brightly, illuminating rooms that had been wrecked by the explosion if not destroyed altogether. The hotel towered twenty-plus stories, a giant among the buildings around it. Whirling high overhead, the helicopter continued to circle like a vulture waiting for its prey's last kick of life.

He looked at Hirschfeld. "They've got ground teams on-site," he said grimly. "They don't intend to walk away empty-handed. We only touched the tip of the iceberg with the people we turned up."

"I know." A thin line of blood ran from the corner of her mouth. "We go in."

Bolan nodded and tapped the transmit button. "Eagle one."

"Go."

"ETA?"

"Now, Striker. That's us coming around the corner."

The panel wagon carrying Grimaldi and two Mossad agents squealed around the corner, braking to a sudden halt when they saw parts of the hotel blocking the street.

Bolan sprinted forwards, taking the lead. There was no doubt in his mind about Hirschfeld's ability. If she wasn't suited to this type of close-in work, her people wouldn't have sent her.

"Ground teams are inside," he said into his throat mike. "They also own the pigeon in the sky."

Grimaldi and his companions left the panel wagon and headed for the hotel. "And to think of the bitches and complaints most people have about park statues," the pilot quipped.

"Captain Hirschfeld," one of the Mossad agents called.

"Here," Hirschfeld said into her mike.

Bolan took up a position outside the warped lobby doors, peering across the jagged remnants of glass in the frames and across the hallway.

"Your orders?"

"For now," Hirschfeld replied, "the American's in charge." She took up a position on the other side of the lobby doors.

Bolan tripped the transmit button. "Jack?"

"Go."

"You and your team have the outside of the building."

"Gonna be tough sledding, Striker. Lot of people are going to be trying to go to ground."

"Can't take the chance our targets are going to be doing the same."

"That's a big helicopter up there."

"Not that big—count on it. The play just got dicey with our arrival."

"Could be Hezbollah is just looking for a few good men."

"Maybe, but I never like the odds on drawing to an inside straight. And maybe with us feeding intel back and forth we'll get a better picture of what it's like inside."

"We're on it now."

Bolan cleared, fisting the Uzi as he turned the corner and slithered through the glassless door. He drew gunfire at once, going to ground in a diving shoulder roll that brought him up locking target acquisition on the Arab behind the main counter. Taking no chances with Hirschfeld already on the move, he stitched a neat figure eight into the man's body.

People streamed into the lobby in various stages of undress, yelling in terror in at least a half-dozen languages. Smaller explosions sounded in the floors above, and plaster dust floated to the ground in waves. Bolan identified the new concussions as grenades, indicating that Hezbollah's itinerary was a program for mass destruction.

The Executioner paused against the bank of elevators. A trio of lights were descending. Another was frozen in place. He caught the door of the nearest one as it opened. Hirschfeld's voice echoed in her ear as she coordinated her team, bringing up the reserves. Bolan motioned the cage's occupants out with the Uzi, and they double-timed it out into the lobby. He stepped inside, followed immediately by his partner, and punched up the twenty-third floor. He hit the transmit button. "Jack?"

"Go."

"Give me a twenty."

"Second floor and feeling like a salmon fighting my way upstream. I've had to bust a couple of guys playing hero. Christ, we've almost been taken out by the good guys. If I'd tattooed a big red *S* on my chest like my mother wanted, I wouldn't have to deal with this shit right now."

"Stats."

"We're hurting, but we're moving."

Bolan cleared. The light indicator showed the third floor as the cage began to stop. Hirschfeld had the control panel cover off. A small throwing knife was in her hand, baring wires. Sparks flew, but she ignored them.

The warrior stepped in front of the opening door as a handful of men and women tried to get on. Most of them saw the weapons and backed away. "This cage is going up," Bolan said, "and that's the last place you people want to go."

A thin man with styled hair muscled his way to the front of the crowd. "American journalist, pal, and the top's exactly where I want to go. I've been dying for an exclusive."

Bolan's voice was graveyard-still as he put a hand on the man's chest. "You might get your chance to do just that someday, but right now you'll have to find your own transportation." He pushed, and the man went stumbling back to land on his butt.

The door closed and the cage started up again, increasing speed past the normal limit.

"I rewired it," Hirschfeld said. "This cage will only be responsive to this panel now. There won't be any more unscheduled stops."

The cage continued to gain speed, pressing down heavily against Bolan's body. Reviewing the list of names Kurtzman's computers had spit out concerning the hotel's guests, the soldier made a mental assessment of which guests would be targeted for a quick snatch. Damien Gray's name headed the list. According to the files Kurtzman had given him, Bolan knew the investigative reporter was somewhere on the twenty-third floor.

A line of bullet holes blasted into the cage, zipping it from top to bottom in an unforgiving assault. The Executioner went to ground at once, rolling into a combat-ready position. Hirschfeld had almost mirror-imaged him on the other side of the cage.

"They know we're coming," Hirschfeld said unnecessarily.

The light indicator showed floor nineteen. The ascent was slowing.

"We're going to be sitting ducks for anyone on that floor when the doors open," the Mossad agent stated.

"Not entirely," Bolan said as he regained his feet.

The light indicator showed floor twenty-one.

The warrior reached above his head with the haft of his Cold Steel Tanto combat knife and broke the light fixture in the elevator's ceiling. Darkness cloaked the elevator cage. He resheathed the knife on the web belt, then pulled an SAS-styled flash-bang concussion grenade from his gear. "We're just going to have to make our shots count."

At the twenty-third floor the elevator cage came to a stop with a sudden lurch that almost threw them off their feet. The doors came open with a bell tone that was almost lost in the sudden barrage of autofire.

A HUMAN TIDE TRIED to wash over Jack Grimaldi despite the obvious presence of the Galil assault rifle in his arms. He cursed vehemently, still blinking his left eye where he'd caught a fingernail while on the second-floor landing. Tears ran down his face, blurring his vision. The two Mossad agents were somewhere below him.

A man reached for Grimaldi, cresting a swell of bodies trying to reach the lobby. They were at the fifth-floor landing now, and people had stopped jumping over the edge and taking their chances with gravity.

Grimaldi assumed the guy was a friendly since he wasn't waving a gun in his face, and that made him tougher to deal with. Using his left arm, he swept across his attacker's arms, blocking whatever chance the man had at seizing the Galil, then lifted his knee into the man's stomach with enough force to drive the air from his lungs. "Sorry, pal," the Stony Man pilot said with genuine feeling, "but my dance card's full at the moment."

Catching the disabled man by the shirtfront before he could fall, Grimaldi paused, letting the traffic flow around him. Spotting one of the Mossad agents, he passed down his burden, then continued on.

The fire escape jogged back inside the building at the sixth floor. Grimaldi halted for a moment to help a woman get her small child back into her arms, then saw her on her way.

The emergency door was open when he reached it, and he passed through with only slight jostling from the escaping guests. Bodies littered the floor—young, old, male, female, black, white, and all colors in between. The thing that hurt Grimaldi most was the handful of dead kids scattered the length of the hallway. In the flickering and uncertain light of the fluorescent fixtures, nothing moved. The sixth-floor hallway had been turned into a bloody graveyard.

He turned and found a Mossad agent on his heels. The man was younger than Grimaldi, and the violence he'd seen thus far was taking its toll. "Here?" the Israeli asked in a hoarse voice.

"No," Grimaldi replied. He led the charge back up the fire escape, feeling his breath rasp in his lungs as his feet rang on the metal steps. The assault rifle was sweat-slick in his hands. He tapped the transmit button on the headset. "Striker?"

The lack of a reply held a world of meaning.

Grimaldi pushed himself harder. The big guy had always been there for him whenever they had a joint mission, had never walked away before the dust settled without knowing what happened to the people he'd been with. The pilot was damned if he was going to do it any different. It wasn't something he'd learned from Bolan, just one of the things they had in common and respected in each other.

The hollow pop of grenades echoed from the eleventh floor.

Grimaldi reached the landing with his heart hammering his rib cage in near rebellion.

Another explosion followed, louder than the first.

Motioning the Mossad agents to the other side of the door, Grimaldi swung it open. Plaster dust filled the hallway, joining with the faulty fluorescent lighting to give the scene a murky look.

Four Arabs swung around with automatic weapons when the sprung hinges of the emergency door squeaked.

"Single-shot!" Grimaldi growled. "I want these bastards down without hurting anybody they might have left alive." He squeezed the trigger of the Galil, wishing he'd had time to unfold the buttstock for more accurate shooting. Focusing on the center of the chest, he put two rounds into two men before discovering the Mossad agents' sniping abilities were directly on target, as well. Only as he moved through the doorway and saw the empty square of glass above him did he realize how close the Hezbollah gunners had come to his own position.

The pilot took a handkerchief from his pocket and tied it over his mouth and nose to keep the dust from choking him. A third of the way into the hallway, a voice caught his attention.

A man covered in blood and plaster dust waved from an open doorway, leaning heavily against the jamb.

"Seal it off," Grimaldi told the Mossad agents. "Get whatever survivors there are left on this floor headed for the fire escape."

The men nodded quickly and sprinted toward the rest of the rooms, covering one another.

"Are you American?" the wounded man called from the door as Grimaldi approached.

"As apple pie," the pilot replied. He took a closer look at the man, noticing the 9 mm Beretta in his hand. The gun had been fired dry, the slide locking back in the open position. Despite the absence of a uniform, the haircut was pure GI. There was no doubt in Grimaldi's mind that the man was close to death. He kept the smile on his face despite the cold chill racing along his spine. He slid an arm around the other man and helped him toward the bed. "Take a load off, soldier. We got everything under control here."

A brief burst of autofire from the hallway made a liar of him. The wounded soldier didn't seem to notice.

Grimaldi pulled his handkerchief mask down, rested the Galil against the bed and started tearing the sheets into bandages. The soldier was young, but the pallor of death settling over him made him look old. The Beretta never left his hand.

Blood trickled from his mouth as he turned to look at Grimaldi. He had to try twice to get words to come out. "They got Major Deering. We were betrayed. They took him."

Grimaldi finished plugging a wound in the man's abdomen to staunch the blood flow. "It's okay, soldier. We'll get him back."

"I couldn't stop them. Rusty died before he could even get his gun out." The soldier's hand gripped Grimaldi's arm tightly. His wild eyes focused on the pilot's. "I shot one of them, sir. I shot one of them dead. I never shot a man before." His head lolled back and his sightless eyes stared at the cracked ceiling overhead.

Grimaldi dropped the bandages. "Goddamn it." He reached up with a shaking hand and closed the soldier's eyes.

BOLAN THREW the grenade underhanded, aiming for the center of the hallway. On the other side of the elevator cage Arella Hirschfeld was a slim silhouette. The warrior counted down as voices screamed at one another in Arabic, then the flash-bang grenade went off, filling the hallway with light and noise.

The Executioner wheeled, squeezing off 3-round bursts. He worked left to right, meeting Hirschfeld's own effective marksmanship a little over halfway.

The familiar *whup-whup-whup* of helicopter blades closed in from overhead.

"The chopper's landed," Hirschfeld said as they raced down the length of the hallway.

Bolan checked the room registered to Damien Gray and found it empty.

"Gray?" Hirschfeld asked as he returned to the hallway.

"Gone."

"He has to be on the roof."

"Yeah." Bolan crossed the hallway and sprinted into one of the rooms overlooking the street in front of the hotel. "They'll be expecting us to try the fire escape," he said as he took a collapsible grappling hook and fifty feet of knotted nylon cord form his web belt. "Maybe they won't be looking for us over here." He leaned out a gaping hole and gripped the ragged lip of the wall, whirling the hook slowly, then pitching it upward. It soared over the top of the building another floor up. Pulling the slack out to lodge the padded arms, he hooked it solidly, slung the Uzi over his shoulder, then swung out over the darkened street and started pulling himself up hand over hand.

As soon as he had an elbow levered over the edge of the building, he felt the cord take Hirschfeld's considerably lesser weight. Wind from the rotating helicopter blades blew small rocks and dust into his face as he peered over the edge.

A cluster of figures hovered near the roof's fire escape door. Automatic weapons were drawn in hard, lean lines in their hands. Another group separated from the fire escape, pushing three hostages ahead of them.

Bolan didn't recognize any of the hostages as they were herded toward the cargo doors of the helicopter. Hirschfeld joined him.

"Down," the Executioner grated, letting himself hang from the side of the building by his hands. "Three feet. This way. There's cover." He slid his hands sideways, moving away from the safety of the rope, forcing himself not to think about the twenty-four-story fall below them.

The woman followed without hesitation.

"Now," Bolan said, pushing himself up. The sheltering bulk of a thrumming HVAC unit hid them from view. He flicked the safety off the Uzi and took up a position beside the big unit on his knees.

Just as Hirschfeld crested the top of the building, a shot rang from the helicopter crew. The woman fell back toward the street. Only one of her hands remained visible on top of the ledge. She didn't make a sound at all.

In one fluid movement Bolan slipped the machine pistol on full-auto and burned a 32-round clip toward the Hezbollah men positioned around the emergency door. The terrorists fell to the rooftop, unmoving.

The backwash of the rotors gained intensity, igniting a whirlwind on top of the building. Someone slammed the cargo door shut as the last of the men got aboard. The helicopter leaped into the night with the engines screaming in protest.

Bolan dropped the empty machine pistol as the Hezbollah survivors tried to regroup. He threw himself at the ledge as Hirschfeld's fingers started to slip, reaching well below the lip of the building to grab her wrist. The hard edge of the ledge cut into his flesh, but he kept his grip on the woman's arm, using his greater weight to lever her up. His shoulder and back muscles burned with the strain. Footsteps sounded in his ears even as he pulled her to the top. His free hand slid the Detonics Scoremaster from his shoulder holster as he twisted on his butt. He brought his other hand away from the Mossad agent and fired from a sitting position, concentrating on the three targets before him and ignoring the bullets whining around him.

The .45 thundered in his fist as he tracked from left to right, unleashing a trio of Glaser rounds. The Teflon-and-shot combo was a terrifying one-shot/one-kill round that sported a ninety-nine percent attrition rate in actual use by American FBI agents. The Executioner went for the rapid-fire torso shot, downing each man instantly with exit wounds the size of pie plates.

The helicopter was a retreating speck in the dark sky.

There was nothing else left alive in the hellzone atop the hotel.

Bolan let his breath out, noticing the burning sensation on his neck for the first time. Then he felt the slow trickle of blood dripping into his collar. He forced himself up and reached into his med-kit for a compress bandage to fit over

Hirschfeld's wound. He opened her shirt and examined it. The bullet had passed completely through just below her ribs. He covered both entrance and exit, using a lot of tape around her slender waist to hold the bandages in place.

With his help she managed to sit up. Grimaldi and the rest of the Mossad team arrived as she rebuttoned her shirt. Her complexion was only a little paler than before. "There'll be no question about the wisdom of exfiltration at this point?" she asked Bolan.

"No," the warrior replied. He searched the night sky in vain for the helicopter.

"Good." She gave orders to her men and set the retreat in motion, limping only slightly as she got to her feet and started moving. She gave Bolan a brief smile. "I'd hate to abandon you after you saved my life."

Bolan looked at Grimaldi, noting the pained look on the pilot's face. "Jack?"

"Busted play, Striker," Grimaldi commented quietly as they fell in behind the Israeli agents.

"It's not over," Bolan said. "Terrorism is a personal war, and these people haven't seen how personal it can get. But we're going to set up a private itinerary to introduce them to the concept. Bet on it."

CHAPTER FIVE

Riyadh, Saudi Arabia

First Day—3:17 a.m.

Jessi Grafton blinked blearily, wondering if it was really the sound of gunfire that had awakened her. The dark hotel room engulfed her, and she tried to remember where everything was but couldn't. Even the location of the light switch eluded her. Bone-aching tiredness coupled with jet lag and a late arrival had led her to bed as soon as she'd checked in. She hadn't even bothered to undress or take off her glasses. Now that appeared to be a blessing.

Gunfire rattled the walls again, and this time she was sure of it. She bolted from the bed and immediately tripped over the plastic case containing her laptop computer. She and it went down with a resounding bang. Her glasses somehow managed to stay on her head, and she pulled them down into place.

Screams punctuated the gunfire now.

"Oh, shit," Grafton muttered as she struggled to find her purse and tennis shoes in the dark. Without her passport she wouldn't be able to get out of the country. Without her tennis shoes she wouldn't be able to make it across the parking lot outside.

She found them and slipped them on while sitting on the floor. At thirty-two and having experienced her share of hot spots around the globe while working for *Worldview* magazine, she'd learned a long time ago to recognize the stink of cordite from expended cartridges. She recognized it now.

Voices shouted out in the hallway. There was a violent disagreement in the works, which was silenced by a short burst from an automatic weapon.

Grafton jumped when someone kicked open the door next to her room. Realizing there was no time to escape by running, she ducked into the bathroom, stood on the sink and pried at the acoustic panels in the ceiling. A fingernail broke, then another, but the panel came free when she pushed it.

Bracing for the effort, Grafton leaped up and pulled herself through the hole. She heard voices at her door as she balanced herself across the panel grids and barely had time to shift the panel back into place as someone kicked the door in.

She crouched in the darkness above the ceiling, wrapping her arms around her legs and holding her breath. Lines of weak yellow light filtered through a vent in the center of the room and she peered through them, blinking rapidly as someone switched on the room's light.

Two men suddenly came into view, both wearing loose, flowing robes and bushy black beards. The weapons in their hands glistened with oil. The smell of cordite became sharper and more intense.

They talked to each other as they searched the room. Grafton understood none of it. She finally had to start breathing again and it sounded like a bellows pump in her own mind.

One of them said something, and this time she recognized her name. The choking fear that held her in thrall was melted by the white-hot heat of a fight-or-flight impulse when she realized they were actively seeking her. Her breath hissed through her nose when she looked down into the bathroom and saw the fine spray of powder from the acoustic tile spread across the counter.

She moved, feeling her way when she couldn't see, guessing at the direction of the elevators. Even if she couldn't get into one, the fire escape was nearby and she was only on the second floor.

Part of her mind, constantly bent with a reporter's curiosity, questioned the Arab faction's presence at the hotel, especially how they'd come up with her name. She was a third-rate journalist with a magazine whose publisher currently had more dollars than sense, and she wasn't too proud to admit that. Her stories for *Worldview* were hardly earthshaking or even really news. As a monthly magazine, all they could hope for was in-depth articles on rehashed events that were already fast becoming history.

She bumped into unidentified pipes and got dust in her eyes. She crawled over electrical cords gingerly, just knowing she was going to be electrocuted before she ever had the chance to be shot. She sneezed, started to again, caught herself, and coughed instead.

Little squares of light beckoned to her, but she avoided them on the operating principle that if she could see them, they could see her. She didn't know how far she'd gone when she heard a plaintive child crying for its mother. Unable to ignore the pain and fright locked in its shrill cries, she paused to track the sound, then headed in the child's direction.

There was no doubt about the source of the noise. She peered through the vent and saw a small black child rubbing angry fists into his eyes. He screamed for his mother again, shaking with the effort.

Unable to abandon the child to whatever fate had in store for him, Grafton hooked her fingers under the nearest acoustic panel and lifted. She slid it aside and dropped through, causing the little boy to scream even louder. She glanced anxiously at the open door, wondering if his louder cries would draw attention.

He tried to run as she caught him up in her arms, fought briefly, then subsided and lay on her shoulder crying.

Grafton reached for a chair, intending to clamber up into the ceiling recess again, but a metallic click behind her froze her on the spot. She looked over her shoulder at the Arab in the doorway, who grinned and shook his head. He said something she couldn't understand.

Holding on to the child protectively, Grafton said, "I don't know what you're saying."

In response the man stepped forward and grabbed her wrist with bruising force. She yelled out in pain, refusing to drop the child. The man pulled her through the doorway and stood her in line with at least twenty other people.

A fierce-eyed man strode the length of the hallway, closing in on them. He stopped in front of the assembled people, glancing over them like a general marshaling his troops. Two younger men with assault rifles stood on either side of him. "You are our prisoners," the man said in heavily accented English. "You will do as we say, when we say, or you will die."

"These aren't exactly the Geneva Convention rules you're playing by here," an older man commented.

Grafton could tell the man was American by his accent.

When the fierce-eyed man growled a command, one of the men beside him stepped forward and let loose a burst at the American's chest, not stopping until the body hit the bloodstained carpet.

Stunned cries and shouts of disbelief tore through the hostages. Grafton automatically tried to soothe the crying child, telling herself to wake up while knowing at the same time that it wasn't just a nightmare.

"The only rules here," the fierce-eyed man said, "are our rules. Pay attention to them. You will get no second chances." He motioned to the gunmen around them.

Grafton followed her fellow hostages, as they were herded onto the fire stairs.

"Want me to carry the little fella?" a man with an Irish brogue asked. "A little slip of a girl like yourself might find it a wee bit discomforting navigating them stairs with him around you." He was a big man, dressed in casual wear, with hands calloused and shaped by years of hard work. His face was broad, burned permanently red by the sun and wind, which contrasted sharply with the reddish-blond thatch of hair and ropy eyebrows.

Numbly Grafton passed the boy over, taking the lead as they went down the fire escape stairs.

"My name's Torin Conagher," the man said quietly. "And who's this little fella?" The boy resumed his crying, wrapping a chubby arm around the Irishman's thick neck.

"I don't know," Grafton replied. "I found him alone in one of the rooms." She flinched from one of the guards as they proceeded down to the next landing.

"Who're you, lass?"

"Jessi Grafton."

"Aye. You were the missing woman these bastards were so flustered about."

"I don't even know these people." Grafton held on to the stairway railing as her legs almost gave way. Ahead of her, a woman tried to help a man staunch a messy shoulder wound. She glanced down and saw the splotches of blood on the metal steps.

"They call themselves Hezbollah," Conagher told her, "and a right nasty bunch of devils they are. I tried to re-build a few structures for the Lebanese government in Beirut back in the early eighties. Got a right smart whiff of them then. You'll have to go far to find a more dedicated group of terrorists than them who stand against the United States and Israel."

Once she was on the basement floor, one of the terrorists grabbed her by the shirt and shoved her toward a waiting van. "What do they want with us?"

"Hostages, lass," Conagher replied. "So mind you step lively when they tell you, or they'll drop you where you stand. When you're moving an operation as quickly as this one, the last thing you need is an uncooperative hostage. A close brush with the IRA taught me that long ago."

Grafton started to step up into the nearest van. A terrorist reached out and seized her shirtfront. Her immediate reaction was to pull away from him, but a rifle butt to her stomach doubled her over and dropped her to her knees. She retched, feeling the sour bile rise in her throat as the terrorist screamed commands in her ear.

The Hezbollah grabbed her hair and dragged her to her feet. She stumbled after him, trying not to get sick again. She wrapped her arms around her ribs, off balance even before he threw her through the cargo door of another van. Scraping her face on the metal floor of the van, she struggled to her knees, holding back tears of frustration and fear. The van door slid shut with a deafening bang only a second before the vehicle sped out of the underground garage.

As she looked around, she realized she'd been consigned to a van of women. Then her sight was taken away as the three terrorists guarding them stepped forward and placed hoods over their heads.

Grafton tried to remember the Lord's Prayer, but the words wouldn't come. Only imminent death filled her thoughts.

CHAPTER SIX

Haifa, Israel

First Day—3:53 a.m.

"Coming up on the drop area now, sir," the Israeli pilot said crisply over the intercom.

Mack Bolan pushed himself out of the cargo plane's seat and hooked an arm through his parachute straps. Jack Grimaldi was already in motion behind him.

The Mossad agents who'd accompanied the Stony Man warriors on the soft probe into Beirut remained quiet in their seats. Arella Hirschfeld, looking wan and drawn belted into her seat, gave Bolan a shadowed smile. "Goodbye, my friend," she said softly, "and may your journey home be a safe one."

Bolan took the hand she offered and squeezed it gently. "Yours, too, Captain. And tell your people we'll be in touch soon regarding our next move." He moved to the cargo door, feeling the vibrations of the big trimotor's engines beneath his feet.

The copilot came back and stood by the cargo door. Shrugging into the chute harness, Bolan slipped on his helmet and swung the mike to his chin. "Jack?"

"Check."

Working with practiced economy, Bolan spot-checked Grimaldi's parachute rigging, then tapped him on the helmet to let him know he was ready. Seconds later the tap was repeated on the Executioner's helmet.

The Israeli copilot unlocked the cargo door and pulled it open, motioning Bolan and Grimaldi forward. The Executioner stopped near the edge, avoiding the suction of the slipstream as he looked down over the city. The golden dome of the Baha'i shrine gleamed dully, like a setting sun grown cold in its own embers. The city rose out of Haifa Bay to the west, climbing in terraces shaped by the wind, time and the sea, covered over with modern buildings and homes that offered nothing of the romantic backdrop of the Middle East.

A moment later the cargo plane sped out over Haifa Bay. The water resembled a hard, dark sheet of glass dotted with small sailing craft. The copilot tapped Bolan on the shoulder. Leaning forward, the Executioner let the wind take him, gliding well away from the tail section of the trimotor. Grimaldi was close on his heels.

Counting down, Bolan yanked the rip cord, watching the chute mushroom above him. It was black, as was the combat skinsuit he wore, discernible only because it blotted out the stars. He checked and found Grimaldi floating above him.

"Sarge?"

"Go."

"Got a fix on our target?"

Bolan scanned the dark water with his night vision goggles and found the thirty-foot Chris-Craft holding steady farther out to sea than he'd expected. "Three o'clock, guy."

A pause, then, "Shit. Aaron's warped sense of humor again."

Bolan knew the pilot was referring to the luminescent grizzly bear painted on the deck of the boat, thinking Grimaldi's comment was like the pot calling the kettle black. He put the NVG away and made adjustments to the chute's spill, aiming for their target. Four distinct figures moved along the lines of the vessel, one of them already using a chemical wash to remove the infrared bear design.

The warrior dumped the chute twenty feet from the water to give himself plenty of clearance from tangling shroud lines that might drag him under. He dropped into the sea feetfirst, and the chill of it struck him as forcefully as a brick wall. For a moment he was lost in the complete blackness, unable to discern up from down. He released a thin stream of air bubbles, feeling them brush against his cheek, then followed them toward the surface.

He broke through quietly. Any sound he might have made was covered instantly by the waves lapping against the Chris-Craft. Two of the men on board were already fishing the parachutes from the water with long boat hooks.

Grimaldi bobbed up a moment later, wiping the water from his face with a hand. He spit out a stream of water, blinked as he looked around, then grinned at Bolan.

Another of the boat hands dropped a folding ladder over the side of the vessel and locked it into place. Bolan swam for the ladder and pulled himself aboard. Two of the boat hands leveled MAC-10s at his waist as he stood.

Grimaldi hauled himself up and saw the weapons. "You boys forgot the brass band."

A man in casual sailing clothes moved between the two gunners. "I was told you'd have a word for me." His eyes were black and as hard as flint.

"Wonderland," Bolan told him.

The man waved the MAC-10s down. "That's the one," he replied with an easy grin, holding out a hand. "Name's Ben Murtaugh. I'm with the U.S. embassy in Haifa."

The Executioner shook hands. "Belasko. This is my partner, Grimes."

"I've got some dry clothes for you below." Murtaugh turned to his men and issued orders, then led the way into the cabin. "You almost took us unawares, Mr. Belasko," Murtaugh said as he flipped on a light switch. The interior of the cabin was small and neat, carefully filled with two chairs, a vinyl-covered couch, a television and a stereo. The embassy man took up a position behind a small wet bar. "Clothing's there on the couch. Details came in scrambled, but I think I got the sizes right. There's a first-aid kit, as well. I was told your condition was questionable."

Bolan stripped out of the wet clothing, dried off with the clean towels provided, then redressed in Levi's and tennis shoes. He peeled the old bandage off his neck, medicated the wound, then made a new one from the first-aid kit. He pulled on the white cotton shirt and rolled the sleeves up. There was a jacket and tie, but he left them off for now. Later, if needed, they could lend a business look to the outfit. He unzipped the Detonics Scoremaster from the waterproof pouch in his gear, tucked it into the waistband of the jeans and pushed the three extra magazines into his pockets. He kept his map case and ID with him. Nothing else remained in the clothing that could tie him to anything that had gone down that night.

"You're a careful man," Murtaugh observed.

Bolan glanced at him. "Yeah." He looked out the port window as the coastline of Haifa Bay came into view. A sprinkling of lights interrupted the darkness. He felt tired, bogged down by the lack of intel concerning the hostage situation. He didn't know how many lives were at risk even now, couldn't begin to guess how many had died. The Mossad team had been lucky in getting the exfiltration to go as smoothly as it had. As it was, three agents had been killed, their bodies left behind in the mad scramble for the waiting plane.

"Can I fix you something to drink?" Murtaugh asked. "We try to keep a good stock on hand. Never can tell when unexpected guests might drop in on you."

"Coffee," Bolan replied, letting the curtain drop back over the port window.

"Me, too," Grimaldi added.

The embassy man poured three cups of coffee and passed them around. "The communiqué I got from the State Department said I was to give you every cooperation," Murtaugh said. "I was informed that this was strictly an eyes-only assignment."

Bolan didn't say anything. He rolled his wrist over and checked his watch. The numbers were falling on a new operation now, one he didn't even have a handle on yet, and lives could be ticking away with them, as well.

"Much as I admit to enjoying being woken up in the middle of the night to go on a snipe hunt," Murtaugh said, "risking my standing here in the Israeli community without knowing why really chaps my ass."

"You're not at risk," Bolan said evenly. Politics, especially the petty politics of pecking order evidenced by Murtaugh, didn't belong in a war zone. Politics were for the containment of military aggression and for settling the dust when the warriors were ready to pull out.

"Goes to show how much you know, buddy," Murtaugh replied. "The Israelis didn't especially cotton to this unplanned night drop of yours. It kind of set their teeth on edge. To them this is America's way of telling them to butt out."

"For now," the warrior said, "that's exactly what it's supposed to mean." He knew it was because Hal Brognola had the President's ear back in Washington. The Justice Department Fed was already thinking along the same lines— that with American hostages involved so soon after the Iraqi crisis, the Stony Man teams were going to figure in as a large part of the hostage recovery operation. And the Stony Man Farm setup had tighter security and a lower profile than the National Security Agency.

Until Bolan's abdication after a KGB mole infiltrated the White House and ultimately was responsible for the death of April Rose, Stony Man Farm had been home to three covert strike teams. Phoenix Force was a band of international freedom fighters who fought the war against terrorists on international fronts. Able Team laid the heavy hand of quick and absolute justice on the criminal element operating within the United States.

As Colonel John Macklin Phoenix, Bolan had watched his old name laid to rest. He'd spearheaded the Stony Man teams, operating independently and in conjunction with Able and Phoenix as the need arose. But with April Rose's death and the devastating attack on the original Stony Man setup, he'd recognized the need for a lone wolf aggressor who wasn't shackled by the bureaucratic red tape that kept a response from being instantly issued. A good general didn't marshal his troops or his battle plans from anywhere but the front lines. Bolan hadn't hesitated an instant in re-taking the field, even though it meant losing the protective umbrella of Stony Man Farm.

The penetration into Beirut had started out as a favor for Hal Brognola, Stony Man's liaison with the White House. There was no doubt in his mind that it would require a sur-gical strike backing a full-scale blitz to put things back in order.

"Bullshit," Murtaugh said. "This is the Mossad you're dealing with here. You don't just tell them to butt out."

Bolan stared at him. "You do for now, Murtaugh, or you'll be on the first plane home."

"You don't have that kind of pull."

"There's one way to find out." Bolan returned the man's gaze full measure.

Murtaugh dumped his coffee into the small sink in the kitchen, dropped the cup in, as well and headed up the companionway.

Bolan poured himself another cup of coffee and watched the coastline of Haifa loom closer. He ached to be doing something constructive, but he'd learned to wait until he had enough intel before going into action. This wasn't going to be any different. But starting out, the stakes seemed a little higher this time.

"THE BEIRUT SITUATION isn't the only thing on tap to-night," Aaron "Bear" Kurtzman said.

Bolan sat in Murtaugh's office in the U.S. embassy on 37 Ha'Atzmaut Street. Regular business hours had ended at four-thirty in the afternoon, but a skeleton crew of special agents with covert intelligence ties were working overtime tracking the hostage snatch in Beirut. The warrior had routed the call through a couple of cutout stations so that it couldn't be traced to Stony Man Farm. Bear had scrambled incoming and outgoing conversation so that it couldn't be monitored. "What else is?" Bolan asked.

"We're looking at copycat grabs in Saudi Arabia, Ku-wait, Iraq and Bahrain."

Bolan absorbed it, making himself think of the geography and stats rather than the people who lived and died behind the numbers. A soldier went into battle with a clear-cut objective in mind and a means to do it. Thinking about the lives that were to be won or lost could make him freeze up at the wrong time. "Who's fronting the operation?"

"We've got confirmed reports that Hezbollah is behind it, but the leadership is picking up some side action from other sympathetic parties."

"This has been in the works for a while."

"Yeah."

Grimaldi lounged against a wall with a cigarette and a cup of coffee.

Bolan flipped open his map case, found a map of the Middle East and marked the snatch cities as Kurtzman read them off. "It's spread out."

"But definitely organized," Kurtzman replied. "These people went in on the numbers, guy, complete with take-down lists of who they were after. All the targets were hotels catering to American and European business interests."

"Have you got any numbers yet?"

Kurtzman sighed. "Upwards of a hundred people, Striker. That's all I can tell you until the State Department gets more intel. I'm tapping their information as fast as it comes in. Counting your action in Beirut, I've confirmed thirteen American and twenty-seven European deaths so far. That list is growing, too."

"Where's Hal?"

"Bending the Man's ear in Wonderland to get us some kind of green light on this."

"And Barb?"

"Working out logistics on her own. I had everybody cleared out of here until I got my finger on the pulse. Distractions right now I don't need."

Bolan picked the lock on the desk's top drawer and pulled it open. Grimaldi raised his eyebrows to express interest.

"Jack got wind of a Major Deering who was taken in Beirut," Bolan said. "What can you tell me about that?"

He listened to the click and whir of Kurtzman's computers as he examined the contents of the drawer. Picking up a large box of staples, glancing at the gleaming rows of them spilled out across the drawer, he shook the carton. A solid object of considerable weight rattled inside.

"No Major Deering listed," Kurtzman informed him.

"Jack figures he's Army. From the looks of things, Hezbollah went in knowing Deering was there, too."

"The only Deering I can find is with military intelligence," Kurtzman replied. "I'm looking at their files now. According to them, Major William H. Deering is on a sensitive assignment in the Philippines."

"Check it out for me. I want to know if the major is there."

"On the QT."

"No other way at this point." Bolan opened the box of staples, and a compact microcassette recorder dropped out into his hand. The red recording light was on. "I've got a feeling we aren't the only ones working a busted play here."

"You got it."

Bolan held the recorder up for Grimaldi to see, then switched it off and popped the cassette out. He checked the cassette, finding both sides were unmarked, and tossed it to the pilot.

Grimaldi caught it, pulled the magnetic tape free of the case and set it on fire with his lighter. He let it burn for a moment, then dropped it into the trash can.

"Anything else?" Kurtzman asked.

"I need a fast trip to the Farm."

"The USS *Winkler* is stationed in the Red Sea. A Sea Horse chopper is en route now that'll take you aboard. Hal's getting the authorization you need for your return flight."

"Where's Able and Phoenix."

"Here. They went on yellow alert as soon as you and Jack kicked the dust off in the States. Hal had a bad feeling about this one."

"He was right."

"Yeah."

"What about the Mossad?"

"Barb's been ducking inquiries since you guys made the drop into Haifa. She did mention that she was surprised the people she talked to weren't more demanding. They gave her the impression they had problems of their own. I did check and found out some action went down in Tel Aviv tonight involving a jail break by someone the Mossad had been sitting on."

"Is it connected?"

"I don't know. They're playing this one close to the vest. I haven't been able to turn over a clue. Somebody dropped a total blackout over the recovery operation."

"They haven't found the guy?"

"No."

Bolan turned that over in his mind to get the feel of it. Things didn't just happen this closely together without being related in some fashion. "Do you know who the prisoner was?"

"Not yet. I'm still working on it."

"One last piece of business," Bolan said, staring at the tape recorder in his hand. "Tell Barb to pull in some outstanding IOUs from the State Department and get a man named Ben Murtaugh bounced from the Haifa embassy. I don't know if he's the leak to the Israelis the CIA has been looking for, but he's definitely a guy who doesn't know when to back off. Since we're going to be scrambling in this direction, I don't want him around underfoot."

"Will do." Kurtzman broke the connection and the scrambler hissed off a moment later.

Bolan put the phone away as someone knocked on the door. "It's open."

Murtaugh stepped into the room. "Hospitality or not, bud, I still got a job to do. I'd like my office back."

"It's yours." Bolan handed the embassy man the tape recorder on his way out the door.

Murtaugh's air of impatience melted away.

"You might want to get a fire extinguisher for your wastepaper basket," Grimaldi told him as he passed by, "before your smoke alarm goes off."

"Did somebody order a Navy helicopter?" an embassy aide asked while holding a phone receiver to his ear.

"Mine," Bolan called. "Have it sit down in front. It's already been cleared through Israeli airspace." He moved toward the building's entrance with Grimaldi on his heels, his mind working furiously. Instead of questions being cleared up when the dust settled after the hostage strike, more had arisen. The falling numbers continued to click hollowly in his head—only they weren't his numbers now. They belonged to someone else's clock, and there was no guessing what the enemy's final objective was. Nor where or how big the battlefield was going to be.

CHAPTER SEVEN

Stony Man Farm, Virginia

Second Day—9:12 p.m.

"Bloody hell, Katz," David McCarter muttered as he climbed through the mud and bushes on his stomach, cradling the AR-15. "My idea of a good time is *not* scarfin' through these woods waiting for one of Kissinger's mechanical beasties to shoot my blinking lights out."

He paused on top of a knoll overlooking the target area. The rain continued to fall, surprisingly chill for this time of year. Autumn was just beginning to color the leaves of the surrounding trees, but the night robbed them of their glory. Dressed in combat black, his face darkened with combat cosmetics under a black beret that was a holdover from his Special Air Service days in Great Britain, he was one shadow among many. He wore combat boots and carried a Browning Hi-Power in a chest rig that also held spare magazines for the assault rifle. A web belt held extra ammunition for the Hi-Power as well as flash grenades.

Water dripped down the back of his collar as he focused a pair of night vision goggles. The night dropped away to shades of green and black. Nothing moved. He tracked through the thick stand of trees with the practiced ease of a hunter.

The dark silence of Stony Man Farm spread out before him. Carved from the Blue Ridge Mountains in Virginia, the Farm didn't look like much to the casual observer. In the center was a three-story main house, two outbuildings and a tractor barn. From a cursory surface inspection, it looked like a functioning farm, complete with denim-clad farmhands and machinery. The outer lands of the Farm featured abundant apple and peach orchards. The fields in closer to the housing grew sweet potatoes, snap beans and strawberries. No trees grew there. It made line-of-sight easier. The orchard trees concealed security equipment as well as roving guards that stayed within the shadows day and night. A small landing field was north of the main house, and it wasn't used for farm-to-market days.

McCarter knew the Farm for what it truly was—the hardsite and headshed of America's premier unknown antiterrorist groups. Instead of a life-style dominated by the seasons and counted down by a sunup-to-sundown schedule, the permanent members of Stony Man Farm were hardwired into their lives by a special satellite 22,300 miles away in space that allowed them to link up with the rest of the world. And they operated twenty-four hours a day.

Wiping the moisture from his eyebrows, McCarter pressed on. Katz would have his hide if he wasn't in position on time. The Phoenix Force leader was a stickler for detail. McCarter preferred a rolling-action plan when he flew solo, with plenty of flex built in. Still, he had to admit that when he called the shots on an operation, he preferred they fall just as sharply on the numbers as Katz's.

Still crawling on hands and knees, McCarter clung to the brush line. He paused when he spotted the first surveillance camera. It was mounted in a tree three yards aboveground, whirring silently as it rotated on its neck.

McCarter identified it as Vidicon, and the dual housings mounted on either side of the camera let him know that it was infrared-equipped. He cursed silently. It was certainly no surprise. As well as having been briefed on the improvements in Stony Man Farm's perimeter defenses, he'd braced units like it before.

He gathered his feet under him, tucked the AR-15 in close and made ready to run for it. As soon as the radius of the mobile camera moved away from him, he dug his boots in, lifted his knees high and sprinted for everything he was worth. When he felt the trip wire go, it was too damn late to do anything except try to keep his leg in one piece.

He fell, rolled out of control and came to a stop on his back, looking at the stars over his head. Without warning his nose turned red, illuminated by a hidden laser sight. "Shit," he said in disgust. As he stood up, one of the hidden gunners added insult to injury by shooting him with a paint pistol. Three fluorescent pink blobs spattered across his chest in quick succession.

"You're dead, McCarter," a young man's voice taunted from the darkness. "Cut down in your dotage."

"Bugger off, mate," McCarter roared as he picked up the fallen assault rifle.

MCCARTER ACCEPTED the bottle of Coke from Kissinger with a nod of thanks. He tilted his head back and drained a third of it with one long swallow. "Ah, now that hits the spot."

"Speaking of spots," Gary Manning said, "that's an interesting wardrobe you've started sporting."

McCarter glanced down at the paint splotches. "Just some bloke's pained idea of a cheap joke. There'll come a return engagement one day, trust me."

They were in Cowboy John Kissinger's private wing of Stony Man Farm. While the weaponsmith was carved from a heritage that denoted the Great American Southwest, his surroundings were the latest in high-tech. Gun cases and shelves displayed all sorts of gleaming deadly beauty. More of it was stored in fire-resistant, impact-resistant cases in this room and in others.

The three remaining members of Phoenix Force were already in the room, wearing chagrined looks on their faces. Gary Manning, a Canadian, was a big man with a barrel chest, dark blond hair and gray eyes. He was the Force's chief demolitions man.

Rafael Encizo stood next to him. He was four inches shorter with black hair, dark brown eyes and coloring that reflected his Cuban ancestry. He was an expert in many forms of death.

Calvin James was the newest member of Phoenix Force, brought on board after the untimely death of Keio Ohara. He was lanky and black, his hair worn in a short trim. Uncle Sam had seen to his training as a Navy frogman in the SEAL, and a few years on a police beat had taught him how to swim with the sharks he met in the street. He leaned against the wall behind Encizo and Manning.

A voice boomed in the small command room. "Maybe they should call you guys Feeble Force after tonight's fiasco."

McCarter sniffed disdainfully, imitating a member of London's high society. He put on a voice to match as he turned to face the verbal aggressor. "If performance against the Farm's security network was any indication, a few months ago you'd have been referred to as DisAbled Team, old chap."

Carl Lyons guffawed and slapped his knee. "Hee haw, McCarter. You and that rapier wit of yours slay me. Really. You do." He was big and blond, an ex-LAPD cop whose path had crossed that of Executioner Mack Bolan during the Mafia Wars, before America's response to terrorism had given birth to Able Team and Phoenix Force. Now he rode with Able, earning his nickname of Ironman by being one of the wildest cards in the deck. And one of the deadliest. Able Team held down the domestic front against terrorists and other hostile aggressors.

Next to him stood Rosario Blancanales, called Politician by his friends for his unique abilities to defuse combustible situations and people who were determined to go ballistic.

Hermann Schwarz sat at the wall of electronic surveillance equipment, poking through the keyboard that connected him cybernetically to everything in the Farm's deadly environs. He'd earned the nickname Gadgets during the Vietnam War when he and Blancanales had formed Pen-Team Able with Bolan. He was skilled at booby traps, surveillance devices, and everything else that was mechanical or electronic in nature. "So where's your fearless leader?" Schwarz asked.

McCarter walked over to the master security board, eyes tracking across the rows of surveillance screens as Schwarz worked through them. Shot after shot of darkened landscaping lit up by infrareds, StarTron and thermal imaging paraded across the screens in almost a blur.

Schwarz referred to Yakov Katzenelenbogen, Phoenix Force's senior member. Katz was a veteran of the Mossad and ran the team with an iron fist, almost literally because he'd lost his right arm in the Six Day War. The prosthesis he'd replaced it with came with any number of deadly attachments.

"Who knows?" McCarter said. "Maybe he's busy out there right now tying up all those young boyos who've got such an atrocious sense of humor. What are you guys doing here?"

"Like you," Schwarz replied. "We're on yellow alert."

"Some big doings going on somewhere," Calvin James suggested. "Otherwise they'd never have all of us together."

McCarter nodded. His teammate was right. With different spheres of influence, Able Team and Phoenix Force rarely meshed operations. "What about Striker?"

"He tripped over the present situation," Cowboy John Kissinger told them. He was tall and broad, his mouth framed by a gunslinger's mustache. He wore a tan Stetson and aviator-style sunglasses and looked as if he'd just stepped off a ranch, thanks to his boots, jeans and a western-styled shirt. A turquoise-and-silver necklace at his throat spoke of his Amerindian heritage. "Where the hell's Katz?"

Finishing his Coke, McCarter glanced back at Lyons. "A twenty-spot, mate, says Katz comes waltzing in through this without being found or downed."

"I'll take that bet. I haven't seen easy money come rolling my way for some time."

"Going to be a while longer too," Blancanales said with a grin, jerking his thumb back to the doorway of the weapons lab.

Katz stood there with his arms folded over his chest, dressed in skintight black. His black beret was tilted rakishly over his forehead, and his light blue eyes twinkled.

"No fucking way, ace," Kissinger growled. He nudged Schwarz aside and took over the keyboard. "No way could you have beat this system legit." He punched buttons, and file names scrolled up obediently.

McCarter laughed out loud and held out his hand. "Pay up, Lyons."

Standing up with a grimace of displeasure twisting his mouth, Ironman reached into his pocket.

Kissinger turned around. A line was highlighted on his screen. "You slipped a virus into the security program. You programmed it not to recognize you as a threat."

"And the human element was decidedly more easy to overcome once all the advantages of sophistication were removed," Katz agreed. "These tests are done to derive any holes within the security network. I found one." He smiled. "And, as I've said before, I don't like to lose."

"The twenty, Ironman," McCarter prompted. "A bet's a bet."

"He cheated."

"He beat the system."

Before the debate could reach a truly boisterous intensity, the computer screens in the weapons lab flickered. The Stony Man warriors put a damper on the festivities as they watched the yellow alert on the monitors shift to full red.

McCarter put his empty bottle down and hustled for the main house with the others. Whatever was going down was going down *now*.

CHAPTER EIGHT

Beirut, Lebanon

Second Day—6:23 a.m.

Dr. Fahad Rihani held the framed eight-by-ten color portrait in trembling hands. He sat at a wooden desk in the small office of what used to be a thriving import-export business before the civil war in Lebanon had killed the proprietor and his family. Many had lived within the walls over the next years. The periods of time had varied. In the end it fell into Hezbollah hands and remained there.

The walls had been reinforced with debris that fell from the three upper stories. Windows had been filled in, as well, turning it into a war bunker. There was no electricity. Tallow candles burned on the desktop and in holders mounted on the wall. Thick black smoke spiraled toward a small flume in the center of the ceiling, leaving behind a wicked scent that burned the sinus cavities. The building now had two hidden exits.

Candlelight flickered across the glass over the picture, highlighting the woman's hair, making the smile on her lips touch her eyes.

Rihani sighed, feeling the pain stir anew within his breast. She was beautiful. Thick black hair cascaded down her shoulders. Her brown eyes showed a mixture of wisdom and merriment. In the picture she was still young, still alive. Still his.

As he closed his eyes, the sharp odor of the candles vanished, replaced by the warm scent of the woman. Rihani breathed in deeply and whispered her name. "Jamila." The echo bounced around the small room and came back to him empty and cold.

He blinked, shutting away the pain. There would be an end to that after he'd brought vengeance to his enemies, after he'd ripped Israel from the face of the world. Tenderly he reached for the supple cloth on the desk and wrapped the picture, binding it with faded yellow scarves Jamila had once worn. He secured it in a safe place in the duffel Faisel had made of his personal things.

A low knock sounded on the wooden door.

"Come," Rihani called, settling back into the chair.

Faisel entered, stepping carefully over the piles of bedding that covered the broken concrete floor. An AK-47 was slung over his shoulder, pointing down. He wore traditional dress now, as did Rihani. The outline of a holstered pistol was under the robe. "Have I interrupted your rest?" Faisel asked.

"No. I can't rest until I've accomplished the mission that burns in my soul. It's a burden for me, and I must shoulder it."

"God grant you wisdom, strength and patience." Faisel reached for a spindly chair. Placing it in front of the desk, he sat, the Russian assault rifle beside him.

Rihani recognized the troubled look on his friend's face. He steepled his fingers before him, resting his elbows on the desk. "There's a problem with the delivery of the weapons?" His voice was quiet, soothing, a pattern he fell into unconsciously once he noticed tension in others. It wasn't so much a consideration, he'd learned, as it was a deadly tool in skilled hands.

"No, the weapons are granted to us freely from the Libyan colonel. They'll be arriving very soon."

"And the payment?"

Faisel waved. "It'll be made at our convenience as was agreed." His eyes flashed. "Our Libyan benefactor also wished us success in our efforts."

"Of course," Rihani said. "They'll be his successes, as well, with no chance of loss to him."

"Yes."

"Then what is it that troubles you, Badr?"

"You know me too well."

"As only I know myself."

Faisel grimaced. "There's talk among the others who have linked their causes to those of the Party of God," he stated.

"And what do they talk of?"

"You, my brother."

Rihani remained silent, shifting his gaze to the tip of a lighted candle because he knew Faisel would find it too weighty to bear. "And what is said?"

"You must realize that you've been gone from us so long."

"It has been as God wills. Now He wills me to return, to take up the sword against our enemies again."

"This I know in my heart, but our comrades think the years have blunted your abilities."

Rihani flicked his deadly black gaze at his lifelong friend. "You know me."

"Yes."

"You know that the years I've spent as a prisoner of the Mossad have left me unbroken and unbent."

"Yes."

Rihani lowered his voice. "I was reborn the day Jamila was killed."

"I know, Fahad. I helped you bury her and shared your tears and grief as my own."

"God has seen fit to return me now. He knows I'll carry the burning brand of retribution to the cursed Israelis. I gladly take up the call of the great war to drive the Great Satan and his puppets from our lands."

Faisel bowed his head. "I know this, but many of our warriors are new to us. They don't know you to be the instrument of God come to smite our enemies. Some among them say you've been away too long, that you've learned how only to be a prisoner. Some say you'll never think as a

holy warrior should and that you'll only continue to fear
your return to an Israeli prison."

"And what do you tell them, Badr?"

"I tell them they're wrong."

"And do they believe you?"

"No. They're guided by fears of their own."

"They fear the retribution of the Americans and Europeans?"

"Yes. Never did they expect so many hostages."

"How many?"

"Dozens of them. And we left dozens of wounded and
dead. They fear we're walking on the edge of a sword."

"That's where a warrior lives," Rihani said simply. "It's
where his heart beats strongest."

Rihani flicked his gaze back to the candle flame. "The
Israelis will never imprison me again. Truly they never
could. The only true prison is a man's mind. If you chop
away all of his bridges to the outside world, let him see only
what you wish him to see, let him feel only what you wish
him to feel, then you have truly imprisoned him. But only
death lies in wait for me if I'm returned to Israeli hands.
And I'll never die until I've brought them to their knees.
God will grant me the strength to do that."

"They'll listen to your words, Fahad."

"But they won't believe."

"I do not think so."

Rihani leaned forward and closed his forefinger and
thumb on the candlewick, ignoring the quick bite of burning pain. "Belief is a powerful thing," he said quietly,
looking up. "And I'll make them believe me. A demonstration is in order, for our people as well as our enemies."

"Yes, my brother."

"I need solitude while I make the preparations."

Faisel slid quietly from the chair, putting it back against
the wall, the AK-47 already back at his side. He paused at
the door. "If you would change your mind about a gun, I'd
see to it you had one immediately."

"No." Rihani's reply was adamant.

"We have many enemies," Faisel reminded him. "They'll all want you dead now. A gun may save your life."

"No. My weapon is here." Rihani touched his temple with tapered fingers. "God has graced me with a gift few men have. I won't dishonor it by choosing not to trust in it."

"As you wish."

Faisel left and the door clicked closed behind him.

Rihani heard the man talking to the guards outside the door as he levered himself out of his seat. His muscles ached from unaccustomed activity, but it was a pleasant pain that served to heighten his awareness. He crossed the room to the black medical bag that had been delivered less than an hour ago. Unlocking the clasps, he peered inside, gazing at the collection of chemicals and syringes.

Closing the bag, he gazed into the mirror hanging from the cracked plaster wall. His magnetic black gaze absorbed him as a candle flame reflected across the surface of his eyes. The dark depths stirred restlessly. No man he'd ever faced on his chosen battlefield had ever possessed the power to defy him. And no man ever would, he vowed silently.

He picked up the black medical bag and carried it with him, as much a part of him now as it had been all those years ago. Only he knew the true horror he could wreak with it. But it was time to reveal some of his abilities and show the hostage nations how much he was able to control.

He was smiling in anticipation by the time he reached the door.

CHAPTER NINE

Stony Man Farm, Virginia

Second Day—12:01 a.m.

"Come on, baby, give it up." Aaron Kurtzman fingered the keyboard diligently, milking the tapped systems for information for all they were worth. At present he had a tagalong connected to intelligence lines stemming out of the CIA, the State Department and a Mossad fringe group. He'd even plugged the system into a CBS newsline satellite feed that had a camera crew working inside Beirut, relaying audio and video. Another sporadic feed was cross-referenced into a KGB outpost operating in Tbilisi and served to pick up further hints of the struggle going on inside Lebanon.

Kurtzman was a big man even in the wheelchair. He was built more along the lines of a nineteenth-century blacksmith than a man whose mind constantly challenged the depths of artificial intelligence and computer systems.

He sat at the helm of his U-shaped desk listening to the clack and whir of his world-within-a-world, captaining his electronic battleship powered by binary fusion as he searched for the elusive bits of intelligence Bolan and the other Stony Man teams would be needing. The fighting took place in the trenches. He knew that. He'd been a trench fighter at one time in his career himself. But for Stony Man the war frequently began here and often depended largely on the amount of information and disinformation he could collate and dismiss.

He sighed, rubbed a big hand over his face, then pushed his palms against the arms of the wheelchair to work the kinks from his spine. Something popped tiredly between his shoulders, and it didn't sound reassuring. He leaned forward, scanning the dozens of monitors mounted along three of the room's walls. Normally they were kept covered behind false paneling, not necessary for the shows he gave the Stony Man warriors. Tonight they were all active, manned by three other members of his crew while another half dozen waited in the wings between shifts.

Carmen Delahunt was old-line FBI material that Hal Brognola had raided from Quantico. Sharp, vivacious and equipped with a temper that matched her red hair, Carmen was someone Kurtzman had counted on for years behind the scenes. She was divorced, with the last of her three children attending college in Maryland. Like the others, she wore a white lab coat and casual dress, favoring a pair of faded jeans, yellow sweater and tennis shoes. She worked her board like a machine, only making casual adjustments to her glasses as she scanned the material.

Akira Tokaido was young, cocky and unconventional in his methods. Rather than regarding the computer hard- and software as a tool, he seemed to think of it more as a prosthesis for his mind. He often followed his own paths of logical reasoning, and Kurtzman let him because Tokaido often came up with off-the-wall solutions that had evaded others. He was lean and compact with a shock of punk-cut black hair. He chewed bubble gum constantly and kept one ear plugged into a mini-CD player that no doubt played the latest in heavy metal. The CD player was another thing Kurtzman had allowed because it seemed to enhance Tokaido's performance rather than detract from it. His fingers blurred on the keyboard as he watched his personal collection of monitors.

Last up was Huntington Wethers, a black professor of cybernetics whom Kurtzman had recruited from Berkeley five years before. Hunt Wethers was the only man on the Stony Man computer team who looked at the computers more as a science than as a means of leveraging information. Tall and well built with gray hair staining his temples,

Wethers and Kurtzman often shared mind-expanding conversation well into the wee hours of the night concerning facets of unexplored cybernetics. He clenched an unlit pipe between his teeth as he worked.

Disgruntled with the progress being made, Kurtzman fed a new command into his keyboard. Instantly the large screen on the wall at the opposite end of the room flickered and changed. A world map skated across the screen's surface in shades of dark blues and dark greens, imaging larger and larger as the focus was aimed at the Middle East. Nearly a dozen yellow-lighted blips pulsed at him in silent accusation.

"Coffee, Aaron?"

Kurtzman wheeled his chair around at the sound of the woman's voice. Barbara Price, mission controller for the Farm, had entered the room. He'd been so involved in what he could and couldn't figure out that he hadn't seen her come in. "Yeah."

Price lifted the stained glass pot and examined it. "It's about time for an oil change, don't you think?" Wearing a dark business suit complete with matching jacket, she had the face and shape of a model yet the keen and decisive wit of a military commander.

"C'mon, Barb, anyone can see it's easily got another thousand hours in it before we have to clean it." Kurtzman grinned in spite of the pressure he felt. His coffee was a long-standing joke between his colleagues, and a source of many scathing barbs from Grimaldi and McCarter. One of them, he couldn't remember which, had suggested Kurtzman made it so bad because he wanted it as a last-ditch effort to stave off sleep. Too much caffeine would give a person a case of the jitters, but the thought of one cup of coffee made that same person reach for a second wind before a second cup.

She poured him a cup and brought it over, sticking with the glass of orange juice she had in her hand. "Anything new?"

"We're still confirming the hostage lists," Kurtzman replied, turning his attention to the keyboard. "Carmen?"

"Yes?"

"Shoot me the roll call."

"On its way."

Kurtzman folded his arms across his chest and watched as the lists obediently scrolled across his master screen—names, places of origin, departure and arrival, and expected periods of stay. A heading containing each hotel, the country and the time of incidence preceded each batch.

"How many?" Price asked.

"Almost a hundred so far." Kurtzman punched more buttons. Other screens filled with more tracts of information. "To the left you have a list of confirmed dead, and it's weighing in close at sixty names, with more coming in as the wreckage is sifted through in Beirut. That isn't counting the domestic casualties I can't pin down. The CBS news team has found over two dozen unidentified bodies, though. On the right are the people we know for sure to be over there but are listed as MIA at the moment. It's tough sledding now because everyone wants to play this close to the vest. They figure the more information they give away, the more the terrorists will have to use against them."

"The incidence times are all within minutes of each other," Price commented.

"Oh, yeah, this thing was planned down to the nines, and they pulled it off like pros. Except for that run-in with Striker."

"Have any of the terrorists he and Jack put down at the scene been ID'ed?"

"Tentatively. They're Hezbollah."

"The Mossad should have files on a number of those people."

"They do, but the Mossad isn't being exactly cooperative at the moment."

"Why?"

"From the layers of red tape I've been able to peel away without being discovered, it looks like some kind of internal security problem."

"What does that have to do with us?"

Kurtzman fingered the rim of his coffee cup. "They might figure we're part of the problem." He raised his voice. "Hunt, give me that file on Major Deering."

"Coming." Wethers shifted his pipe as he inscribed instructions.

"Who's Deering?" Price asked.

"Jack drew a wild card during the infiltration of the hotel in Beirut," Kurtzman said, bending to his board. "Found a U.S. soldier in civvies who said he was there with Major Deering before he died." A color still popped up on the master screen.

The man in the picture was in full Army dress. He looked to be in his late fifties, with close-cropped iron-gray hair and a neatly trimmed full mustache.

"Major Deering?" Price asked.

"Major Deering." Kurtzman confirmed. He punched more buttons, and the military man's record began flipping through.

"Decorated." Price observed.

"Very," Kurtzman said. "A real career man."

"Where does he fit?"

"Beats me. According to the Army's file on Major William H. Deering, the man's in the Philippines now on a sensitive assignment."

"Have you been able to confirm that?"

"No. But then we haven't been able to confirm that he isn't, either."

"Our missing major has spent a lot of time in Lebanon," Price said. She sipped her orange juice thoughtfully.

Kurtzman glanced at the man's TDY sheet and nodded. "And this is only what's on the surface without counting covert operations." He let her think about it. Wherever Brognola had recruited the woman—and Kurtzman wasn't sure because he made it a point never to spy on friends or associates unless there was blood involved—she'd learned her trade well. He guessed from somewhere in one of the never-to-be seen arms of the National Security Agency. Not only was she careful, organized and daring, but she had an intuitive streak that he wouldn't have bet against in the face of stacks of hard evidence. His world dealt in facts and figures; Barbara Price's often dipped somewhere over the horizon for surprising results.

"We need to find him."

"We will." Kurtzman sipped his coffee again and watched as Carmen Delahunt slipped two more confirmed names onto the hostage list. She also added three more dead and another twelve domestic casualties.

"Where's Striker?"

"En route," Kurtzman replied. "I've got a message waiting for him and Jack on the USS *Winkler*. I've added a little knowledge to what we had before, but I didn't dare pump it over to him at the Israeli embassy."

"You can also let him know Murtaugh's been pulled and should be on a chartered flight out of Haifa—" she glanced at her watch "—twenty minutes ago."

"The State Department?"

"Surprisingly polite about the whole matter."

"Despite the fact that we fielded a team into Beirut without their knowledge?"

Price gave him a sugary sweet smile. "It's still without their knowledge, Aaron. At least they didn't feel they had enough to call me on it."

"And if they had?"

"Hal's in with the President now. They wouldn't have gotten far."

"Hey, Aaron."

Kurtzman looked up at Akira Tokaido.

The young man blew a pink bubble and popped it, revealing the white smile underneath. "I think I found our military intelligence bogey."

"Don't just sit there with that self-satisfied smirk on your face," Kurtzman growled. "Run it onto the screen."

"Coming at you." Tokaido tapped his keys with the rapidity of an assault rifle at full-throttle.

Kurtzman watched as passenger lists to and from the Philippines shuffled back and forth across the screen.

"We know Deering took a flight out of Dulles to the Philippines," Tokaido said as he continued to work the keyboard. "And we know according to military files he's still there. So I worked on uncovering another common denominator. Assuming the Army manufactured a cover for our missing major, I poked holes in the passenger lists leaving the Philippines in the past three days. After all, we knew where Deering was for sure three days ago."

The lists shortened as Kurtzman observed them, already guessing Tokaido's next moves. The different airlines coalesced into one list.

"Here," Tokaido said, "you have a list of regular passengers who fly to the Philippines on business. I figured military intelligence would want a name that was known to the computers and wouldn't draw attention to itself. Once I let myself play with that, I also assumed they'd pull a civilian out of the pot and give him the 'for God and country' speech." The screen rescrolled with fewer names. "Here you have only the male names." The screen rescrolled. "Names of people who were verified at later stops than Beirut, where there was a brief landing, are left off this one." Another list appeared. "I used insurance carriers purchased at the airport to find out the ages of some of the remaining male passengers. Anybody who wasn't Deering's age was automatically dropped off the list."

Only a half-dozen names remained. "One of those is a confirmed casualty." The screen rescrolled, leaving five names. "Two of them are at the rescue site awaiting airlift out." Obediently three names were centered on the screen.

Tokaido's grin widened. "The rest is a simple matter of trial and error. I tapped AT&T records, researched the calling card number of George Timmons and found out it had been used less than an hour ago at Manila." He held up his arms like goalposts. "TD, Coach, and the kid's not even breathing hard."

"Good work, Akira." Kurtzman couldn't suppress a smile as he scrolled through the hostage list and found George Timmons's name. His team meant a lot to him, and he took pride in their efforts. "Now if we can figure out what Deering was doing there and how Hezbollah found him, maybe we'll be in business."

Hunt Wethers turned in his chair and tapped the stem of his pipe against his teeth. "Perhaps I can venture some guesswork on the why."

"You penetrated military intelligence files?" Kurtzman asked.

"No, but I've shadowboxed with them enough that I feel qualified in assuming."

"So give."

"Deering's been involved in political and military affairs in Lebanon before. That's a fact. He's also been called on to do some sensitive hostage negotiations for the embassy people. Fact again. Deering knows who to grease over there for information. That's supposition, but I accept it as a given. However, the Israelis are suspicious of us for more than just Striker's movements alone. They couldn't fault the man for wanting to keep the integrity of his operation. That much is guesswork, but I think it hangs with the structure I've got going."

"You feel it's something other than Striker's operation?"

"From a peek at Deering's jacket, I'd say, yeah, I not only feel it, but I believe it, too. I think Deering went to Beirut to get something Israel wouldn't want him to have. It's no secret that the Mossad has planted spies within our intelligence networks before. And we've not exactly been shy about doing the same ourselves."

Kurtzman didn't bother to mention Murtaugh. As senior over the intelligence network at Stony Man, he was privy to a lot more intel than was normally released to anyone. "You think the Israelis made Deering?"

"Yep. Either during or after the Hezbollah raids." Wethers stuck his pipe between his teeth.

Kurtzman looked over his team. "Deering's a negotiator on special assignment. Okay. It's a scenario I'll buy until something else comes along. If I was military intelligence looking for a buy-back, what would the prize be? Hunt, Akira, that's your assignment. Carmen, stay on those lists. I want to build some kind of data base concerning the hostages so that our guys can take some of the guesswork out of what they'll find when they go in after them.''

The three computer techs turned back to their screens.

"I can tell you how Hezbollah knew Deering was there." Barbara Price commented quietly.

Kurtzman looked at her expectantly.

"The case of the purloined letter, Aaron. He wasn't hiding from *them*. No mystery involved at all.''

"You think military intelligence was putting something together with Hezbollah behind Israel's back?"

"I don't think it was just the Israelis who were caught with their pants down," Price said. "I'm betting Hal and the President are going to be interested in this, too.''

"Still doesn't tell us what the prize was.''

"No, but knowing who might have had access to it means a lot, doesn't it?''

"Yeah.'' Kurtzman sipped his coffee and turned back to his keyboard, thinking about correlations and possibilities. His temples throbbed. He hadn't even felt the headache coming on.

"Where's Able and Phoenix?" Price asked.

"In the war room since you had me flash the red alert,'' Kurtzman answered.

"I'll go down and bring them up to speed on this. If you find out anything, let me know.''

"Count on it.''

"I am.''

Kurtzman pushed his frustration away. The answers were there. Somewhere in the tangled skeins in the overlapping fields of cyberspace, they were all there. They couldn't evade him forever. Doubt clouded his thoughts. Even though they couldn't escape his reach forever, the answers could be long enough in coming to make a difference. How much of a difference remained to be seen. The problem was, a difference at this stage of the operation was usually measured in lives.

CHAPTER TEN

Beirut, Lebanon

Second Day—7:43 a.m.

Jessi Grafton focused on her skills as a reporter to keep the fear away. She couldn't sleep. When she tried, the panel truck would invariably hit another rough place in the road and bounce her skull into the metal sides. Her butt ached with fatigue brought on by her posture, but there was nowhere to move. The van floor was covered by women who were every bit as cramped for space as she was.

Two guards sat in the back with them. Instead of firearms, the men held wickedly curved knives that were almost long enough to be called swords. Both men had a reptilian look about them, like lizards sunning themselves on rocks. The knives were never relaxed from their grips, and were held resolutely in hard-knuckled hands.

Grafton shifted her shoulder. It had gone to sleep even though she couldn't. But it had help. The fourteen-year-old British girl who'd sought her out lay almost catatonic in her arms. From time to time the reporter smoothed her hair and talked to her, trying in vain to elicit some kind of response. All she'd been able to find out was the girl's name: Beth.

Abruptly the panel truck slowed, drawing the attention of the prisoners in the form of fearful glances and turning heads. Most of them were clad in nightclothes and robes, contributing to the feeling of dehumanization. Grafton felt sorry for the women. A sudden turn threw some of them off balance, scattering them in a twisting of arms and legs and starting a new chorus of frightened shrieks.

The guards got to their feet at once, taking up positions by the sliding door. They made motions with their free hands, waving everyone to their feet. Struggling to disentangle the girl long enough to get them both up, Grafton watched as the door slid open. Three more men filled the rectangle, carrying the black hoods. The prisoners were shoved out to the waiting men one at a time where they were hooded and bound. No one tried to fight.

Grafton held the girl until she was taken from her. Beth kicked and screamed for a moment, then tried to curl up into a fetal ball. They carried her away. Grafton turned her attention to her surroundings. Early-morning sunlight filtered through a haze of dust. The panel truck had been parked at the rear of a multistoried building that reached high into the blue sky. Rubble lay all around them. Broken walls formed a narrow cul-de-sac that ended at the building. More of the terrorists hid along the walls and empty windows, their weapons out in the open. Evidently they considered themselves to be on safe ground.

An older woman fell down in front of Grafton. She knelt immediately and tried to examine her. One of the guards stepped forward, raising the knife menacingly.

Unable to control her anger, Grafton snarled, "She can't get up, you bastard. Can't you see that?" The arm felt light and brittle in her hand.

The guard retreated and conferred with the others.

Grafton checked the woman's pulse and found it thready and weak. "Hang in there," she said to the woman. "It's going to be okay." The woman's heart fluttered its last beat under the journalist's fingertips. Reacting instinctively, she rolled the woman on her back, doubled her hands up and began CPR.

"Oh, my God!" another woman screamed.

Grafton ignored the confusion, concentrating on her inner count. She pushed against the sternum, then pushed again and again. Straining with the effort now, she reached for the woman's mouth, intending to make sure her tongue hadn't become an obstruction before starting artificial respiration.

One of the terrorists grabbed her elbow and tried to pull her away.

Grafton jerked free. "No, goddamn it. If you don't let me do this, she's going to die." She opened the woman's mouth with effort.

A guttural voice ordered her to stop in English, but she ignored it.

She had an impression of something moving, then pain slashed at the left side of her face. She rolled away from the force of the blow, tasting blood inside her mouth. Dazed, she tried to get her feet under her, thinking that the woman was dying.

Before she could get her tearing eyes open, she was yanked out of the panel truck. She fell full-length onto the heaps of rock-edged rubble, and the air was forced from her lungs. Her head spun dizzily. Flesh tore on her palms as she tried to force herself up. Rough hands grabbed her and pulled her arms behind her back. As one of the terrorists bound her wrists, she watched another use his knife on the throat of the older woman. Blood seeped out slowly, thick and dark. There was no heartbeat to propel it on its way.

As much as she'd learned to hate the black hood earlier, it was almost like tender mercy as they dropped it over her head now. Someone led her away and she went, stumbling over the refuse.

CHAPTER ELEVEN

The Red Sea

Second Day—8:08 a.m.

Bolan watched the gray bulk of the USS *Winkler* come into view. Smaller craft moved around the aircraft carrier, support vehicles going about their day-to-day business. His eyes felt grainy, and they ached despite the aviator sunglasses Grimaldi had passed over from his kit earlier at sunup.

Grimaldi pointed. Bolan followed his line of sight and saw the F-14 Tomcat sitting on deck in the ready position, a flight crew attending to last-minute details of the attack plane. He felt his seat belt snug tighter as the helicopter heeled over and dropped altitude.

"I'm on the wings as soon as we touch down," Grimaldi said, cupping his hands to be heard.

Bolan gave him a thumbs-up and a nod.

The helicopter's skids touched down lightly despite the ocean's movement. Curious deck hands turned to watch Bolan and Grimaldi disembark, fanning out along the lines of the other aircraft and gun emplacements. Holding his jacket over his arm and knowing the Detonics Scoremaster was clearly revealed to the crew, Bolan moved for the tower. Grimaldi trotted toward the Navy fighter, and the flight crew made room for him.

An older man in admiral's dress came around another line of Tomcats with three aides in tow. The admiral had his hat tucked under his left arm, and his white hair blew in the wind. He offered a hand as the helicopter moved off again. "Admiral Pete McGill. We've been expecting you."

Bolan took the man's hand and shook it. His first impulse—from a life he could never quite forget—had been to salute. The older man was covered in brass and looked to be the epitome of spit and polish. "Belasko." he replied. His cover didn't provide a title. It didn't need to.

"Don't know who you are, soldier..." McGill said as he waved him toward the tower, "but I got a call from the President himself to get you on board and see to anything you wanted as quick as I could."

"Just the bird," Bolan replied, "and lift-off soon as you can get it."

"Say the word, son, and it's yours."

"Fair enough, Admiral." Bolan followed the man through the heart of the tower to a small room outfitted with a desk, two chairs and a bookcase.

"Got a message a few minutes ago," McGill told him. He handed over a slip of paper with a number on it. "Didn't leave his name. I figured you'd know who it was."

"Yeah."

"I've got a ship-to-shore line scrambled and standing by for you."

"Thanks." Bolan lifted the handset while the admiral showed himself out. He cleared the number through the communications officer, then waited for the connection.

"Striker?" Hal Brognola's voice asked.

"Yeah." Bolan seated himself in the office chair across from the admiral's desk, feeling fatigue flood through him. Only memories of the blood and death, and an instinctive reaction to preserve life kept him going. He knew he was going to have to grab some sack time quick or he wasn't going to be of use to anyone.

"Any problems with your connecting flight?"

"We go on my say."

"Bear told me he'd clued you in to the other hostage situations that developed after your soft probe into Beirut."

"Right. How many people are we looking at?"

"As of last count, one hundred seventeen with another twenty-three to be sorted out. But we're turning more casualties than hostages at this point."

Bolan ran the figure through his head, calibrating the complexities that faced the Stony Man teams.

"All hell's breaking loose out there, Striker. Every one of those people were taken by factions of Hezbollah or sympathy groups we didn't know existed. This is the biggest damn example of terrorist networking we've ever encountered. Aaron's even turned up a whiff of a rumor that part of the hostage raid is being bankrolled by Libya."

"That's not surprising in that corner of the world. Has any contact been made with the terrorists yet?"

"No. And that seems to be the most unnerving thing of all. They had a game plan, and it went down by the numbers. So why the holdup in negotiations or demands?"

"Maybe that's in the game plan, too."

"Ah, batshit, Striker, it's the waiting for the other shoe to drop that kills you."

"What about Deering?"

"Still among the missing. But Bear thinks he's got Deering as definitely being pegged on some covert operation in Beirut."

"The Man doesn't know anything about it?"

"He tells me no. I believe him. We've got some tracers out at this end, but none of the generals on the Hill want to lay claim to their pigeon."

"Understandable in light of the situation."

"Yeah, well, the mood's pretty ugly here on Pennsylvania Avenue, too."

"Have Aaron stay with it and see what turns up."

"I am. I've got a feeling we're going to be turning over some really nasty rocks before everything's said and done."

"Yeah. I know."

"The Israelis may offer only token assistance at this point until we get the Deering situation squared away. Seems they lost a high-priority prisoner themselves last night."

"Who?"

"Don't know. Yet. Aaron's still working on that question, too."

"Have you heard anything about where the hostages are being held?"

"Nothing's firmed up, but we think Hezbollah have them holed up somewhere in Lebanon. It's a position of power for them, especially if some of the other Shiite factions are backing their play."

"That's the way I had it figured, too. Have Aaron pour as much satellite recon into the area as he can."

"Already done, guy. We're pulling out all the stops on this one."

"Able and Phoenix?"

"Waiting on your call."

"It's going to be made as soon as I hit stateside."

"Fair enough."

Bolan made adjustments to his lists of ideas and possible alternatives to infiltration of Lebanon. Either way it went, with the Israeli support groups blowing hot and cold, they were severely undermined for a mission of this magnitude.

"The Man wants you to head this up," Brognola said, breaking into the silence. "He told me to ask."

"You knew what my answer would be."

"Yeah, I told him that, too, but he wanted me to ask, anyway. This is going to be a high-profile score, Striker, and there's no escaping that. The blowup with Iraq has already primed the media for this kind of thing. There's news teams already grounded in Beirut with more on the way. We've held up as many passports through the State Department as we were able, but a lot of free-lancers are willing to hit the dirt for the kind of money the networks are going to throw at them."

"We're going to need temporary bases of operation once the infiltration goes through," Bolan said. "And weapons. Extracting that many people isn't going to be a cakewalk."

"No problem. The Soviets have already offered us full support, and they're working out some other details, as well. Could be we'll end up with more than what we'd expected."

"It won't come together without the Israelis."

"I know." Brognola sighed. "The Man and I are working on that now. If we can clear up some of the mystery concerning Deering without tipping our hand in case they suspect it's something less than what it is, we think we have a shot at putting everything together. Exfiltration is going to be goddamn impossible without them."

"Where's Deering?"

"On the hostage list for now. There were confirmed sightings besides the soldier's report that he was taken."

"But he *is* alive?"

"Yeah. I know. Whatever the man's mission, he's another loose cannon we have to worry about."

"Get Aaron to run me hard copy on the reports he turns up. I want to look it over for a while on my own while I get things in perspective."

"You got it. Anything else?"

"Tell Barb I want two alternate routes for every primary route we choose—one ground and one air—and backup supplies ready for airdrop if we need it. If the Russians are supporting us in this, have her work out the logistics through them. It'll give her something to work out while she's waiting on Jack and me. If this is going to be a surgical strike into the heart of this new terrorism, the ability to travel and change routes can't be a question."

"I'll pass it on."

Bolan softened his voice. "Up front, Hal, no matter how this thing goes down, it's going to be bloody all the way around."

"It already is, big guy, but I don't want those people we lost to have died for nothing. Neither does the Man."

"Stay hard," Bolan said, then broke the connection. He folded his jacket over his arm and headed for the deck. He found Admiral McGill surveying the flight deck with a practiced eye.

McGill turned at his approach, the brim of his hat shading his eyes. "Find everything, son?"

"Yes, sir. I appreciate the loan of your office."

The admiral waved it away. "It's just an office. Now this lady you're standing on, that'd be a different matter entirely."

Bolan grinned at the pride he heard in the other man's voice. "Yes, sir."

Squinting up at him with one eye, McGill asked, "Military?"

"Yes, sir. A long time ago."

"Haven't forgot your training."

"No, sir. I suppose not."

"Well, son, I still don't know what it is you're doing here exactly, but I got me a hunch. I'm not a betting man, but I'd bet on this one. I just want you to know, if you get back over this way real soon and happen to need a hell of a ship to back your play, me and the lady will be right here."

"Yes, sir. I'll remember that."

"You do that."

Bolan held out a hand and the admiral took it.

"Godspeed, son."

"You, too, sir." Bolan trotted over to Grimaldi and the waiting Tomcat. The F-14 was already snugged up in the catapult, waiting to claw into the air. He dropped into the back seat and belted up in the parachute and harness rigging as the flight crew locked the canopy down.

Grimaldi's voice crackled into his ears over the radio. "Ready?"

"Hit it."

Grimaldi called for the launch.

The flagman dropped his fluorescent banners. Explosive g-force dropped an anvil on Bolan's chest as his peripheral vision blurred with the motion. The flight deck fell away beneath them, gunmetal-gray giving away to the dark emerald of the Red Sea.

Grimaldi rolled expertly as he brought the Tomcat around, bringing the USS *Winkler* into view a final time before kicking in full burn and getting out of there.

CHAPTER TWELVE

The Oval Office, Washington, D.C.

Second Day—1:10 a.m.

Hal Brognola walked through the quiet hallways of the White House. He didn't bother to wear a name badge. All the Secret Service people had been briefed about him, and his clearance had come from the top office itself. Reporters manned the pressrooms at all hours, awaiting the latest news. From time to time some of the more aggressive ones made it out into the halls and forced a confrontation with the military advisers who were also on call. A name badge would have let them know immediately who he was, and it was no secret that Brognola was figuring into the present scheme of things in a big way. The people just weren't aware how. He breathed a silent prayer that they never would as he popped another antacid tablet and ground it between his teeth.

Reluctantly he rebuttoned his suit coat and straightened his tie as he came to a stop in front of the back door to the Oval Office. Despite the lax stand on formality this late at night, he was a man who believed in showing respect to the Man and the office. No matter what the clearance or the support he got from the Man who worked inside, he still felt odd sporting the Chief's Special .38 on his hip. Yet it had been at the President's request. So far they hadn't clearly identified their enemy, and the covert nature of Stony Man Farm demanded that Brognola and the President spend much of their time planning alone.

Brognola nodded at the fresh-faced Secret Service woman standing guard at the door. She looked prim and proper in her business suit, like a college student going for that all-important first interview rather than someone who had hired on to take a bullet for the President of the United States.

She nodded back and opened the door, stepping out of his way as she kept him out of her line of fire. Her smile was slight, perfunctory. He went in and she closed the door behind him.

The President stood behind his desk, looking through the slatted blinds and bulletproof glass. His hands were clasped behind his back and his shoulders slumped. Highlights danced off his glasses as he turned to look at Brognola. "Is he coming?"

"Yes, sir. He's never let you or this country down before." The big Fed glanced down at the cluttered desktop. The coffee service wasn't the only thing new. Bulging files had been added to the stacks already there.

"To paraphrase a colleague of mine many years removed," the President said, "these are the times that try men's souls."

"I know."

The Man lifted the coffeepot and glanced at Brognola. The head Fed nodded, still not completely relaxed about the Man's easy manner after the years they'd served together. He took the coffee.

Maps of the Middle East and surrounding countries had been taped to all the walls, filling every available space. The President had insisted on seeing the logistics for himself.

"While you were gone," the President said, "I was notified concerning the identity of Major Deering's ultimate commanding officer on this mission. General Ernest Dwight, I've been told, is en route to this office, accompanied by an Army colonel I trust implicitly. I want you here when I confront him."

"Yes, sir." Brognola didn't mind that in the slightest. The rescue teams were going to be culled from his people, and he wanted every bit of information concerning the situation he could get his hands on. "Have you found out what Deering was doing in Beirut?"

"Not at this time." The President sipped his coffee and walked along the row of maps. The intercom squawked. The Man touched a button. "Yes, Becky?"

"Sir, another of the CBS special reports is getting ready to air."

"Thank you." The President flicked off the intercom and took a remote control from his desk. A panel rolled back in the wall and revealed a twenty-five inch console with attached VCR. The set hummed and crackled as it came to life, and the red recording light of the VCR winked on.

The well-known face of the anchorman seemed gray with age and fatigue. Breaking into live transmission, the anchor posed questions of the journalist team in Beirut as the cameraman panned the area where they were. Broken buildings, smashed and burned cars, refuse, empty shop windows and bodies were revealed to the viewing audience. Thick black smoke shifted on a gentle wind as orange and yellow flames curled and twisted in the wreckage. Somewhere in there Brognola thought he could see the burning remnants of a van.

The cameraman zoomed in on a running pair of men dressed in ragged robes. The men's faces were full of fear, marked by scabbed-over injuries. Shots rang out, amplified and strangely flattened by the pickup mike of the Camcorder. The two men pitched facedown onto the street, vanishing under the wheels of a government truck that barreled around a corner. The reporter's voice suggested to the cameraman that they get the hell out of there and the transmission ended abruptly.

The news anchor came back on. He seemed caught off guard, and as he gathered his thoughts, he shuffled the pages in front of him. "We'll try to reestablish communications with our ground crew as soon as possible. Until then let me recap the events leading up to the current situation."

The President triggered the remote control, and the panel swallowed up the blank television again. "God in heaven," the Man said quietly. "That whole country's a war zone."

Unable to resist the urge any longer, Brognola unwrapped a cigar, stuck it in his mouth and fired it up. He released a steady stream of smoke, feeling some of the pressure go with it. "It has been for some time. This isn't going to be an easy assignment to bring off."

"Neither was Just Cause, but it's something that has to be done, no matter what kind of political backlash comes of it. We're going to stay the course on this one and get those people to safety if at all possible. Are your people willing to get involved?"

Brognola gave him a wintery smile. "Sir, I don't think you could keep them out of it at this point if you tried. Striker's already proved he stands ready to walk the walk no matter which side of the political fence it puts him on."

The President sighed. "I know, Hal. When you work in this office, it gets hard to remember there are people out in the world who don't let their existence hang on political winds." The intercom buzzed again. "Yes, Becky?"

"General Dwight is here to see you, Mr. President."

"Thank you. Send him in. Alone." The Man stood away from his desk.

Brognola flanked him on the other side, watching a cool demeanor settle over the nation's chief executive officer.

Dwight entered the room and closed the door behind him. He saluted sharply, carrying his hat under his arm, then stood at full attention. He was nearing retirement age, and his hair had long since faded to snow-white. Bushy eyebrows partially obscured pale blue eyes that would have looked at home on a killer wolf. His face was full and florid, and the broken veins of a career drinker stained his cheeks and nose. "Good morning, sir," he said crisply.

"At ease, General," the President directed, "and have a seat." He waved at one of the plush chairs in front of the desk.

Dwight's gaze swept the accumulation of maps and photographs strung across the walls. "No, thank you, sir. If you don't mind, I prefer to remain standing."

"As you wish," the President replied. His voice was casual, soft. "I suppose you're wondering why I called you here."

"Yes, sir."

Brognola could feel the hostility radiating from the Army general and judged the man to have been well into a bottle when he'd gotten the order to go to the White House. The big Fed repositioned himself out of habit, readying himself to move quickly. As a rookie patrolman starting out on a beat in the nation's capital, he'd nearly had his guts shown to him by a knife-wielding man he'd figured was too drunk to stand, much less move quickly. It was a lesson he'd never forgotten. A whisk of those ice-blue eyes let him know his movement hadn't gone undetected. He cursed himself silently when he realized rebuttoning his suit coat had put his .38 even farther away if it came down to sudden violence. And the scent of it was definitely in the air.

"It's about this man," the President said, taking a photograph from a file on the desktop. He consulted it briefly himself, as if to verify he had the right one, then extended it across to the general.

Dwight took it and glanced at it quickly before handing it back. "Yes, sir."

The Man accepted the photograph. He held it to his waist, picture out, and there was no way to take it other than as silent accusation. "Tell me about this man."

"That's Major Deering, sir, as you are no doubt aware. William Harding Deering, of military intelligence."

"Yes, General, I'm aware of that. What I don't know is why this man is in Beirut."

"He's in the Philippines, sir, on special assignment."

"That's bullshit and you know it." The President's voice hardened, ringing off the soundproofed walls. He threw the picture down. "I'm only going to tell you this once, soldier, so you'd damn well better listen good. I'm going to ask you some questions, and if you don't come clean with me, I'll have your balls for a pair of rearview mirror knick-knacks."

Dwight blanched, and Brognola had to fight to stifle a grin in spite of the serious nature of the conversation.

"Now tell me what you had this man doing in Beirut."

"Sir, maybe I'd better have my lawyer present while we talk."

The President crossed his hands on his chest. "You're government-issue, mister, not a civilian. Your ass is already hanging from the barn door on this little midnight excursion. If you want some breathing room, you'll have to earn it."

Dwight flicked his gaze toward Brognola. "Who's this man?"

"As far as you're concerned, he's my shadow."

"Brognola, right?" Dwight asked.

Brognola didn't respond. There was a time and a place for everything, and for now it was the President's show.

"Yeah, you're Brognola, all right. You head up your own little dirty tricks division, don't you?"

Brognola returned the fierce gaze full measure.

"General." The Man's tone of voice was an order to attention.

Dwight squared his shoulders from force of habit. "Yes, sir."

"I want a verbal report on Major Deering's mission now."

Eyes focused on the wall behind the President the way the instructors taught at officer candidate school, Dwight said, "Major Deering was in Beirut by my order, sir, to obtain a political prisoner I judged to be a menace to the security of the United States in the hands of any country not our own."

"And you took this upon yourself, General?"

"Yes, sir, I did. I'm familiar with the man in question, and I didn't want to take a chance he'd escape if the order went through the proper channels. Too many things become public knowledge before they can even be acted on."

"Who was the man?"

"Dr. Fahad Rihani."

The President looked at Brognola, who shook his head. The name didn't mean anything to him, but he committed it to memory to give to Kurtzman and his team.

"Who is Rihani?" the President asked.

"He was a Hezbollah leader at one time. He was also on the CIA's payroll."

"I don't remember the man."

"He was slightly before your time, sir, and you can bet any bridges connecting the Agency to Rihani were hard to trace then, and completely gone by now."

"What makes him so important?"

"His capabilities."

Brognola was surprised by the response but didn't let it show.

"What about his capabilities?" the Man asked.

"I don't know, sir. I'd say it's possible he could sabotage some of our standing in the Middle East."

"So you chose to do that yourself?" the President asked.

Dwight didn't try to make a reply.

"If this man Rihani is so dangerous, what was he doing loose until now?"

"He was a prisoner, sir."

Brognola's interest pricked up, knowing the other shoe was about to drop now. His stomach gurgled sourly. He reached down and stubbed the cigar out in an ashtray on the desk's corner.

"Of whom?" the President asked.

"The Mossad, sir." Dwight didn't blink when he said it.

The President turned away, moving back to his window. "Are you telling me, General, that we're responsible for trying to take a prisoner from the Israelis?"

"Only indirectly, sir. Major Deering went to Beirut to hire mercenaries to do the job. Apparently he was double-crossed. When he gave the merc team the location of the prisoner, they evidently betrayed him to Hezbollah."

"When was this?"

"Two days ago."

The President clasped his hands behind his back. "And when, exactly, did Major Deering know he'd been the victim of a ruse?"

"I assume at the time of his capture."

"Do you know where Dr. Rihani is now?"

"No, sir."

"But he's the man who escaped from the Israelis?"

"Yes, sir. I believe so."

"And how do you think they're going to feel when they find out we were responsible for the loss of their prisoner? Assuming, of course, that they don't already know."

"They'll be pissed off as hell," Dwight said without hesitation. Then he added, "Sir."

The President stood in silent, frozen fury.

"It's not as if they're entirely guiltless in this matter themselves," Dwight said. "They had Rihani as a prisoner for years and let us continue to believe he'd been killed in 1983. Rihani's a menace, one that needs to be terminated on sight. Trust me on this."

Facing the general, the President said coolly, "I'm a little lean on trust where you're concerned in this matter. You understand my position, of course."

"Yes, sir."

"Good. As of this moment, General, consider yourself under house arrest. You will speak to no one of the matters we've discussed in this office, or I swear I'll have you in Leavenworth before you can find your butt with both hands."

"Yes, sir."

"Dismissed."

Dwight saluted and executed a crisp about-face before he marched through the door.

The President put his hands in his pant pockets as he worked his jaw uncertainly. "You still want this one, Hal?"

"You got somebody in mind who can do the job better?"

The Man shook his head. "No, of course not. It's just that your teams are going to walk into this with dirty hands.

At this point I can't sanction any of this officially. It just wouldn't be prudent. Too many other people and other countries are involved. And from Dwight's own admission, we're just as guilty as the next man. But I don't want these murderous bastards to get away scot-free with this."

"No, sir. They won't."

"I want our people safely out of the hands of those terrorists as soon as possible. This country isn't going to knuckle under to outside pressures. I want a hard-line protocol established with this operation that will serve as a warning to anyone who even thinks about taking another American hostage."

Brognola nodded.

The President looked at him with tired eyes. "You realize we may be betting the Farm on this one?"

"Yeah, but so far we've always drawn to a winning hand." Brognola couldn't help but think that all streaks came to an end sooner or later. He excused himself to relay the latest information on to Kurtzman and get a new ETA for Bolan, trying to see a way through the confusion that lay waiting for the teams in Beirut. His thoughts built no more than a tunnel, dark and confining, and the only way to find the other end was to enter, come what may.

CHAPTER THIRTEEN

Beirut, Lebanon

Second Day—4:36 p.m.

"We're being followed," Numair announced.

Rihani lounged in the back seat of the ten-year-old limousine with his black bag between his feet. Two guards sat before him with M-16s across their laps. Faisel was beside him, his M-16 canted across the seat. "How many follow us?" Rihani asked, catching the driver's eyes in the rearview mirror.

"One car. Perhaps another."

"Don't draw attention to yourself," Rihani instructed.

"Of course." Numair drove carefully, staying to the right of the traffic.

"Don't search for them," Rihani ordered the guards. The two facing him nodded slightly, mirrored by the bobbing head of the man in the front passenger seat. "Badr."

"Yes?"

"Please take care of it."

"As you wish."

"But I want to speak to the men, to know who they are and who sent them."

Faisel removed a walkie-talkie from his robe and spoke into it briefly.

Rihani flicked his eyes to the rearview mirror. The familiar calm control that locked into place was a welcome sensation. It had been too long since he'd felt in command of his destiny. "Numair, how many follow?"

"Only the one vehicle."

"Don't lose it."

Rihani watched the narrow streets pass with their broken buildings filled with shattered windows. He chafed his wrists unconsciously at the missing weight of the manacles, caught himself and made his hands lie still on his thighs.

"They're in position," Faisel said.

"You know of an area where this can be done?"

"Yes."

"Then let's do it. But remember, I want at least one of the car's occupants left alive."

"As you wish." Faisel gave brisk commands into the walkie-talkie. Numair turned right at his request, taking the corner slowly so that their tail could drop back and follow at a comfortable distance.

The limousine took up most of the alley that wasn't filled with trash cans and makeshift tents. Frightened faces peered out from gathered flaps. Even with the air conditioner on in the luxury car, Rihani could smell the filth and excrement. It offended him and his sensibilities. He steeled himself against it, focusing on the coming confrontation. "Now, Badr," he said in a low voice. "Do it now."

Faisel relayed the command, dropping his walkie-talkie as he scooped up his weapon. "You will remain in the car," he said to his old friend.

Rihani nodded. His chosen time of death was upon him, but it wasn't now.

"And you," Faisel continued, pointing to one of the guards, "will stay with him to protect him."

The guard touched his forehead. "It shall be as you say."

Faisel reached forward and rapped sharply on the seat behind the driver. "Numair, as quickly as you're able."

The big man nodded and whipped the wheel around, spinning the rear of the big car until it came about ninety degrees. When it rocked to a standstill, it completely blocked the road. Faisel and the other three guards climbed from the vehicle and closed the door behind them.

Rihani turned in the seat as a staccato roar of autofire rippled through the alley. Both front tires on the midsize sedan behind them flattened even as the driver threw the transmission into reverse and tried to make an escape. A yellow taxi skated around the street corner, sideswiping one side of the alley as it barreled toward the sedan. Robed and bearded members of Hezbollah leaned out the windows and shouted in savage glee, denouncing all enemies of God.

The taxi driver spun his vehicle around and smashed into the rear of the sedan. The back window of the car exploded in pieces as autofire raked the taxi. Two members of Hezbollah collapsed from the windows and fell to the grimy street.

Faisel paused, kneeling for just a moment, then squeezed off a single round that cored through the windshield and killed the passenger. Before the driver could move, one of the Hezbollah terrorists reached through the open window and put a curved knife to his throat. The driver threw up his hands at once.

Rihani waited as Faisel took control of the prisoner and brought the man out of the wrecked vehicle. The man was dressed in European clothing, cheap, lightweight summer stock that spoke instantly of the KGB to Rihani. He was young, his face a pale and narrow moon that was rapidly going white. A close-cut shock of brown hair was matted with blood from a scalp injury.

Faisel wasted no time, firing off instructions to his men as he marched the prisoner at gunpoint back to the limousine. He paused only for a moment to yank the man's suit coat back from his shoulders and pin his arms in a makeshift straitjacket.

"Help Faisel get the man inside," Rihani ordered the remaining guard, "then assist the others in seeing to the wrecked vehicles."

The guard moved at once.

Faisel pushed the captured man inside, seating him on the foldout rear booth. The man breathed noisily, sucking in great drafts of air, shaking in his fear.

Scanning him with the experience gleaned from years in American and Russian intelligence work, Rihani knew the man before him was still a child in the ways of espionage and covert death. Up close the prisoner definitely had a Slavic cast to his features. He didn't look Israeli, but with the influx of Soviet Jews, Rihani didn't rule out the possibility.

Faisel put the assault rifle away and drew a .357 Magnum, resting the butt of the big pistol on his thigh while he searched the man for weapons. An empty shoulder holster dangled uselessly under one arm. Through with his inspection, Faisel pushed the man back against the booth seat, the muzzle of the Magnum never wavering.

"Numair," Rihani called.

The big driver looked up.

"Take us away from here."

The engine caught smoothly, and Numair guided the car through the alley and onto another street.

"Who are you?" Rihani asked in English. He brought the full intensity of his gaze to bear on the man.

"Dmitri Chekov," the prisoner replied in a thick accent. Scarlet ribbons trickled down his face and across his lips from the bleeding scalp wound.

Numair drove slowly, checking his mirror frequently.

"You're in much trouble, young Dmitri Chekov," Rihani said in a patronizing voice.

"This I know."

"You're Russian?"

"Yes."

"Why were you and your partner following me?" Rihani stared into the blue eyes, seeing the flicker of desperation light their depths. Chekov's hands trembled against his thighs. "If you try anything against me, he will shoot you. Never doubt that for a moment."

Chekov's gaze wavered for a moment, drifting to Faisel, then locking back on Rihani. "I don't."

Rihani smiled, putting false warmth into the effort. "Good. You will live longer." He checked the flow of the traffic, giving the silence time to coil tightly in the Russian's bowels as he knew it would. "Why were you following me?"

"We had our orders."

"What were those orders?"

"To follow. To observe. Nothing more."

"You're sure these orders contained no commands to terminate me or my followers?"

"Nyet," Chekov said, shaking his head.

Rihani pulled a gauze bandage from his kit and mopped blood from the man's head. "You're doing very well."

Chekov's reaction showed that he clearly did not know how to take the praise.

"Who are you working for?"

"I can't tell you that."

Rihani kept his voice soothing, capturing the man's eyes with his. "Of course you can. You can only *choose* not to."

The young KGB agent bit his lip in indecision.

Closing his hand around the bloody bandage, knowing the movement would draw the man's attention to it, Rihani turned it up so that it faintly resembled a blood-red rose. It would serve to create new feelings of insecurity. A scalp wound was notorious for its capacity to bleed. If the younger man was unfamiliar with such things, he could be persuaded he was injured far worse than he thought or felt himself to be. "You're with the KGB." He made it a statement, flat and damning.

Raising his eyes from the bandage, Chekov nodded. "Yes."

"How many other KGB agents are in Beirut?"

"I don't have that knowledge."

"And all know of me?"

"I think so. Information about you came through general intelligence restricted to this area."

"What were you to do when you found me?"

"Notify our superiors."

"They have a special team waiting to take over if I'm found?"

"Yes, I think so."

Focusing his black gaze on the KGB agent, Rihani asked, "Do you know why the KGB wants me?"

"Nyet."

Rihani looked at Faisel.

"I believe him," Faisel said.

Nodding, Rihani replied, "So do I." He raised his voice. "Numair."

The driver pulled over at once, frightening a crowd of refugees away from the curb as a government-marked panel van rolled into sight. The occupants of the van stared at the limousine for a moment, then went on, trundling down the street.

"They're as useful as the fowl hunting the falcon," Faisel remarked as the vehicle disappeared. "They know they'd only be targets if they dared to step out onto the streets."

"God grants success only to wise and brave men," Rihani said. "Release him."

Faisel opened the door and motioned the Russian out with the .357. As if not trusting his good fortune, Chekov made his way out of the rear of the car in a crablike maneuver, using his arms and legs to go sideways. When one foot touched the pavement, Faisel shot two rounds into the man's chest, which pitched him onto the broken sidewalk. People scattered as the corpse rolled to a stop.

The limousine's tires shrilled as the big car shot away from the curb. Faisel pulled the door shut and used a piece of yellow cloth to wipe drops of blood from the window. The .357 disappeared into folds of his robe. "The KGB fears you, my brother."

"As well they have reason." Rihani pulled at his beard, running his fingers through its length. It felt cleaner than it had in years. He remembered how Jamila used to grin at him when he purred like a big cat while she stroked his beard. Then he forced the memory away. Digging up the past now when he was moving would only slow him down. He'd vowed against all restraints that would hold him back from his vengeance while a prisoner of the Mossad, and he wouldn't give in to his own emotions. "The KGB knows what they, in their stupidity and prideful foolishness, have unleashed upon the world. And they have told no one of it."

"This you know to be true?"

Rihani nodded. "This I know to be true. As you saw for yourself, they aren't even telling their own people. No, my brother, our secret is safe. Even when we destroy Israel as we have planned, the KGB will offer no testimony as to how it happened and seek only to avoid blame."

"If we told the others of the power you wield," Faisel suggested, "perhaps they'd come around sooner and be more willing to shoulder their part of the burden."

"No!" Rihani's denial was sharp. He softened his voice as he resumed speaking passionately. "Badr, my brother, *this* is the true and holy war. You and I and our chosen few, we're God's true and holy warriors who shall give our lives to the struggle so that others may build on our triumph. He has given this fight to me, given me the knowledge to use against our enemies, and taken Jamila from me so that I may be strong enough to break down the doors of their houses. I can't tell the others because it would only lessen the power of God's covenant with me. All it would take is one man among us who isn't what he seems, or who doesn't truly believe as God wills, and our holy battle could be doomed. The Great Satans have power, as well. As a warrior, you should know it is best never to challenge the strength of your sword against that of another's. You should kill quickly and cleanly and become the victor." He paused. "And that is what we shall be."

"As God wills." Faisel touched his forehead in supplication.

"Yes," Rihani agreed, his passion for vengeance smoldering like burning coals in his stomach, "as God wills."

RIHANI SAT in the silent hall of the abandoned clothier's building with only the telephone and the burning candle on the badly listing table for company. He stared into the flame, concentrating his energies, recalling the essence of the man he waited to speak to. He also recalled the fears the man held and separated each one in his mind until each became a strong strand independent of the others.

The phone rang, and he picked it up without losing his train of thought. The focus was his again. He had submerged the outer world in the interior world that was his domain.

"Your call is now being completed," the overseas operator told him in English.

He remembered to say thank you, maintaining the candle's brightness in his mind's eye. This pirated phone line was used infrequently by Hezbollah, kept secret as most things were. After today it would never be used again.

The telephone receptionist at the Russian embassy in Washington, D.C. was polite and enthusiastic. For a moment he wondered at the enthusiasm, thinking changes had really occurred in Russia while he'd been held captive. "Comrade Fyodor Khromeyev, please," he said. The sound of his voice in the abandoned room was powerful and compelling even to his ear.

"Just a moment and I'll switch you over."

He waited, savoring the pause. Faisel had charted Khromeyev's movements and promotions while the Mossad had held him prisoner, just as he'd tried to with the others on Rihani's lists. Some had dropped through the cracks as time passed, swallowed up by bureaucracy and retirement. But enough remained. And the passage of time hadn't been only an enemy. It had been a friend, as well. Many of the people on those lists had stepped into even greater positions of power. He smiled at the candle flame.

"Comrade Fyodor Khromeyev," a full basso voice rumbled at the other end of the connection.

Even with the prevalent static on the line Rihani had no problem recognizing the man for who he was. He made his voice sibilant, weighing his words as the power came back into him. As he spoke, he kept up a measured cadence of his syllables. "How are you feeling, Colonel?"

"I'm fine," Khromeyev said, switching from English to Russian as Rihani had. "Who is this?"

"An old friend."

"I have many old friends."

"Don't you recognize the voice. We've spoken on many occasions, but not in some time."

Khromeyev paused.

Rihani forced himself to remain patient. His voice was an instrument, the tuning fork of the power he contained in his mind. "Do you know me now, Colonel?"

"Yes," Khromeyev replied in a much lower and slower voice. "Yes, I do. You're Luchok."

"I'm your friend."

"Yes. You're my friend."

"Your best friend."

"Yes. My best friend."

"Do you trust me, Colonel?"

"Yes. Of course."

Rihani concentrated on his voice, feeling perspiration bead on his forehead in the still air of the abandoned building. "I would never lie to you."

"No. You wouldn't."

"Lying would only hurt us all."

"Yes. I understand."

Rihani imagined the Russian's mind as a lock with the combination spinning. Already two of the tumblers had clicked into place: Khromeyev knew who he was and knew only to trust him. "You know they're out to get you."

Static buzzed through the heavy silence.

"They'll kill you if you let them."

"Yes. They'll kill me."

Rihani didn't allow himself to smile at his success at getting the safe that was Khromeyev's mind to open at his request. "You must not let them."

"No."

"They'll kill your family."

"No." The terror in the man's voice was genuine.

Savoring the fear he detected at the other end of the connection, Rihani reached for another strand, pulling it tight. "You can stop them."

"I must."

"How will you stop them?"

"I'll kill them first."

"Good. It's only self-defense. No one's worth the lives of your family."

"No one," Khromeyev echoed with empty passion.

"Now go. And hurry before they stop you."

The phone clicked dead.

Exhaling a shuddering breath, Rihani hung up the receiver and mopped his brow with a shirtsleeve. Sometime during the conversation the candle had gone out. He got another from his pocket, lit it and began the phone chase that would give him American financier Walter Carson, who was in Russia on business. He knew Carson would be easier to reach. Americans were always available for the phone.

AN HOUR AND A HALF later Rihani walked tiredly out into the open air of the alley where Faisel and Numair waited for him. The limousine was safely hidden away. Night had fallen and covered the rubble with shadows.

"Success, Fahad?" Faisel asked.

"God was with me and in my thoughts," Rihani replied. "Tell the others they'll have their proof now and instruct them on where we want the hostages."

"As you wish." Faisel hurried off into the darkness.

Rihani followed much more slowly, unbelievably drained by his mental exertions and emotions. He glanced up at the star-filled sky as Numair stepped over the fallen debris with uncanny ability and catlike quiet. "It's a good time of the day to be alive, isn't it?" he asked.

Numair grinned. "We're this much closer to the holy war, and that's the best time of all to be alive."

Rihani silently agreed as he went on.

CHAPTER FOURTEEN

Fyodor Khromeyev sat at his desk and watched his hands tremble while rats' teeth gnawed at his stomach. He didn't look at the telephone receiver that lay on the carpet buzzing. The fear raged through him worse than any fever he'd ever known. Every stinking, sweat-soaked minute of the nightmares he'd thought himself cured of came back in force.

Disorientation gripped him like a vise and refused to let him go. He didn't recognize the office, didn't know for sure where he was. The only discernible thought in his mind was that he had to get away. He had to get out of this strange building and save Yevka and the children.

The framed picture to his left caught his attention. Yevka sat on the wooden steps of their house, Mark standing straight and tall beside her while little Cesia sat in her lap, a gap-toothed grin spread across her face. His trembling fingers brushed against the glass surface as torn and twisted visions of blood filled his head.

"No!" He moaned, his throat mangled with the passions gripping him, and swept an arm across the desk, toppling everything to the floor. Standing up, he felt snarled in an immediate sense of vertigo. He caught himself on his palms, leaning heavily on the desk and breathing hard.

He squeezed his eyes tightly, waiting for the blackness to settle over his inner vision. Instead, the twisted and writhing bloodthings painted themselves on his eyelids again, filled with garish color. He snapped his eyes open, blinking against the sudden glare of the fluorescent lights.

Barely able to restrain the impulse to flee, he pulled the drawer open on his desk. He mouthed Yevka's and the children's names in a silent litany that kept him moving. His hand closed around the handle of the small pistol he stored there. Without releasing the weapon, he slipped it into his jacket pocket and started for the door.

He forced himself to breathe out, striving against the hyperventilation that would rob him of his stamina. Then he opened the door and stepped out into the air-conditioned hallway, where he stood for a moment, the door still open behind him, his pistol clasped tightly in his fist. The steady clacking of typewriters filled his ears while subdued conversation underscored the office noises. A telephone rang. He caught himself just as the pistol came out of his pocket, made himself put it away again.

Perspiration gathered in his heavy brows, despite the coolness of the hallway, and dripped down his nose. He shut the door behind him and started forward, noticing for the first time how dry his throat was.

Everyone is a potential enemy. Luchok's voice rustled in his mind like a snowdrift tumbling across the Siberian wasteland. *The KGB is everywhere. And they know what you have done.*

Khromeyev shuddered again. He didn't need Luchok to tell him that. Then he wondered if the words in his mind had been Luchok's or his own. They both voiced the same fear.

He rounded a corner and came upon a secretarial pool he didn't recognize. He still wasn't sure how he'd been moved from his current position in Moscow. Perhaps the KGB had drugged him and left him here to see what he'd do once he discovered himself in a strange place. But that left the question of how he'd known his gun would be in the drawer. He stopped pursuing the questions in his mind; they only led to a kaleidoscopic whirl of confusion. The fact that most of the secretarial pool seemed to be female instead of male only placed another rift in his fragile stability.

He lowered his head, tucked his chin down and strode across the open space like a man on a mission.

"Comrade Khromeyev," a woman's voice called after him.

He stopped, turning slowly to face the woman as his heart exploded in bursts within his chest. The woman seemed somehow familiar, like someone he'd perhaps met in a dream.

She held a sheaf of papers out to him as she approached. Her smile beneath her glasses was perfunctory and skilled, her hair tied back in a severe bun. "I rang your office, but you weren't there. These require your signature so that we can put them out in today's mail."

He looked down at the papers. His name was typed there at the bottom in English. The realization that it wasn't in Russian ran through his veins like ice water. He knew now that this was no KGB test. This was torture of the most maddening kind. And, as always, the trademark KGB cruelty ran through it—instead of his real title of lieutenant colonel, they'd shown him as a full colonel in the documents.

"Comrade?" the woman asked.

"Take them away," Khromeyev ordered in a hoarse voice that sounded as if it had been squeezed through skeletal lips.

The woman blinked, resembling a shocked owl behind her glasses, and stepped back. "Comrade?"

"Take them away," Khromeyev repeated, then turned to go.

"These are important papers, Colonel. They require your signature. Today. If I don't have it, I'll have to go over your head for approval."

Yevka and the children, Luchok's voice reminded. *Yevka and the children have no knowledge of your betrayal or of the consequences of your discovery. Only you can save them.*

"Do what you must," Khromeyev said. He stopped at the next desk and glowered at the secretary sitting there. Her hair was long and loose, not proper at all for a military secretary. "Where's the nearest exit?"

She stared at him, glanced back at the secretary standing in the middle of the floor, then back again.

Unable to restrain his rage and frustration, Khromeyev reached out and batted her typewriter to the floor. Papers fluttered everywhere. She cowered in her chair, raising her hands to fend off any blows directed at her. "Where?" he roared.

"There," she said, pointing. "Follow the corridor to the end. It's marked."

Khromeyev straightened and glanced quickly around the room. The secretary who'd been so insistent was already on the phone.

"I need security," she said into the mouthpiece.

Without hesitation Khromeyev pulled his weapon and shot her through the head. She fell back without a sound as the other people in the room dived for cover. Sadness touched some inner part of him, and Khromeyev wondered about that. Perhaps he'd known her. Things were so uncertain.

Yevka is in danger.

Self-doubt faded from his thoughts as his primary responsibility reasserted itself. He turned and ran down the corridor as the screams and wailings spilled out behind him. His legs seemed impossibly heavy and his breath came in troubled gasps. Yevka would never understand why he'd worked with American military intelligence. Perhaps she wouldn't even want to go with him as they fled for sanctuary at the American embassy. But she would. Once he explained the danger the children were in, she would come.

He used his hands to push off around a corner, stumbling over two men in uniform. Neither wore side arms. They gave way instantly once they saw the pistol in his fist. Pain flared to new life in his chest as he forced himself into a run again. He heard the thumping of military boots in the hallway behind him. Salty perspiration stung his eyes, and he brushed it away.

Without warning the next turn brought him to the glass doors overlooking a street scene that couldn't belong to Moscow. Realities became mixed in his mind, a strange blending of old and new that took away all hope. He came to a halt at the top of a short flight of stairs. The pistol dangled loosely in his hand. Dozens of cars swished by on the sunny street, vehicles he'd never before imagined. He glanced around at the score or more of people filling the foyer. Luchok continued whispering things in his mind, making him restless.

"Comrade Khromeyev!"

He wheeled at the sound of his name.

Two men stood in the hallway he had just left. Both wore security uniforms he wasn't entirely familiar with. One knelt on the floor, holding a short assault rifle. The speaker held a pistol wrapped in both hands.

"Comrade Khromeyev," the security guard said in a quieter voice. His eyes were hard, and as bright as ball bearings. "You will put down your weapon and come with us. Now!"

You might as well put the gun to Yevka's head yourself, Luchok said softly.

Khromeyev's voice was a pain-filled howl. "No!" He swept the pistol up, triggering shots automatically. The standing officer went spinning away, punched back by his bullets. A hammer dropped over his heart and pushed him over the edge of the stairs. When he landed, he couldn't regain his breath and he'd lost his weapon. He turned his head to look out on the street to try to make some sense of what he saw and felt. A ghostly reflection of a man much older than he knew himself to be looked back at him. The warm trickle of blood ran down his cheek even as the metallic taste of it filled his mouth.

The young security guard he'd shot came and knelt beside him. His shoulder was covered with blood. The strident orders of more security men yelling at the passersby to get back combatted the sound of the ocean that tried to drag him under. "Why did you do this, Comrade?" the young guard asked.

Khromeyev struggled to make his mouth work, found the words. "To save my wife and children. It was all I could do as a man."

Confusion covered the security man's face.

Khromeyev died before the pain and loss ever reached him, taking with him only the intense fear.

CHAPTER FIFTEEN

U.S. Embassy, Moscow

Second Day—9:47 p.m.

Walter Carson was lost in the Korean War as he hung up the telephone mechanically. The voice on the other end had been soft and soothing, but it had conjured up fears that chilled him to the marrow.

He was in Seoul. He was sure of that despite the way things looked. His large apartment was just another cover the CIA had given him. He wasn't sure how the man who'd been on the phone was connected with the Agency, but he didn't doubt it for a moment. Luke had proved himself to be an able companion before on other missions. A mental image came to Carson's mind as he retreated to his bedroom. Luke's voice, soft and as smooth as silk, made him remember a combination of the cartoon figure of Uncle Sam and Humphrey Bogart.

He dressed quickly, choosing dark clothing and a dark trench coat. He reached overhead for the small oilskin pouch he knew was there but didn't remember placing there. It was heavy and blunt. Once opened it revealed a stubby Russian automatic with two spare magazines. The lock-and-load procedure was done on sheer reflex, then he dropped it into a pocket of the trench coat.

Swallowing the fear and the feeling of certain death, he opened the briefcase on the bed and reviewed his cover ID. Evidently the Agency had done a thorough job on the setup because they'd entered him in-country under his own name. He didn't know why he couldn't remember it, but some of the figures and technical terms on the papers even made sense to him. Though what didn't make sense was why he'd be negotiating a trade agreement with the Russians. A surer bet would have been selling bomb shelters in Midwest America. But, according to the papers, he'd just made a hell of a deal.

Carson left the briefcase open, doused the contents with fluid from the bottom of his lighter, then ignited it. Blue-yellow flames spread over the papers like quick-moving fog. Probably there wasn't anything in the case that was worth concealing, but it would slow down his pursuers.

The North Koreans know who you are, Walter. They will kill you if you don't escape.

He cringed inwardly, tasting bile at the back of his throat. A sudden headache pounded at his temples. He spit phlegm in the hallway as he left the room. His hand curled around his weapon, moving it so that he could fire through the pocket if he had to.

Outside, the cold metal bar of the stairway railing felt hard and unforgiving in his hand. He turned up the collar of the trench coat and stayed with the sidewalk. He knew there would be no rendezvous until he could signal that he was in trouble.

Few people were on the streets now, and they were bundled up as warmly as he was. He wouldn't recognize his enemies until they'd made their move. Fear clenched his stomach with a madman's fury. He breathed out slowly, then patted his pockets for a cigarette. When he came up empty, a hollow voice in his head reminded him that he'd quit. He shook his head. The voice couldn't have been his own. He'd been smoking solidly, a two-pack-a-day man, since 1944, eight years ago. Being stationed here in North Korea had upped that to almost three packs on most days.

He wrapped the trench coat more tightly around him, trying to remember if Korea had ever been so cold. Usually he only wore the trench coat for the sweltering rainy season.

He ran a hand over his face, felt his sweat-slick cheeks slide under his palm. Images played over and over in his mind. He saw young Barry Jonas, who'd been partnered with him for a time, as his team had discovered him. Jonas's body had been ravaged by the North Koreans—his teeth had been knocked out; he'd been blinded by a blunt instrument; his fingernails and toenails had been torn away; he'd been cruelly unmanned. Tied to the table as they'd found him on the salvage operation, with enemy soldiers ringing the intelligence fortress, there had been no real choice. Not once they'd seen the shape Jonas was in.

Without saying anything the other members of the team had left Carson to finish the job.

Vertigo swirled around Carson, and he had to stop for a moment. He wanted to release the gun, knowing it was causing part of the sickness he felt. But he couldn't. It was also his salvation. With it he could never be tortured as Barry Jonas had been.

For a moment memory of the past came back to him as if he were reliving it. *Smell the blood, Walter? Smell the urine and the foul stench a dying body leaves behind? This is death. But you know there is something worse than death, don't you?*

Carson could picture Luke standing beside him as the words tumbled through his mind.

This is death, Luke went on. *Hanging on to life only by a thin thread of agony.*

"Oh, Christ," Carson moaned, rubbing his free hand across his forehead. The memory held him a little longer, letting him relive the heaviness of the gun as he'd lifted it. He'd talked to Jonas in hoarse, broken words, whispering with breath he didn't think he had, promising him the team would get him out. In a way the blindness had been a blessing. Jonas didn't see the pistol, only felt the pillow brush against his face as Carson had raised it. The pistol's report had been muffled in the bulk of the pillow.

Carson shuddered as the memory released him. He made himself go forward again, staying well within the shadows of the sidewalk.

The wail of a fire truck sounded behind him. He glanced back and saw the gray smoke funneling up from his apartment building. Evidently it had gone up faster than he'd expected. He put more effort into his steps.

Luke's voice dogged him, hurrying him along.

Wheels screeched as a car pulled onto the street. Small U.S. flags fluttered on both front fenders. Men in full-dress Marine uniforms spilled from the doors, their white gloves and white caps almost glowing in the dark. Two of them halted in their approach to the building he had just left. One of them pointed in Carson's direction.

Blind with panic now, Carson gave up trying to appear nonchalant and ran. He reached the street corner as rubber burned on pavement.

They aren't Marines, Luke said in his mind. *They're North Koreans, Walter, and they won't stop with just stripping the flesh from your bones.*

He turned down the alley, his heart exploding in two-to-one rhythm with his pounding feet. Fisting the small pistol tightly so that he wouldn't lose it, he attempted to leap a line of trash cans and went sprawling in the alley. Skin shredded from his hands and knees. Blood trickled from his nose and ran down over his lips. He hacked and coughed as he breathed it in.

He got to his feet just as the car turned into the alley. The bright lights took away his night vision and jarred into his optic nerves.

"Mr. Carson!"

He barely recognized the Marine standing next to the car. He kept telling himself it was a trick, that they only wanted him alive so that they could torture him. Barry Jonas's mutilated body was close enough to his mind that he could smell the scent of scorched flesh. Nausea threatened to overwhelm him.

"Mr. Carson, wait up. We only want to help." The Marine came forward, flanked by the car as more people and vehicles followed. His white gloves were empty. In the shadows Carson was sure there were Asiatic features.

Tears blurred his vision still more. He fell to his knees, unable to run anymore.

You know what they'll do. Even if you live, you'll never truly be a man again.

"We're going to get you out of here, Barry," Carson said. The words had haunted him so long, bringing with them guilt and a sense of betrayal. He'd lived his life on the edge so long, expecting something to happen to him, somehow managing to conquer the fear each time he'd been in the field for the Agency.

"Mr. Carson, are you all right?" The man in the Marine uniform was less than twenty feet away.

Carson was amazed. The accent was perfect. It sounded exactly like English. Something glinted near the Marine's wrist. Part of Carson's mind told him it was a polished cuff link on the uniform. The other part assured him in Luke's soft voice that it was a knife.

Without hesitation he leaned forward, slid the barrel of the pistol between his lips, closed his eyes and pulled the trigger.

CHAPTER SIXTEEN

Stony Man Farm, Virginia

Second Day—2:18 p.m.

"Not another sight in the world like it, is there?" Jack Grimaldi asked. He had the F-14 Tomcat heeled over so that Stony Man Farm was spread out only hundreds of feet below them.

"No," Bolan replied as he watched the dark green foliage and carefully cultivated fields race by.

"Miss it?" the pilot asked.

"All the time, flyboy."

"Me, too," Grimaldi said somberly. "There was a time, Sarge, when I had the occasional social moment with you down there."

"I miss that, too."

"Yeah."

Bolan watched a farmhand turning dirt with a tractor, then moved his glance on to the main house. Three stories aboveground, there was nothing in its appearance to suggest the firepower and defensive measures it was capable of unleashing. Three stories high, another story underground, and at least a thousand untold stories locked within its walls. Once it had been a place he'd called home.

Grimaldi rolled the Tomcat over and put them on a path to the landing strip north of the farm. Bolan watched the ground rush up at them as the pilot's skilled hands controlled the jet. The runway wasn't long enough to allow a normal drop, so the portable catapult line had been raised. Flight crews stood by in readiness. A bright red emergency fire suppression van was on the east side, a Medevac unit was on the west with a military jeep parked just behind it.

"Ground team doesn't appear to be too confident," Grimaldi grunted as he went full flap.

"They know it's been a long flight," Bolan replied, feeling the negative g-force pull him forward.

Grimaldi snorted derisively. "The day I can't put down a skysled I got into the air is the day I'll start thinking about a career in submarines."

Bolan relaxed, waiting for the impact.

"Hang on," the pilot said. "We're going into it—now."

The clank of metal on metal was dimly heard above the jet engines, but the stopping force was incredible. Bolan went with the motion and let the restraining straps do their job. He unbuckled as Grimaldi popped the canopy, then followed the pilot down the ladder.

"Jenkins, sir," a young officer in a flight suit said to Grimaldi. "I'm responsible for taking the bird back,"

Grimaldi returned the crisp salute. "It's yours, ace. Tell the Admiral many thanks when you see him."

"Yes, sir." The pilot stepped up the ladder to the cockpit, trailed by his navigator.

Bolan handed his helmet to one of the ground crew and stepped out of the flight suit. Hal Brognola, Stony Man's liaison with the White House, waited behind the wheel of the jeep. The Executioner took the passenger side seat as Grimaldi levered himself over the side onto the rear deck.

Brognola was dressed in a suit, as usual, looking out of place in the jeep. A heavy five o'clock shadow stained his lower face, and black-lensed sunglasses covered his eyes. He popped the clutch and guided the jeep forward over the rough terrain between the surrounding trees, then held out his hand. "Good to see you, Striker."

Taking the hand, Bolan said, "Good to see you, too, Hal." And, despite the circumstances that had brought them together, it really was. The Justice man had been one of Bolan's closest friends since the early days. Brognola and Leo Turrin had worked behind the Justice Department's back to help the Executioner in his war against the Mafia when the opportunities had been there, then worked just as hard to take him off the street when pressure came down from the top. "The others?"

"Waiting on you."

"Give Jack and me fifteen minutes to prep," Bolan said, "and we'll be there."

Brognola nodded. "Fair enough. We're going to have to disseminate a lot of information to everyone, and Bear's still on a collection drive even as we speak."

The thunder of jet engines drew Bolan's attention. He watched as the F-14 screamed into the sky and disappeared, knowing Stony Man Farm was going to be as much of a way station for him as it had been for the fighter jet.

"SCRUB YOUR BACK?"

Bolan blinked his eyes open as he recognized the feminine voice, hovering in that peaceful never-never land that was only briefly attainable at the Farm. Warm water cascaded from the shower head, splashing down his nude body.

Barbara Price stood behind the shower curtain, poking her head around the corner and smiling at him. The warrior grinned back. A lightness touched his heart when he saw her. They were friends. Nothing more, nothing less, with no strings attached. Both—by nature and by profession—were loners, carrying personal burdens as well as the ones they accepted from other sources. At times, schedules permitting during the frantic moments at Stony Man, they stole a few of those minutes for themselves. "Sure," he said.

Price swept the shower curtain back and, already nude, stepped into the small cubicle. Bolan gathered her into his arms as she hugged him, luxuriating in the hot and scented female flesh that pressed against him. Despite the fatigue from the last desperate hours, his body reacted instantly to the electric contact. He kissed her deeply while his hands refamiliarized themselves with the smoothly rounded terrain.

"It's been a while, soldier," she whispered into his ear, her nails trailing along his spine.

"Makes it better," he said softly, nuzzling her throat. His hands cupped her buttocks, causing her to moan gently.

She pressed against him eagerly, pulling away to look deeply into his eyes. Her hands framed his face. "I don't want to be the one to mention it, but we're facing a deadline here." She smiled. "Personally I'd prefer it if we had more time."

"So would I." He bent and gathered her in his arms, carrying her dripping wet to the bed. She pushed him over onto his back as he joined her.

Barbara straddled him slowly, and he could tell she was smiling at the look of anticipation that had to be on his face. Water dripped from her face and hair as she massaged his chest with her palms. He returned the effort with enthusiasm, watching the smile disappear as a quiet need took its place. Sliding backward, slick skin against slick skin, she drew him in, then began the climb to mutual ecstasy.

DRESSED IN BLACK jeans, joggers and a short-sleeved sweatshirt, Bolan made it to the war room fifteen minutes late. No one mentioned it as the group came to quiet attention.

Brognola was at one end of the table, leaving the other open for him. Kurtzman sat at a table of his own that was covered with computer equipment. McCarter, Lyons and Grimaldi peeled back from a raucous three-part harmony that had dominated one corner of the room to join the others at the table. All the warriors were dressed combat casual in jeans, pullover shirts and joggers. All wore side arms. Since the assault that had ground the original Stony Man Farm into the land from which it had sprung, all members were required to be personally armed at all times. Bolan's own borrowed Detonics .45 was sheathed in a paddle holster at his back.

Pausing at the coffeepot, Bolan took a ceramic cup from the tray beside it and drew off a cup. He looked at it in speculation. "Aaron's?"

"Guilty," Kurtzman confessed.

McCarter's voice followed on the heels of the admission. "I've been talking to Kissinger about the possibilities of hooking up a compressed air rig to a container and using it for crowd dispersal."

A light rumble of laughter rippled through the room.

"Can't do that," Lyons said in mock seriousness. "The motor pool crowd told me they use the leftover coffee to clean crankcases. Roberts informed me that once they immerse an engine in a vat of it, the only thing that comes back up is the metal."

"They even have to repaint," Rosario Blancanales added.

Bolan seated himself while he waited for the kidding around to die away. They were hard men facing a hard job, and a few minutes of levity might help to ease the tension. He sipped the coffee and immediately fought a quick grimace. Bear had outdone himself this time. He set the cup to one side as he pored over the two-inch stack of hard copy before him. A quick perusal revealed maps, histories of Hezbollah members and background on the hostages.

Heads turned as Barbara Price entered the room, outfitted in slacks and a dark blue blouse. She bypassed the coffee and took a glass and a container of orange juice from an ice tub. Calvin James and Gary Manning made room for her at the table. Gadgets Schwarz slid her hard-copy packet over to her.

Brognola stood at his end of the table, his fingers already busy unveiling a fresh cigar. "One hundred twenty-two people," the head Fed said somberly. He let the number hang in the air.

Bolan sipped his coffee, his thoughts churning with the logistics of the problem presented to the teams.

"One hundred twenty-two people," Brognola repeated, "and somehow we've got to find a way to bring them home."

"Do we know where they are?" Rafael Encizo asked.

"No." Brognola glanced at Kurtzman. The lights went out and mirror projections lit up all four walls. "Not exactly, to answer your question, Rafael, but we do have enough to do more than simple barnyard guesswork."

Bolan watched the projection across the room from him as Brognola approached Kurtzman's desk. The head Fed took a metal pointer from his pocket and extended it. The projection was a color-coordinated map of the Middle East, and multicolored lines extended from the different kidnapping areas to touch the border of Lebanon.

Brognola tapped each line in succession. "We owe this much information to the CIA, the State Department and the satellite network Aaron was able to establish. From the looks of things, Hezbollah has brought the surviving hostages to Lebanon."

"Surviving hostages?" Schwarz echoed.

"Yeah." Brognola's face was a tight, grim mask. "Some of the routes the intelligence people have followed had bodies along the way. Some appeared to have died of wounds, others of heart attacks and other physical ailments. A handful of them were executed."

"They're cutting out the deadwood," McCarter said coldly.

"That's what we think," Barbara Price agreed. Her beautiful face couldn't quite conceal her horror at the thought. "Of the remaining hostages, Hezbollah has a group of people who can be moved and transported fairly easily. That includes men, women and children."

"Rotation of hostages and guards is fairly standard over there now," Calvin James said.

"Right," Brognola replied. "I'm willing to bet that's what's going down. They weeded out the weak ones because once they go into seclusion with their captives they can't be bothered with having to dispose of bodies."

"There's still been no contact from Hezbollah?" Bolan asked.

Brognola shook his head. "No. But we're expecting it anytime."

"And in the meantime?" Carl Lyons asked.

The big Fed spread his hands. "We wait. It's as simple as that. If it's too long, we start kicking doors open."

Bolan watched the disgruntled looks swapped between the members of Phoenix and Able, knowing it didn't sit well with Grimaldi or the others, either. He put his personal feelings on hold, just as he knew the others would. There was a time for war to be up close and personal, and others when it had to be kept distant before the losses became mentally insurmountable. "What's Israel's stand on the hostage situation?" he asked.

"They're being very closemouthed about the operation, but there's a reason for that." In terse words Brognola sketched the events concerning military intelligence's attempt to get their hands on Dr. Fahad Rihani.

"Israel would naturally withdraw after something like this," Katz said quietly. He tapped an unfiltered Camel on the back of his prosthetic hand and lit up.

"Right," Price said. "At this point we can't blame them for being hesitant to work with us. But the Mossad has a lot of domestic information we could use."

"Who is Rihani and why is he so important?" Gary Manning asked.

Brognola looked over at Kurtzman.

"I'm working on it," Bear replied. "Apparently there's more to Rihani than surface value alone."

"And just what is the surface value, mate?" David McCarter asked. He reached back into the ice tub, pulled out a canned Coke and cracked it open.

"In the early eighties," Kurtzman said, "Rihani was the head of Hezbollah. Then he was captured by the Mossad."

"The early eighties?" Politician repeated.

"Yeah."

"The Mossad's been sitting on him for a while then."

Kurtzman nodded.

"Doesn't seem so coincidental that Hezbollah would break Rihani free at roughly the same time they seized all the hostages, does it?" James asked.

"No," Brognola said. "Evidently even after all these years Rihani's name still carries enough weight to get things done. My main question is why?"

"Charisma," Lyons suggested with a grin.

A ripple of laughter moved through the room and died away.

"If it was only that easy," Brognola said, "we could already have this show on the road."

"There's another mystery attached to this, too," Kurtzman informed them. He punched buttons on the keyboard, and the scene on the walls changed.

Bolan finished his coffee and watched the silent videotape play out against the walls. The building was an embassy. When he saw the security guards' uniforms, he knew it was Russian. The subject of the tape was completely unknown to him.

"I tagged computer inquiries coming from a Mossad outpost in Washington," Kurtzman said. "I've been keeping watch over everything I could find that they were doing in the fringe areas. Surprise, surprise when this one turned up."

On-screen, the man whirled and brought his gun up only to be shot down by the guards.

"His name was Fyodor Khromeyev," Kurtzman announced. "He was attached to the Russian embassy in Washington. Before that he'd been active in the KGB."

"He was also a prime source of information for military intelligence at one time," Price put in. "In the days before Gorbachev and *glasnost,* Khromeyev fed information through channels that kept the U.S. apprised of activities in Afghanistan so that military forces and covert operations could watch them more closely."

"I trust the man was never discovered," McCarter said.

"No," Price replied.

"And where does he fit into this?" Bolan asked.

Kurtzman shook his head, punched a button and replayed the tape from the beginning. "That I don't know, Striker, but it's connected. Khromeyev was assigned to the Middle East during the early eighties. That's another tie-in besides the Israeli interest."

Khromeyev was shot down again in silence.

"I don't have the audio tracks for this," Kurtzman said. "Maybe there weren't any. But I picked up another tidbit of information through other channels. Before he died Khromeyev asked that his wife and children be spared from the KGB."

"He thought the KGB were onto him after all these years?" Encizo asked.

"That's the way it looks."

"Were they?" Katz asked.

"From what I've been able to find out, the KGB still doesn't know about Khromeyev's betrayals."

"Curiouser and curiouser," Grimaldi commented quietly.

"That it is," Brognola said. "According to the files we were able to get on Khromeyev, his wife died almost six years ago."

A thick silence dropped over the room.

Bolan took the time to get another cup of coffee.

"Now there's a brave laddie," McCarter observed.

As Bolan returned to the table, the scenes on the walls changed. News footage of a business meeting in Moscow took over.

Brognola tapped the pointer against the projector so that four shadows appeared on the walls. "Walter Carson just finished negotiations on a business deal in Moscow a few hours ago. Now he's dead."

"In Moscow?" Schwarz asked.

"Yeah."

"How?"

"He shot himself," Brognola answered. "In front of two Marines he put a gun in his mouth and blew the back of his head away."

"Like the Khromeyev episode," Kurtzman said, "this one doesn't make much sense, either. Before leaving his hotel room Carson set his briefcase on fire, burning all the trade documents and his ID."

"Standard intelligence reflex when you think your cover's been blown," McCarter said.

"Yeah," Brognola agreed. "Only Carson wasn't working the side streets for anyone that we can tell."

"That you know for sure," Lyons put in.

"True."

"What was his background?" Bolan asked. The answers were there; it was just a matter of fitting the pieces together so that the right questions appeared.

"OSS," Kurtzman replied. "He moved on into the CIA when the Agency was formed. The only action he ever saw was in North Korea. For those of you who aren't old enough to remember, General Douglas MacArthur handled the troops over there, and he wasn't too fond of covert ops. Carson was part of a rescue team that tried to recover a captured agent. Instead of getting the man out Carson had to kill him. Less than six months later Carson had a breakdown that mustered him out of the Agency. He went into private business and never looked back."

"What about his ties to the Middle East?" Bolan asked.

Kurtzman grinned. "I see you're staying up with me, Striker." More news footage rolled on the walls, showing Carson at a business meeting in Beirut in 1981. "Four years, people. Carson spent that time shuttling back and forth across the globe, and he had major investments and interests in and around Lebanon before the attack on the U.S. base there in 1983."

"We have a connection," Katz said, "but where does that leave us?"

Kurtzman laced his fingers as he rested his elbows on the arms of his wheelchair. "At the moment it leaves us digging into a vacuum of information. I've got a tape coming in from Moscow that's supposed to have Carson's phone calls on it. He taped almost everything he did by phone for secretaries to type up later. The intelligence guy wasn't happy about giving it up, but his orders were cut from on high."

"The President's backing this play with everything he can," Brognola said. "Still, you're looking at ten men against an unknown army with 122 hostages as the biggest door prize of the century. Officially the U.S. is going to appear willing to negotiate at this point, but we've got some other avenues working for us now. I think we can bring Israel around when our rescue attempt goes down, and there are others involved."

Katz crushed out his cigarette and blew smoke through his nose. "When all is said and done, Israel will be there for the hostages. They won't willingly let innocents die. The growing friendship between the U.S. and Russia has made Israel more suspicious of her allies these days, and that feeling has been compounded by Major Deering's efforts, no doubt. The promise of world peace has served to blur some of the fail-safe lines protecting Israel, and they know it. Many of them believe they will be left to fend for themselves rather than risk another world war."

"And I believe Hezbollah is planning to use that psychological strategy against Israel before this is over," Brognola told them. "I don't believe for a moment that the U.S. is the only target. If they can push Israel into the aggressor mode, it'll be harder for the U.S. to step in and clean up without threatening everything we've worked for. Our world image suffered a lot with the Panama invasion and the Iraq crisis. We're definitely playing for high stakes here."

Something rang at Kurtzman's keyboard. The big man wheeled around to attend to it, holding a receiver to his ear. He looked up at Brognola. "You'd better take this. Hezbollah has just made contact."

Brognola dropped his cigar into an ashtray. "Put it on-screen."

The walls flickered, then changed as the video link with the White House kicked in. Bolan watched a Camcorder attached to the wall move into life and focus on Brognola.

The face of the President, ten times larger than life, filled the screens. "Gentlemen," he said softly, "the shit's just hit the fan."

CHAPTER SEVENTEEN

Beirut, Lebanon

Second Day—10:30 p.m.

Dr. Fahad Rihani stood before the group with a confidence he hadn't felt in many years. Besides himself, Badr and Numair, almost thirty men occupied the empty warehouse. They represented different factions of the Shiite and Palestinian hard-liners who'd rallied to the cause he championed so fiercely.

The low rumble of conversation abated as he took his place before them. He remained standing, meeting the gazes of the men he knew. Some of them quickly looked away, as if afraid of the power of that glance.

Rihani cleared his voice as he pulled the hood of his robe back to reveal himself. "God truly watches over His believers," he said, pitching his voice so that they'd have to listen carefully to him. "I see among you many who have fought the holy war for many years, and still the struggle and thirst for victory haven't died within you."

"We fight a holy war," a young man's voice called from the back. "No mortal man may turn us aside. We're merely God's hand and desire made mortal to wipe the cursed Jews from the face of the earth."

"Agreed," Rihani said. He raised a clenched fist and shook it as his voice took on more fire. "We're God's instrument, striving to make His dreams come to pass. Never forget that. We're brothers in our holy war, and we shall make the Great Satans listen. They're weak. They don't choose to know their God as we know ours, nor do they choose to serve only Him. They struggle instead for their own glory, sacrificing one another to attain it."

A ragged cheer passed through the ranks.

"There was some question about my abilities to once again be the leader of Hezbollah," Rihani continued more softly, "I had Badr give you the names of people who were to be examples of the power I still wield in our efforts. Now you shall see the results of what has come to pass."

Numair went to the corner and yanked the cord on a portable gasoline-powered generator. Faisel unveiled a nineteen-inch color television set and VCR they had liberated in one of their raids. The TV came on at once, spreading a rainbow of color in the uncertain light of the warehouse.

"It's in English," Rihani explained. "Those of you who speak the infidel tongue translate for those who can't."

The crowd surged forward, focusing on the television. When the tape was played, several voices spoke, translating English to Farsi and Arabic.

Rihani watched silently, feeling the power locked inside him seethe restlessly. The two pieces had been taped at different times from different news stations. The reporters detailed the deaths of Khromeyev and Carson without alluding to any reasons for the men's actions. When the tape ended, Faisel turned the television off and Numair killed the generator.

"Those people are examples," Rihani said. "For you to know that I can still control the minds of some of our enemies. They hold no secrets from me. Through them we have even more power besides the hostages we hold. If not for the interference of the Mossad years ago, Israel would already be only a memory. I pledge my life and the lives of my comrades to doing God's work and to bringing an end to the Israelis." His gaze swept the crowd, finding the excitement there that he could feed on. He had them. Just as surely as a fly caught in a spiderweb, he held their dreams and desires in the palm of his hand. "Do you give me your allegiance, my brothers?"

A resounding affirmation rattled from the walls of the empty warehouse.

"ARE YOU SURE you'll be all right without me?" Faisel asked.

He and Rihani stood outside the limousine, watching the bustle of activity as the cargo plane readied for takeoff.

Rihani looked at his friend, then placed both hands on the man's shoulders. "You must go. God has already given us both our tasks to do. We must not stumble."

A dozen men approached the belly of the cargo plane, carrying a tarp-covered crate.

"I've thought of this day before," Faisel said, "and I've longed for it never to come. Forgive me. I've been weak."

"This is as it should be."

"I know, I know. But to realize that this will be the last time we see each other...."

"Only in this lifetime."

The propellers began to spin wildly, creating a backwash of noise.

"There's no one to whom I'd give more trust," Rihani said.

"This I know, too, Fahad." Faisel's hands closed tightly around his elbows.

Rihani pulled him close and embraced him, then kissed him on both cheeks. "Go with God, and remember that the timing is critical. We must smite our enemies together and destroy the stability of the Great Satan."

Faisel released him and stepped away. "It will be done." Then, turning, he strode toward the waiting plane without a backward glance.

Numair stepped back and opened the limousine's door. Rihani climbed inside and watched through the window as the cargo plane taxied into place, then raced for takeoff speed. He stared after the retreating lights until they vanished. Now the die was truly cast.

He sat back in the plush seat of the limousine and ordered his thoughts, knowing there was still much to be done before morning.

RIHANI STOOD and looked down at a third of Hezbollah's hostages. Roughly forty men, women and children huddled together in the near twilight below.

The building had once been a factory and had once turned a tidy profit. But that had been before the civil war ravaging Beirut. Now it was empty and barren. Armed guards watched from the ramparts. The bottom floor was underground, designed before business interests had totally given up on the idea of peace in Lebanon and fled elsewhere for profit and stability. The lower exits had been welded shut with blowtorches, while the two stairways leading to the floor above had been cut away and replaced with rope ladders that could easily be raised and lowered.

The rumble of conversation died away as the hostages saw him standing there. Numair and another guard, both carrying assault rifles, flanked him.

"The light," Rihani ordered.

A mounted spotlight flared to life, throwing a three-meter circle of yellow glare into the midst of the hostages. Most of them held their hands up and leaned away from the bright intensity of the light.

Rihani nodded at Numair. The big man moved with pantherlike ease to the end of the balcony and kicked down a coiled rope ladder. He left his assault rifle with one of the guards, then began his descent.

Rihani placed his hands on the railing and leaned over to watch as Numair swept through the cowering crowd. One of the hostages moved suddenly, seeking to take the big man from behind. Numair whirled without warning, slashing a huge hand backward that crumpled the man to the floor. The sound of drawn rifle bolts froze the hostages in place.

The spotlight tracked Numair as he closed in on the fallen man, struggling weakly to get away. Blood trickled over the hostage's lower jaw. Obviously satisfied with the retribution he'd exacted, Numair went once more into the crowd with the light following him. The man he stopped in front of was reluctant to come with him.

Rihani recognized him at once. Damien Gray had never looked less sartorially perfect. The hair was a twisted mess and his clothing was torn and gaping. Numair wordlessly pointed to the rope ladder, then shoved Gray from behind. The reporter took a few stumbling steps before catching his balance.

Numair's second objective was ensconced within a small circle of men. There was no mistaking the military haircuts and quiet way they worked together to protect the man in their midst. Numair halted just outside the circle, then lifted his hand full in the spotlight.

The men ringing their leader couldn't mistake the warning as the guards raised their weapons. A heartbeat later the man within their protection stepped forward despite their hushed words.

Retaining a military posture that was unbowed and unbroken, the man led the way to the rope ladder. Gray had already managed the climb with some difficulty, being assisted the last few feet by the guards closest to him. The reporter stood at the end of the balcony, drawing shuddering breaths as he watched the tableau below him.

Rihani drew back from the railing, tucking his arms inside his sleeves. The second man's head drew above the edge of the balcony and he stopped. His grin was bare and mirthless as he continued climbing. "I'll be goddamned," he growled. "It's you, you son of a bitch. And all these years we thought you were dead."

"You were wrong, Major Deering," Rihani replied.

Deering threw himself into motion as soon as he cleared the rope ladder, but Rihani didn't flinch. Even as quick as the military intelligence man was, Numair was quicker, leaping like a great cat to bring the man down. He landed on Deering's back, and light gleamed on the curved dagger that suddenly flicked under the major's throat.

"Oh, shit," Damien Gray muttered hoarsely. The reporter pressed back against the railing as if afraid he'd be next.

One of the guards drew up the rope ladder as if nothing had happened.

"You're a foolish man, Major Deering," Rihani said as he moved closer. "You were when I first knew you, and you are now."

Deering spit at him, the effort landing only inches from Rihani's feet. Numair reacted instantly, taking his dagger away as he grabbed a handful of the intelligence man's hair and slammed his face into the concrete floor. Blood spurted from his chin and lips.

Rihani looked at Gray, who quailed visibly under his dark gaze. He gestured to his men. "Take them and clean them up. Then bring them to me. We have much to talk about."

OREN CATHER'S VOICE had changed very little over the years. Rihani had no trouble recognizing it at once. He pitched his words soft and low, aiming for the metronomic rhythm Cather had always been so susceptible to. "Oren, how are you doing?"

"I'm fine. How are you?"

"Well, my friend, very well indeed." Rihani could tell from the cautious tone in Cather's voice that he was having difficulty placing him. Cather's stature and position on the international scene had grown and changed as had the others. Instead of being a political aide in Beirut, Cather was now a sensitively placed American diplomat in Tel Aviv.

"Maybe I'm a little tired," Cather said cautiously, "but I'm having trouble placing your voice. I'm sorry about that."

"Think nothing of it." Rihani ignored the office surroundings, concentrating on the image of the mousy little man he'd gotten to know almost fifteen years ago. "It's been a long time since we talked. My name is Lucien."

"Lucien."

"Yes."

"We're friends."

"Yes." Rihani could tell by the deepening of Cather's voice that the hypnotic conditioning was taking over. "We often talked of your parents."

"My parents."

"Yes. Remember them?"

"Yes, Lucien, of course I remember them."

"They're in danger."

"I know."

"The Nazis have them. You must escape to save them."

"I will."

"Do you know where you are?"

A momentary pause emphasized the static clinging to the telephone connection. "I'm at Gestapo headquarters. I've been brought in for questioning. Someone has broken my cover."

"Yes, Oren, and you must hurry or your parents will be sent to the gas chamber with the other Jews."

"But they're Germans." Cather's voice contained a teeth-on-edge whine.

"In the eyes of the Führer they are Jews first."

"Yes, of course. I must go at once." Cather broke the connection.

Rihani replaced the receiver on his desk unit and leaned back. He took an embroidered cloth from his pocket and mopped his forehead. Perspiration was already threatening to trickle into his eyes. He chided himself for being so weak. It was all a matter of focus, of lulling his subjects into the otherworld he'd created for them so long ago. He exhaled deeply as he put the cloth away. Cather's attack in the American embassy in Tel Aviv wouldn't cripple the forces gathering to face Hezbollah, but it might buy more time as their enemies tried to sort through everything.

Someone knocked on the door.

"Come."

Numair entered, leading Damien Gray. The reporter had been bathed and given fresh clothing.

Rihani stood and waved toward one of the two chairs in front of the desk. He even put on a false smile to relax the man. "Please. Accept my hospitality."

Gray sat, a look of sick anticipation staining his face.

Rihani looked at Numair. "And the major?"

"He'll be joining us shortly. He wasn't as compliant as this one."

"Of course. Try not to damage him any more than necessary."

"As you wish." Numair left, closing the door behind him.

Rihani walked around the desk and sat on its edge. "Would you care for a cigarette?" He took a pack from the desk and held it out.

Gray's hands trembled as he shook one out and handed the pack back. He accepted the light Rihani offered but had trouble holding the end of the cigarette still long enough to get it ignited.

"You're a famous reporter," Rihani said after Gray expelled his first breath of smoke. "You work for the American television stations."

Gray nodded.

"You're also noted as being something of a...muckraker, I believe it's called."

The term sparked a nerve in the reporter that overrode his fear for a moment. "Hey, I just show the news as I see it," he said in an obviously ritualized statement. "I don't make it up." The fear in his eyes showed that he thought he'd overstepped his bounds.

"I want to offer you a job. In return for your skills as a journalist you'll be given better treatment than your comrades. A room, a bath, clean clothes, food when you wish and a limited amount of freedom. You'll get two stories. The one I give you, and the one going on around you. The first I want you to assemble now. The other can be assembled at your leisure after your release."

"My release?"

"Yes. In time the Israelis and Americans will have no choice but to accede to my demands. Once they've done this all the hostages will be set free."

Despite efforts on the reporter's part, his face clearly showed doubt that Hezbollah's goals could be achieved.

"Are we in agreement?" Rihani asked.

"Sure." The look in Gray's eyes was cold and calculating. "What's the story?"

Rihani smiled to himself, finding the amusement reflected automatically on the reporter's face. Manipulation was so easy when the manipulator had everything his subject could ever wish for. And television personalities—especially newspeople—were victims of their own egos. He'd learned that a long time ago, as well. He looked away as another knock sounded on the door. "Come."

Numair entered, dragging Deering. The major's face had been washed, but there was no hiding the injuries he'd received. Bruises were already showing up around his eyes. His hands were manacled behind his back, drawing a grimace of pain from the man as Numair ungently put him in a chair. The young Hezbollah fighter stood close by, holding a pistol in his hand, well out of the major's reach.

"The story," Rihani said, "will be yet another coup for you concerning the atrocities the American government has perpetrated in this part of the world."

Deering swiveled his head toward the reporter. "What the hell are you doing, Gray? Are you cooperating with this mad son of a bitch? Are you intending to sell out your own people to this lunatic?"

Gray looked back at the intelligence man and blew smoke at him. "Hey, look, GI Joe, I'm sitting here now, a prisoner in a foreign country not through any fault of my own. It's you fucking war hawks in the capital that keep the world in such a mess. If you get caught with your pants down around your goddamn ankles, don't blame me for showing it on national TV."

"The story," Rihani repeated, "is about an agent of the United States government who hired a mercenary force to wrest a captive from the Israeli Mossad."

Gray's face was rapt with interest at once. "No kidding?" He dropped his cigarette butt, crushed it underfoot and helped himself to another without asking.

"You're going to interview Major Deering concerning these matters," Rihani told him, "and you're going to hear the truth from him."

"You can piss up a rope, buddy," Deering said with vehemence. "You're not getting jackshit out of me."

Gray ignored the man, focusing on Rihani. "Maybe we don't need him. Have you got any other proof? Even if it's not so good, I can promise you that it'll come across like gangbusters on television when I get finished with it."

"Major Deering will be only too glad to talk when I'm through with him." Rihani reached down and picked up his black bag, placing it on the desktop and opening it. He took out a hypodermic syringe, tapped it experimentally on the sides and squirted out a thin stream of colorless liquid. "After all, Major, getting people to talk when they didn't want to was one of my chief responsibilities when I worked for your government." He looked at Numair and nodded.

Numair barked orders and three men entered the room. There was a brief struggle as Deering tried to escape, but it was all wasted effort. In the end they held him as Rihani shoved the needle into his arm and depressed the plunger. Deering bellowed in rage, managing a final show of resistance before the drug started to take effect.

The Hezbollah leader disposed of the syringe and sat back on the edge of the desk. In the end the taped interview the reporter would get confirming the mercenary action against the Israelis would only amount to yet another smoke screen. But it would keep attention diverted from the real plan as long as the Russians kept their silence.

The lighter snapped as Gray lit another cigarette, drawing Rihani's attention. "Hey," the reporter asked as he released a plume of smoke, "do you know where I can get a good cameraman? I want this to be choice stuff when we send it out.''

"Of course," Rihani replied. "I appreciate a craftsman who takes pride in his work."

CHAPTER EIGHTEEN

Stony Man Farm, Virginia

Second Day—3:31 p.m.

"We've just been given the ransom notice," the President said grimly.

Bolan looked up at the screen, aware that the video cameras were broadcasting his image back to the Oval Office. "What are the demands?"

"We're to bring home our diplomats and our military people and our hardware from Israel immediately." The President's eyes kept flicking down to what appeared to be a list on a piece of paper he held in one hand. "Hezbollah wants us to break off all military and economic aid. No more funds are to be transferred from Israeli support groups based in this country, and we're supposed to freeze Israeli assets already here." He sighed and put the paper away. "Gorbachev tells me he's been given the same ultimatum in view of the present Soviet Jew emigration."

A tense silence fell over the Stony Man group. Bolan knew everyone was assessing the information in his or her own way. The demands threw all thoughts of a timetable to the winds. There was no way the U.S. could forfeit relations with Israel.

"They're insane," Brognola said softly.

"There's no way that can be done," Barbara Price added.

Yakov Katzenelenbogen interrupted in a voice filled with emotion. "Even a slight pullback of military aid would exact a great toll. The perceived weakness will only encourage extremist enemies of Israel to join in the attack begun by Hezbollah. They'll be like vultures gathering for the kill.

We're talking about a very nasty, bloody war here. If we start out by giving in, it will only be the beginning.''

Bolan glanced at the head of Phoenix Force. Of them all, Katz was the most closely tied emotionally to Israel's fate.

"Rest assured, Yakov," the President said, "that I'm not ready to throw the towel in, even if only for a subterfuge to buy time."

"How much time *do* we have?" Bolan asked.

"Seventy-two hours as of 1700 hours today," the President replied. "And the clock is ticking, gentlemen. Once the deadline is passed the hostages will start dying." He hesitated. "I don't know. Maybe, with no attempts being made to go along with the demands at all on the surface, Hezbollah might start killing them off even sooner. There's just no way of knowing."

"When are you going to turn us loose on it?" Brognola asked.

"Now, Hal." the President told him. "Whatever help I can give you is yours, of course, but I can't go public with any of this yet. Officially I can't sanction anything you people do, but unofficially I've already set the wheels in motion. You're going to have help on this one."

"Help?" Brognola repeated.

Bolan watched the Stony Man teams trade uneasy glances. Even as he carried on his own war, set up his own battle lines and objectives, so had Phoenix and Able been given the same latitude. They'd worked together before, but never with others when the stakes were so high.

"Too many other people are involved in this for us to think we have to play a lone hand," the President said. "You've got ten men who can go local on this one. Ten men against an army. I can't be responsible for sending those men into odds like that. I spent my time in the CIA, and I've seen my share of futile operations. And this damn well isn't going to be one of them."

Brognola remained silent, choosing only to fish a fresh cigar from his pocket.

"The British have already told me they're sending in a crack SAS team," the President continued. "And you know the Israelis aren't going to take this lying down no matter what we do. Mikhail has volunteered a Spetznaz unit. We're looking for a big win here, people, and I don't give a damn how we pull it off. Rather than having units of the SAS, Spetznaz and Mossad crisscrossing one another's trail in Beirut and getting in one another's way, the heads of state involved figured we could get more mileage out of deploying them together and dividing up the footwork between us. If this all blows up in our faces later and the truth comes out . . . Well, we'll just face that tune then. Together. What I want you people to do with your counterparts over there is nail this ruthless son of a bitch's hide to the barn door before we lose any more people."

"In view of everything that's happened," Carl Lyons said, "with the fact that Israel was concealing a political prisoner from the U.S., Britain and Russia, and the fact that American military intelligence saw fit to get this guy back through whatever means possible, how much trust do you see developing over there once the troops are grounded?"

"As much as it takes, Mr. Lyons," the President responded immediately. "Despite what's happened, the important thing is the survival of the hostages. Do you see your goal as being anything else?"

"No, sir."

"Well, then give credit where credit is due. These people have been in this same situation before, as well. Maybe the scale's a little grander than they're used to, but the bottom line remains the same."

Bolan nodded. It didn't matter what flag they flew when it came down to the wire. A soldier's job remained a constant, just as surely as death and taxes. And their job in Beirut would be the same no matter what country was called home.

Kurtzman wheeled into motion in his corner of the room, putting a receiver to his ear as he pecked at the keyboard. "Got a hot one coming in Hal," the computer man said as he looked up at the walls. "Going on-screen with it now." The President's face faded. "Coming your way with it, too, Mr. President."

The interior of an office came into view, shot at a forty-five-degree angle. A silver-haired man wielding a big pistol occupied the upper right corner. Two male secretaries were taking cover behind a small metal desk and a row of filing cabinets. Three shots rang out.

"Where?" Bolan asked.

"American embassy in Tel Aviv," Kurtzman replied. "I tapped into the computer security network. This is live."

"Who's the shooter?" James asked.

"I'm running it."

The man turned and fled, his back coming around to the camera.

Kurtzman's fingers clacked on his keys. A small rectangle appeared in an upper corner of the wall screen as the main picture was reduced to make room for it. The small rectangle froze with two pictures in its center—one of the man in full frontal and the other of him in profile; a third window opened up below, a series of faces blurring through it.

The camera angles changed, picking up the fleeing man as he charged into a hallway. A quick dash took him out of view again. The computer cycled through the linkup, flipping through cameras until it found the man again. This room was larger, containing two tables surrounded by chairs. Four people were inside, their startled voices amplified by the security system.

"What's going on?"

"Oren?"

"Gun! He's got a gun!"

The ID window came up with a matching picture just as the man leveled his weapon at the horrified group.

Bolan read the name printed below the rectangle—"Oren Cather, American diplomat assigned to Israel, based in Tel Aviv" was printed in neat block letters with right-margin justification.

Cather fired, and bullets scarred the top of the wooden table the group had used for cover. One of the women screamed.

Bolan felt his stomach knot in helpless rage. There was something obscene about watching the scene unfold and being unable to do anything about it. "Where are the security teams?" he asked.

"They've been alerted," Kurtzman assured him.

"There," Barbara Price said.

Three men in security uniforms halted at the doorway opposite Cather. Their guns were drawn, but they seemed reluctant to fire on the man.

Cather raised his weapon, and they ducked behind the doorframe as he fired again.

"What's his story?" Katz asked.

"He's been assigned to the Tel Aviv embassy for the past eight years," Kurtzman said, consulting a private monitor screen for a moment.

"There's no reason for them to expect this?" Lyons asked.

Kurtzman shook his head. "None."

A man raised his head behind the conference table. Cather fired instinctively, tracking the movement. The man went down, drops of blood spraying across the wall.

"Son of a bitch," Jack Grimaldi gritted.

Cather reloaded, dropping the empty magazine onto the carpet as he slammed another one home. He aimed at the doorway and fired three times in rapid succession, showering the area with plaster dust.

Another window opened on the wall screens, focusing on Cather's throat. Medical stats printed out immediately below.

"Heart rate and respiration are way above normal," Kurtzman announced.

"Drugs?" Blancanales asked.

"Hard to say," Bear responded. "The software can monitor his pulse and breathing through visuals." The bio-window zeroed in on Cather's eyes, blowing them up to ten times their size and holding the image even as the man turned away from the camera. "The retinal prints show it's Cather and not a ringer, but he's definitely in an agitated state."

One of the security guards whirled around the doorframe, his arms falling naturally into a weaver's grip. His eyes were grim and hard over the barrel of his weapon. The pistol barked twice.

Cather jerked with both impacts, spinning as the final bullet caught him in the upper chest and spread-eagled him over the other conference table. His pistol tumbled from his hand. "Nazis," the man croaked as a trickle of blood oozed out the corner of his mouth. He shivered and was still, his eyes sliding into the thousand-yard stare that was so familiar to the Executioner.

The other two guards came around the doorway, leaving the man who'd pulled the trigger staring at the body. The three people behind the conference table helped the wounded man to his feet. He didn't seem to be seriously injured.

"Nazis?" David McCarter echoed. "Did the bloke think he was being trailed by Nazis in the middle of Israel?"

Kurtzman consulted his private monitor as the wall screens presented the image of the President. "Cather served in World War II. Of German heritage, he shifted over to the OSS during the war after his parents were gassed at Auschwitz."

"There was no reason for him to believe the Nazis were after him," Barbara Price said.

"Maybe he thought he was shooting Nazis instead of coworkers he'd known for years," Bolan suggested. Some of it was making a sickening kind of sense. He was just guessing at this point, but they were guesses built upon a soldier's observations of a world at war. And they had a foundation in the memory of American soldiers he'd seen who'd been taken captive by VC and tortured into a world that existed only in their own minds.

"Got something, Striker?" Brognola asked.

"A hunch." Bolan glanced at Kurtzman. "Where's the Beirut connection?"

"Two years," Kurtzman replied. "Between 1979 and 1981 Cather was a liaison for the United Nations peace-keeping force."

"All roads lead to Beirut," Grimaldi said somberly.

"What's the hunch?" Brognola asked.

"Posthypnotic suggestion."

Brognola appeared to be considering it.

"Try mind control," Kurtzman said, "and you'll hit the nail on the head."

The attention of the Stony Man warriors instantly shifted in his direction.

"We just made Dr. Fahad Rihani," Bear said. "He was a mind control specialist employed by the CIA and the KGB during the late seventies and early eighties."

"What's the rest of it?" Bolan asked.

"Still sorting through it, guy. As soon as I get the skinny on his file, it's yours."

Bolan nodded and gave his attention to the President. "Who's heading up the teams in Beirut?"

"You people are," the President replied, "and the operation is going to be controlled from Stony Man Farm. I had to pull some strings and rake in some IOUs to get it done, but that's how it's going to be. With primarily American hostages and an American ally at stake, I couldn't risk it any other way. The Brits and Mikhail were understanding about it. So were the Israelis, surprisingly, in light of the circumstances."

"But they'll be playing their own game, as well," Katz put in.

"That's to be expected," Bolan said, "and I can't fault them there."

Katz nodded and crushed out his cigarette. "If there's no problem with it, I'd like to be the liaison for the Israeli team. Perhaps my insights into their workings will keep us on a more even footing."

"Fine." Bolan glanced at the camera. "If there isn't anything else, sir, I'd like to get moving on this. We can set up rendezvous points for the various teams from here as well as start moving tactical gear into position."

"As you wish, Striker," the President said. "I wish there was more I could do for you at this point. If there's anything later..."

"You'll hear about it."

"Fair enough." The President gave them a grim smile. "Godspeed, gentlemen." The wall screen went blank, and mechanisms whined as the wall units slid under concealment again and the overheads flickered into life.

"Stay with Rihani's file," Bolan said as he headed for the door. "Let me know the minute you have something you feel I can use. Barb?"

"Yes."

"It's fourteen hours' flying time from here to Beirut. See what you can do about getting some hardware that can cut that down. Hours are passing too damn fast."

"I'm already on it. When you get with Kissinger, fax me a list of the equipment you're going to be taking."

"Right." Bolan stepped out into the hallway, already feeling better just to be on the move.

KURTZMAN WAS HOLDING the debriefing in the war room, and Bolan took his seat without preamble. The air inside the room was cold and electric even before the lights went out and the displays were brought up on the walls.

"Dr. Fahad Rihani," Kurtzman said. He covered the man's background from birth until his disappearance in 1983. Rihani's college experience, his family, what he'd done for the KGB, CIA and other world espionage groups that was available through Sensitive Operations Group channels were all included. Pictures splashed across the wall screens, showing Rihani with different dignitaries and agents over a span of ten years. It was a lesson and brief history in how cold the cold war had been during its heyday.

Bolan memorized the man's features, burned the man's black eyes into his mind. Hundreds of deaths had been attributed to Hezbollah while under Rihani's control. CIA file tapes were available on some of the subjects who'd faced Rihani's more personal skills. It was a collage of madness and perversity, an endless stream of men and women who'd been reduced to mere shells of humanity through drugs, sustained terror and hypnotic conditioning. Bone-thin corpses lacking the will to die with case numbers instead of names paraded across the walls.

"Bloody hell," McCarter commented quietly.

Bolan agreed. It was hell, fashioned by a man who had found he could kindle a desire inside himself for it. There was no other answer.

"You say Rihani was Soviet-trained?" James asked.

Kurtzman nodded. "During his day, Rihani was reputed to have been one of the KGB's finest."

"Could explain the presence of the Spetznaz," James continued sourly. "Goodwill be damned. It could be a matter of political CYA—Cover Your Ass."

Katz broke in, his voice smooth and reassuring. "Let's not forget, Calvin, that it was the United States that started the funding for mind control and its usage. Rihani learned many of those skills from his CIA contacts, as well."

"Yeah," Blancanales said, "and LSD was a by-product of those same fine folks who were struggling to know what evil lurks in the minds of men."

"Sounds like the Shadow," Lyons commented.

"Nah," Schwarz replied, "he only knew what evil lurked in the *hearts* of men."

Despite the attempts at lightheartedness, Bolan knew what they'd seen had affected all of the Stony Man warriors. The bad jokes, the black humor and the light touch in the face of adversity were all methods they'd learned over the years to relieve the stress and strain of their dark world.

"I found your tie-in to the three men," Kurtzman said. "The problem is, it throws another monkey wrench into the whole deal. While he was in Beirut, Rihani worked as a consulting psychologist under at least three different names that were verified by the CIA in undisclosed reports. Rihani saw Carson, Khromeyev and Cather in that professional aspect. That's evidently where and when he programmed them to become berserkers."

"And the CIA thought he was dead." Encizo said.

"Exactly," Kurtzman replied. "They investigated his patients, including Carson and Cather, but didn't find anything out of the ordinary, so they let them pass. The problem is, they never got their hands on Rihani's personal records under these names."

"Boiled down," Brognola said, "we've got potentially dozens of people—Americans, Russians, Brits, French and Israelis—who could be walking around, programmed as these other men were. There are a lot of other possible time bombs Rihani could choose to set off at any time. Even if we knew for sure who they were, the manpower plus the high profile required by the operation would be staggering. We'd be blown before we ever got started."

"And there's this," Barbara Price added. She tapped a keyboard at her side. "This is just in, Aaron, so you didn't know about it."

The displays changed, melting down into a grainy black-and-white picture. Price hit more keys and the picture exploded, enhanced by the computer system until it was more than a picture and became generated by the computer alone. A light gray circle wrapped around the bearded face of an Arab in business clothing. The scene was shot in an airport lobby.

"That's Heathrow," McCarter said.

"Right," Price replied. "These are airport films sent to us by Interpol. We're coordinating some of our surveillance through them because they've already got the manpower in place over there."

"And the chap we're looking at?" the lanky Briton asked.

"Badr Faisel. He is, according to our sources, Rihani's right-hand man."

"When was this taken?" Katz asked.

"Less than a few hours ago," Price answered. "Interpol had no orders to detain him, only to verify movement Kurtzman picked up that was headed this way."

"Where's he going?" Grimaldi asked.

"Here. To Washington, D.C." Price turned to face the group. "Carl, Pol and Gadgets, Faisel is your part of the joint assignment. Interpol also ID'ed part of his entourage, but you can bet they didn't get them all. We need to know why Faisel's here and what he's up to."

"No good is a safe bet," Lyons said laconically.

"In which case you'll stop him," Price replied. "But to do that you're going to have to find him and the terrorist cell he's brought with him. If you take him out too soon, the cell will probably scatter and be even harder to run down."

"We understand," Blancanales said. "Slow and easy does it."

"Able Team's going to be dealing with a glitch over here, too," Kurtzman said. "I've tracked a Mossad hard team coming this way. Until now I didn't know what they were coming for. They're traveling incognito and they're traveling light and quick."

"So we don't want to rock the boat early," Schwarz concluded.

"Right."

"If these people are in contact with Hezbollah back in Beirut," Brognola said, "taking them down early could kick off a bloodbath over there. Treat the situation with kid gloves until you see that you have no choice."

"And the Israelis?" Lyons asked.

"If it comes to it," Brognola replied, "slow them down, too. We're on home ground here, and they should respect that."

Lyons nodded.

Brognola looked around the room. "Anything else?"

Price and Kurtzman shook their heads.

"Okay, people," the big Fed said, "this is the way it breaks down. The Spetznaz team is awaiting rendezvous at Baku, where Kissinger's going to set up your temporary base. The SAS team is already en route to Riyadh, Saudi Arabia, and will touch down before any of you do. And the Mossad team is waiting in Tel Aviv.'' He looked at Katz. ''Yakov, you said you wanted the Israeli link. It's yours. To cover the three teams properly with our people, Phoenix is going to have to split.''

Katz turned to McCarter. ''David, you and Gary pair up and meet the SAS team. Rafael and Calvin will remain with me.'' He moved on to meet Bolan's eyes. ''Mack?''

''Agreed,'' The Executioner replied. ''Jack and I will take the Russian front.''

''We'll coordinate as much intel to you as we can from here,'' Price said, ''but we'll be depending on your information from the field. So will the other teams. Aaron's secured a covert channel for the operation through a weather satellite system that will be in place over the Middle East most of the time. Don't hold back anything. Let us make the decision from here as to how important it is.''

''Barb's got the hot seat here,'' Brognola told them. ''I'll be manning the one in Wonderland with the President as we try to keep the State Department and other bureaucratic agencies off your backs. It's going to be impossible to keep a low profile on this one, so you're going to have to be damn quick about it. When you find the hostages, it's going to have to be a coordinated blitz. In and out and gone. The pickup sites have already been designated and will be reassigned when we know where our people are.'' He paused to look around the room. ''Other than that, all I can tell you is good luck and God keep.''

Bolan pushed his chair back and stood. ''The only choice we have is to shut Rihani down as soon as possible. This is a dirty war. The stakes are too high to think of it as anything else. And it's going to have to be fought on their terms. We're just going to have to be better at it. We're going in late and behind, and we have to catch up if we're going to do the hostages any good. Starting now.'' He looked at the men he would be leading into battle, meeting level gaze after level gaze. ''Let's do it.''

CHAPTER NINETEEN

Beirut, Lebanon
Third Day—10:43 a.m.

Place des Martyrs had once been the prime area of commerce before the beginning of the fourteen-year civil war that had leveled so much of the city. Some real business was still attended to, but a lot of it had changed over to black markets and clandestine meeting places.

Bolan, dressed in his brown bomber jacket and jeans, remained in the shadows of an alley as the sun crept toward the noon hour. The two Russians with him were indistinguishable from the sparse human traffic wading through the ruin of the street.

The Executioner shifted uneasily. The flight to Baku had taken a little over ten hours. It had been a puddle jump for the Soviet air force to drop him and the Spetznaz team into the city. The whole procedure seemed more like a milk run to the Russian team, but there was no denying the training evidenced by their special forces teams. Grimaldi had been familiar with a couple of them from different stints at Stony Man Farm.

A battered red Chevy compact rattled through the streets, belching smoke. Men and women gave way reluctantly before it, scattering harsh curses in its wake.

"He will come," Zhenka Kalinin said quietly as Bolan checked his watch.

"He's taking his time." Bolan growled. They were working a soft probe for the mercenary team transporting the weapons to Hezbollah, looking for the thread that would take them back to the storehouse before the munitions hit the streets.

Kalinin shrugged. "These are trying times, Comrade Belasko, filled with desperate men and desperate acts. No man will easily trust another. Even a man such as Tuholske who has the correct papers and history."

Bolan nodded. The Spetznaz commander was right, and they both knew it. The helplessness of sitting on the sidelines was grating on his nerves. The SIG Sauer P-226 hung comfortably in breakaway leather under his left arm. He had a duplicate sheathed in an ankle holster. Both men had been targeted in at Baku. He missed the Beretta 93-R and the Desert Eagle .44 Magnum that were his usual weapons on missions, but had opted for the availability of the same gun and caliber with all three teams. All magazines were transferable in hostile situations, and the 9 mm round was plentiful in Beirut.

Kalinin was big and dark. A broad mustache framed his upper lip, tucking into corners of his dimples. His dark hair was cut short and ragged without being conventional. Pavel Karpov was a smaller man with dusty blond hair and light blue eyes. He was at least ten years Kalinin's senior.

"Here he comes now," Karpov said.

Bolan watched as Demyan Tuholske left the bombed shell of a building at the end of the street. The young Spetznaz trooper made his way across the street like a man with no particular place to go. The Executioner tracked the movement in Tuholske's wake at once. "He's got company," the soldier stated, and waved the other men deeper into the alley.

Kalinin and Karpov responded at once, hands slipping inside their jackets to get their weapons. "There's the signal," Kalinin said as he freed the safety on his SIG Sauer. "Demyan knows he's been identified."

Tuholske stood on the opposite street corner and fired up a cigarette.

"How many men do you count, Mr. Belasko?" Kalinin asked.

"Three on foot," Bolan replied. "And there's a car."

"Two men in the car," Karpov added in a wintery voice.

"Check." Bolan watched as Tuholske guided his entourage away from the alley. The medium-size black sedan rolled along behind in quiet pursuit. Sunlight glinted from the short radio aerial. The Executioner unleathered the 9 mm pistol and flicked off the safety.

"Five men," Kalinin said.

"Yeah." Bolan jogged back along the alley, keeping the pistol out of sight. "Any idea who they are?"

"No," Kalinin replied as he jogged close behind.

"PLO members," Karpov stated flatly.

Bolan paused at the next street corner. "You know that for a fact?"

"Yes."

Bolan turned to Kalinin for confirmation.

"I don't know those men, Mr. Belasko," the Spetznaz leader replied. "But Comrade Karpov has had many experiences outside my own field of operations. I was told this would be an asset to our present assignment."

"They are PLO," Karpov insisted quietly.

The warrior read volumes into the unspoken aspect of the conversation. Karpov had looked too old to be regulation Spetznaz, and Kalinin's comment only confirmed it. Exactly what the slender man ultimately was remained to be seen. The Executioner dipped a hand into his jacket and brought out the ear/throat communications gear. He unfolded it and snapped it into place, thumbing the transmit button. "Jack?"

"Copy."

"Got our guy in sight?"

"Check. He brought back company."

"Yeah. Is your team in position?"

"Sure. We'll dust them off on your signal."

"Head count?"

"I make five."

"Check. Any cross-references?"

"Two. According to Aaron's mug shots, those guys are PLO."

"You got confirmation at this end, too."

"How do you want to play it, guy?"

Bolan eased around the building and walked at a normal gait. The broken cityscape had too many hiding places. "I want the vehicle taken out first, and I want at least one of the ground troops left intact."

"Roger."

Kalinin and Karpov nodded, showing that they understood the instructions.

Bolan kept the lead as they skirted the building. He cleared the corner and waved Kalinin and Karpov to ground behind him. Their breathing rasped close at his elbow. Glancing around the corner, he saw Tuholske leading his tail along as if oblivious. The man's hand was tucked into his jacket pocket. Bolan keyed the mike. "Give me five, Jack, then hit it." He pocketed the ear/throat set and moved out, mentally counting down the numbers.

Tuholske's eyes met his briefly, then hardened as he threw his cigarette away. Bolan marked the fire zones as the numbers fell, moving to keep the lanes open around the Russian agent. When he was twenty feet from Tuholske, a double boom of sniper rifles drowned out the street sounds and the glass windows in the tailing sedan spiderwebbed.

The vehicle veered out of control and smashed into a leaning streetlight, flattening it to the ground. A door popped open as the Executioner raised his side arm and brought the closest man into target acquisition. He squeezed off three rounds as Tuholske dived to the ground, clawing for his weapon. Bullets chipped the broken sidewalk as the Spetznaz officer rolled across the rubble.

Bolan's three rounds took his man full in the chest and flung him back as his weapon cleared leather. The hollow boom of Grimaldi's Beretta sniper rifle filled the air again and the surviving member of the car team sprawled across the hood.

Rubber shrieked on the pavement as the team's mobile unit, a Ford Econoline van with a patchy gray-and-brown paint job, roared onto the street.

A bullet whipped by Bolan's head as he took a Weaver's stance and lined up his next man. He fired coolly, making the shots count, and the shooter went down in a twisting heap.

The remaining man fired a loose collection of shots in Bolan's general direction, then turned to flee. Tuholske pushed himself from the ground, quickly climbed a pile of broken concrete slabs separating him from his running target and launched himself at the man.

The Ford van twisted sideways in the middle of the street. Someone slid the panel door open to reveal a tripod-mounted M-60 screwed into the floor.

Bolan raced forward as the gleam of a knife appeared in the PLO man's hand. Tuholske had lost his weapon in the tackle while disarming his adversary. The Executioner grabbed the man's knife arm as it descended, stopping the motion short of Tuholske's throat as he screwed the hot barrel of the SIG Sauer into the man's neck. He shook the arm meaningfully. English or no, it was something the guy could understand. The knife clanged to the pavement. The Executioner shoved his prisoner to the ground, keeping his pistol against the guy's spine as he put a knee on the man's back.

Tuholske gathered the loose weapons as Kalinin moved forward to make a quick frisk. Karpov stood nearby holding an Uzi. The crowd on the street had frozen for a moment, hypnotized by the action, then hurriedly got under way again before they became part of it. Kalinin moved away, fisting his side arm. "Nothing," he said.

Bolan nodded, then grabbed a fistful of the man's jacket and yanked him into a stumbling run toward the waiting van. Even as the prisoner's hand closed on the frame of the panel door, an invisible force slammed him inside. The Executioner heard the rolling boom of the shot a heartbeat later as he scrambled for cover. He took up position at the rear of the van, tracking the buildings on the other side of the street where the shot had to have been fired from. Nothing moved. There were no other shots.

Kalinin and Karpov were hunkered behind rusting hulks of automobiles. Bolan fitted his communications gear into place and hit the transmit button. "Jack?"

"Not one of ours, Striker."

"Pursuit?"

"Pretty damn quick, guy. The Syrian peacekeeping units have already been notified. We've been picking up their broadcasts."

"Break it off." Bolan ordered.

The warrior put the ear/throat set back in his pocket, cutting off the pilot's quick "Roger." Ducking into the van with Karpov and Kalinin close at his heels, he clambered over the body of their prisoner. He rolled it over as Tuholske and Karpov boarded and the driver got the vehicle out of there.

The bullet had gone in neat, just right of the man's spine, and blew out a plate-size section of the chest. Bolan released his hold on the corpse, which slumped to the floor. He guessed the caliber at 7.62 mm—the same size as the sniper weapons the team had been issued. He holstered his pistol and met Karpov's light blue gaze full measure. The man didn't blink. "Somebody killed him to keep him from talking," Bolan stated.

"That much is evident," Karpov said. "Perhaps he had comrades we didn't see who wished to speed him on to meet his God. These people, with their religious propaganda and dogmas, are all too willing to sacrifice their lives and the lives of others."

"Yeah," Bolan replied, "I guess you could look at it that way. If you were inclined to take things at face value. Me, I'm not so ready."

"And a paranoid man flees when no one follows, Comrade," Karpov said.

A flicker of resentment passed through Kalinin's eyes, but he said nothing.

Screams of sirens tore through the streets behind them as the van's driver whipped through the predetermined course. When he jammed on the brakes, the door crew quickly slid the panel open and let Grimaldi and two of his team through. The pilot was breathing hard from the run to meet the van.

"Where's Svoboda?" Bolan asked.

Grimaldi shook his head. "Lost touch with him as this thing started going down."

"There." The driver pointed, stopping the vehicle again as the panel door slid open.

Andrei Svoboda ran flat out, keeping his weapon close to his body so that its weight wouldn't slow him down. Like Karpov, Svoboda was an older man, but slim with a squarish face and a brush cut. He leaped into the van as the driver popped the clutch.

Bolan reached out and took the Beretta sniper rifle from the man without explanation. Svoboda drew back a fist immediately.

"Sergeant!" Kalinin barked, his voice freezing the action.

"How many shots did your team fire, Jack?" Bolan asked as he ejected the box from Svoboda's rifle. He freed the action and dropped the shell in the chamber onto the metal floor of the van.

Grimaldi conferred with the other two men in his group. "Seven shots between us."

The tension in the back of the van was almost palpable.

"I counted nine from the sniper unit," Bolan said. He glanced at Karpov and smiled thinly. "You know how it is, Comrade. A military mind is constantly at work sorting and keeping track of details." He returned his attention to Svoboda. "How many did you count, Captain Kalinin?"

The answer came slowly. "Nine."

Bolan held out the rifle's magazine at shoulder height. The rounds rang out as they hit the metal floor of the van. "Seventeen," he said in a graveyard voice. "You're one short, Svoboda."

"Perhaps the magazine was short to begin with," the man suggested.

"Perhaps." Bolan agreed. He flipped the empty magazine back to the big man. "Now I have to wonder which is worse to have standing at my back—a spy or an incompetent soldier."

Svoboda's cheeks flamed with the insult. Only a soft command from Karpov held the man in check.

Turning to Tuholske, Bolan asked, "Did you get the name of the mercenary handling the munitions transference, Corporal?"

"Yes, sir," Tuholske said, squaring his shoulders. "Nick Leighton. He's a man known to us and our intelligence staff."

"That's enough, Corporal." Kalinin glanced at Bolan. "We'll go into that in short order."

"Yes, sir."

Bolan nodded. The Spetznaz officer's words were enough to let him know new lines were being drawn across the mission's membership. He sat beside Grimaldi and wondered how soon it would be before Karpov had to make his next move. At the same time he wondered how many of the Spetznaz team really belonged to Karpov instead of Kalinin. And what orders they ultimately followed.

CHAPTER TWENTY

Washington, D.C.

Third Day—3:07 a.m.

"It's my town," Leo Turrin explained with a smile. "I don't know how you guys thought Hal would turn you loose in the nation's capital without a chaperon."

Lyons shook his head as he looked at the little Fed. "Tad bit overdressed for the gala event, aren't you, Leo?" They were in the underground parking area of the Justice Department. Gadgets Schwarz sat behind the wheel of the three-year-old bronze Lincoln Able Team had been issued courtesy of Stony Man's motor pool. Blancanales sat in the rear seat with a grin on his face.

Turrin looked down at the black tuxedo in mock astonishment. "Hal did mention you guys were in covert action, but, hell, Carl, the only way you can go covert in this town is in tails and top hat."

"The only time Carl's ever fully dressed is when he's in tail and pitchfork," Schwarz said.

Turrin grinned, while Lyons scowled and crawled back into the front seat.

"Actually," Turrin told them as he slid into the back, "I've been engaged in helping keep heavy artillery from hitting the streets in pursuit of your target."

"Faisel?" Lyons asked.

"Exactly."

Schwarz put the Lincoln into gear and headed for the exit.

"Rumors have already hit Washington that a pack of wild-eyed gun-toting Arabs landed somewhere in one of our suburbs. So far Hal and the President have managed to contain the information. Still, Hal and I have been working our asses off to shut down a troop buildup over here.'' Turrin sighed as he unbuttoned his coat. ''The last place I crashed had a party going on. I got stuck dressing for the part to keep from arousing suspicion.''

Lyons flashed his Justice badge at the security guard, and the heavy, reinforced doors rattled up at once.

''So give, Leo,'' Blancanales said. ''Hal said you had some big scoop on where we might find Faisel. We've been breaking our butts for hours without turning over a single clue. Don't tease if you can't please.''

''Like I said, gentlemen, D.C.'s my town. While you were getting a case of flat feet out rattling doors, I've put a few old contacts onto the scent.''

Lyons knew about Turrin's old contacts. While working the special unit detail during Bolan's Mafia wars, he'd been given some information on Turrin through Brognola's old office. Turrin had been in Sergio Frenchi's Family in Pittsfield, Massachusetts, where the Executioner's first self-declared war had started. Turrin had been in charge of prostitution then and had inadvertently turned out Bolan's younger sister into the Life. Bolan had initially targeted Turrin as a casualty of his war until he'd found out Turrin was a deep-cover Fed. Somehow the two men had forged a friendship that ran soul-deep. Now Leo operated out of an office in the Justice Department under the name Leonard Justice and took piecework from Stony Man. Still, there were a lot of Mafia connections who thought Turrin had voluntarily taken a powder but was still linked with Family business.

''I figured it would take a system already in place to bring Faisel and his men into the city,'' Turrin continued. ''So I went hunting the system, not the man.''

''We already tried that,'' Schwarz said. ''Didn't turn up shit there, either. Carl practically tore down a head shop on Fourteenth Street when the owner was being uncooperative.''

''They don't call them head shops anymore,'' Lyons said.

Schwarz shrugged. "Whatever."

"I heard about that," Turrin said.

"That's no surprise," Blancanales replied. "Hell, there were two news teams and a half-dozen squad cars there before we broke loose."

"Somebody got a damn nice cocaine collar out of the deal," Lyons said in his own defense.

"But you didn't turn up anything in the way of Hezbollah," Turrin said.

"There is that," Lyons admitted with a tired smile. His eyes burned, so he blinked, then finally gave up and used the eyedrops he'd bought earlier.

"We going anyplace in particular?" Schwarz asked, "or are you just fulfilling your man-about-town image?"

Turrin gave him a Georgetown address.

Lyons knew the general area from the maps Kurtzman had provided. He also knew from Turrin's voice that whatever lead the little Fed had turned up, it felt pretty solid. "Going shopping, Leo?" he asked. "A new pair of cuff links or a tie tack?" He glanced over the seat.

Turrin smiled. "Let's just say we're doing a little market research."

"Are you packing anything besides an extra hanky?"

"Actually I did come prepared." Turrin reached inside his jacket and brought out a hammerless stainless-steel Smith & Wesson .38 Bodyguard. There was no front sight. He slid it back into its shoulder harness. "And this packs a hell of a punch."

LYONS TOOK foot recon as they neared the target area. He was dressed in jeans and a chambray work shirt under a Washington Redskins windbreaker. His Colt Python hung in a rig at the small of his back. Speedloaders were tucked into the windbreaker pockets.

A cool wind blew in north from the Potomac River, dusting M Street free of litter. The city's night denizens were out in force, drawn by the scattered neon lights. He counted the street addresses down as he took the side street near a shop featuring Madonna wear for imitators. A neon light pulsed in a strobe effect that threatened to screw up his night vision.

A middle-aged black woman with tinted red hair stepped out of the shadows of a doorway. She still had a nice body, which was wrapped in an emerald strapless dress that was three inches shy of being presentable in mixed company. The lithe blond girl who joined her didn't look eighteen.

The older woman put a cigarette to her lips. "Got a light, sugar?" she asked in a thick Southern accent.

"Yeah." Lyons stopped and lit her cigarette, keeping his gun hand near his hip.

The blonde wet her lips too slowly for the action to resemble natural reflex. "My name's Kitten," she said in a throaty voice, "but you can call me anything you'd like."

"Beat it, Kitten," Lyons growled without looking at her.

The blonde started to protest.

"Do it," the other woman snapped.

Immediately the blond girl dropped back.

"You're a cop, aren't you?" the woman asked.

"I've been one," Lyons replied.

The woman expelled smoke. "I could tell. Your eyes give you away, Mr. Policeman. You got that hard look that says you got a badge where a man's heart ought to be. Don't tell me you're out here tonight rousting girls who're trying hard to make a living."

Lyons smiled at her straightforwardness. Street people still held a special place in his heart. When it came to cops and citizens, street people would lie, cheat, steal and break hearts to make it through another day. Or, by the same turn, they could be a beat cop's best friend. "I wanted to leave you with a word of warning," he said. "This end of the street's going to get red-hot in just a few minutes. Maybe even attract all kinds of attention."

"Uh-huh. I hear you talking, and I thank you for the tip." She crossed her arms over her breasts and shivered. "It was about time I dragged these old bones to my crib, anyway. The business that's still out here, well, it belongs to them sweet young things. I don't go for the rough trade kind of stuff no more." She dropped her cigarette and crushed it with the toe of her high-heeled shoe. "And you be careful out there, Mr. Policeman."

"You take care, too, lady. And from here, those old bones look just fine."

"You're too kind and too silver-tongued to be a cop," the woman replied as she walked away. "But if you're ever this way again and need something, you just put the word out for Kismet and I'll be there." She disappeared into the shadows with the young blonde in tow, the clicking of her heels fading after her.

Lyons studied the front of the business as he approached it. It was Turrin's call, but a gut feeling put in a quick agreement. He drew the Python and held it against his leg.

Scattered empty cars dotted the curb on both sides of the street in the building. The lower half was set up in true souk style from the way Turrin had described it, offering a varied selection of hand-painted pottery, Phoenician glassware, steel and copper cutlery with handles in the shape of animal and bird heads. One window was given over entirely to handloomed rugs and tapestries with a wide color range. Streetlights glinted from inexpensive jewelry draped over T-shaped displays. The name on the door was blockprinted in unassuming black letters: Mideastern Imports and Antiquities. The building was three stories high. Somewhere in there, Turrin's Mafia connections had said would be Faisel and other members of Hezbollah. Or at least the team that had slipped the terrorists into Washington, D.C., would be there. A little interrogation would at least give them a new lead.

He waited for the traffic to pass, then jogged across the street. He did a quick recon of the storefront and tested the door to make sure it was locked.

Tucking the .357 back into its holster, Lyons crossed the sidewalk to the metal awning in front of the building that housed the clothing store next door and pulled himself up. The heavy tarp stretched precariously as he tumbled onto it.

He breathed a sigh of relief as he gained the ledge and reached back for the second story over the Mideastern Imports store. The brick felt rough and grainy under his fingers. He edged back toward the narrow expanse of space between the buildings, aiming for the dark window almost ten feet back.

Without warning glass exploded from the window frame as gunshots echoed between the buildings. Lyons yanked his hand back and drew the Python as a body came tumbling through the window, dragging the draperies with it. The trash cans below flattened with the impact. Thinking that Pol, Gadgets or Turrin had inadvertently triggered a silent alarm in their assault on the building, he peered around the window, tracking the .357 inside.

Another volley of gunshots rang out, but these were deeper inside the building, coming from the top floor.

Lyons threw a leg over the window, wondering how the hell the others had gotten so far ahead of him. Before he could get his feet solidly under him, a dark-skinned man carrying an Uzi burst into the room. The Stony Man warrior threw himself forward, skidding across the worn carpet of the bedroom as the Uzi cut a trail of 9 mm parabellums into the walls above his head. He snapped off two 180-grain loads and watched the shooter crumple to the floor with a rush of scarlet staining his chest.

His ears ringing from the sudden thunder trapped inside the room, he forced himself up and into motion, pausing at the doorway with both hands gripping the Python. Two more bodies lay on the carpet of the dimly lighted hallway. Dark patterns on the walls told him someone was using a sawed-off shotgun.

Lyons stepped over the bodies, heading for the short stairway at the end of the hall that led up. He saw Blancanales below him. "Pol."

"Ironman."

Gadgets stepped out of the shadows near Blancanales with Turrin on his heels. "You start the party without us?" Schwarz asked.

"Not my party," Lyons growled. "I thought it was you guys." He moved cautiously up the carpeted stairway with the other three men flanking him. The screaming and shotgun explosions died away as he found the first body on the stairs. He used a penflash to scan the corpse.

A shotgun blast had almost ripped the man's right arm off, but it was the two holes between the man's eyes that had killed him.

"Goddamn .22," Lyons swore. "Son of a bitch." He turned to the others. "They beat us here!" He drove his legs hard, lunged up the staircase and hit the landing at the top, wheeling neatly into place beside the closed door. Checking with the others to make sure they'd had time to set themselves, he groped for the doorknob, found it, then whirled and put a boot near the lock. The metal separated from the wood with a shrieking groan as the door flew inward.

Lyons went in low, both hands around the .357's Pachmayr grips as his elbow and foot blocked the rebound of the door. Gadgets took the door high, leveling his cut-down Mossberg 500 Military shotgun to give coverage.

Two men stood with their hands behind their heads in the small bedroom. Three more bodies sprawled across the floor.

"One flinch," Lyons warned, "and you guys are dead."

"We understand," one of the men said in formal English. "But I assure you, the enemies you would have found here have already been dealt with."

Lyons stepped into the room, centering his revolver on the speaker's chest. Turrin took his place at the door while Blancanales followed him into the room.

"We have identification you will be interested in," the speaker said.

"Quiet," Lyons snapped. He waved them to the wall, kicking the SPAS-12 and Ruger Mark II Bull Barrel .22 out of reach with his foot. "You two seem like guys who know the position. Do it."

The men fell against the wall with outstretched hands high above their heads. They were dressed casually, boating slacks and knit shirts under light jackets.

"Pol?"

"Dead, dead and dead," Blancanales responded in disgust. "These guys are very thorough."

"Couldn't expect anything less from the Mossad, could you?" Lyons holstered his revolver and stepped toward them. He frisked the men, then told them to turn around.

Both were dark and lean, seeming to be college age but already possessing a cold gleam in their eyes that came from seeing too much death up close.

"We have identification," one of the men said again.

Lyons nodded. "Slowly, ace, because you guys have a lot to answer for here tonight."

The man nodded. He hooked a finger under the collar of his shirt and pulled out a stainless-steel chain attached to a laminated rectangle. It unclipped easily, and he passed it over.

Lyons took it and read it with his penflash.

"Actually," the man said as he lowered his hands, "I think you'll find we have nothing at all to answer for here." His smile was thin.

"Ironman," Gadgets prompted.

Police sirens poured into the streets below, then died as the vehicles came to a stop. Reflections of red and blue lights chased each other against the closed windows of the buildings.

Holding up the laminated rectangle, Lyons said, "Diplomatic immunity, guys, from the Israeli embassy."

"A real license to kill," Turrin said quietly as he put his gun away.

"And a hell of a get-out-of-jail-free card," Schwarz added.

"There's no reason to be angry," the speaker said as he took back the card. "Your enemies are our enemies. We have only—"

Lyons cut the Mossad agent off, stepping up for a face-to-face as he thumped a big forefinger into the man's chest. "You've only fucked up is what you've only done," he growled. "We came here after Faisel. I didn't happen to see him when I was turning over the bodies you guys left behind. That means he's still loose to do whatever he was sent over here to do. And he knows somebody's turning over rocks trying to find him."

"He will be stopped," the Mossad agent said.

"Well, I'm not convinced of it," Lyons snapped.

"Ironman," Blancanales said quietly. He stood at a window, looking down.

Lyons joined him, noticing the ropes hanging from the side of the building.

"They weren't alone," Blancanales stated.

Lyons shook his head. "Dollars to doughnuts, guy, these jokers didn't make this place until we were headed this way."

"Maybe so, maybe no."

"That's it, isn't it?" Lyons asked, turning to meet the Mossad agents' gazes. "You guys didn't even have a handle on this place until you made us."

There was no reply.

Lyons looked at Turrin. "We got a rat in the pack, Leo, and we'd better turn him up quick before these clowns disrupt anything else we get a lead on."

A voice filled with authority ripped into the room, ordering them to put their guns down. Lyons and the others complied, joining the Israelis in putting their hands behind their heads.

Blue suits flooded the room, taking command instantly. The smell of sweat and fear overlaid the scent of fresh death from the three corpses.

Lyons let the officer behind him push him against the wall, then felt the cold steel of the handcuffs encircle his wrists and click into place. He was spun around roughly and marched toward the door.

A heavyset black cop in plainclothes met him at the door. "You," Detective Sergeant Rollie Maurloe said in disbelief.

A brief, humorless smile twisted Lyons's lips. "Me," he agreed quietly, and turned so the detective could get at the cuffs.

"Word I got from the Hill," Maurloe said as he unlocked the bracelets, "was that you were supposed to be some kind of covert agent out of Justice."

Lyons massaged his wrists while the officer took back his handcuffs. "If you want, you can see my buzzer again."

"No. I had you checked out after the head shop thing earlier. Took a reaming from my captain for even bothering anybody with asking."

"They don't call them head shops anymore, Sarge," one of the younger officers called.

Maurloe ignored the man. "I thought you people were supposed to be doing the Navy submarine thing on this. You know—run silent, run deep."

"That's not exactly my forte."

The detective tipped his hat back with a broad thumb as he looked around the room. "No, it damn sure ain't."

CHAPTER TWENTY-ONE

Riyadh, Saudi Arabia

Third Day—12:12 p.m.

David McCarter scanned the buildings with the binoculars until he found the one Kurtzman had tipped them to. Waves of heat undulated in front of the lenses.

"Got a bit of a hot on today, doesn't it, sir?" Sergeant Hoskins of the SAS commented.

"That it has, mate," McCarter replied. "But we'll be making a few spots hotter."

"Aye." Hoskins grinned and spit a blob of tobacco juice onto the tarmac of the building where they'd set up their lookout. He scuffed it with a boot.

McCarter stood and stretched, still working out the kinks of the enforced inactivity of the flight in from Virginia. He wore Arab clothing, as did all of his team, and had let his reddish beard grow to avoid a clean-shaven look. Perspiration beaded his face despite the shade offered by the *ghutra* covering his head. Gathering the folds of the ankle-length robe, he threw a leg over the side of the building and followed the squeaky fire escape down, Hoskins in his wake.

Gary Manning was waiting with the three jeeps the SAS team had commandeered for the operation. The Canadian looked pale and uncomfortable within the confines of his robe.

The other Britons came to a semblance of attention which, considering the habitual unconcerned manner McCarter knew the special forces people usually employed when dealing with superior officers, was impressive.

"Okay, lads," McCarter said as he took up the passenger seat in his jeep, "let's look sharp and step lively out there. We won't be getting another go at this in our lifetime." He took out an ear/throat communications set and fitted it under the headdress. Hoskins slid in under the wheel and hit the starter. The jeep's engine caught at once, and sand spilled out behind the wide tires as Hoskins let the clutch out. "Mr. Manning?"

"Roger," Manning's voice came back.

"Mr. Parker."

"Here, sir."

"Fine," McCarter said. "Then let's do this one by the numbers, shall we?" He slipped a pair of amber-tinted aviator sunglasses from an inner pocket and put them on. Glancing over his shoulder, he watched the other two jeeps head out in different directions, following their own routes to the target area. Each transported a three-man team. The remaining twelve members of the SAS squad were already in place around the outer perimeters of the strike zone, ready to assist with the exfiltration once the mission was accomplished.

It was a simple in-and-out maneuver, designed to develop information from someone in the group they could take as prisoner. Textbook stuff, really.

As the jeep rolled to a rocking stop, McCarter clambered out quickly, touching the SIG Sauer P-226 beneath his robe. He missed the Browning Hi-Power, but realized the wisdom of matched armament for the teams. Halting beside the wooden door, he pressed the transmit button on the headset. "Team one."

"Set and ready," Manning's voice whispered back.

"Team Two."

"On your mark, sir."

"The mark is now," McCarter said. "Go!" He aimed the Remington riot gun at the door and triggered a load of double-aught buck that knocked a hole where the doorknob used to be. As he pumped a fresh round into the breach, Hoskins kicked the door open and heaved a flash-bang into the room.

Startled yells were cut off by the sudden explosion of force, thunder and light. McCarter peeled around the corner as Hoskins and the other member of the team backed him with AK-47s.

GARY MANNING rappeled down the side of the target building, coming to a skidding stop by the second-story window on the opposite side of the entrance attacked by McCarter and his team. The explosive charge he affixed to the window frame was one of his own construction, as were the ones the other team would be using in its assault on the third floor.

He started the electronic timer as he swung clear of the window. The explosion sounded only a heartbeat after he had his AK in hand and the sling looped over his arm. He pendulumed back to the window and aimed himself inside.

Three men were already starting to respond to the noise downstairs when they saw Manning crash through the buckled remnants of the window. The Phoenix warrior released the rope as he rolled onto the floor, his AK-47 up and chattering a death stream that raked across the men. At least two bullets from the Hezbollah guns slammed into the Kevlar vest under his robe, punching him to the floor.

Grunting in pain, he pushed himself to his feet, listening to the autofire above and below him. A quick scan of the three men who'd confronted him told him they were dead. He opened the door and ducked as bullets thudded into the wooden panels. One of his teammates flipped a flash-bang into the hallway even as he faded back into a defensive posture.

Manning ripped the *ghutra* from his head to open up his peripheral vision. He stepped back into the hallway, drawing the attention and the fire of a staggering Hezbollah warrior. A figure eight on full-auto from the AK-47 blew the terrorist down like a straw man.

The echoes of trapped gunfire made hearing impossible. The ear/throat headset squealed in Manning's ear as other frequencies jammed it. He jogged down the hallway and stopped as a terrorist at his feet started trying to fight his way back to consciousness.

Planting his foot and using his weight, Manning fisted his free hand in the man's loose clothing and lifted the terrorist up. A quick visual confirmed that there were no wounds. The man had been stunned by the grenade.

The Hezbollah fighter's hand darted for the handle of a wicked-looking knife scabbarded in the folds of his robe. Manning shifted, slamming the terrorist into the wall and following it up with a rough elbow that brought a return to unconsciousness. The man tumbled to the floor. "Wilberton," he yelled.

The SAS man nodded and knelt at once, using a pair of plastic handcuffs to bind the terrorist's hands behind his back.

"Get him out of here," Manning ordered.

"Yes, sir."

A terrorist appeared on the stairway and fumbled for his weapon when he saw Manning.

Squeezing the AK-47 in two 3-round bursts, Manning watched the 7.62 mm spray hose the man back into the wall. He tapped the transmit button on the headset, hoping he could be heard above the frequency disruptions. "Mc-Carter."

"Yeah."

"Got a bird in the hand, buddy."

"We bagged one ourselves."

"Unless you're out to set a new record, I'd say we've got our limit."

"That's a roger. All units—the goal's been secured. Let's clean house and kick the dust off."

Manning charged down the stairs, falling in with Mc-Carter's group as they did a room-to-room search.

"McCarter," a calm voice said over the headset frequency.

Manning fell back, checking to see the rooftop team coming down with a wounded man.

"Acknowledged," McCarter called back.

"Saudi troops, sir, and they're headed this way."

"Can you slow them down a wee bit, mate?"

"Yes, sir."

"Then don't bloody well stand there telling me about it. See that it's done."

"Yes, sir."

McCarter looked up at Manning and the other team. "That the lot of them?"

Manning nodded.

"Then let's blow this pop stand."

Following the ground team out, Manning glanced at his watch. Less than five minutes had passed since they'd hit the perimeters of the building. It amazed him. He'd seen how well Phoenix Force could cooperate to achieve an objective, but he was amazed at the showing the SAS had given. And most of them weren't even breathing hard.

He pulled himself into his jeep as the first explosion went off. His trained ear for demolitions told him Parker and his unit had opened up with the claymores they'd brought in from their desert base camp. They'd be under orders to make sure none of the Saudi security people were hurt, but the explosions would sure as hell scare years off their lives.

Manning tucked the assault rifle away and drew his SIG Sauer as the driver let out the clutch. Glancing over his shoulder, he saw the outline of their prisoner under a drab gray tarp in the back. His stomach clenched at the thought of what lay ahead. It was important that the Hezbollah gunners talked. Kurtzman's computers had ID'ed the terrorist cell as being part of the group that had taken the hostages from the downtown hotel. Whatever they knew could be added to what was already known and what was being found out by Bolan and Katz. It would give the rescuers a better shot at finding the hostages in time.

The jeep headed for the rendezvous point where the Russian transport plane could be flown in to pick them up.

Manning had no doubts that McCarter and the SAS unit could be as brutally efficient about interrogation techniques as they were about the assault on the building. They'd wring as much information out of their prisoners as there was in whatever fashion was demanded. The Geneva rules governing prisoners of war had been laid aside as soon as the terrorists had fired the first shot.

CHAPTER TWENTY-TWO

Kuwait, Kuwait

Third Day—1:03 p.m.

Rafael Encizo knew prisons intimately, knew the horrors that were perpetrated within their gray slab walls. He'd been a prisoner at El Principe Prison in Cuba. There were still scars, physical as well as mental. An old and cold chill rippled down his spine as he watched the guards cross the walkways above the prison grounds.

He stood in the back of the canvas-covered truck the Mossad agents had turned up to use in the recovery of the Hezbollah terrorists. A hot, dry breeze curled around him, stirring the canvas flaps listlessly. Perspiration trickled down his face and neck, soaking the collar of his khaki shirt. His sleeves were rolled to midforearm, already sweat-stained darker than the rest of the uniform.

"Damn, it's hot," Calvin James groaned.

Encizo nodded. "Yeah, but according to the travel notes Aaron packed in our kit, the average temperature in this city often gets over 120 degrees. That's a lot hotter than it is now."

James took a quick sip from the canteen lying on top of his kit.

Ignoring his own thirst for the moment, Encizo took a handkerchief from his pocket and wiped his face and neck. He crushed it in his hands when he was finished, looking at the looming gray structure and remembering. The nightmares had gone away for the most part now. They interrupted his dreams only occasionally. Most of those times he was able to control the remembered fear enough so that he wasn't forced from his bed. When he was in action, they never lingered. He knew why Katz hadn't asked him to go inside while retrieving the prisoners.

Encizo chided himself for letting personal feelings and memories get in the way of the job. He was too professional for that. If only it hadn't been for that damn gray wall of a building with the barbed wire crown looming over the operation. He knocked the dust from his uniform cap, slicked back his damp hair with his fingers and put the cap on. "I'm going to take a walk around to see what I can see."

He stepped down and out into the full blast of the searing sun, feeling its fingers pry deeply into every opening of his shirt and whisk hotly across exposed skin. His boots grated on the grains of sand spread out over the worn pavement. He carried his AK-47 on a military sling over his shoulder. His 9 mm SIG Sauer rode butt forward on his right hip in a military button-down holster that completed the overall effect of the uniform.

Three of the Mossad agents were inside with Katz, finishing the negotiations for the Hezbollah prisoners. Eight more of them helped to outfit the two transport trucks and blocker car. The other nine manned and guarded the sleek speedboat waiting in the harbor that would take them to the rendezvous point where they'd be picked up by the Israeli air force.

He glanced down at his boots and saw the dust covering them. Reflexively he raised each foot in turn and wiped it off on the back of his pant legs. He sighed when he realized what he was doing. Military training and his own vanity were only part of it. A prisoner in an eight-by-eight cell didn't have anything if he didn't have his own sanitation. Memories of the times he'd torn the tail out of his shirts to make cleaning rags, of the hours he'd spent detailing the concrete floor and cinder-block walls, would never go away. Proximity to the prison only brought them into sharper focus in his mind.

He whistled to himself, turning to his love of music to take the bad images away. Surprised by the choice of songs that came to mind, he couldn't help but grin when he recognized it as "Summertime Blues."

"Rafe." Calvin James's voice came in crisp and clean over the ear/throat headset he wore.

Encizo hit the transmit button. "Yeah?"

"We got company coming, buddy. Gurion and Akiva just called it in."

"Where away?" Encizo turned to face the highway expectantly.

"Nine o'clock, and closing fast."

Encizo made the placement immediately, turning to face the prison as the helicopter rotors drummed into his hearing. "Where's Yakov?"

"Inside. There's too much radio interference for me to reach him on the throat mike. He's going to be coming out of that building with no idea that trouble's closing in."

"Lavi," Encizo snapped, drawing the driver's attention in the second transport truck. He waved toward the main gates.

The Israeli nodded at once. The truck gave a full-throated roar as it came to life, belching out a black plume of oily smoke, then jumping forward like an impatient horse fighting the bridle.

Encizo leaped, catching hold of the large mirror mounted on the passenger side, then unslung the assault rifle. He squinted, making out the black dot of the helicopter in the distance as the transport truck closed in on the gates.

RUNNING A PRACTICED eye over his four charges, Katz picked his weak link. The man the others called Sofian would be the first to break once the interrogation began. The man was older than the others, scarred in previous battles. Katz nodded to himself. Sofian had already been dispelled of his illusions that Hezbollah's members were the true and chosen soldiers of victory.

Their footsteps rang against the walls of the wide prison corridor. The rumble of voices from the prisoners had subsided to the intensity of retreating waves in a cove.

The four prisoners were shackled together by ankle chains and moved in a shuffling step. Their beards were matted and dark hollows shadowed their eyes. The olive-green one-piece prisoner's uniform made them look small and harmless.

Katz never let himself believe that for an instant. He paused at the last checkpoint as the barred door clanked back to allow them passage.

"It's almost like old times, isn't it?" Ranon Goldberg asked.

Katz returned the Mossad chief's gaze. "Almost, my friend, but they say you can never go home again."

Goldberg looked resplendent in his imitation uniform and held his baton with just the amount of cockiness needed to pull the role off for those not aware of the deal between Israel, the United States and Kuwait. He pulled at one of the flared thighs of the pants. "Still, perhaps it's something you should be giving some thought to. Our war here is far from over. Your skills and knowledge are invaluable."

The station guard checked them through with only casual interest.

"The world isn't just about one place anymore, Ranon," Katz said as they resumed their walk toward the warden's office and doors to the outside.

"Bah. You have only felt this way since your wife's death, my friend."

Strangling the quick anger that filled him, Katz met the other man's eyes. "You presume much on a friendship."

Goldberg sighed. "I'm sorry, Yakov. I see that I have. I was only thinking that if the two of you had had children who yet lived, perhaps you wouldn't have let so much of Israel go to the grave with her."

"But it wasn't that way."

"No. And it's our loss, too, believe me." Goldberg clamped a hand on Katz's shoulder.

The warden's office was neat and efficient, and—when he'd dismissed his secretary to negotiate the final bit of business—surprisingly empty. Warden Harithah fumbled through the security code on the big safe that held their weapons. As he did so, the third Mossad agent stepped forward and placed a briefcase on the small desk.

Katz holstered his pistol at his side and felt immediately better. Even with the arrangements made by the U.S. State Department and the Israeli government, it hadn't been easy to go naked into the lion's den. But then he hadn't truly been unarmed. Since he'd lost his own arm in the Six Day War, he'd substituted prostheses that often provided him with more than adequate fire power. The arm he wore now had a built in .22 in the forefinger, and it was solid enough to use as a club.

The two small clicks of the briefcase's locks drew everyone's attention. When the lid was lifted, stacks of Kuwaiti currency were revealed. A high spot of color burned on the bridge of the warden's nose.

"For your trouble," Goldberg said, "to be shared as you see fit."

One of the Hezbollah prisoners spit, and it landed on the money. A Mossad agent stepped forward and gave the prisoner a warning glance.

Katz took measure of the emotion trailing through Sofian's eyes. Despair and hopelessness were predominant. It was enough to let him know the sight of the money involved had affected the man. He knew he'd been bought and paid for.

The agent handling the briefcase clicked it closed and handed it over.

"Thank you," Warden Harithah said with a small bow.

Goldberg returned it smartly, his heels together.

Katz knew the money had been a face-saving gesture for the Kuwaiti government. This way everything was kept on a business level. With the havoc that Saddam Hussein and the Iraqis had wrought in recent months, it was enough for the Kuwaitis to know that Israel and the U.S. would consider the release of the Hezbollah prisoners as a favor.

One of the younger agents led the prisoners out, flanked by the other man. Katz and Goldberg brought up the rear. The Phoenix team leader fired up a cigarette as they neared the final set of doors. He tapped his ear/throat headset experimentally. Only the continued low buzz of static filled his ear.

Bright sunlight stabbed into his eyes as they exited the building. He became aware of the approaching helicopter rotors even as Calvin James's hurried voice clipped over the receiver.

"Bogey, Katz, coming in at twelve o'clock high!"

Katz reacted instinctively, reaching forward to shove the prisoners into a run. He was aware of the other three Mossad agents going to ground to provide covering fire. Reports from small-arms weapons blasted into his hearing even before the .50-caliber thunder rang out overhead. Tufts of grass and dirt clods jumped from the prison grounds in an erratic line.

Then the helicopter was gone.

"Where?" Katz demanded as he hit the transmit button, then gave the Hezbollah prisoner at the rear another shove. Small-arms fire continued to snap and pop around him.

"Nine o'clock, Yakov," Encizo's calm voice came back.

The rotor wash descended, blowing stinging sand from the yard. Katz wheeled, bringing up the SIG Sauer as his arm formed a straight line. He squeezed off shots methodically, aiming for the pilot as the chopper swooped like a chicken hawk, spreading out .50 caliber talons. The Plexiglas, already chipped and cracked, splintered under more of his shots. Sparks scattered from the skids as it shot by again.

"No! No!" a man's voice shouted.

Turning, Katz saw two of the Hezbollah men come to a stop in the center of the yard. The Kuwaiti prison guards were returning fire, as well. Beyond the front gates Encizo leaped from the running board of the transport truck and took up a position between the heavy bars.

The helicopter heeled about before Katz had the chance to force the prisoners on. The two men who'd stopped the progress of the Hezbollah terrorists were grimly holding on to the ankle chains while the other two tried in vain to take cover. As the helicopter bore down on them, they raised their arms in triumph.

The big .50-caliber rounds chopped through the knot of men, dousing the sandy ground with blood. Katz emptied his pistol at the Plexiglas bubble, wishing he had a machine pistol instead. He moved at once, wanting to verify how many of the Hezbollah prisoners, if any, still remained alive.

The unmistakable yammer of Encizo's AK-47 chewed into the fray, and the helicopter moved on, the pilot unwilling to hold his position against the onslaught. Katz knelt to check the prisoners. Sofian was still alive. A .50-caliber bullet had torn through the fleshy part of his thigh, the wound generating a lot of blood. Two of the other men were dead.

A flicker of movement out of the corner of his eye was the only warning Katz got as the other Hezbollah man who'd tried to sacrifice all of them attacked. He looped the chain between his wrists around Katz's neck, clasping his hands behind the Phoenix team leader's head.

The helicopter spun and headed back, a fresh line of .50-caliber bullets tracking across the prison yard. Katz tightened his throat muscles instinctively.

"Now, you Jewish cur," the Hezbollah terrorist said with venom, "now you will die."

Instead of fighting the force at his throat, Katz lifted his prosthesis and jammed his index finger under the man's chin. He fired off three rounds, and the man's features went slack as he crumpled slowly to the ground.

Katz rammed a fresh magazine up the pistol's butt, tripped the slide and aimed at the chain holding Sofian to the line of dead men. The chopper's rotors fanned over them. He squeezed the trigger five times, blasting the chain in two. "Run!" he ordered. "Get up and run for your life!"

The man scrambled, hands manacled together in front of him as he ran as best he could with his injured leg.

"Down, Katz," James transmitted. "Got a 40 mm warhead coming in your direction that's gonna slap that sucker out of the sky."

"Make it good, Calvin."

Katz gathered his feet under him and threw himself out of the line of the big .50. A whoosh, discernible only because he was listening for it, cut loose from the front of the prison.

The explosion overhead was deafening. Bits and pieces of the helicopter wafted downward, followed by a sizable chunk of the chopper that hit, slid across the ground and thumped into the retaining wall of the prison with enough force to chip away cinder blocks and mortar.

The two younger Mossad agents were up at once, closing in on the helicopter wreckage to check for survivors. Evidently there were none because the pistols in their fists remained unused.

"Yakov?" Encizo called.

"I'm fine. See to the prisoner. He has a wound that needs tending if we're to get anything from him."

"Right."

CHAPTER TWENTY-THREE

The Oval Office, Washington, D.C.

Third Day—7:15 a.m.

"Yakov's man confirmed it. All of the hostages have been routed back to Lebanon."

Hal Brognola listened as Barbara Price laid it out for him. He sat at his desk in the dim light of the makeshift office the President had ordered set up for his use during the Mideast crisis. A gnarled cigar sat on the blotter beside an open pack of antacid tablets. "Where are McCarter and Yakov now?"

"En route to Lebanon. Yakov will get there first. He's got a list of Hezbollah hiding places and plans to follow up on those unless something else turns up."

"Why has McCarter been slowed down?"

"Flight arrangements had to be changed. The interrogation took longer than he expected. And the SAS team took a casualty on the raid."

"That brings them down to what?"

"Eighteen men plus Manning and McCarter."

"Any chance of beefing up the roll call?"

"A chance, sure, but realistically if McCarter gets something to roll over on, you can bet he's not going to be wasting time waiting for substitutions."

"I know."

"This is the SAS we're talking about, Hal. They invented hardship duty."

Brognola rubbed his lower face with a big hand. "Yeah, yeah. I read you. I just want to get a handle on this thing as quickly as we can."

"That's what we're all working for. You're just feeling the sideline pressure."

"You sound like you're handling it okay."

"I've got Aaron to yell at when things get too tense."

"True."

"Somehow I have a tough time picturing you doing the same to your present company."

"The President wouldn't like it."

"No. Probably not." Price laughed.

Brognola couldn't help but laugh with her. He was surprised at how good it felt to be able to join in. When they finished, he said, "This doesn't read right."

"You mean the hostages all being in one place like that?"

"Yep."

"It's ringing a few warning bells at this end, too," Price agreed, "but I'm damned if I know what to do about it now."

"They'd have been better off keeping the hostages spread out. That way the rescue teams, if thought of any came up in their planning, would have had to risk taking indecent liberties with international borders on a large scale and for a lot longer time period."

"They considered rescue teams. Bet on it."

"I am. That's why this doesn't scan. The Hezbollah factions in Lebanon have to know about the takedown operations McCarter and Yakov have pulled off."

"I think so, too."

"So why aren't they on the phone raising hell about it and threatening the hostages? Or going ahead with some kind of physical retaliation?"

"I haven't got any answers for you, Hal. I wish I did, but I don't. Then again, the President could be taking that call this very minute."

"Unless they're too busy to worry about it right now." Brognola turned the thought over in his mind and found a dank darkness he truly didn't like. "Does Striker know?"

"Yes."

"And?"

"And he's going to get back to us on it."

"He's drawing a blank, too."

Price agreed.

Brognola leaned back in his chair and heard it groan in protest. The sound was sharp and hard in the empty room.

"Striker's also working on an internal security problem of his own," Price said.

"The Russians?"

"One of them terminated a prisoner they'd taken in Beirut who could have possibly had some information about the hostages."

"Why would they do that?"

"I've got Aaron digging now. Mack said he had the feeling the KGB slipped a ringer team into the Spetznaz ranks."

"What does the Spetznaz chief say?"

"At this point, nothing. It's the same old game of paranoia and reflexive cover-up despite *glasnost*."

"Terrific." Brognola exhaled noisily and popped an antacid tablet. "There's a gang of renegade Mossad agents playing cowboys and Indians with Leo and Able Team here, and the KGB is circumventing Striker's operation in the heart of Beirut."

"What's this about Able Team?" Price asked.

Brognola gave her the gist of Able Team's crossing of swords with the Mossad in Georgetown.

"When?" Price asked.

Brognola flicked an eye at the notes he'd taken on the call-in from Turrin and gave her the time. "Should have called sooner. My fault."

"It's okay."

But he knew from her tone that it wasn't okay. He'd been trying to avoid dividing her attention on two fronts while she juggled the events taking place in the Middle East. Overprotecting his people was still a hard habit to break. Even when, technically at times, they weren't his people. "I'll have Lyons get in touch with you concerning the specifics."

"Don't. I'll take care of it." Her tone said that was exactly the way she wanted to handle it. "You might," she

added, "put a bug in the President's ear and get him working on the KGB angle from the Moscow end. Whatever secret storm is brewing in the Russian ranks, Striker stands a
good chance of being swept away in its eye. Unless we can
put enough pressure on to break it early."

"Agreed. I'll get on it now."

She said goodbye and broke the connection.

He stood and gathered the loose pages of notes into a
coffee-stained manila folder and dropped them into his
briefcase. He might have office space in the White House
for the moment, but experience had shown him a wise man
always took the important office work with him.

He stopped briefly in the lavatory to wash up and shave,
and still figured he'd be early for his eight o'clock meeting
with the President.

A knock sounded on the office door. When he answered
it, a man held out a garment bag and said, "Compliments
of Miss Price."

Once inside he unzipped it and found two freshly pressed
suits in his size, proving she knew how it was with him and
how his mind worked. He'd wanted to pack a bag himself,
or have his wife bring something up, but either way would
have left him open to the reporters who'd managed to uncover his connection with the hostage situation.

After finishing the quick Marine bath he'd started, he
dressed in a fresh suit. The tie was a little more colorful than
he'd have preferred, but he felt refreshed.

The Secret Service man on the door to the Oval Office was
new. He watched the guy's eyes flick over him as he approached, obviously comparing him to a mental checklist.

"Good morning, Mr. Brognola."

"Morning." Brognola adjusted his tie and took a firmer
grip on the briefcase. "Is he in?"

"At least since I got here at four."

Brognola knocked and entered when he was asked in.

The President sat behind his desk, chin propped on his
fingers, palms pressed together. His eyes were watery and
red behind the glasses. "Morning, Hal."

"Morning, sir."

"Tell me you have good news."

"Can't."

The President sighed.

Brognola stopped by the coffee service and poured himself a cup. "Tell me *you* have good news."

"Can't."

"Coffee?"

"Thanks. I already have some."

Brognola made himself sit in one of the chairs before the desk. The last thing the Man needed to do was try to keep up with him while he paced out his anxiety.

"In fact," the President said, "I've only got more bad news to share with you."

"Maybe we'll still be even after this meeting then."

"Really?"

"Really." Brognola blew on his coffee, knowing the antacid tablets were going to spoil the taste.

"Take a look at this," the President said, "then decide whether you want to call or raise." He took the remote control out of a desk drawer and punched buttons.

The wall opened up as Brognola swiveled, revealing the TV/VCR combo. CNN blinked off, sweeping the anchorperson away as a tape played. He recognized Damien Gray at once from the times he'd watched the reporter on different major news networks. Major William Deering looked enough like his file pictures to be identified. The military intelligence officer also looked as if he'd stopped short just this side of hell. Dark bags were tucked under his dull, bloodshot eyes. His hair was uncombed and in wild disarray. Someone had dressed him in an Army uniform but didn't get some of the medals and insignia in the right places. But the uniform would have fooled most of the people the makers had wanted the tape to fool.

"My experts tell me he's been drugged," the President related in a neutral voice.

Brognola nodded. He'd seen men who'd been subjected to a lot worse than Sodium Pentothal, the drug movie spies always used. It gave him pause, though, when he realized where he'd seen most of them lately—in Dr. Fahad Rihani's files.

By contrast Damien Gray looked well groomed and freshly shaven. The men sat in chairs in front of a make-shift soundstage.

"If you look closely," the President said, "you can see the belt they used to keep Deering in the chair."

Brognola looked and found it at once.

"This is Damien Gray," the reporter said solemnly.

The President tapped a key on the remote control and the volume increased.

"Most of you out there know me," Gray went on. "For those of you who might not, I'm the anchorperson on Washington, D.C.'s *Capitol Headlines*." The reporter paused dramatically to shuffle the three-by-five index cards he held in his hands. "Those of you who've followed my career know I've always been in the forefront of the news teams in the capital. My staff and I have been instrumental in keeping the American people aware of the waste and overspending our government has been guilty of, and I've personally uncovered a few of the dirty tricks engineered by the CIA and other secret enforcement arms of our government."

Deering wobbled unsteadily in the chair, his eyes rolling wildly.

"The guy's not pulling any punches, is he?" Brognola asked as he unwrapped a fresh cigar.

"It gets worse."

"By now you should all know about the present crisis in the Middle East," Gray said. "Many of you have loved ones over here. Some of you may have already lost someone close to you. My sympathies if that's the case." The reporter cleared his throat.

Deering spoke, his face looking apoplectic. Nothing was audible. A string of spittle ran down the side of his mouth.

"They've got Deering's mike turned off at the moment."

Brognola nodded.

"Even now the lives of more than a hundred more people hang in the balance," Gray went on. "This is jihad, the Arabic holy war. But this isn't a war that was declared by the peoples of the Middle East, who—ultimately—are the victims as much as you at home are. It was declared by the American government, and I mean to prove that to you here today beyond the shadow of a doubt."

"Christ," Brognola said softly.

"Oh, Gray's only getting warmed up."

"With me is Major William Harding Deering of the U.S. Army's Military Intelligence branch." The camera angle shifted, zooming in on Deering. "Tell the viewers why you were sent out here, Major."

"I was ordered to get Rihani." Deering's words were slurred and slow. His eyes looked unfocused.

"They spliced the tape," Brognola said.

"Yes." The President sipped his coffee and pushed the cup aside. "But tell me how many viewers are going to stop and think about that."

Brognola remained silent.

"You're speaking of Dr. Fahad Rihani?" Gray prompted.

"Yes," Deering responded immediately. "He's a Commie bastard."

"They also edited out all the dead space between Deering's responses," Brognola said.

"To make it appear he was more coherent than he really was." The President sighed. "Until we're able to give the American people more of the truth about what's really going on over there, this tape is going to be very damaging."

The camera zoomed in on Damien Gray as he faced his viewing audience. "For those of you unfamiliar with the name, Dr. Fahad Rihani was a significant leader of Hezbollah here in Beirut. He disappeared in the early 1980s, apparently the victim of foul play, but the body was never recovered. However, now that all of this has come to light, we now know that Dr. Rihani was taken prisoner by the

Israeli Mossad, that country's covert enforcement agency. Dr. Rihani was kept away from his family and friends from that moment until recently when a mercenary force hired by Major William Deering botched an attempt to steal Rihani from the Israelis.''

"Israel's not coming out of this smelling like a rose, either," Brognola commented.

"Gray doesn't bother explaining why the hostages were taken," the President said. "But he takes care to see that the American government takes the blame."

"What were your orders concerning Dr. Rihani?" Gray asked.

"Supposed to get the Commie bastard."

"And if you weren't able to accomplish that?"

"Kill him," Deering said vehemently.

Brognola threw his cigar into the wastepaper basket beside the President's desk. "Shit."

"We've really screwed the pooch on this one."

"How many copies of this tape have gotten out?" Brognola asked.

"I don't know. I've got some people working on it, but it'll be hours before we know for sure. But that doesn't really matter. With the satellite hookups between the news services, they've all got it by now."

"Has it hit television here yet?"

The President nodded. "All three of the majors and a handful of the independents have been running it."

"Public opinion?"

"Hard to say at this point. Depends on what we're able to achieve in the next few hours. Gray's reporting has a huge following by today's standards from what I'm given to understand."

On-screen Gray kept tossing questions at Deering, drawing thick-voiced answers.

"Is there anything else I should see in this?" Brognola asked.

"You've got the gist of it."

"Fair enough. Let's move on to new business." Brognola threw a couple of antacid tablets into his mouth and chewed. With a skilled economy of words he laid out the Stony Man probes in the Middle East. The President already knew about Able Team's in-town problems.

"I don't want to believe Gorbachev is involved in anything underhanded," the President stated when Brognola finished.

"He's probably telling his aides the same thing right now concerning the Deering situation."

"True."

"However, that still leaves us a wasp nest to deal with."

"Two. Counting the Mossad angle."

"Yes. Well, it appears we've almost brought that one on ourselves." The President removed his glasses and rubbed his eyes. He checked his watch. "I've got a meeting in the pressroom at 9:45, and I don't know what I'm going to tell those reporters. Stepping forth at this moment to say anything about the missions we've got in play over there will only compromise the Stony Man teams."

"I agree."

"I was vice president before I stepped into this office. I knew what I was letting myself in for. At least I thought I did. There's been too much happening, though, for me not to question our abilities concerning what we're now facing." The President put his glasses back on and looked Brognola square in the eye. "And the most important thing I'm wondering about now is whether those men, linked with allies they may or may not be able to trust, will be able to bring this one home."

Brognola gave the Man the truth because it was something he had to face himself. "I don't know, sir. But what I am sure of is that if anyone can do it, those men can." *Or they'll die in the attempt.* He left the last unsaid because that was something he didn't want to face.

CHAPTER TWENTY-FOUR

Beirut, Lebanon

Third Day—5:24 p.m.

"Get Up."

Jessi Grafton lifted her head with effort to look up at the big guard towering over her. She sat with her back to the metal wall of the abandoned factory. For a blessed moment she'd been asleep with her head resting on her crossed arms on top of her folded knees. Dreams had taken her far away, but the perceived security melted away as quickly as the darkness before the guard's flashlight.

"Get up," the man repeated. He reached down and clamped a hand around her bicep, hauling her painfully to her feet.

The crowd around her surged forth protectively as the men separated from the group to help her.

The guard released her and drew his knife. Overhead the sound of at least a half-dozen rifle bolts being primed filled the tense silence.

The crowd fell back uncertainly. A handful of children cried, waking still others who joined in.

Bright steel glinted in the guard's fist as he backed away. "Come," he ordered.

She followed, pulling at her torn clothing and wishing she knew what was about to happen. She kept her eyes away from those of the other prisoners because she didn't want to see the fear on their faces. It was hard enough to keep from letting her own fears consume her.

Once she was under the balcony another guard kicked the rope ladder down. "Up," the first guard commanded, pointing.

She placed shaking hands on the outsides of the swaying ladder and started up. After two false starts, she got the hang of the rhythm and made it to the top.

A guard pushed against her shoulder, forcing her back to the wall. "Stay."

She placed her arms across her breasts as an unexpected chill of fear raced along her spine. She stayed. There was nowhere she could go.

The guard made five more trips into the crowd of prisoners, selecting two more women and three men.

As the last man made his way over the edge, Grafton recognized him as Torin Conagher, the Irishman who'd been taken hostage with her in Saudi Arabia. He looked disheveled and worn. Grafton knew she couldn't look much better. Scabs had formed on her mouth and palms from the rough treatment she'd already received.

"Hi, lassie," Conagher said with a slight smile. Once in better lighting, the dark circle around an eye that had swollen shut was visible. "I see you're still hanging in there. Got a bit o' sand about you, don't ye?"

She tried to smile and felt her bruised lip pull crookedly with the effort. "Maybe I'm just not smart enough to lie down and die!"

"Faugh! That's no way for a lassie as handsome as yourself to be speakin'. Where there's life, there's hope."

"Shut up," one of the guards said.

The rope ladder was pulled up and pushed out of the way. Then one of the guards removed sets of handcuffs from a canvas bag and secured each prisoner in turn.

The handcuffs felt cold, hard and heavy at the ends of Grafton's arms. She had to quell the sudden rush of bile and panic that threatened to choke her. Being restrained to a specific area was one thing, but to be physically restrained like this was something she'd never before encountered. Her hands shook. She knotted them into fists, but it didn't help.

"Go," one of the guards ordered, waving at the corridor to their right.

"Buck up, lass," the Irishman said quietly. "Don't let these bastards see that you're afraid of them. Don't give them that satisfaction."

Gathering her courage, Grafton straightened her spine and made herself walk, falling into place second in line behind a red-haired woman old enough to be her mother. She forced herself to think that when she got out of this she'd have one hell of a story, a first-person view that not many other news services would get. *When,* she reminded herself, not *if.*

She counted her steps mechanically, her mind tuned for details that she could use in a news story. She made notes of the fact that the woman before her wore a long dress and went barefoot, that the guard leading the procession had a burn scar just under his right eye that quirked up that corner of his mouth, that Torin Conagher smelled of Old Spice and slept-in clothes and had a voice as smooth as Tennessee whiskey.

They didn't stop until they were outside. She held up a hand to shade her eyes from the evening sun already staining the sky a shade of crimson that brought back unpleasant memories of the past two days. Loose sand stirred by the salty breeze wafting in from the Mediterranean slithered over the broken tarmac of the driveway in front of the building. Sections of the six-foot mesh fence defining the parking area hung haphazardly or were missing completely. Beyond it the wreckage of the city began. A patched and battered lime-green-and-white Winnebago sat idling before them, showing scars of earlier battles. The passenger side of the windshield was starred over so badly that visibility was impossible.

"Inside," the guard commanded, grabbing each prisoner in turn by the handcuff chain and yanking them toward the RV.

Grafton stumbled forward and might have fallen if Conagher hadn't caught her shoulder and helped her regain her balance. The extended courtesy earned the Irishman a gun butt in the back that drew a muffled curse of pain.

She went inside, feeling the chill bite of the air conditioner at once. Hands reached out to push and pull her roughly to the rear of the vehicle. She took a place beside a small cracked window and looked out as four jeeps with armed men rolled into view. A black Chevy van with a four-wheel-drive undercarriage followed a moment later. She watched as Rihani got out of the van and began giving orders to his men.

"Sit." The guard made a motion toward the floor.

Grafton sat, scooting around to make room for the other prisoners. She made sure she was still able to see out the window as she clung to her reporter's curiosity as a means of self-preservation. Conagher sat beside her, his manacled hands hanging loosely in his lap.

Then the four jeeps and the van headed out in single file, followed by the RV.

"This surely isn't shaping up to be no Sunday drive," Conagher whispered.

Glancing at the hard-eyed men sitting in front of them in the makeshift seats, Grafton silently agreed, wondering what it was all about. And where it would end for them.

CHAPTER TWENTY-FIVE

North of Beirut, Lebanon

Third Day—8:37 p.m.

Outfitted in night-black camouflage fatigues, Mack Bolan trained his infrared night glasses on the strike zone. The foothills of the Lebanon Mountains were alive with noises, from the west wind whipping in off the coastline less than five miles away to the insects that lived in the grass nearby. His eyes ached from the constant effort of searching the stark landscape before them, made even harder by the snowcapped mountains in the distance that reflected the slight moonlight. He was fatigued from the forced five-klick march with full pack that had brought the strike team this far.

"Anything?" Jack Grimaldi asked.

"It's there," the Executioner replied. "Right where Tuholske's man said it would be."

"Where away?"

Bolan called out the coordinates, then checked his watch. Precious time had been spent getting here under the cover of night. He felt the constant fall of the numbers on the mission, knowing those could soon be measured in lives instead of heartbeats.

"I make it at almost three thousand yards," Grimaldi said.

"Agreed."

Grimaldi put his field glasses away. "The way it's situated, it's not going to be an easy nut to crack."

"I know." Bolan eased back down the hill, taking care to stay within the shadow of the tree they'd used for shelter.

Like Grimaldi and the members of the Spetznaz group, his face was covered with black combat cosmetics.

"So give," Grimaldi said as he followed.

"Quick penetration," Bolan answered. "Full blitz. We get in, create as much damage as possible, gather as much information as we can and make sure Leighton's transport teams are crippled for the duration at least."

"Kalinin's not going to like it."

"He doesn't have to. He's not going to find another way to get it done." Bolan replayed the scene in his mind as he walked back to the rest area, rebuilding the land around the hardsite in his head layer by layer. It had three sides, constructed low and long and heavy. The fourth side was the steep incline created by the foothills. The outer perimeters were covered by foot patrol and stationary guards. The reduction of native foliage within one hundred yards of the hardsite was too complete to be natural. Nick Leighton was a cautious man. Everything contained in the merc's profile that Kurtzman had been able to scrape up screamed that fact.

He paused, drawing his map case from a pocket in the leg of his fatigues. When he found the topographical map he wanted, he flicked his penflash on and studied it. His neat handwriting covered different areas of the map, recording observations he'd made earlier and the information they'd gleaned through Tuholske. Satisfied they had all that was possible before going in, he refolded the map and put it away, then shouldered the sniping rifle and walked back to the temporary encampment.

THE EXECUTIONER SLIPPED through the night, taking care to remain a part of the landscape. The ground near the hardsite was broken and hard with bare patches of sandy loam scattered through the grass. The islands of near-light and darkness made it easier to be seen if a man wasn't careful.

Four Spetznaz sharpshooters made a ragged line behind the assault group.

Bolan counted the numbers off silently as he continued his advance. His AK-47 was secured across his back. The twin SIG Sauers rode in their holsters at armpit and ankle. A Cold Steel Tanto knife was sheathed down his other leg.

Thirty-seven seconds out from the attack time, he crossed the path of one of the merc guards. The Tanto hissed from its sheath as it filled his palm. He waited in the shelter of a bush, up on one knee as he coiled his muscles. When the guard came within reach, he moved up, fisting the knife as he shoved it into the man's heart and twisted. The Executioner's free hand pressed against the man's lips, stifling an outcry. The guard tried for his pistol as Bolan took him to the ground. The warrior twisted the knife again, and life left the body. He wiped the knife clean and returned it to its sheath.

He freed the AK-47 as the first of the sniper rounds cored into their chosen targets. With the specially tooled silencers Kissinger had equipped the rifles with, there was no sound at all.

One man dropped heavily from an outcropping less than twenty yards from the slanted roof of the shack Leighton had chosen for his temporary headquarters during the transit work for Hezbollah. Before the body had time to completely come to a stop, a Spetznaz soldier moved out of the cover of darkness and dragged it into the brush. Only one of the targets required a second shot.

Not a sound was made during the attack.

The shack's windows were cut at irregular intervals, as if the building had been put together without any real blueprints of anything more than just a thought for more space. There were no lights.

Bolan hit the transmit button on his headset. "Kalinin?"

"No movement inside the building, Mr. Belasko."

"Fair enough. Hit the door."

The whoosh of the LAW's 94 mm warhead was audible a heartbeat ahead of the cataclysmic explosion that ripped the front door from its hinges as well as huge sections of the walls surrounding it.

Bolan moved out, crouching to keep a low profile. Startled shouts and cries of pain rang out in the aftermath of the detonation. A Chevy Suburban jumped skyward and rolled over as another warhead slammed home just beneath it. Two flame-wreathed bodies staggered out of the wreckage of the shack and were dropped almost immediately by sniper fire.

Firing from the hip, the Executioner placed a series of tribursts across the flaming cavity created by the LAW. He continued running, drawing no fire as he dropped behind a low ridge. Thumbing the transmit button on the headset, he whispered, "Jack?"

"Here."

"Peripheral."

"Nothing moving guy."

Bolan studied the fires as new ones took root in the wooded parts of the structure. "Kalinin."

"Yes?"

"Pull back your troops to secure the area," Bolan commanded. "They've gone rabbit. There has to be a rear entrance. I want them covered when they show up again."

"At once."

As some of the Spetznaz fell back to take up secure positions, Bolan raced for the burning building. He hit a wall of smoke, and a blast of heat almost seared his exposed flesh. He switched the AK-47 for one of the 9 mm pistols and jammed a handkerchief over his lower face. Movement to his left attracted his attention. He fired at point-blank range, blasting three hollowpoints into the merc on the floor. The guy's gun dropped from nerveless fingers.

A dark rectangle reflected nothing from the center of the floor. Hardwood planks had ruptured and splintered from the explosion, making it impossible to close the trapdoor behind.

The heat threatened to consume Bolan. The clock was ticking, taking Leighton and his mercenaries farther from capture and closer to setting up another rendezvous to deliver the Hezbollah arms. He leveled the SIG Sauer and stepped down the ladder into the darkness of the bolt hole. The third stair gave way beneath him, dropping him roughly to the uneven floor.

Faint illumination lit the stone corridor ahead of him, creating black ghosts of the fleeing men. Bolan trailed his free hand along the wall, following it. From the uneven and hard angularity, he guessed the tunnel had once been used for quarry work.

He moved his pace up to a jog when he heard an engine turn over and catch. The lighting was better, suggesting a powerful artificial source ahead.

The quarry tunnel kept opening up as it sank back into the foothills. Then it was no longer a tunnel at all, but a cave. The sound of the first engine was joined by another, and the din inside the confined area was incredible.

Unable to hear, the Executioner wheeled around as two 4X4 trucks revved up and took off, heading for what looked to be a solid wall. Autofire sent him back into hiding as bullets ricocheted and sparked from the stone walls.

The wall in front of the trucks broke away as they passed through, leaving behind only the boards, lengths of canvas, brush and dirt that had been used to camouflage the cave's entrance.

Bolan tried the headset but got only static. He sprinted toward the entrance and the three motorcycles that had been left behind. They were hard-driven dirt bikes, something Leighton's mercs could use to ferry back and forth to Beirut for short bits of R and R.

The warrior straddled one of the bikes, tossing the AK-47 to the ground because he wouldn't be able to use it on the rocky terrain. Brief seconds later he had the ignition hotwired and the four-cycle engine pumping away like a chain saw. He stamped the gear lever into first, twisted the accelerator and released the clutch. The front wheel came up in response as he rushed for the opening. He stood up on the pegs as he shot over the pile of refuse scattered before the cave entrance. The landing was jarring and violent, uncertain as the driving back tire twisted for traction on loose rock.

He shifted into second, then third, closing in on the two trucks. Thumbing the transmit button, palming the headset to his ear and mouth so that he could be understood, he called for Grimaldi and Kalinin.

"Here, buddy."

"Here, Comrade Belasko."

"I'm on the bike behind them. I'll see if I can cut them off. We can't let them get away. In order to neutralize the threat of those weapons being shipped, we've got to take them out here."

"Understood, guy."

Kalinin checked out, then moved on with a brand-new set of orders to his men.

Bolan scraped the headset from his face and pocketed it. He geared down and stood up on the pegs as a track of 7.62 mm slugs from the rear truck forced him off the trail. He'd closed the distance to something less than a hundred yards, but it was still too far away for the SIG Sauer to be truly effective. The motorcycle roared up the side of the foothills, becoming airborne as it skipped across the uneven rises.

The warrior geared down, sticking out a foot as he brought the motorcycle around to his left, then gunned the engine, aiming for higher elevation. Shots continued to issue from the trucks. A man fell out and sprawled in a loose-limbed fashion that announced his death.

Bolan felt satisfaction. Evidently Kalinin had thought to position the snipers so that someone was constantly harassing the mercs and chopping at the numbers.

The front wheel of the motorcycle hit a rut and tried to follow it. Bolan wrestled with the machine, pulling it back on course as the rear wheel spewed out dirt and rock behind. The moonlight and shadows played hell with his depth perception and judgment.

He ran the strike zone through his head again, blowing up his mental map until he remembered what he was looking for. The trucks were headed away from the Mediterranean, away from the limited hiding places afforded on the coast. With the northeasterly course they'd set, there was only one road they could be headed for. Between them and that road, less than a quarter of a mile away, was a pass that had been cut by a stream. If they could get that far, it was a safe bet the four-wheel-drives would allow them to get across.

The edge of the pass came within sight almost too quickly. Timing his approach, Bolan shot up on top of the hill as the first truck headed into the narrow gap where the shallow stream wound around.

Bullets whistled by him as he started back down on the parabola of his climb. He jerked up on the handlebars as the front wheel cleared the ground, feeling the sensation of weightlessness wrap around him. The motorcycle's engine strained in loose confusion.

Satisfied the thousand-pound projectile was on target, the warrior kicked loose, readying himself for the coming impact. The motorcycle hit first, and he had a momentary impression of the spinning front wheel smashing through the lead truck's windshield as the driver tried to swerve.

Bolan hit the ground hard, losing his breath, not pausing to draw one as he rolled in the sand and pebbles of the streambed. Agony speared his body, but he refused to give in to it. He flailed in eight inches of icy water, freeing a spherical grenade from his harness. His first breath screamed into his lungs as bullets chopped into the water beside him.

The first truck, with the motorcycle still embedded in the cab, slammed into the gap, effectively blocking the second truck less than thirty feet away. Bolan pulled the pin on the Misar MU 50-G hand grenade, lobbed it in the direction of the second truck, then submerged. The brief autofire was lost in the grenade's detonation, which had an effective kill radius of fifteen-plus feet.

The Executioner pushed himself up, drew the SIG Sauer and fired smoothly. He didn't try for groupings or head shots, aiming instead at the center of every body that came within his sights. When the magazine blew back empty and locked, he transferred the weapon to his other hand and grabbed the spare pistol at his ankle as he raced for the bank.

Hugging the ground, Bolan concentrated his fire on those mercs still able to return fire. When the second magazine blew back empty, he knew for sure five of his targets wouldn't be getting back up.

He hunkered down, rolling over on his back as he shoved fresh magazines into the pistols. Ahead of him was the slope of the foothills. Behind him were the running footsteps of the deploying mercs. There was no way he could make the climb before enemy fire raked him back down.

One grenade remained on his combat harness. He shoved one of the 9 mm pistols into the shoulder rig, then freed the grenade as he dropped within the shelter of the low bank. Heavy footfalls echoed over his head. Firing left-handed, he snapped off four shots in his attacker's general direction. He heard a groan of pain as he sprinted along the bank, paused, peered over the three-foot-high embankment and lobbed his last grenade toward the second truck again.

As the explosion blew hunks of wet sand high into the air, Bolan reached over the top of the embankment and shot two men who'd tried to advance on his position during the confusion. Autofire drove him back down and sent him scrambling for cover.

Nearly a dozen men were still operational. The Executioner reloaded his pistol and immediately triggered two rounds into a man who'd jumped into the stream.

Movement caught his eye and drew his attention to the top of the hill. Three Spetznaz officers threw themselves onto the ground and laid out a blazing pattern of fire. The mercs dived for cover.

Bolan palmed his headset and slipped it on. "Kalinin?"

"Here, Comrade Belasko."

The ghost of a smile hovered on the Executioner's lips as he waded through the stream. "Did you ever see an American cowboy movie when you were growing up?"

"We are the cavalry, yes?"

"Hell, yes!"

More Spetznaz crowded the immediate vicinity, and the firing died off as the mercs realized what had happened. Grimaldi broke in a heartbeat later, saying, "You think these guys wised up as to who the Indians are?"

"HOW MANY DID WE LOSE?" Bolan asked.

"Three," Kalinin replied. "Vanek just died."

They stood near a knoll six klicks from the mercenary hardsite. Loose coils of smoke still hung above the hell-zone, but no one with any authority in Lebanon had chosen to investigate.

"They were good men," Bolan said.

"Yes," Kalinin replied, "they were." He sighed. "At least I'll be able to send them home to their families. These days, as terrible as they appear now, aren't the old days where young soldiers simply disappeared and families knew only what the government wished to tell them."

"Maybe some things aren't so far removed from those days," Bolan suggested softly.

Kalinin's eyes narrowed. "You speak of Karpov and Svoboda. I have told you—"

"Excuse me, sir," a young Russian soldier said. "The prisoner is ready to speak now."

Kalinin nodded and led the way.

Bolan trailed behind. Nick Leighton had died in the trucks, but his second-in-command, a rough Irishman named Sean Dalton with a record even longer than his commander's, had agreed to talk. First, though, he'd had to have a compound fracture seen to before he bled to death internally.

Dalton was rough and grizzled, his short, clipped red hair matted to a high forehead. His left leg was in a splint and his complexion was almost as pale as the bandages. He lay on the ground and used his arm as a pillow.

Bolan squatted before the merc, well out of reach of a sudden lunge. Kalinin remained standing, his back ramrod stiff.

"Are you the head boyo?" Dalton asked.

Bolan returned the man's level stare.

"I told your johnnies I wasn't about to talk to anyone 'cept the head man himself."

"So talk." Bolan prodded.

"American?"

The Executioner nodded.

Dalton sighed with relief. "Lord loves an Irishman."

"Doesn't mean it's going to get any easier," Bolan warned.

"Maybe not, boyo, but I feel a lot better about it. I'd not be talking at all 'cept that Nick's dead and gone. The rest o' this team, they can vanish. Me, Hezbollah will remember some, but I don't plan on returning to this little garden spot anytime soon." Dalton leaned forward.

"You boyos did that right and proper back there, you know."

"Cut to the chase," Bolan growled. "I'm burning a candle at both ends now, and I'm not about to let you set fire to the middle."

"What's the deal?"

"You talk, you walk."

"You make it sound simple."

"That's the way it is."

Dalton grinned, but it quickly faded to a grimace of pain as he tried to shift his leg. "You and Walter Cronkite."

Bolan stood and started to walk away.

"Here now," Dalton called after him. "Don't just go off like that."

"I don't have time for games, Dalton. I'm operating on numbers that leave you in or out damn quick."

"All right, all right. What do you want to know?"

"I want to know where the munitions shipment is that Leighton handled for Hezbollah, and I want to know where the hostages are being held."

"The weapons are in Damascus," Dalton replied. "As for the hostages, I got maybe one place in mind for sure. Leighton, he didn't just figure on good faith with Hezbollah. Nicky had that bugger, Rihani, followed by a couple of our boys. The way we pieced it together, Hezbollah's holding two groups of hostages in Beirut, with a third somewhere farther south for insurance.''

''No idea where?''

''None. God's truth.'' Dalton raised his hand on it.

''Give me the addresses in Beirut and Damascus.''

CHAPTER TWENTY-SIX

South of Baalbek, Lebanon

Third Day—11:08 p.m.

Halting the caravan at the top of a gentle hill overlooking a lush valley, Fahad Rihani concentrated on turning the clock back years. With painstaking effort he overlaid the entire area with a mental map he'd charted long ago. The stream in the valley twisted more than he remembered. For a moment he thought it was a trick of the moonlight, then quickly realized he was seeing it at low ebb, at a time when the summer season had almost succeeded in sucking it dry. Judging from the sandy embankments, when the stream was more full it flowed straighter. Only a cattle trail scarred the hillsides, twisting over outcroppings and between trees and bushes.

"Take us down," Rihani ordered as he reseated himself in the jeep.

Numair nodded and put the vehicle in motion.

"Call the men in the Winnebago," Rihani said to the man in the back seat. "Tell them to stay there beside the road. The hostages will be just as accessible."

The man lifted his radio and spoke softly.

Rihani braced himself against the dash of the jeep. More of his sense of direction was coming back. Memory washed over him, bringing with it the anger that had nearly consumed him all those years ago.

Rihani held up a hand. "Stop here."

The jeep rocked to a stop fifteen meters from the streambed. The other vehicles made a semicircle behind it.

Rihani got out of the jeep to get his final bearings. A lightning-blasted evergreen tree hung precariously on the edge of the stream, its exposed roots gnarled and dark as they stabbed into the black water. He glanced at the tree, making an effort to control the excitement and hate that threatened to overwhelm him. "There should be a pile of ruins."

The men spread out at once, trailing the barrels of their weapons through the brush. A few minutes later one of them cried out, "Here. I've found them."

Nervous anticipation chewed at Rihani's composure. He forced himself not to run and tried not to think that his prize had been recovered by those who had lost it. Still, the one Faisel had taken with him had remained in place. His memory had proved correct.

The man hacked and slashed at the overgrown brush and long grasses twirled around the disheveled stack of limestone building blocks. They were remnants of a structure built by the Mamluks in the fifteenth century. He'd never known what they once might have been.

Rihani knelt slowly as he stared at the stones. Instead of the past he saw only a future for vengeance, a means for the holy war to be released.

"Under here, Dr. Rihani?" Numair asked.

"No. These only mean that our quest is sure to be fruitful." Rihani traced his fingers across the cool surface of the stones. He dug in the grasses until he uncovered the top of a broken column that had been buried in the ground. "Go get the shovels."

A half-dozen men dropped their weapons and ran back to the vehicles. Gathering his robe about him, Rihani stepped off the distance marked indelibly in his mind. There could be no forgetting. On days when the Mossad interrogators waxed eloquent, he had focused on the time when this would come, denying the pain they had given him.

He stopped and looked at his feet. Black soil, overgrown with brush and grasses, shifted beneath his weight. A light film of perspiration masked his face and left gleaming droplets in his mustache. He ran a hand across his lower jaw to clear them away. The sound of booted feet tearing through the undergrowth let him know the men had returned with the shovels.

"It's here," Rihani said when they'd joined him. "Begin digging." He stepped away.

Fifteen minutes later someone's shovel struck an object in the ground.

"Enough!" Rihani ordered. He walked to the edge of the hole and looked down. "Only two men now."

Numair selected another man and ordered the others out of the pit.

"Carefully," Rihani instructed.

Numair called for a bucket and one was passed down. He and the other man began filling it with their bare hands, handing it up when it was full, then repeating the process. Gradually the outlines of a wooden crate came into view.

Excitement flared anew in Rihani. Like some earth goddess of ancient lore, the land was giving birth to the weapon from the seeds of destruction he'd planted so long ago.

When the crate was revealed, it was a four-foot square still partially buried in the dirt. Rusted metal bands held it securely. The words stamped into the moldy wood were in Cyrillic script.

"Numair," Rihani called.

The young man looked up, then put his shovel to one side and helped Rihani descend into the hole.

"Your knife." Rihani held out his hand for the heavy blade, then used it to pry at the metal bands. Once they were cleared, he thrust the knife under the edge of the crate's lid and pulled. Nothing happened. Silently he cursed his weakness. He used both hands this time but still couldn't summon enough force to pry the lid free.

"Doctor," Numair said softly, "allow me."

Rihani stepped away and gave the younger man room.

Corded muscle stood out in sharp relief under the thin fabric of Numair's white shirt. Perspiration dripped from his face, and he groaned as he exerted himself.

Nails screamed as they broke and tore loose. Grabbing the lid in one hand, Numair yanked it loose from the crate and held it for Rihani's inspection. Blobs of white Styrofoam packing blew away in the wind, scattering artificial snow across the bottom of the hole. Numair dug within the packing and uncovered the contents.

The device was thirty-five inches wide, twenty-six inches high and twenty-six inches long, covered by a transparent plastic bag with two zippers.

Rihani stepped forward to claim the prize. He ran a hand down the cool plastic, savoring the hard angularity of the device. He looked up at the men gathered around the hole, some on their knees and some standing to see what was revealed. He held his hands out to them. "My brothers, I give you the one and true Sword of Hezbollah, and the means with which God shall smite the cursed Israelis from our world forever." He extended a hand.

A man reached down and caught it, bringing him up easily.

"What is it?" one man asked.

Numair lifted the device reverently and placed it on the edge of the pit.

The words of the Russian captain had never left Rihani's mind. He studied the group spread before him. "This, my brothers, is a weapon God has seen fit to place in our hands. They call it a Special Atomic Demolition Munition— SADM." He tried to relate to them what a .01-1 kiloton of explosive power was. Some of them were old enough to remember the horror of Hiroshima and Nagasaki, and he witnessed the fear as it creased the faces of the older men.

"With this no one can stop us. We'll show these unbelievers and desecraters what a true holy war is. We'll demonstrate for them what our love of God and His ways empower us to do." He paused, catching the eye of every man there. "For God!" he roared with as much vigor as he could muster.

They echoed him, breaking into wild abandon for a moment as elders among them spoke of the rewards God would no doubt give to His disciples who marched for His glory.

Rihani watched them, knowing he'd chosen well. These men believed in him, and they believed in the cause he spoke for. His inner strength soared and washed away the tiredness that had clung to him.

Turning to Numair as the clamor died away, he said, "Quickly, my brother. There are two more of these devices buried beside the first. Here and here. As speedily as you're able."

Rihani smiled in satisfaction as the men set to work. Now those around him who'd pleaded for retaliation against the West's efforts to make war with Hezbollah would understand why he'd chosen not to divert their energies. While the Americans, Britons, Russians and Israelis struggled with one another and tried to maintain their own secrets, he and the members of his select group could take the war where it really belonged—to Israel.

And the nuclear edge of the Sword of God could sweep them all away. A lightness of heart Rihani hadn't felt in many years touched him. "Soon, Jamila," he whispered. "Soon."

CHAPTER TWENTY-SEVEN

Sidon, Lebanon

Fourth Day—4:53 a.m.

Dressed in combat black, a light jacket and his black beret, Katz trotted quietly through the tangled landscape of the banana grove. He paused at its perimeter, concealed by the bole of a banana tree. A silenced Uzi hung over his shoulder, and the SIG Sauer he'd been issued was holstered at his hip, butt forward.

Katz raised his infrared binoculars to his eyes and focused on the target area. Two towers with a crumbling wall spread between them were all that remained of the castle that had been built during the crusades of the thirteenth century. Christianity had clashed with the Muslim world then, too, and scars of those battles remained.

Katz couldn't help wondering what scars would be left by the present engagement.

He trailed the binoculars along the towers. The castle had originally been constructed at the edge of the ocean and was used to defend the port. Now it lay abandoned, an occasional stopover for tourists and photographers.

The towers stood almost three stories high, blacker than the night that framed them. Time and salt air had provided the coloration. Once, perhaps, the castle's stone might have been white and the structure something to marvel at. Now, in Katz's mind, it was only a charnel house. Somewhere in that tumbling wreckage were the seventy hostages they'd been sent to rescue—or so they'd been told.

He unlimbered the ear/throat headset and keyed the transmit button. "Rafael?"

"Here."

"Calvin."

"Yeah."

"Ranon?"

"Yes," the Mossad chief replied.

Katz continued, calling out the names of the other two men who were part of the team. When all were present and accounted for, he asked for a report on the security defenses.

"Two men," James radioed back. "Both on the left tower."

Katz focused the binoculars and found them. Both were dressed in traditional Arab garb. They carried Soviet machine pistols.

"How do you wish to handle this?" Goldberg asked.

"I want to look at them," Katz replied, "without them looking at us. Before we do anything we have to verify whether the hostages are there."

"Hezbollah wouldn't waste time guarding an empty castle," the Mossad chief pointed out.

"Have you never worked a decoy, Ranon?"

There was a hesitation, then the Mossad agent asked, "What do you suggest?"

"A boat," Katz answered. "Rafael?"

"On my way, Yakov."

"Calvin?"

"I'm in your shadow, Rafe," James said, "so be sure to count noses before you come up firing."

Katz stayed with the tree line, closing in on the dock area. Creaking mast lines and men's conversations as they worked penetrated the rush of the sea. Diesel engines fired into throaty life. It would be dawn soon, the Phoenix team leader realized, which would curtail their chances of approaching the castle under the cover of darkness.

Crates were stacked on the dock to be loaded later. He slipped between them effortlessly, staying away from direct contact with any of the dockhands. He kept his prosthesis tucked into his jacket pocket. With the hook in place instead of the artificial hand, he knew he'd draw more attention from a casual observer. And a man with a hook would be easily remembered. Yet the hook was more serviceable for the "personal" involvement the probe might demand.

The scent of brine and percolating coffee mixed with the smells of drying fish and diesel fuel. He pulled his beret lower as he turned a corner around a stack of pallets containing sacks of sugar. At the end, sandwiched between rows of chemicals, cement and packaged fruit juices, a forklift clattered to sudden life.

The driver waved happily and switched on his overhead lights. Katz waved back and hurried on before the forklift operator could get a good look at him. The wooden dock vibrated underfoot as the forklift went into motion. Hydraulics groaned and wheezed behind him as the first load was lifted.

Ranon Goldberg stood beside bales of paper and cardboard. Like Katz, he wore black, and it served to blend him in with the seamen from a nearby merchant marine vessel.

"Your men?" Katz asked as he walked over to him.

"Nearby."

Katz nodded and pulled out a pack of cigarettes. He passed them over, then shook out one for himself. Goldberg lit both. "You act like a man with something on his mind."

"We both do."

"You've talked with your superiors concerning the Mossad team in Washington?" Katz knew he had, but there had been no time to talk in private before this.

"Yes." Goldberg looked him square in the eye. "But they won't relent. Those men have their orders. Just as I have mine."

"And those are to get Rihani no matter what the cost."

Goldberg didn't reply.

Katz turned away from the man. He watched the fishing boats set sail and tried to find a handle for the anger that threatened to erupt inside him.

"Yakov," Goldberg said a moment later.

"Yes?"

"This man is very dangerous. If he isn't stopped, it could mean a catastrophe for Israel."

"This I know already."

A forklift lumbered by, carrying a pallet of sugar. Another man yelled as he quickly dodged out of the way.

"There," Katz said, indicating Calvin James at the stern of the dark blue Chris-Craft bobbing slowly toward the dock area. Goldberg transmitted directions to his men and followed in the Phoenix team leader's footsteps.

The boat butted into the rubber tires lining the edge of the dock, well away from the current flow of activity. Keeping an eye on the other boats and people to make sure no one took extensive notice of them, Katz stepped into the boat. He kept the Uzi canted across his chest, concealed by his jacket.

Encizo was in the wheelhouse. "There's been some movement in the castle, Yakov."

Katz thumbed the transmitter on the headset. "What kind of movement?"

"A small powerboat with two men," Encizo said.

Using his binoculars, Katz scanned the crumbling towers. At the base, pulling away from the ragged coastline filled with jutting black rocks, he spotted the powerboat. The vessel moved slowly, bouncing over the breaking waves. "Bring us around for a look-see."

The Chris-Craft turned slightly, and Katz tracked the suspect craft through the mast and rigging of a half-dozen fishing vessels pushing out to sea. Three hundred yards out the powerboat came about and stopped. The two men leaned forward and pulled a long, tarp-covered object from the boat, then tipped it over the side.

A cold fist closed around Katz's heart as he lowered the binoculars. "Rafael?"

"I saw it."

"Bring us about."

"Doing it now."

Katz leaned heavily on the railing and watched the powerboat start back for the castle. "Give them time to clear the area."

"Understood."

"Calvin?"

"Yeah?"

"We'll have need of your diving abilities."

James skinned out of his blacksuit and shoes.

"And if they have someone watching over that area?" Goldberg asked quietly.

"It's a chance we have to take." Katz reached back for the Beretta sniping rifle James carried. He checked the action, flicked off the safety and went to join Encizo in the wheelhouse. A buttstroke cleared the Plexiglas from one of the small windows. He lined up behind the rifle and scanned the castle through the StarTron.

The powerboat's crew disappeared into a hidden cove.

"Here," Encizo said as he cut the engines.

Katz tapped the transmitter button. "Calvin."

"On my way."

The Phoenix team leader watched as James dived into the water, keeping the sniper rifle at the ready. He counted time automatically. Less than a minute later James surfaced with difficulty, dragging the tarp-covered object with him. Goldberg and the two Mossad agents went to help him aboard.

"Now, Rafael."

Encizo nodded and engaged the twin diesels. The Chris-Craft moved forward.

Satisfied that the recovery maneuver had gone undetected, Katz went back on deck. James sat on the wet deck, arms crossed around his shoulders as he stared at the contents of the tarp. "Well, Katz, you got your verification on where the hostages are being held."

Katz looked down at the corpse. The girl couldn't have been much over fourteen or fifteen, with honey-blond hair and a dusting of freckles under pale blue eyes.

"Cover her," Katz said in a neutral voice. He passed the sniper rifle to James, then headed for the wheelhouse without another word.

CHAPTER TWENTY-EIGHT

Washington, D.C.
Fourth Day—1:08 a.m.

"I don't like it, Carl," Blancanales said from the driver's seat of the Chevy Lumina van.

Lyons slipped into the shoulder rig with practiced ease and mounted the Colt Python in an upside-down breakaway rig. "What's not to like?"

"The fact that you're going in by yourself," Schwarz said from the passenger seat.

"Guys, look, I'm a big boy now. Even my mom thinks it's a good idea that I go make wee-wee by myself." Lyons was dressed for the street—jeans, hobnailed boots, black turtleneck and short-waisted denim jacket. He dropped his feet experimentally, making sure the Derringer Semmerling LM-4 was secure in its boot holster. The little pocket pistol packed a quintet of .45 ACP rounds in five inches of blued steel. It wasn't accurate at a distance, but it wasn't designed to be. For Lyons's purposes that wasn't necessary. What *was* necessary was that the Semmerling put down whatever it needed to. He didn't have any doubts about that.

"With a guy like August Terranova," Leo Turrin said from the rear of the van, "you make a mistake and you won't end up with anything left to make wee-wee with."

Lyons turned up the cuffs on the jacket, then flared the collar just to watch Blancanales blink in sartorial dismay. He peered through the van's one-way glass at the posh nightclub on the other side of Wisconsin Avenue. It was bracketed by a dozen other neon-encrusted watering holes for the nation's capital. However, the carefully tended

Japanese garden outside set the Blue Note apart from the rest.

"I thought you didn't know this Terranova, Leo," Blancanales said.

"I know of him," Turrin replied. "Just didn't figure he'd be so connected."

"That's life on the street," Lyons said. "You cruise with it, you're in the know. The instant you step inside, you're three steps behind looking at maybe never getting back in the stride."

"Still—" Schwarz began.

Lyons cut him off. "Still, I know what I'm doing. I was a cop for a lot of years. This is cop's work. Detective Maurloe knew that when he gave me this bit."

"He gave it to you because he was afraid you were going to level his town before he could get you out of his hair."

Lyons ignored the sarcasm.

"You don't have to go in alone," Turrin reminded him.

"Yeah, I do. Terranova's got to think about me. He's got to think he's inside my skin when I let him see my face. He's got to believe I'm capable of doing whatever I say I'm going to do."

"Let me go with you," Turrin suggested. "I've played the good cop/bad cop routine before."

Lyons made a buzzing noise. "Wrong. When you played, you took up space on the other side of the table. You were working deep, Leo, and the cops pulling a number on you didn't know that. You were never part of the up-front organization. That's a whole different smell, brother. And I can't allow Terranova to smell nothing but cop when I go in there. Federal agents won't spook him. That's what he's got his lawyers for. But the one thing guys like him respect and want to shit needles over when they see it is a nightmare cop over the edge sporting a hard-on for justice. You may know the song and dance, buddy, but it's a whole 'nother thing when it comes time to walk that walk and talk that talk."

Lyons glanced at Blancanales and Schwarz. "Look, guys, I appreciate the concern, but there are times I only know how to get something done by myself. Back when you were running through the jungle in Vietnam with Mack, I'll bet there were plenty of occasions the big guy dealt himself a lone hand.''

"Too many," Schwarz said.

"Spent a lot of days wondering if we'd ever see him again," Blancanales agreed.

"Yeah, well, this isn't going to be days. Only minutes. So stand down and do us all a favor by relaxing until something goes wrong.''

Lyons hit the door release on the van, got out, then jaywalked across the street against the light and drew curses from the late-night drivers. He hit the opposite sidewalk by the numbers, already digging up his cop's mental armor and locking it into place, a street radar that had never failed him.

The street people had already noticed Lyons and gave him a wide berth on the sidewalk. Their eyes bored into his back, and he could feel it. It was like stepping back into something he could never truly leave. Too much of what he was now had been built back inside a patrolman's uniform.

He stepped inside the nightclub and moved to the left until he had the wall to his back. The decor was Japanese—marble tables, oil lanterns, bonsai trees in huge clay pots, privacy walls made of rice paper and paintings all set a subdued visual tone. A hidden DJ spinning blues platters set the audibles. The clientele was a mix between yuppies and older patrons who might have experienced some of the Jazz Age's vibrant years themselves.

"May I help you?" a waiter inquired as he materialized from the after-dinner gloom.

"No thanks," Lyons replied. "I'm kind of used to helping myself." He stepped around the man, scanning faces for Terranova. The file Maurloe had slipped him had come with dozens of pictures. He didn't feel he'd have any trouble recognizing the man.

"May I ask what this is about, Officer?" the waiter insisted, moving quickly around to confront him again.

Lyons sidestepped the man and took off, moving around the rice paper walls and drawing a mixture of stares and glares. "You can ask, but don't get in the way."

Seeing that he wasn't getting anywhere, the waiter turned and moved away.

Lyons knew the guy was going to the management. He stepped up his speed, not wanting civilians to gum up the works or lessen the impact he wanted to have on Terranova.

He found his quarry at a large table in the back. Nine other people sat in chairs around it, half of them women. Lyons recognized working girls when he saw them. The men were dressed casually, but all sported jackets.

Terranova sat at the head of the table. He was a big man, well toned by vigorous exercise. Maurloe's records showed that he was some kind of belt in tae kwon do. Lyons couldn't remember the color and hadn't been impressed. A shark's smile, full of white teeth, twisted Terranova's mouth. His shoulder-length black hair was pulled back in a thin ponytail.

Lyons noted that the two heavies eating dinner at a separate table had put their gun hands under their jackets.

"Do I know you?" Terranova asked as he leaned forward and placed his hands on the table.

"No," Lyons replied as he moved closer. "No, you don't know me, but I know you."

The two heavies started to get up.

Terranova waved them back down. "Maybe you should introduce yourself."

"Maybe we should go someplace private," Lyons said with a smile of his own. "Shouldn't confuse the ladies with business talk and screw up their digestion."

A couple of the younger women giggled but were quickly silenced by glares from their "dates."

"If I don't know you," Terranova said softly, "that means I don't have business with you." He picked up his fork and turned his attention back to his meal.

Lyons knew from Maurloe's files, a collection of police and private conjectures, that Terranova was a regular handyman in the slimier levels of city life. If a defendant needed a witness removed, he contacted August Terranova. If a shipment of cocaine had hit a snag and the DEA was about to pounce on it, the traffickers called Terranova for a quick disappearance and a quicker return to the market area. If there was side action to be made on a fight or a horse race, Terranova was there with chests of money to lay out on the street to pick up the local slack. The man was an entrepreneur working the dark side. His cleanest business was moving information, and he made sure he had plenty of it to move and to use. Maurloe's personal files were filled with notes concerning deals the detective had been sure Terranova had negotiated. The man sold to both sides and often resold the information, adding the names of the people who were acting on it.

"Oh," Lyons said as he stepped up to the table, "we got business. Trust me."

The heavies were coiled springs in their chairs.

"Maybe you haven't met my lawyer," Terranova said, holding the fork in his fingers. "Mr. Gregory Latham, meet Mr.— Sorry. I guess I don't have your name, Detective."

Latham was the third man at the table, an older guy with white hair and round-lensed bifocals. His expression was one of solemn distaste.

"I don't have time for all these social amenities," Lyons growled. "Let's say we blow this pop stand."

Terranova grinned. "Let's say we don't."

Lyons flipped the bowl of soup into the man's lap, smoothly drawing the Python as the two heavies stood up. He pulled back the hammer on the revolver with a callused thumb. "Uh-uh, boys, not nice." He motioned with the barrel. "Get 'em up."

The bodyguards complied slowly.

"I want to see your badge," Latham demanded, forcing his way up out of the seat. "I'll have your ass in a sling for this. You can't treat citizens this way."

"Sit down, Pops," Lyons said in a hard voice.

"Easy, Greg," Terranova soothed. "Ain't nothing going down here that can't be fixed."

Keeping an open hand, Lyons slapped Terranova across the face and knocked him to the floor. "Shut up and stay down." He removed a pair of handcuffs and tossed them to the bodyguards. "Do the honors, boys, and link it through that table. I don't want to think about you wandering around unsupervised."

A wild yell drew Lyons's attention. He turned in time to see Terranova spin at him in a roundhouse kick. He dodged, letting the foot slide by, weaved around two follow-knuckle punches, sidestepped a hammer blow directed at his temple, then shot out three left jabs followed by a hook that robbed Terranova of his breath and split his lip. Lyons wasn't even breathing hard. His gun had never left the matched pair of heavies. They put the handcuffs on reluctantly and sat down. "Now the guns."

They tossed them onto the floor. Lyons picked up the weapons and jammed them barrel first into a potted bonsai tree, filling the barrels with dirt. As he bent and grabbed a handful of Terranova's shirt, the man made a grab for his wrist.

Lyons let him have it, then stepped into the pull and brought his knee up into Terranova's groin. Grabbing the back of his prisoner's collar, Lyons steered the doubled-over man toward the washrooms, kicking the door open with enough force to slam it against the inside wall.

Three men stood at the urinals, all wearing surprised expressions.

Lyons held up the gun, maintaining his hold on Terranova's collar. "Everybody out—now!"

The men complied without a word, and Lyons swung Terranova toward the first stall.

"You're a dead man, cop, and nothing's going to be able to keep you alive." Terranova spit blood when he spoke.

Lyons punched him in the face. He caught Terranova by the ponytail as the man went down, then shoved his face into the toilet bowl. The cold water revived him immediately. Lyons kept the man's face under for a full fifteen-second count, then yanked the ponytail up. "I need some answers, tough guy, and I need them damn quick. I don't have time to waltz around like this all night."

"God, God," Terranova screamed hoarsely when his face came up out of the water. "You're going to kill me."

"I used to be a badge," Lyons said in his ear. "I made a living out of putting guys like you away. Then a deal you had your goddamn paws on broke that badge. You reading me, pal?"

"Yeah, yeah," Terranova gasped. "I don't even know you."

"You don't have to know me. You do business out there on the street and don't give a damn about who gets caught in the cross fire. Hell, you don't even remember the names." He shoved Terranova's face back into the bowl.

Terranova fought back, but his efforts were becoming weaker.

Lyons pulled him back. "A drug deal, scumbag. Seven years ago. You fenced it through Eddie Marchetti, burned four cops in the process with your man inside the evidence room. Two of us got jail time. They broke my badge and stuck me inside. You got any idea what prison's like for an ex-cop?" Lyons spoke from the heart. All that had been in Maurloe's files. Maybe there had been an innocent cop in there, and maybe they'd just gone along with a successful operation until they were caught. "The way I figure it, you got everything I got coming, only I don't have the time to give it to you." He thumbed the hammer back on the .357 and held the barrel to his prisoner's head.

"Stop!" Terranova shivered in fear. "Stop it, man! There's gotta be something I can give you back."

"Don't fucking lie to me, puke." Lyons shoved the man's head back into the bowl, holding on for a long count. He had Terranova on the ropes now. The man was skidding toward disorientation, filled with the fever of self-preservation. He held himself in check, not giving in to the nausea he felt at his own actions. It took memory of the twisted bodies left by Hezbollah to keep him hard. He yanked Terranova's head up.

Terranova coughed and spluttered. "Deal...let me...let me deal with you. Christ! You can't just kill me."

"You're lying."

"I'm not. I swear on my mother's grave!"

Lyons forced a chilling laugh as he tapped Terranova on the head with the gun butt. Faces occasionally popped through the washroom door, then disappeared just as quickly. "Did I tell you I'm a section-eight, Augie-boy? I can pull this trigger and wait for them to come get me. The worst I get out of the deal is a rubber room. Can you top that?"

"Christ, give me a chance. There must be something."

Lyons screwed the barrel of his revolver to the back of Terranova's head.

"Don't do it, man."

"Maybe there's something." Lyons made it sound like a sudden thought from nowhere.

"Anything. Name it."

Lyons hesitated, letting Terranova believe there was no way out, let him wait for the sound of the shot that would burst his skull and spill his blood into the toilet. There was no turning back now. If it was going to play, the time was now. "The Arabs," he breathed softly. "Give me the Arabs. I can be a hero if I turn them for the Feds."

Terranova said nothing.

Lyons yanked on his collar, gagging the man. "You handle anything for them?"

"Yeah," Terranova said in a voice that cracked frequently. "Handled some transport problems they had."

"Where are they?"

"Don't know. Christ, man, I swear it. I got an address. A place they're supposed to go to pick up some stuff."

"Give it to me."

Terranova did, holding on to the bowl and shaking with the fear that held him in thrall.

"Who're they planning to whack?"

"The Jewish lobbying groups at the Capitol. AIPAC. Something like that. A couple of my guys overheard them talking. I sent in some ringers, some guys who could speak Farsi in case they tried to double-cross us. Christ, that's all I know. I swear it, man."

Lyons stood and headed for the door. He holstered the Python as he walked toward the entrance, then keyed the transmitter in his pocket. "Copy?"

"Got it," Blancanales said.

"Send in Barb's troops."

A siren screamed to life in the street. At least a half-dozen patrol cars and almost that many unmarked vehicles flooded Wisconsin Avenue.

Lyons met Detective Maurloe as the compact Washington cop hit the sidewalk. He wore a tan trench coat that, like the man, had seen better days.

"Quite a stir you created in there," Maurloe said as he flicked a wooden match to life with his thumb and lit his cigarette.

Police officers and young FBI agents poured into the restaurant, setting up roadblocks and securing the entrances. Lyons knew Barbara Price had gone for overkill on the arrest to draw attention away from Able Team and the events preceding the arrival of the Feds. And there would be an interesting little twist added to keep the lawyer, Latham, from complaining too loudly. "How'd you find out about this little shindig?"

Maurloe grinned. "An old war-horse like me? Hell, I kept my ear to the ground. When I heard this rumble going down, I bummed a ride off a feeb I knew and here I am."

"I didn't work this to cut you out."

"No hard feelings, son. I may be a local cop, but I keep up with the papers. You still got your work ahead of you."

Lyons nodded.

"So tell me. What dirt did you get on Terranova that I couldn't find?"

"Tax evasion," Lyons replied. "Terranova's got a few undeclared bank accounts tucked away in the Bahamas that he's going to have to answer for." That had been Kurtzman's contribution to the takedown. "He's going to end up out of circulation for a while."

"You people work quick." Maurloe held out a hand. "Good hunting, son."

Lyons took the hand and shook it. "Enjoy the show."

"I plan to. I'll have my VCR on when the news hits tonight. This is one I'll want to watch again."

Lyons smiled and left Maurloe there, unimpeded by the FBI agents who'd been briefed about him. Blancanales met him with the van, already prepared to sweep on to the next theater of operations. If things were working out as they'd hoped, they were a step ahead of their Mossad counterparts. As he stepped up into the van, he wished there was a way they could be sure.

CHAPTER TWENTY-NINE

Damascus, Syria

Fourth Day—9:24 a.m.

"There's our boy," McCarter announced, pointing at the approaching white limousine.

"I see him," Gary Manning replied.

McCarter trained his binoculars on the vehicles again, moving from the lead limousine to the pair that followed. Yellow dust streaked all of them, billowing in clouds behind them as they followed the dry two-lane road from Damascus. The tip of the city could be seen behind them, needles of tall buildings nestled in the rolling foothills of the Anti-Lebanon Mountains. Waves of shimmering heat distorted the view.

"Got a bird in the air, too," Manning added. They stood near the last hangar in the small row facing the private airfield. Flat land spread out around them, dotted with sparse vegetation. A small plane buzzed energetically on the flight path and hopped into the air. Ground crews and aircrews cycled through usual morning activity. With the multinational backdrop and clandestine business agreements taking place around them, the members of Phoenix Force and the SAS soldiers attracted no undue attention.

McCarter dropped the binoculars and scanned the sky until he spotted the helicopter. It wavered in the distance, hanging like a dragonfly, then dipped in closer to trail the limousine caravan on a parallel flight path.

"It has Syrian military markings," McCarter observed as he focused on the chopper.

"And a gun crew."

McCarter raked his gaze across the side of the chopper and studied the mounted M-60 in the bay door. "Leaves an ugly question in the air, doesn't it, mate?"

"Literally," Manning replied.

"Don't think they'll want to take part once the actual party gets under way, though."

"Syria's not exactly pro-Israeli here, David. They've taken an active part in all three wars against Israel."

McCarter put his binoculars in their case on his hip. "That's true, mate, but then this isn't a purely Israeli issue we're involved in. American and British hostages paint quite a different face on the whole matter."

"Still, I'm keeping a weather eye peeled."

McCarter grinned. "Keep one for me, too. I've got a feeling I'm going to be too busy to keep one of my own." He hit the transmit button on the headset. "Mr. Hoskins."

"Here, sir."

"This needs to be swift about, mate, and no matter the spit and polish the regular military chaps fret about."

"Yes, sir."

Resettling the SIG Sauer snugged into the waistband of his pants, McCarter swung himself into the passenger seat of the Jeep Cherokee they'd purchased after hitting ground zero. Manning slid in behind the wheel. The big Canadian's fingers brushed against the metal stock of the M-249 SAW tucked out of sight between the seats, then moved on to key the ignition.

"Okay, Mr. Hoskins, Mr. Parker, let's roll out the barrel for our guests, shall we?" McCarter braced one foot against the dash as they moved to intercept the three limousines. He belted himself into the combat harness and drew the AK-47 from beneath the seat, checking it over automatically. Cowboy Kissinger's drops had been on time and on target even as the fire zones shifted without warning. There was no doubt about the quality of the weapons involved, only a routine that had to be served as the Briton girded for battle.

He glanced up at the helicopter and watched as it pulled into a circular holding pattern. "Looks like an official escort to the border."

"That's the way I read it, too," Manning replied.

McCarter looked back. Hoskins and his crew were in the dark blue Dodge van coming across the hot tarmac. Parker and his team manned the ten-year-old station wagon with plastic-covered windows. The rest of the SAS members were staked in various positions around the jet they intended to seize for their escape.

The Briton considered their plan one last time as the few remaining numbers fell toward doomsday. They'd been on the scene less than an hour, enough time, armed with the intel Kurtzman had relayed from Bolan, to see the thing done and set up. It was ballsy, it was skeletal and it was bloody well going to slide into no-man's-land from one heartbeat to the next.

He looked back at the three limousines approaching the outside fence of the airport. Aswad, the Libyan end of the munitions connection, was in one of them. He flicked the safety off the assault rifle. It didn't really matter which one the man was in. They were all going down when the team took the munitions out. He hit the transmit button on the headset. "Mr. Sinclair."

"Here, sir."

"Secure your perimeter."

"Yes, sir."

Small-arms fire broke out when there was less than one hundred yards separating the limousines from the Cherokee. The lead vehicle swerved, generating roiling dust clouds as the driver brought it to a sliding stop.

"I'd say they were a mite bloody well skittish about coming to the ball," McCarter remarked dryly. He didn't take his eyes off his target.

"Could be they've heard about a few of the things going on down south," Manning commented. "Mack and Katz haven't exactly been able to keep their movements low-key."

"Get around them, mate. Can't have them running off before the real festivities begin."

Manning nodded and downshifted as he hit the shift-on-the-fly four-wheel-drive control. A line of autofire dug up dust devils from the baked yellow ground. More rattled into the back body of the Cherokee, taking out the rear window.

Holding on as Manning swerved hard to the left, McCarter returned fire, firing off several short bursts at the limousines. Glass shattered in two vehicles, and a corpse sailed through a windshield, propelled by an unbroken line of 7.62 mm rounds.

"All secure, sir," Sinclair announced.

The Cherokee bounced over the hill, the fat desert tires digging into the sand. McCarter recharged his weapon, snapping the fresh magazine into place with the heel of his palm. "And their reaction, Mr. Sinclair?"

"The buggers are going bloody crazy."

"Satisfactory, Mr. Sinclair. Now if you'll just announce our intent."

"Of course, sir. Been waiting for this after seeing your mate in action with those explosives. Talented lad, talented lad."

"At least you've got one fan," McCarter said.

"The man's no slouch when it comes to demolitions work himself," Manning replied as he fought the wheel. "You could've let him do it."

"I make it a habit to use the best man available for the job."

The three limousines formed a ragged line as they came about. The helicopter skimmed closer to the ground, falling into a tighter circle.

The explosions from the hangar area eliminated everything on ground level in the immediate vicinity. Orange and black curls of flames belched from the hangar as the munitions detonated in quicker and quicker waves. Petroleum-based products left dark smoke smudges against the blue of the sky, which were quickly ripped away by the next explosion.

"Damn fine work, mate," McCarter commented as he shouldered the AK-47. "Now let's get these blokes stopped in their tracks." He thumbed the transmit button, looking past the limousines to the station wagon and dark blue van. "Mr. Hoskins."

"Yes, sir."

"Your privilege, Mr. Hoskins. Announce our intentions."

"Yes, sir."

The limo drivers hesitated, uncertain of their next move as they were suddenly confronted on two sides. Manning tapped the brake and brought the Cherokee to a stop sixty yards away. McCarter watched as a man broke free of the halted van and shouldered a tubular weapon. There was a puff of smoke a heartbeat later.

The shock wave of the 94 mm warhead propelled by the LAW slashed into the Cherokee and generated a temporary deafness. McCarter blinked and swallowed hard to equalize the pressure in his ears, but the ringing persisted.

The lead limo turned into fiery debris. Flaming bodies twisted free of the wreckage and ran.

McCarter flicked the assault rifle to single-shot and spaced mercy rounds into the three men in doomed flight. They crumpled to the yellow desert sand and were sheathed in flames.

The two surviving limousines jumped forward, barreling down on the Cherokee. Fifty-caliber rounds thudded into the hard-baked ground, raking a jagged line across the hood of the 4X4. The windshield starred from three wild rounds fired by the gun crews of the luxury cars.

Wiping blood from a nick on his face, McCarter said, "Step on it, Gary. These bastards aren't getting through."

Manning floored the accelerator, and the 4X4 set down as the tires grabbed hold. The defile between the two rolling hills was narrow and filled quickly. Rather than challenging the limousines in a head-on confrontation and unwillingly giving way to their greater weight, the Canadian tapped the brake, popped the clutch, shifted out of four-wheel-drive, double-clutched again and threw the rear end of the Cherokee into a sliding skid. It connected brutally with the lead car, slamming into the vehicle with enough force to drive it into the other limousine.

Buffeted by the combined greater weight, the Cherokee lost its equilibrium and rolled. McCarter had a quick impression of topsy-turvy landscape, then the 4X4 came to a rest on its roof. "Bloody hell," he grunted as he lifted his feet to kick the shattered windshield free.

Both limousines had skidded out of control and rammed into the embankment that lined the road. Staggering to his feet, McCarter shouldered his assault rifle and flicked to full-auto. He squeezed the trigger as a Libyan soldier brought a pistol up in a two-handed grip, a stream of 7.62 mm rounds chewing through the man's face and dumping his corpse over the hood of the car.

The Syrian helicopter dropped in a blazing run, leading a trail of hellfire across the overturned Cherokee.

"Son of a bitch," Manning snarled as he pushed himself to his knees. Blood leaked from a shoulder wound. Lifting the Squad Automatic Weapon, he sighted in on the helicopter as it banked for another run. It moaned like a band saw as it took up full-auto.

The helicopter broke off the attack, black smoke trailing from the rear rotor section. It wobbled enough so that McCarter didn't think it would make it back to the city. He also realized that didn't say anything about the electronics on board or the Syrian army that would be rapidly deployed in their direction. Never mind the final upshot of the matter; at this point they could be executed as an invading army.

"Sir."

McCarter thumbed the transmit button on the headset. "Go, Mr. Hoskins."

"Trouble's headed your way."

Looking back toward Damascus, McCarter saw the line of military vehicles barreling down the road. He glanced at Manning, who stood holding the M-249 SAW across his chest. He'd already found his backpack and pulled it on. The big Canadian nodded. "Acknowledge, Mr. Hoskins. Mr. Sinclair?"

"Yes, sir."

"Our target?"

"Hardly a stick left standing. Mr. Manning did good work. Real good work."

Manning grinned.

"These blokes," Sinclair went on, "wouldn't have enough for a decent fireworks display if they pooled their resources between 'em."

"I read you, Mr. Sinclair." McCarter looked at the Cherokee. "What about our transportation?"

Manning shook his head. "Leaking fuel like a damn sieve, buddy. Even saying the ignition would turn over, we'd more than likely go up in flames."

"Fair enough." McCarter looked back for the van and the station wagon. They were two hundred yards away. "Mr. Hoskins?"

Hoskins's reply was lost in a thunderous boom.

Knocked from his feet, McCarter spit out yellow dust and reached for his binoculars. He heard the whistle this time, just before the explosion, and managed to remain standing as he swept the terrain, stopping when he found it. "They've got a fucking tank in the area," he said to Manning. He thumbed the transmit button. "Mr. Hoskins. Mr. Parker. Clear those vehicles at once and proceed on foot. They've got a T-62 in position to the east."

He swung the binoculars around as the 115 mm gun belched another whistling round. He didn't have time to count, but it looked as if everyone had cleared the vehicles. The blue van was swallowed by smoke and fire, then tossed back to earth fifty yards away.

"We got to buy them some time, mate," McCarter said. He shifted the SIG Sauer to his waistband as he ran for the Cherokee. The back door was jammed.

Another 115 mm round slammed into the ground near the abandoned vehicle as Manning sprung the lock with a booted foot. McCarter opened the door and pulled out equipment cases until he found the one he wanted. He knelt, snapped open the locks and withdrew the RPG-7 that was packed inside.

Manning scooped up the four extra rockets, then grabbed McCarter by the shirt and propelled him up the nearest hill. "Incoming!"

Hearing the whistle, McCarter knew they'd become ground zero for the tank attack. His feet dug into the loose, shifting yellow sand as he sprinted for the protection the hill offered. He threw himself over the top and rolled down, Manning on his heels.

The tank round hit the Cherokee dead on. McCarter knew it from the sudden explosion of heat and black smoke. The Syrians either didn't give a damn if the Libyans lived through the attack or they figured they were all dead. He thumbed the transmit button. "Mr. Sinclair."

"Here, sir."

"Get that plane out of here as soon as those men reach you."

"You lads had best hurry along, then, sir, because it's about to hit the fan at this end, too."

"Get Hoskins and Parker aboard, then lift off."

"Sir?"

"Do it. I can't sacrifice the mission on account of two bloody laggards." McCarter ripped the headset off as he elbowed his way forward. "How far?" he asked Manning.

"Three, four hundred yards."

"Closer, damn it. I can't work with a hundred-yard near miss." McCarter flipped up the sights, drawing down on the Russian tank. "I want to at least worry those buggers a mite."

"Call it 375," Manning said as he dropped his binoculars.

McCarter marked it on the sight, then elevated the windage. He settled down, rested the tube on his shoulder and drew in a breath, working on becoming part of the weapon. The tank's cannon belched smoke again. He squeezed the trigger before it could dissipate, thinking that he wanted to get at least one round off before they were hit.

The tank round landed on the other side of the hill, still on-line with the road. Dirt spewed up and over them as they buried their faces in the sand.

When McCarter looked up again, he saw that the rocket had landed behind the tank, which was now in motion. The turret floated easily, marking the threatened direction. "Rocket." He held the tube up.

Manning got to his knees, loaded the weapon, then tapped his friend on the head. "Go."

McCarter drew down on the tank again and breathed out slowly. He estimated the tank's speed, ignoring the fact that the military jeeps were getting closer. He squeezed the trigger, watched the white flare of the rocket, then lost it in the sudden eruption of dirt and noise in front of them.

"You got it!" Manning yelled. "Son of a bitch, you got it!"

"Yeah, well, mate, there's still plenty of them out there to get us." McCarter looked back at the airfield a quarter mile away. There were some knots of hand-to-hand fighting as the SAS took the plane they'd agreed on. "Rocket."

Manning loaded.

Squinting, feeling the rush of adrenaline flooding his system, McCarter aimed in front of the lead jeep. He squeezed off and felt the push of the rocket leaving the tube. It flew true, smashing into the front of the jeep and exploding, throwing the vehicle into the others following close behind.

"What now?" Manning asked.

McCarter dumped the useless rocket launcher. "I make it a quarter mile to the airfield, Gary. You up to a foot-race?"

"I figure it beats the hell out of hanging around here."

"Then let's do it." McCarter dumped the AK-47, shifted his pistol to the front of his pants, clamped his headset back into place and took off at a run.

Manning fell in beside him. "Pace yourself, guy. Despite what your head's telling you and what you think all that adrenaline's going to let you do, you've been pushed hard lately. If you're not careful, you're going to end up on your face waiting for the hounds to catch up."

"I read you, mate." McCarter hit a comfortable stride, working on breathing in through his nose and out of his mouth in shallow breaths rather than deep ones. He kept his arms in rhythm, kept them in, let his legs do the majority of the work.

Hollow echoes of helicopter rotors and small-arms fire pursued them. McCarter raced down the side of the hill away from the road. The going was tougher in the loose sand, but the decrease in visibility made up for it. Sand worked its way into his boots, quickly chafing his toes and ankles despite the socks. He ignored the pain as he studied the airfield.

Evidently the SAS team had made their objective, though there were still scattered pockets of resistance across the tarmac.

Keying the headset, McCarter said, "Mr. Hoskins."

"Sir."

"Are you aboard?"

"Yes, sir."

"What the hell are you waiting for? Take off."

"Can't hear a word you're saying, sir. Must be some kind of interference in the area. Be best if you saved your breath for running. Looks like you rowdy young bucks are bringing in quite a lot of the buggers."

McCarter didn't waste his breath arguing. Perspiration streamed off his face as they ran through the gates and turned sharply toward the idling jet. The heat shimmering over the tarmac was incredibly oppressive and almost overwhelming. Bullets skipped, dodged and whined all around them. He led, calling Manning's attention, ducking behind a sleek Piper Cub for protection. The heavy rounds from the helicopter's .50-caliber machine gun slammed into the small aircraft, punching in fist-size holes.

The jet was less than a football field away. The familiar strain of an M-60 rattled off in response to the helicopter's .50-cal bark. Surprised, the pilot heeled away.

Four jeeps dodged over the broken gates in hot pursuit of the two Phoenix fighters, spreading out among the damaged and undamaged planes. Their gunners were firing on anyone who came into their sights. Small explosions came from the hangar where the Hezbollah munitions had been stored, adding to the general confusion. The helicopter had dropped back out of target range of the M-60 in the captured jet.

McCarter hit the transmit button in frustration. "Damn it, Hoskins, get that plane in gear or I'll shoot you myself. Two of those jeeps have already triangulated your position through the chopper."

The jet got under way, cruising slowly down the length of the runway. The side door was still open.

"Hurry, mate," Hoskins replied. "We haven't been a bunch noted for leaving blokes behind when things get to be in a nip."

Whirling around the tail section of the Piper Cub, McCarter drew to point-blank range on the driver of a jeep rounding a corner. He squeezed off four rounds, starring the windshield as the bullets drove home. The rear gunner tried to bring his weapon to bear, but a 3-round burst from the SIG Sauer punched him to the tarmac.

McCarter ran a parallel course to the jet as it gathered speed. Then a bullet caught him just above his left ankle, burning through the flesh as it knocked him off balance. He fell, barely able to catch himself on his hands to prevent his face from smashing against the runway.

Manning didn't break stride as he caught up to his comrade. His hands reached out, roughly grabbing McCarter's clothing. "Is it broken?"

"Don't think so," McCarter replied. Another jeep fell into line behind them. He struggled to stay up with Manning as he swiveled his gun arm in the jeep's direction. He fired without looking, ignoring the sights and going for the target. A line of bullet holes skated across the hood of the jeep and the men in the front two seats as he fired the clip dry.

"Hurry up!" Hoskins yelled in his ear.

McCarter looked up as they drew abreast of the jet's open door. Hoskins held out an arm, supported by two men behind him. McCarter reached, slid his fingers around the man's thick wrist and felt his feet leave the tarmac as he was yanked inside. Hoskins fell across him and they both went down in a tumbled heap. Manning and another man joined them a heartbeat later. Someone closed the door and the pilot applied full takeoff thrust, throwing them toward the rear of the aircraft.

Hoisting himself up, McCarter limped toward the pilot's cabin. It was cramped in there, and the copilot left his seat immediately, squirming through the door as he handed over the headset.

"Sergeant Hoskins said you'd be interested in this end of things," the man said in passing.

"Right as rain," McCarter replied as he took the copilot's place. Whoever had owned the plane had installed a smuggler's miniradar screen, and it was manned by another SAS warrior. "Anything?"

"Three," the man said, not looking up from the green screen. "Six o'clock. Coming bloody hard."

"I've got it, Corporal," McCarter told him. He rolled over and twisted back into a 180-degree turn, bringing the three fighter jets into view. Dropping altitude, he skimmed dangerously below a safe floor. The yellowed and sunblasted terrain streaked by. He felt the blood trickling inside his boot but ignored it. Heeling over, he rolled the jet as a fighter tried to come up under him. "Guns?"

"Here." The corporal pointed at a button next to the altimeter. "Twin .50s, built below the cowlings. Figure line-of-sight for two or three hundred yards. Can't tell you what the payload is, but figure it's a thousand rounds apiece."

"Good enough, Corporal. Let's see if I can't make the bloody buggers respect this old war hawk's claws." He shot across the bows of the fighters, making their numbers work against them. Two of the aircraft peeled off, giving the shot to the third. A handful of rounds rattled into the rear section of the jet, then McCarter was rolling, losing altitude as he tapped the flaps and lost airspeed. He brought the nose up as the underbelly of his target came into view. Guessing the cyclic rate of the twin machine guns to be somewhere in the neighborhood of eight hundred rounds, he touched the firing stud and held it for five seconds.

Bullet holes danced down the side and underbelly of the fighter, stitching a line of jagged metal craters. Black smoke trailed from the jet as it veered out of control. McCarter shot by beneath it, running for the Israeli border at full throttle, pursued by the two Syrian jets.

"Four bogies, sir," the navigator called out. "Coming at twelve o'clock high."

"Roger," McCarter acknowledged. He wheeled and dodged, knowing the Syrians had pulled back because they were confused by the sudden turn of events. Even as the lead attacking jet raced for position, an Israeli F-15 streaked out of the sun and hammered the Syrian jet from the sky. The remaining aircraft turned tail. Working the controls with a light hand, McCarter lifted to join the two-by-two formation of the Israeli jets. He found the Israeli frequency and said, "You lads are a bit of a ways from home, aren't you? I figure the Israeli border to be miles from here. Over."

The Israeli pilot next to him gave him a thumbs-up. His face was hidden by the oxygen mask, but McCarter could hear the smile in the man's voice. "Perhaps we wandered off course. From time to time it happens. And those people back there, they're in no position to cry foul. Pictures were taken of the munitions your team destroyed that they had allowed to exist. It will be, as you say, settled out of court this time. Over.''

"Fair enough, mate." McCarter signed off and settled into the routine of the trip home. The sky was a friend he'd known for a long time. What was waiting for them on the ground in Beirut was still a mystery.

CHAPTER THIRTY

Beirut, Lebanon

Fourth Day—3:46 p.m.

Mack Bolan pulled into traffic and followed the black limousine from two car lengths back. He touched the transmit button of the headset. "Jack."

"Go, buddy."

"We're in motion."

"I'm on it. Where away?"

"Going south. Black limo. Three hardguys and Rihani."

"You ID'ed him?"

"Affirmative."

Six blocks farther on the limo turned left.

"East," Bolan said when he keyed the transmit button. "They're going east on Rabi."

"I have them in my sights," Kalinin reported.

Bolan broke off the pursuit, letting the traffic net they'd set up do its work. The team had spent the past several hours keeping the abandoned factory that Sean Dalton had given them under surveillance. Confirmation on the hostages' presence there had been slow in coming until the RV and jeep caravan had arrived. The hostages aboard the RV had been taken inside the factory at once.

Bolan listened to the broken string of brief contact sightings communicated by the different units as he moved into his next position. They had six cars working the traffic, and a van for collating intel.

Flipping his map case open, he unfolded the section depicting downtown Beirut, tracing the possible streets with a forefinger and trying to guess the eventual destination. It had to be someplace with good visibility and relatively limited access. The factory area had both in the form of the flat loading docks and parking spaces slotted all around it.

He left the map open as he leaned onto the accelerator and cut through the two lanes of traffic. At the moment he was running parallel to the limousine three blocks north. He was guessing the limo would cut a slow spiral south back into the heart of the city.

"We got a problem," Grimaldi announced.

"What?" Bolan asked.

"Karpov and Svoboda just took a powder."

The Executioner slipped one of the SIG Sauer pistols under his thigh with the butt in easy reach. "Kalinin?"

There was a brief hesitation. "Comrade Belasko, there's no reason to believe they're planning to do anything wrong."

Bolan cut in before the Spetznaz chief could continue. "Jack."

"Yeah."

"Shut them down."

"Wilco."

Bolan tossed his headset to one side as Kalinin began to protest. Spotting a blank stretch of sidewalk, he steered the car onto it. The vehicle bucked and stuttered as it accelerated around the slower moving traffic. The muffler scraped and scattered sparks when he yanked it back onto the street. Metal shrieked. His rear bumper collided with the front fender of a sedan and caused the driver to brake suddenly, bottlenecking the traffic behind it.

He ran the streets through his mind in block sections, searching for the weakness where Karpov and Svoboda would try their ambush. No doubt remained in his mind now concerning the goal of the two men. Only the reasons why were obscured.

He also knew that Karpov and Svoboda wouldn't have jumped the gun unless they were certain where Rihani and his entourage would be heading. When he remembered the overpass two blocks away, he glanced at the map to confirm his coordinates, then floored the accelerator, tapping the brake and gearing down as he took a wide right.

He hit the on-ramp at sixty-plus, feeling the shimmy of the left front tire threaten the vehicle's controllability as the shocks gave way beneath gravity and rolled the car like a soap bubble across bathwater. He overcontrolled the steering to keep it on track, narrowly avoiding a collision as he topped the rise overlooking the street Rihani's limousine was currently traveling.

Karpov and Svoboda had already left their vehicle and stood at the stone wall, looking down at the approaching traffic. Karpov had a LAW settled over his shoulder, and Svoboda stood beside him with an AK-47 in plain view. Traffic gained speed as it passed them. No one appeared to be looking back.

Karpov responded to Svoboda's warning, swinging the LAW around as Bolan sped up the incline. Two dozen 7.62 mm rounds scattered across the windshield and grille of the Executioner's vehicle.

Cutting the wheel hard and stomping the brake, Bolan brought the ancient vehicle around with shrills of protest, presenting it broadside as the LAW leveled off. He grabbed his jacket as he leaped out, bringing his map case and two pistols with him.

The car exploded with a furnace blast of heat that punched the Executioner to the pavement. Tires shrieked in his ears. He rolled, narrowly avoided the sliding bulk of a flatbed truck that skidded where he'd been a second before.

He placed a hand against the truck as he forced himself to his feet. Svoboda lifted the assault rifle and squeezed off short bursts on full-auto. Karpov was already hunkered down, extending another LAW from the pack at his side.

The sleek black limousine appeared in the distance, maintaining a sedate speed as it flowed with the traffic. Driven by a hail of bullets, Bolan ran, firing a string of shots from his pistol as he sought cover. At least two rounds hit Svoboda in the chest but only succeeded in ripping the shirt away to reveal a Kevlar vest. Svoboda stepped in front of Karpov, changing his empty magazine for a fresh one.

A car in the oncoming traffic lane pulled out, the acceleration of its engine audible even over the roaring flames consuming Bolan's car. Karpov stood, aiming the LAW with deliberation.

The Executioner dropped his jacket, map case and extra pistol as he stepped into a Weaver's stance to face Svoboda. He squeezed off the rounds methodically, centering on the big Russian's face. The heat of Svoboda's bullets burned his cheek and plucked at his sleeve. Another dug a bloody furrow along his left forearm. Then Svoboda fell backward, his face a mask of blood.

The car that had turned from the traffic smashed into Karpov's abandoned car, which became a missile in its own right, riding the front of the charging vehicle to slam into Karpov from behind before the man had a chance to fire the rocket launcher.

Bolan grabbed his spare gun and brought it up as Karpov turned to face his assailant. The Russian was pinned against the stone wall by the wreckage; the LAW was six feet from his outstretched hand. Bloody spittle covered his mouth and nose. He clawed for his side arm and brought it up.

Kalinin, bleeding from a scalp wound, stepped out of his car and leveled his own weapon. His pistol cracked three times, and Karpov slumped against the wall.

Bolan watched Rihani's limousine come out on the other side of the underpass. One of the Spetznaz cars was still in quiet pursuit. He reached down for his jacket, map case and empty gun, then trotted over to join Kalinin.

Metal screeched as Kalinin backed away from the crushed vehicle. "Get in," the Russian said as he surveyed the traffic.

Bolan had to yank the sprung door, then had difficulty in shutting it once he was inside. "Didn't figure you for the cavalry this time."

"A decision had to be reached," Kalinin said as he wheeled around and accelerated. The front end wobbled treacherously. Steam escaped from punctures in the radiator. The regular flow of traffic was cut off by the burning car, and a handful of drivers got out to investigate. "I was assured by a prominent KGB official and my supervisor that the assignments of Karpov and Svoboda wouldn't conflict with my own duties here. All I had to do was enable them to get in-country and provide them a base station until their work was done."

Bolan remained silent.

"As you can tell, I was lied to. How far this deceit has spread, I'm unable to guess. My original orders, handed down from President Gorbachev's office, are to assist and effect the rescue of the hostages. I don't know where this move will leave me given the current climate of politics in my country. But this, this was something I *had* to do."

"You did the right thing," Bolan said. "We still have a chance at rescuing the hostages. That's the job you were given, soldier. Together we'll get it done." He held out his hand.

Kalinin took it. "Agreed. With no more distractions or secrets between us."

Bolan settled into his seat and accepted the headset when Kalinin offered it. He braced himself against the dashboard as the Spetznaz chief drove with a frantic economy of motion.

"Striker?" Grimaldi said.

"Go."

"Our teammates?"

"Down and out."

"Fair enough. Got some more good news for you."

"Let's have it."

"Tuholske just scored the second hiding place of the hostages."

THE RUSSIAN SOLDIERS sat in groups inside the empty apartment building cleaning their weapons. They covered the top two floors, the fourth and fifth, and maintained a security perimeter on the ground.

Bolan watched them in satisfaction. Even with the forced pace, the downtime and knowing they were about to exchange their present weapons and gear for others, they'd been trained to take care of their arms. They were professionals to the core, adapting without question to the elimination of the two KGB agents within their ranks, concerned only with their own objectives.

Night had fallen, and street activity had changed from the defensive to the aggressive as the predators came out to feed.

Bolan surveyed the city while maintaining a low profile against the window. He was dressed for the night and had mentally slipped into it hours ago.

"Comrade."

He turned to face Kalinin.

"There's a new problem." The Spetznaz chief set a bulky instrument on the scarred table against the far wall. "Petru found this among Karpov's belongings."

The Executioner surveyed the device under the shielded light they'd set up to study the street maps and architectural blueprints Kurtzman had sent them. "That's an AN/PDR-43."

Kalinin nodded. "Precisely." It was as big as a computer monitor, with an intake and exhaust port. A clear plastic tube almost two feet long held a ball that stayed in place inside. Kalinin wiped the meter face where the needle was buried under zero. "It's used for detecting low-level beta and gamma radiation to make sure nuclear areas are safely sealed."

"It can also be used to track fissionable materials," Bolan said.

"I know."

Bolan gazed at the device, uneasy with the string of possibilities that suddenly confronted the teams. "Is there any reason to believe Hezbollah has access to nuclear weapons?"

"None that I'm aware of."

"Evidently somebody was." Bolan looked up as Grimaldi entered the room.

"Ready," the pilot said as he switched on the satellite communications gear. A coaxial cable led to the small dish antenna on the roof.

Bolan took the mike as the attention of every man in the room centered on him. "Stony Base, this is Stony One. Over."

"Stony One, this is Stony Base," Barbara Price answered. "Go ahead. Over."

"Have you talked with Phoenix One and Two? Over."

"That's affirmative, Stony One. Both teams are in position and ready for your go. Over."

"There's been a slight change on the shopping list they'll be needing," Bolan said. "Equip both teams with AN/PDR-43s and have them sweep the recovery areas when the time comes. Can do? Over."

"Can do. Why the change? Over." There was no mistaking the concern in Price's voice.

"Unforeseen wrinkle. Over."

"Roger, Stony One. Does this mean what I think it means? Over."

"Don't know at this point. Just received the news ourselves. Over."

"I'll notify Packrat," Price said, referring to Cowboy Kissinger's code name for the operation. "He'll see to it those two items are shipped. What about your unit? Over."

Bolan looked at the AN/PDR-43 on the table. "For better or worse, Stony Base, we're already equipped. Over."

"Understood, Stony One. Are you ready for the logistics? Over."

"Yes." Opening his map case and war journal, Bolan laid out his paperwork on the table as Kalinin and Grimaldi closed in on him. "This is how the rescue's to be done...."

AARON KURTZMAN GAZED at Barbara Price with respect. The woman looked as fragile as a Dresden doll, yet in her own way, on the mental battleground she chose as her own,

Stony Man Farm's mission controller was one of the toughest people he'd ever had the privilege of working with.

Torn between fatigue and impatience, Kurtzman flicked his gaze back toward the huge screen at the other end of the room, where a map of Lebanon and Israel was displayed. The pale blue dot signified Bolan, Grimaldi and the Spetznaz. An orange dot nearby denoted Manning, McCarter and the regrouped SAS. Katz, James, Encizo and the Mossad were represented by ruby.

He released a pent-up breath and glanced at the clock readout on the monitor to his right. Counting down in hundredths, the numbers fell faster than pasteboards from a professional cardsharp's fingers. He knotted his hands around the wheels of his chair and strained the muscles to relieve tension.

With all the technology at his command, with the satellite linkups that would enable him to photograph the license plates of the vehicles the rescue teams used, with the feedlines that would pick up some of the communications between the three independent teams, he still wasn't there with them. It was *not* the next best thing to being there. It was hell.

"Did you contact Able?" Price asked.

"Right after you mentioned it. Lyons seems convinced they're narrowing the distance between themselves and Faisel."

"And the Mossad unit?"

"Breathing down their necks."

"Maybe Hal can buy them some space."

Kurtzman shrugged. At the moment that possibility appeared to be a moot point. Able was going to be on target, or they weren't. The same rules applied to their mission as to the ones being carried out in the Middle East. Close only counted in horseshoes and hand grenades.

A buzzer whined for attention.

Kurtzman flicked a toggle, bringing the satellite relay online.

"Stony Base, this is Stony One. Over."

Price put down her coffee cup and fitted the headset into place. She adjusted the wire-thin mike in front of her mouth. "Stony One, this is Stony Base. Go ahead. Over."

"We're in position," Bolan's calm voice said, "awaiting your go. Over."

"Phoenix One, this is Stony Base. Over."

"This is Phoenix One," Katz said. "We're set. Over."

"Roger, Phoenix One." Price glanced at Kurtzman. "Phoenix Two, this is Stony Base. Over."

"Affirmative, Stony Base," McCarter's voice came back.

Kurtzman automatically reached for the damper controls, cutting back on the audible roar of the airplane rotors coming through McCarter's linkup.

"Let's give it hell, mates," McCarter went on. "Over."

Kurtzman studied the white spot that appeared on the bridge of Price's nose. He'd never seen it before.

Her voice was calm and assured when she spoke. "Then let's rock and roll, gentlemen. Stony Base out." She stripped off the headset and laid it down gently. "And God be with each and every one of you," she added in a whisper.

CHAPTER THIRTY-ONE

Sidon, Lebanon

Fifth Day—5:45 a.m.

Calvin James drew the Randall survival knife from its sheath on his right calf and swam up toward the guard's position. He paid attention to his breathing as he fisted the haft of the knife. The rebreather pack across his shoulders let him remain underwater without the telltale bubbles from regular scuba equipment.

The guard had his attention focused on the ships and boats in the distance. He sat on a boulder near the mouth of the cove leading under the castle. His assault rifle was tucked under one arm, and he had his hands in his jacket pockets as if the chill blowing in across the ocean were affecting him.

James cleared the surface in a lunge, grabbing the man by his shirt and dragging him under. There was no time for the guard to scream. He raked the broad blade of the Randall knife across the guard's jugular and held on until the death spasms left the body. He swam down with the body in tow until he found an outcrop of rock that suited his purpose. He jammed the dead man's foot between a pair of large rocks and the body stayed submerged.

Satisfied, he let himself drift up past the outstretched arms of the corpse, using his hands to turn his body until he could bring the four other men assigned to him within view. They followed him, dressed as he was in the Nomex one-piece black jumpsuits, staying less than a yard above the pebbled bottom of the channel cutting under the castle. The faint green glow of their night vision goggles was visible to his own.

He hung suspended in the water as they came around him. Using hand signals, he directed two men to the north side of the channel and two to the south. Sheathing the Randall knife, he unlimbered the Barnett crossbow and took the middle road for himself.

James let the current do most of the work the way the Navy had trained him to do. They'd had a long, hard swim in from their drop point, and the chill of the water had taken its toll.

Peering up through the water, he spotted the remaining guard they'd planned for. He surfaced slowly, drawing the butt of the crossbow to his shoulder as he shifted his other hand to bring up the front end. The crossbow broke the surface first, centered on the guard's chest. He squeezed the trigger as the guard turned around on the narrow shelf of space edging the submerged corridor. The recoil of the bolt leaving the weapon pushed James back under again. Reacting instantly, he struck out for the rocky shoreline, pausing only to pull the Randall from its sheath.

The quarrel took the guard full in the chest. Only a few wisps of feathers protruded over his heart. The man fell forward into the water without a sound.

Operating on reflex, James grabbed the man's hair and took him under, drawing the knife across the unprotected throat automatically. When the movement stopped, he surfaced, spitting out the mouthpiece. He passed the corpse to the nearest Mossad agent, then scrambled to the shore.

He recocked the Barnett as his team came out of the water on either side of the twenty-foot corridor. Water gurgled and splashed at the sides of the tunnel. He dumped the rebreather into the water. If everything went as planned, he wouldn't be needing it again.

Signaling for a buddy check, he counted down seconds to keep a mental tab on Katz's and Encizo's probable movement. One of the men behind him checked his gear, then clapped him on the head to let him know everything was shipshape.

James stepped out of his flippers and fought back a chill from the slow breeze pushing its way into the tunnel. Besides the crossbow and knife, he carried a silencer-equipped H&K MP-5 slung over his shoulder, a SIG Sauer 9 mm pistol in a shoulder rig and explosive, tear gas and smoke grenades at his belt. The body armor under the Nomex jumpsuits had provided the weight to keep them submerged, though it had also cost in the effort needed to reach the cove.

The black Phoenix fighter held up his arm as the man behind him reached out with a white scarf and tied it above his bicep. Bolan had borrowed a page from the French Foreign Legion. In the dark, with Hezbollah fighters wearing possibly similar clothing, the scarves would make it easier to identify friend from foe. The hostages would be the people without guns.

A pair of slip-on tennis shoes from his abandoned chest pack covered his feet. They were wet from the water but afforded protection from sharp rocks underfoot.

He took point, easing into the shadows with the crossbow leading the way. The tunnel echoed with the voice of the sea, gradually leading upward. The Phoenix warrior kept his sense of direction only through sheer effort. Kurtzman's computers had been able to tap the blueprints of the castle from archaeological studies done by American and British scientists and historians. The catacombs beneath them were quite another matter. One theory referenced by Kurtzman in his search had been that Spanish pirates and looters at a later date had enhanced the system of caves already in existence. As such the historians weren't as interested.

Light spilled from around a curve in the tunnel. James faded back into the stone wall, breathing shallowly. He watched the uneven glare as it bounced along the sea surface. Two long, skinny shadows trailed out across the water. Since there *were* shadows, he knew the lead man was carrying the lantern, otherwise the shadows would have gone in different directions. He also knew the man carrying the light would come up with the lantern on his side of the wall.

He reversed the crossbow and set the safety. Just as the illumination was about to reveal the hiding place of the two Mossad agents on the other side of the channel, he swung the stock into the Hezbollah fighter's knee. Bone cracked, but before the man could scream, James swung the crossbow again and slammed him into the water. One of the Israelis behind James hit the water cleanly only a heartbeat later, a knife glinting in his hand.

The remaining Mossad agent fumbled for the gun at his waist, closing his hands around the butt and yanking it from his holster even as James flipped off the Barnett's safety and launched the bolt. Blood spewed as the quarrel passed through the second Hezbollah man's throat. James slid the body into the water and helped the Mossad agent shove both corpses under the narrow shelf of rock left by the passage of time and water.

He gathered up the crossbow and nocked another bolt, then continued on. For a few minutes he thought he was lost. Then the sound of voices above the gurgling of water drew his attention upward. Scanning the general vicinity, he found the stone steps leading up to a huge iron-and-wood door. Peering around the corner, he also found the dark hulks of two boats with their sails furled.

He led the way up the steps, exchanging the crossbow for the silenced H&K MP-5. Once inside the hostage holding area proper, there was no way they could hope to remain undetected for long. He passed through the unlocked door with his team on his heels, not letting his thoughts touch on the losses that might confront them.

"Go!" Katz ordered.

Three men stepped up out of the darkness and swung grappling hooks over their heads in front of the outer wall of the castle.

"One down, Yakov," Rafael Encizo called softly through the headset. "Now two. And three. We can't find the fourth tower guard."

"Stay with it," Katz transmitted. He stood clothed in the Nomex jumpsuit as were the rest of the rescue team. He held a silenced H&K MP-5 in his left hand. A mat-black hook with carbon edges was his right. Dark combat cosmetics shadowed his face.

The three men with grappling hooks let fly within a heartbeat of one another. The padded prongs knocked almost silently against the other side of the uneven wall twenty feet overhead. Quick nods followed as each man pulled his line tight successfully.

"The fourth man has been accounted for," Encizo whispered.

"Hold your position," Katz instructed, "until the new line of snipers are able to take up their weapons." He waved to the team of snipers holding the grappling hook lines. They scurried up at once, the sniper rifles hung barrel down across their backs. Less than a moment later they disappeared into the darkness hugging the top of the castle. Katz hit his transmit button. "Now, Rafael, bring your team forward."

"Acknowledged."

"Goldberg?"

"I'm here."

"And ready?"

"And ready."

"We've penetrated the perimeter."

"We only await your call, my friend."

Katz gestured to the rest of his team and took the lead in the quick jog to the most obscured part of the crumbled castle. He scrambled over the piles of masonry blocks, ready for a hiss from one of the hidden snipers that would alert him to a guard on the ground.

Goldberg and three men manned the three large transport trucks they'd liberated during the dead of night. They'd only be called in when the actual extraction had begun.

Calvin James's success or failure would remain a mystery until they were inside the castle.

Katz raced forwards, the H&K MP-5 canted across his chest in the ready position, already locked on full-auto. Maps and blueprints shifted in his mind as his viewpoint changed. They'd chosen a window on the second floor as a primary means of egress. One of the eight Mossad agents gathered around Katz drew out a smaller grappling hook than the snipers had used. His first toss sailed cleanly through the window.

"Rafael," Katz whispered as the line was pulled taut.

Encizo nodded and scrambled up the rope, making only slight noise as his rubber-soled boots made contact with the stone wall.

"Colonel Katzenelenbogen."

Katz hit the transmitter as the men continued the climb. "Yes."

"I have one of the terrorists in my sights."

"Take him down only if he becomes a threat."

"He appears to be searching for someone, sir."

"The tower guards?"

"Perhaps."

"Yakov," Encizo whispered.

Katz looked up. The last man had cleared the window unnoticed. The rope dangled with a stirrup already fashioned at the bottom.

"Colonel, the guard *is* searching for the tower guards."

"Take him down," Katz ordered as he stepped into the stirrup. Encizo and two of the others hauled him up effortlessly. He held on to the rope with his real hand, the H&K draped at his waist, while he used his elbow to guide his ascent.

"He's down, sir, and no one appears to be the wiser."

"Good job, Sergeant." Katz stepped through the window and motioned Encizo to take point to the left and a Mossad agent to take right point as they left the small room.

Katz dropped the Nomex bulletproof hood over his head and became indistinguishable from the rest of the group. He resented the loss of peripheral vision but recognized the additional safety and terror factor the blank black mask lent.

They moved quickly, following the westerly path Katz had mapped out with Bolan and Kurtzman. According to the intel they'd been able to get on the structure, the only suitable holding place for the hostages was at ground level on the sea side. The blueprints had also revealed the exit leading to the dock area below the castle's foundation. If everything had gone as planned, James would already be in control of that area.

The sound of voices warned Katz of their nearness to their objective. He waved the group down and joined Encizo as they hunkered over to peer through the darkness on the first floor. Three men carrying assault rifles stood before the closed double doors, smoking and talking.

Katz pictured the large room in his mind as he studied the double doors. Wooden shutters had covered the room's only window when they'd studied the perimeter earlier, allowing no view of the interior. He painted it in his mind, filling it in with the fifty to seventy hostages it might hold. Once, perhaps, it had been a room akin to the Great Hall that had crumbled away into the sea. Parties and other social functions may have been given there. Now it was a prison, framed by solid stone walls that allowed a large number of people to be held captive by only a few.

"The three come first," Katz said, "and it must be silently."

Encizo nodded and waved to two of the Mossad agents who carried sniper rifles. He shouldered his own, then indicated their targets with hand signals.

Taking the other six men with him, Katz halted at the top of the stone stairway that led down to the door. An expanse of empty floor stretched west of the door, creating a vast battleground should it come to that. He nodded to Encizo and the other snipers.

Three muffled coughs sounded and echoed in the great stone hall. The three guards spun and fell, all victims of head wounds.

Leading the charge down the stairs, Katz covered the hall area with the submachine gun. Two men, previously designated for the job, lifted the wooden plank holding the iron-clad doors locked.

Katz stepped inside and they closed the door after him, giving him time with the hostages. Only some of them were awake. Most sat or lay on the cold, hard floor. Mothers clasped their children to them as fathers and the other men rolled into defensive positions. The stench and odor of fear in the room was unforgivable.

Pulling the Nomex mask from his face, Katz spoke in English. "I represent a joint effort of the American, British, Israeli and Russian military forces sent here to effect your rescue. Please get to your feet with as little noise as you can manage. Notice the white scarf on my arm. This is the only badge of unity that my team has. Whenever someone with one of these scarves tells you to do something, do it. Immediately. This area is still highly dangerous to all of us, and we have yet to leave Lebanon."

A mutter of relieved cries, tears and bits of prayers rolled through the room as the hostages who were awake turned to wake others.

"If there are those among you who can't walk or need aid in walking, please depend on your comrades for that. The team we have tonight is of necessity small. We'll have everything we can do in fending off any terrorist response."

When all of the hostages were on their feet, Katz rapped sharply on the door. It was opened and he stepped outside.

The hostages were hesitant at first, then as they saw the dead bodies of the guards, they were galvanized into action. One of the Mossad agents took the lead, trotting well ahead of the hostages as two more Israelis fanned out around him forming a spearhead to repel any attacks. A few of the men divided up the weapons of the dead men among themselves.

"Ranon," Katz called.

"I'm on my way."

"Rafael," the Phoenix Force leader said, "rather than be content with letting the rest of Hezbollah learn of the escape gradually, perhaps we should put out notice of our own."

"I agree."

Katz gave instructions to the remaining three Mossad agents, then turned to cross the great hall. The sound of the hostages' feet slapping against stone sounded intense. A door opened as they made the opposite wall, and a shadow stepped out of a rectangle of lamplight. Without hesitation Katz squeezed the trigger of the MP-5 as soon as he identified the man as Hezbollah. A dozen silenced bullets chopped through the flimsy protection afforded by the door. The man went down at once and stayed down.

Pulling the pin of a grenade with his hook, Katz whirled around the edge of the door, got a brief impression of a bunk room with at least a half-dozen men in various stages of wakefulness and tossed in the deadly orb.

The explosion was a thumping basso trapped inside the castle. The door came off its hinges and was thrown to the floor, chased by a thick cloud of smoke.

Encizo added another grenade, then readied his own MP-5. A terrorist, cut and bleeding, came through firing blindly. Katz chopped him down with a short burst, and the body sprawled across the blood-smeared hall. A hail of bullets dug stone slivers from the masonry near his cheek. He spun to face the new threat, lowering the MP-5 to waist level, only to see three Hezbollah terrorists go down before the guns of Calvin James and his team as they brought up the rear.

Drawing his side arm, Katz walked into the room and fired at anyone who moved. Eight men were dead when he finished. None of them were Rihani. Disgusted, he left the room and glared back at the hall. The hostages had all made good their escape. At least from the interior of the castle. There was still a small army of fanatics standing between them and true freedom.

"This post was undermanned," the Phoenix leader stated. He looked at James for confirmation.

"There weren't any real surprises below," James said. "We ran into a small group after we made ground level, but it was a skeleton crew like this."

Katz kept his pistol in hand as he paced and thought. "Rafael, break out the Radiac Set and scan the area."

Encizo shrugged out of his backpack and put the unit to work.

"Still haven't been told why Striker ordered the Radiacs sent along?" James asked.

"No."

"Well, you can bet it wasn't just for added ballast."

Keying the headset, Katz said, "Ranon."

"Here."

"The hostages?"

"We're loading the last of them now. There appears to be no sign of pursuit."

"Apparently we've encountered and nullified all who were present."

"This doesn't sound good, my friend."

"No, it doesn't. Begin transportation now. We'll catch up with you in short order."

"Right. Just don't tarry for long. There are still many miles to be traveled."

"I know," Katz said. "I want to spend some time here to get the measure of what we can expect to encounter." He broke off the transmission and tried to ignore the cold fist around his heart.

CHAPTER THIRTY-TWO

Beirut, Lebanon

Fifth Day—5:47 a.m.

David McCarter fell through the night like a modern-day Icarus. The wind velocity pressed his oxygen mask and goggles into his face. Somewhere in the uneven darkness twenty-five thousand feet below was the building that was the team's assigned target.

The arms and legs of his jumpsuit billowed up and slowed some of his descent. He knew from experience that he was building up to a terminal velocity of a 120 miles per hour. Spread out in the traditional starfish pattern, he tracked toward his target, guided by the Russian navigator tied into the homing frequency built into his suit. The man's voice in the helmet receiver sounded wintery and alien, and a million miles away.

The cold ate into him like a living thing despite the insulated jumpsuit, gloves and crash helmet. He blinked to clear his eyes as the lights of Beirut became visible. Adjusting his tracking path in accordance with the circling navigator's instructions, he smiled grimly. Even as big as the building was it would take a hell of a parachutist to think about making the descent. But then that was an SAS specialty, after all.

At thirty-five hundred feet, confirmed that he was on track for his approach, the automatic opening device deployed his parachute. The black silk spilled out above him, mushrooming toward the clouds.

The target building wavered into view below. He glanced up, counting from habit the chutes following him. He reached fourteen, leaving eight questionable, but they might have been hidden by his own chute. Or some of them may never have opened. Sometimes it happened. Airborne lived with that realization. On this excursion, with as much gear as they were already packing, extra chutes had been out of the question.

The Russian tracker let him know he was at ground zero as far as the instruments were concerned. He had no trouble recognizing the building. Kurtzman had faxed over dozens of aerial photographs, blueprints and ground shots of it.

The Seif Building had once been a prime resort of tourists and businessmen. Standing sixteen stories, a full five stories more than its concrete neighbors, it had once held spacious rooms, garden atriums, glass elevators and luxuries fit for kings, whom it had often entertained. Now it was a mere husk of its former self. McCarter had seen pictures of its faded glories, some of them taken by Striker and Grimaldi only hours before.

The hostages were being kept on the fourteenth and fifteenth floors. Bolan had confirmed that, as well as redrawing as much of the existing interior as they could see. When the Executioner finished, McCarter had had to admit it was an accurate and nearly completely detailed picture. But he'd learned a long time ago that Bolan wasn't the type of soldier to leave anything to chance if it could be helped.

The building's roof came up rapidly. McCarter centered his thoughts and spilled air from his chute, angling for the rooftop. A sudden gust of wind blew him off target. He cursed with real feeling as he raked a hand across his face and removed the goggles and oxygen mask to improve his field of vision.

He spilled air from his chute in desperation as the rooftop slid by him quickly. Then he was over the street, knowing there was no way back. He yanked the shroud lines and spilled the rest of the air from the chute, watching the black silk collapse over a corner of the building. For a moment he didn't think it would hold, then he was dangling from the harness against the brick skin of the building.

Skinning out of the crash helmet, he dropped it and fitted the headset into place. He keyed up and called for a countdown as he grabbed fistfuls of the shroud lines and started pulling himself up. All of them had made it, and he grinned in spite of his present predicament. Fourteen men were on the rooftops. Eight more, two to a side, surrounded the building on rooftops of other buildings on all four sides.

"Snipers," McCarter called as he grabbed a handhold over the edge of the roof.

The men responded at once, letting him know they were in position. With the StarTron scopes they would be a devastating part of the attack, but their primary objective was to keep as many Hezbollah fighters away from the escape path as possible.

McCarter pulled himself over the edge of the building. Manning was already in motion with the SAS men, running out rappeling lines and stripping out of the chute wear. "Ground support," he called as he chased the zipper of his suit down.

"Ready for your go, sir," an Israeli-accented voice responded. Ground support in the form of transport trucks and flank protection had been arranged through Mossad agents already in-country. They lay in wait blocks away.

"All right, gentlemen, let's get it done." McCarter checked his weapons. The SIG Sauer was in place under his left arm. Another rode his right hip. A third was jammed at the back of his waistband. The MP-5 was slung over his left shoulder, and a Gerber knife was thrust into his left boot. Various grenades covered his combat rigging. The flight suits were left piled on the rooftop.

Wearing a pair of thin black leather gloves, McCarter grabbed a rappeling line and braced himself against the side of the building. After verifying that every man was wearing the canary-yellow scarf for identification around his left bicep, the lanky Briton nodded and dropped his Nomex hood into place.

The rope raced through his gloved fingers. He counted the seconds down as he rappeled, flanked by other men. Perspiration gathered on his face and made the headset slippery under his chin. He halted three beats ahead of schedule, standing between windows.

On the first beat he readied the H&K. On the second he propelled himself away from the building, arcing his swing to bring him back toward the window. Shadows moved on the other side of the glass. He had a brief impression of a Hezbollah soldier bringing up an Uzi, then he fired from the hip, using the instinctive target acquisition that had been burned into him during his SAS days.

A line of 9 mm bullets stitched across the glass, punching holes into it before slamming into the man on the other side.

McCarter smashed through the window, spilling through the weakened glass easily. He released the grappling rope as he threw himself prone and brought the submachine gun into play.

The floor had once been leased by an American investment company prior to the Beirut Massacre in 1983. The walls had been mounted on swivel tracks so that office space could be made as it was needed. Few real walls remained.

McCarter stitched a figure eight into the line of terrorists turning to face him. Three men went down at once. Another short burst took care of the fourth. He changed magazines, then got to his feet and removed a flash-bang grenade from his harness. He stepped to the nearest wall, glanced around the corner and saw a knot of terrorists running from a cross fire engineered at the other end of the building. He pulled the tab on the flash-bang and hurled it ahead of the men, then turned away and counted down. The magnesium-based concussion grenade went off with a dull roar, splashing light against the walls.

After flipping the MP-5 to selective fire, McCarter whirled and triggered rounds into his targets. The subsonic slugs punched the Hezbollah gunners to the floor. The

Briton spread his men out with a hand signal as he stepped toward the modular prison that had been formed with the movable walls. He heard terrified screams on the other side of the door, alerting him at once that something had gone wrong.

"Gary," he said, keying the transmitter button.

"Go."

"Got a bit of a problem, mate, so figure on a delay at this end."

"What is it?"

"Don't know at this point. How are things there?"

"Secured. Battening down the hatches now."

"Good. You boys get a move on and get those people to safety."

"Can't leave you."

"Yes, you can. Do it. You start looking back and you're going to lose lives. Seventh floor, mate, just as we planned. Radio the transport chaps when you're in position."

"If you're not there when we get this cleaned up—"

"We will be. Now move your arse." McCarter took a small chunk of C-4 from a pocket and applied it around the door lock. He used a press-in detonator. When it popped, all that remained of the locking mechanism was the hole and a fistful of metal on the floor.

He kicked the door open and ducked inside, the MP-5 up and ready. The room was in darkness, filled with the smell of captivity and close quarters for too many people. Someone lit a candle. McCarter followed the hands and saw the old man's face that came with them.

A harsh bark of Farsi drowned the frightened cries of the captives. The old man looked over his shoulder, then said, "They say they'll kill the women if you and your men don't surrender immediately."

McCarter looked past the man. Draped in shadows in the center of the hostages lying on the floor were two Hezbollah terrorists, each holding a pistol to a woman's head. One of them was framed by a window. He counted windows in his mind, structuring the building from his memory.

The man standing nearer the center of the room said something in Farsi. "He wants you to put your weapon down," the old man translated. "Please. He's holding my wife. He'll kill her. You don't know what these animals are like."

"I know exactly what they're like," McCarter replied as he knelt to place the submachine gun on the floor. He twisted his head and activated the transmit button. "Mr. Barker," he whispered.

"I have him in my sights, sir."

"And the other?"

"Not from me or my mate. The man near the window has to go down first."

"Then I have him. These men are going down now. No bargaining."

"Understood, sir."

The terrorist holding the old woman shouted again. "He says—" the old man started.

"I catch the drift. Mr. Barker—*now*!"

Glass tinkled and the gunner nearest the window tumbled to the floor. McCarter swept the 9 mm pistol from his hip and fired as soon as the weapon cleared leather. A neat round hole appeared off-center between the terrorist's eyes. His nerveless fingers dropped the pistol and he fell away from the woman. The old man cried out in alarm, then ran across the room to hug his wife.

"Good shooting, Mr. Barker," McCarter said into the headset.

"You, too, sir. That was a bit of a squeaker."

Removing his mask, McCarter identified himself and, with help from the other men who'd secured the floor, got the hostages moving. Holding to the rescue plan, they guided them down the stairway and ignored the elevators. It was too easy to booby-trap the shafts, to frag a passing cage. Six people had to be carried, and many of the hostages were too weak with physical and emotional exhaustion to help.

McCarter helped carry one man as they brought up the rear. They'd cut sections of the carpet to use as makeshift gurneys.

"David," Manning called over the headset.

"On our way, mate."

"We've started evacuation now."

"The terrorists?"

"Holed up in the bottom of the building. The ones that are left. There can't be many. We made a clean sweep of our floor."

At the seventh story McCarter followed the rush of people down the hallway to the escape window where an inflatable fire escape slide had been triggered. It looked like a giant canvas vacuum hose. People slid down its length to street level almost eighty feet below, where they were rushed into the waiting transport trucks manned by the Israelis. The inflatable ramp had been Kurtzman's idea, discovered in his perusal of the blueprints.

Passing his hostage along, McCarter hit the transmit button. "Mr. Hoskins?"

"Finishing up now, sir."

"Find anything?"

"No, sir. Clean as a whistle."

"Then get down here, mate, and stop lollygagging about up there." He peered out another window to watch the ground-floor evacuation process. The SAS snipers ran full tilt from the surrounding buildings and set up a defensive perimeter around the transport trucks. When the first vehicle pulled away, four of the SAS joined it as a protective guard. The other four did the same with the second.

Hoskins came out of the stairway in a staggering run, still carrying the Radiac Set. Two men followed him.

"Rihani?" McCarter asked.

"Not among the dead, sir."

"That would have been asking too much," Manning said.

"Get aboard, Mr. Hoskins," McCarter directed.

Hoskins nodded, taking the Radiac and his two men with him. They vanished quickly down the mouth of the slide just as a small group of Hezbollah terrorists came up in an elevator.

The dinging of the arrival bell alerted the Stony Man warriors. McCarter and Manning dived to either side of the window, going to ground as they yanked their weapons into target acquisition. Forty-five-caliber slugs from the Hezbollah Ingrams ripped plaster from the walls and threw white dust all over the corridor.

Triggering the MP-5 on full-auto, McCarter pinned the gun crew back inside the elevator cage. Manning lobbed a grenade, initiating a full flight out of the cage a heartbeat before the explosion. Flames and the concussive force blew the quartet of gunners to the ground. Combined fire from the two submachine guns put the Hezbollah fanatics down for the count.

McCarter forced himself to his feet.

"McCarter!" Hoskins's voice bellowed in his ear. "Get your arse out of the building! *Now!*"

Peering over the edge of the window, McCarter saw the group of terrorists pour from the lobby of the building. Withering fire from the SAS commandos sent them scurrying back for the moment, but the exchange of fire rapidly escalated. "Gary, get moving."

Manning hit the slide in a flying leap. Hot on his heels, McCarter felt a second of disorientation as the canvas tunnel swallowed him. Then everything consisted of gravity and acceleration, giving him a sense of being even less in control than when in a dive from an airplane.

"Hold tight, mates," Hoskins called out. "Those bastards have got themselves a grenade launcher."

"Son of a bitch," Manning said, flailing for control.

A shiver ran through the tunnel, rippling under McCarter just before an explosion of sound chased them down the circumference. Fire ate away the canvas walls they'd just passed through, then rushed down at them like a settling cloud.

McCarter hit the street feetfirst, stumbling from the combined confusion and momentum. He felt a big hand clamp around his shoulder as someone gunned an engine nearby.

"Begging your pardon, sir," Hoskins said as he dragged McCarter onto the running board of the transport truck getting under way.

"No disrespect taken, Mr. Hoskins."

"As you say, sir." Hoskins unlimbered his submachine gun and sprayed the lobby area of the hotel.

At least a half-dozen bodies were strung out in the street.

McCarter began to fire his weapon as soon as Hoskin's magazine cycled dry. Manning was on the other side of the truck cab firing above the heads of pedestrians to clear the way for the truck.

The Israeli driver cut his turn wide, jarring the truck and its contents. Alarmed screams sounded from the people in the back. Manning cursed. So far there was no sign of vehicular pursuit.

"I trust we got them all out, Mr. Hoskins," McCarter said.

"Aye, sir," the SAS replied as he rammed a fresh magazine home while he clung to the truck's mirror. "But I'm thinking we still got us a bonny little chase ahead."

"That we have, Mr. Hoskins," McCarter agreed. "That we have indeed."

CHAPTER THIRTY-THREE

Beirut, Lebanon

Fifth Day—5:48 a.m.

The tunnel was an outdated sewer line. It smelled equally of use and disuse and the bottom was covered with a thin film of slick molds that would never truly disappear until the whole line was excavated and bared under the sun. Six feet across and dead-ending near the underground section of the abandoned factory where the third group of hostages was being held, it made an ideal escape route.

Mack Bolan squatted, balanced on the balls of his feet, and watched the two Spetznaz commandos applying thick lines of thermite to the metal wall that blocked the tunnel. He held his Beretta sniper rifle at the ready, canted forward for instant use. There would only be a couple heartbeats of time that would truly be theirs before Hezbollah regrouped and arranged a counterstrike that would result in the loss of hostages' lives. He breathed easily, concentrating on the skills he needed rather than the possible outcome.

Kurtzman's blueprints had been complete up to a point. The latest update on them had been seven years ago when a realty company had the factory on the market. When he'd first seen the plans, the Executioner had been certain of where the hostages would be held. But there was no way to account for the changes or additions that might have been made during the intervening years.

He pictured it in his mind again as the two men finished their prep work. When the metal wall went down, the main entrance to the rest of the factory would be east, to his left, and twenty feet above him. With the main entrance marked as 12 on a clock face, two more observation posts were at 4 and 8. A narrow railing ran around the room.

He wore a black Nomex jumpsuit with a light blue scarf above his bicep. SIG Sauer 9 mm pistols rode in shoulder leather and in his right boot. Smoke, CS gas and flash-bang grenades were attached to his harness. He'd vetoed explosive grenades because of the enclosed space. The concussive force of the flash-bangs would be disorienting enough. The team didn't need to deal with trauma-induced casualties this early in the play.

Zhenka Kalinin squatted next to him, an identical sniper rifle across his knees. In the darkness and dressed in the Nomex suit, the Spetznaz commander was one more black shadow crouched with the others.

The Spetznaz team moved away from the wall and took up a pair of matched flare guns. "On your command," Kalinin said softly.

Bolan nodded. "Let's do it." He leaned forward, resting his knuckles in the muck to give himself forward momentum when the time came, not wanting to get his palm slippery. When it came down to his sniping ability, that palm was as much a part of the machinery as the rifle. He sensed the movement of the men behind him.

One of the Spetznaz commandos ignited the thermite. Bolan looked away. Even without direct sight the glare was damaging his night vision. He'd known it would when he set up the assault.

"Burn through achieved!" one of the commandos yelled.

Launching himself forward, Bolan slammed his left shoulder into the circular area and felt the heavy round of metal give way before him. Frightened shrieks, curses and demands to know what was happening met him on the other side just before superheated metal clanged onto the concrete floor. Off balance, he went with the momentum, falling into a roll that spilled him closer to the center of the room. He came up on his feet, lifting the sniper rifle to his shoulder as he aimed in the direction of the main entrance.

A shadow carrying a gun and wearing traditional Arab robes hurried to the railing to see what was going on. The Executioner triggered three rounds in selective fire as quickly as he could, the noise echoing like rolling thunder inside the enclosed room. The shadow grabbed its chest and fell slowly over the railing.

The screams and cries of help drowned out all other sound. Bolan was aware of Kalinin coming up beside him to set up a full periphery of fire.

Two flares, one emerald-green and the other cherry-red, exploded against the ceiling almost forty feet overhead. The room was lighted instantly in seething color.

Using open sights instead of telescopic ones to provide a better sweeping field of fire, Bolan located his next target. He worked in quick succession, going for torso shots in groups of two. The butt of the rifle smashed again and again into his shoulder. He rode out the recoil as naturally as breathing, settling into his next shot immediately.

Autofire raked the ceiling for brief seconds as the Hezbollah fighters reacted to the flares as if they were a physical threat. Sparks flew from the metal girders.

A bullet smashed into Bolan's Kevlar vest, but he ignored the pain of its impact. A head peeped above the concrete footing of the railing. The Executioner squeezed the rifle's trigger and put a round between the man's eyes. He followed up with another bullet to the man's throat as the body tumbled backward.

Within seconds the railing was clear of live enemies. Bolan recharged his weapon as he checked on the progress of the containment team. The three men had already reached the main-floor observation post. Two of them pulled nail guns and braces from their chest packs. The third man was dropping the yard-long metal reinforcement bar into place as the other two fired their nail guns to set the braces. The third man swung his MP-5 loose to provide coverage from any threat left in the room. When the nail gunners had the last of the concrete spikes in place, they dropped the power tools and raised their weapons.

More of the Russian commandos were moving full out, checking the remaining doors they were aware of. Apparently all the other entrances had been sealed shut.

Bolan wasn't surprised. The hostage operation had been efficiently planned. He looked over his shoulder and saw Grimaldi already urging the hostages up onto their feet and into the tunnel. Asbestos blankets had been thrown over the charred metal edges to protect the hostages.

They had to use two of the body bags they'd brought along. The victims were a fiftyish woman who'd died from a heart attack and a young boy who'd succumbed to advanced blood poisoning. It had been decided that the bodies were coming out, too. Nothing would be left behind to further torture the minds of the people who had been victimized by the crisis.

Strapping the sniper rifle across his shoulders, Bolan clambered up the rope ladder hanging from the observation deck, followed by Kalinin. At the top he dismissed the men guarding the door. Bullets thudded into the steel plates but didn't penetrate.

He used his fighting knife to rip the air-conditioning duct work from the wall. The ventilation shaft was large enough for him to pass through. He crawled into it without hesitation, checking what he could see against the memorized blueprints. Even with the hostages safely out of the way, there remained the question and threat of Rihani.

His own breathing and that of Kalinin echoed in his ears as he climbed. Dull thumpings from repeated assaults on the barred door rattled around them. Greasy dust adhered to his fingers and palms. He flicked on a dim penlight and continued on.

An explosion jarred the ventilation shaft and sent hot air billowing around him, letting him know the Spetznaz group had cleared the hostages and had set off the C-4 surprise package they'd left behind to dissuade any pursuers who weren't killed outright.

Moments later he found the access panel he'd been searching for. Set near the ceiling, it opened up over a small office containing a desk, a cot and three chairs. The smell of incense and burning wax hung heavily over the room.

Levering the knife, he strained arm muscles until fastenings popped under the pressure. Then he swung the grillwork over his head and dropped down into the room.

Footsteps echoed out in the hall as fleeing men raced by. Kalinin opened the canvas bag one of the Spetznaz had given him. The metal surface of the Radiac Set gleamed in the penlight's beam. He clamped the earphones on his head as he detached the wand and ran it over the room.

Bolan took up a position at the closed door, holding the rifle across his chest.

"It's still hot," Kalinin said as he ran the wand around the room.

"They had it here," the Executioner stated in a flat voice.

"So it would appear. But it's not here now."

Judging the hallway to be clear, Bolan swung the door open. Confirmation of the existence of something radioactive had been reached. Identification and safe destruction of the nuclear property remained. And to do that they were going to have to find Rihani to uncover what exactly it was they were looking for.

He slung the sniper rifle and palmed the silenced 9 mm pistol from his shoulder rig, then stepped out into the hallway. Urgency whispered in his ear, but he ignored it. They were already straddling a fast-breaking play. Any move on his part to speed up things had to end in disaster. He slipped the headset out of a protective pocket and slid it on. "Jack?"

No one answered.

He tried again, then figured when he didn't get a response that Grimaldi and the hostages were still deep in the tunnel. He left the frequency open and jogged toward the area of the factory Hezbollah had converted into their motor pool. Maybe Rihani had only left when the assault on the hostage area began. He could still be nearby.

With Kalinin flanking him on the other side of the hallway, Bolan followed the hallway automatically, mapping his path in his head through the maze of blueprints he'd absorbed prior to the operation. He jogged right, then cut through what had once been a cafeteria to the door on the opposite wall that opened out into the shipping area from the small warehouses in back. He paused only to sweep away the lighted fluorescent tubes illuminating the room. They burst with hollow pops as they struck the scarred floor.

Taking shelter beside the doorframe, he twisted the knob and pulled the door open. The sound of engines turning over and tires screeching filled the room.

He stepped out onto the small railed porch five feet above ground level. A short series of stairs stretched away to his right. The large room was unlighted, but headlights from three different vehicles stabbed into the darkness.

"Striker," Grimaldi called.

"Jack," Bolan responded. "I need a mobile team now. Get it to the on-site motor pool and let's shut it down."

"Roger."

A warning cry in Arabic rang out above the din of engines. Bolan broke left, heaving himself over the railing. He landed on his feet and pointed the pistol like a finger. It chugged against his palm five times in quick succession, taking down the two men pulling at the chains to take up the folding garage door.

Kalinin had already dived for the bottom of the stairs as a stream of autofire ripped sparks from the cinder-block walls where they'd been standing. Metal ripped as bullets punched through the door leading back to the cafeteria. The Spetznaz commander was coolly squeezing off shots from the Beretta sniper rifle with deadly effect.

Bolan ripped a smoker free of his webbing and tossed it against the wall on the other side of the room. It popped and exploded an inky black cloud that seemed to absorb the headlights. There were at least nine vehicles inside the room, including the massive bulk of an RV.

A sedan shot forward, aiming for the stalled garage doors. Breaking from the scant cover he'd been using, Bolan drew his boot gun and ran to intercept the car. He stepped in close as gunners in the passenger and rear seats struggled for a shot at him. Bringing up the SIG Sauer, he leveled it across his other arm and emptied the double-stacked magazine, scoring so closely on his target that he chipped a plate-size hole out of the windshield.

The sedan skidded out of control, broadsiding the garage doors as the Executioner rolled out of the way. Steam escaped from the burst radiator. Still on the move, the warrior leathered the empty pistol and yanked a flash-bang from his rigging. He tossed it into the sedan as the gunners struggled to recover from the impact, then unloaded the rest of the magazine of his other gun as the explosion of light and concussive force suppressed all other sounds.

Bolan reloaded both pistols and checked on Kalinin. The Spetznaz commander was holding his own, but just barely. Both of them stood a chance of being overrun by the Hezbollah fighters remaining in the motor pool.

"Striker," Grimaldi called.

"Go."

"Coming through, big guy. Don't be anywhere near those garage doors."

Bolan hit the transmit button. "It's blocked, Jack. You can't come through there."

"Trust me, pal, it ain't gonna matter who's standing there."

Before Bolan could say anything else, a titanic *whomph* of force screamed into the garage doors and punched on through to the sedan. It halted for just a moment, then gears ground and the force became irresistible again, emerging through the smoke and wreckage as a Land Rover with a full metal cage stretched around the nose.

Spetznaz poured out of the Rover dressed in full Nomex, looking like escaped wraiths from hell as their MP-5s flared to burning life.

For a moment confusion and death reigned inside the warehouse. Nine-millimeter signatures signed a finale to the Hezbollah unit stationed within the factory. Autofire trickled down to selective shots, then died away entirely, leaving only the stench of cordite, blood and death.

Despite their body armor two of the Spetznaz commandos were down with serious wounds. Kalinin tended to them with his men, then joined Bolan in the search of the dead.

"Rihani's not here," Grimaldi stated. "One of the hostages I talked to in the tunnel said Rihani and a group of his men had taken six hostages and left some time ago."

"He took his prize with him, too," Bolan said grimly as he stepped out of the RV. He wiped blood from his cheek, surprised to discover it was his own.

"But it was here," Kalinin said, waving the wand of the Radiac Set. "And some of these men handled it."

"What about Gray and Deering?" Bolan asked.

"Got 'em both. Gray was a little more happy to see us than Deering. The major seemed to be a little miffed that it turned out the Russians had rescued him." Grimaldi smiled at the memory. "But he got over it quick. Then he developed a bad case of take-charge-itis. I had to help him over that one myself. If I was regular GI-issue, I'd be headed for Leavenworth when we get back." He rubbed his knuckles absently.

"The transport team?" Bolan asked.

"Already en route. I split up the team and they're riding shotgun on the vans."

"Then let's move it," the Executioner said as he gazed around the cooling battle zone. "We're losing time. Rihani's still out there. When we get the hostages to safety, then we'll work on ferreting him out." He shouldered the sniper rifle and took the lead.

He could almost feel the madman in his mind, could almost follow the path of twisted logic that had to be propelling Rihani. It was breaking down quick now—hunter and hunted—and he knew he had to maintain his warrior's edge to see his mission through.

CHAPTER THIRTY-FOUR

The Pentagon, Washington, D.C.
Fifth Day—10:41 p.m.

At any other time, Hal Brognola supposed, he'd have been amused at the alacrity with which the security guards jumped to attention.

The corridor was wide and soundproofed. Not even the tread of the President or the half-dozen dark-suited Secret Service men who trailed him was audible. A chill permeated the air.

Brognola knew it was primarily to protect the electronic equipment in the Pentagon war room, but it lingered inside his bones. That part, he knew, stemmed from his own fears.

A general the Justice man almost recognized stepped around the door to the war room and fired off a snappy salute. Two captains flanked him, young enough to be his sons. "Begging the commander's pardon," the general said, "if you'd let us know you were planning on coming, we could've made more proper arrangements."

The President returned the salute but never broke stride. "Yes, I know, General Eastep, but if I'd let you know I was coming, it wouldn't have been a surprise, would it?"

"No, sir."

Brognola stared in fascination at the amount of activity bustling through the large room. Dozens of people were at different chains of desks monitoring private screens. Still more displays lighted up whole walls. The tension inside the room almost crackled.

"Have your chief communications officer meet me upstairs," the President ordered, nodding toward the balcony overlooking the entire area. "Then see if you can rustle up General Howard and Admiral Keeler to join me on the QT. I've got a few surprises to spring on you boys."

"I figured you might when I heard you were here after all those warning lights flashed on in the Middle East." Eastep turned and made his way through the crowd.

"Your first time here, Hal?" the President asked as he ascended the metal stairs leading to the balcony area.

"No, sir." Brognola followed, checking his watch. So far the rescue operations had been in effect for just slightly over half an hour. Questions zinged through his mind, but he had no answers. The major one was if Hezbollah had access to backpack nukes, why hadn't they used them yet? Even as sharp as the teams were that they'd sent in for the recovery, he couldn't fool himself into believing the danger had passed.

"I don't like it here," the President admitted as he came to a halt on the balcony.

Below them the work continued at a frantic pace. Voices buzzed into a confused monotone. It always reminded Brognola of the Houston space shot footage he'd seen. There was nothing else to compare it to. The scenes on the walls changed as different satellite tracking stations were used.

The President leaned on the balcony railing. "This is too much at the heart of things. Like a sentient organism's central nervous system. Only buttons are punched here to signal a fight-or-flight response. That takes conscious thought. I don't like making that choice." He paused, lowering his voice. "Don't get me wrong. I'll make that choice if it comes to that. But there's something wrong about so much power, such vast destructive capabilities being jammed into one little place where so much could go wrong."

"I know what you mean," Brognola said. "It's a little like sitting on top of a powder keg with a match in both hands."

"It's a lot like sitting on top of a powder keg with a match in both hands." The President shifted, taking in a view of the screens. "I know it's never been far from your mind since we heard. How do you think it's going?"

"I don't know. With the addition of the nukes, how can you call a win a win unless you have everything in hand?"

"The nukes have clouded the issue."

"That's putting it mildly."

"I know."

"We haven't even got them out of the country yet."

"Well, we're here to do something about that right now."

A young communications officer double-timed it up the stairs, coming to prompt attention in front of the President. His salute was crisp and neat. "Sir, I've been assigned to see to your needs."

"I want a modem-equipped computer system installed up here immediately, and at least five telephones with separate lines."

"Yes, sir."

"And I want covert patch-throughs to the leaders of the Soviet Union, Britain and Israel."

"Yes, sir."

"You're dismissed, son."

The communications officer saluted, executed an about-face and vanished. He passed two men in Army and Navy dress on his way down the stairs, firing off a salute in mid-stride without missing a step.

The President shook hands with the new arrivals, then made introductions without specifying exactly what interest Brognola represented. Four privates muscled up a rectangular table and five chairs with General Eastep close behind. Generals Howard and Eastep sat down, along with Admiral Keeler.

Brognola took his seat a little apart from the others. Another band of men arrived and quickly installed the equipment the President had requested, bringing the computer on-line with a splash of color. Someone left a pitcher of ice water and a coffeepot on the table. A stack of cups sat beside the service.

The President remained standing. He put his hands together in front of him. "Gentlemen, as you're aware, there's a situation in the Middle East that's been on all of our minds these past few days. Things appear to have come to a head in this matter."

"I'll say," Admiral Keeler said. "That goddamn electric toteboard scoring military activity in those countries is lit up like a Christmas tree. Something big is going on over there."

"I've been in contact with the State Department, sir," General Howard said. "From what I've learned several of the Middle Eastern countries are up in arms about possible American military involvement over there. However, I can tell you that none of our boys have anything to do with it. We've stayed well within our designated boundaries since the Kuwait crisis."

"If you ask me," Eastep stated, "it's those Israelis. I've heard they're creating some kind of confusion over there. I wouldn't put it past them for a moment to be acting on their own in this present situation."

The President leaned forward and spoke into a microphone mounted near the railing. A raspy rattling drew Brognola's attention. As he watched, curtains pulled back to reveal a large-screen TV mounted in the wall even as other curtains moved around to shut off the room below.

"Gentlemen," the President said as the screen came on, detailing troop movement in and around Lebanon, "It's not just the Israelis. It's all of us."

Brognola could tell from the expressions of the other men that he was the only one there who wasn't surprised.

"The Israelis, the British, the Russians and the United States all have covert teams operating within Lebanese borders tonight. It's called Operation Desert Lance, and its purpose is the safe extraction of the hostages held by Hezbollah."

"Where did you find the men for something like this?" Howard asked.

"At this point, General, that's unimportant. I found them. They're there. And we're working on an exfiltration route through the Israelis."

"Mr. President," Keeler said as he leaned forward and placed beefy arms on the table, "don't you realize you're offering those Middle Eastern nations unfriendly to the United States, not to mention Israel, every excuse they need to shoot down those hostages where they find them?"

"Of course I realized that. So did the leaders of the other countries involved. We elected to take the chance and bring those people home."

Howard started to say something.

The President held up a hand and silenced the man. "There's no time to go into all of this now. At a later date, perhaps, there'll be a full debriefing. For now I want you to make sure those people have every chance we can give them. Operation Desert Lance is a joint venture involving the Russian navy and air force, and the American Army and Navy in the area, as well as British units around Saudi Arabia. The Israelis have already beefed up their border guards along the exfiltration point."

"How come I've never heard of Operation Desert Lance?" Howard asked.

"This was put together strictly on a need-to-know basis, General. Bluntly put, until now you didn't need to know. Don't agonize over it. Accept it."

"But, sir," Keeler protested, "how could any operation be put together without the Navy's knowledge? And when you're speaking of Middle Eastern affairs, I *am* the Navy."

"The people I used have resources beyond your wildest imaginings," the President replied.

Brognola resisted a slight smile, wondering how Kurtzman and his team would feel about being referred to as resources beyond someone's wildest imaginings. He figured Price would share his humor even if Bear didn't.

"But the positions of my ships," Keeler said.

"And the strength of my men," Howard added.

"Are all known to those who need to know," the President said. "Trust me. Hal, if you please."

Brognola stepped forward, picked up the telephone, punched out the special number Kurtzman had arranged to feed through and clipped the receiver to the computer modem. He two-fingered his way across the keyboard, conscious of the attention he was receiving. Once he had the file name punched in, he pressed Enter.

The monitor scanned through an electronic mountain of material, flipping faster than eye blinks through maps, intel and conjecture.

"Gentlemen," the President said, "you now have Operation Desert Lance in your hands. Orders in your names have already been sent to your squadrons. I want it reviewed, implemented and fully operational within thirty minutes. Dismissed."

Brognola was appreciative of the professional attitude displayed by the men as they got up to leave. It was like having an atomic bomb dumped in your lap and being told to shove it through the nearest window and hope for the best. The comparison, in light of recent discoveries, left him cold. He poured himself a cup of coffee and hoped it would melt some of the chill. "We're pushing this thing right to the edge of war, handling it this way," he said softly.

The President sighed. "I know. But at this point there's no other way to handle it. If I went to Congress and pushed for anything more direct on the part of all the military, they'd waffle around with it for days, searching for every pro and con they could find. The nuclear devices are the wild card in this. If we don't recover them, we can still lose even after we've won. And that's putting the cart before the horse by assuming we'll recover those hostages without further loss. No, on this we've just got to stay the course, follow our own strategy and pray for the best." He glanced at Brognola. "Are your teams aware of the existence of the nuclear arms?"

"Not yet. Since we've learned of it, there's been no direct-line communications between Stony Base or any of the men in the field. Striker's aware of the possibility, though, because he requested Radiac Sets from the Russians and has implemented them with the teams. The soonest they'll know for sure is at the rendezvous at Damour."

"And by then they may be too far away to effect a successful counterstrike against Hezbollah."

"I know those men, sir," Brognola said. "And I know that once they're aware of those weapons they'll turn over every rock in Lebanon until they find them."

"Yes, but if that part of the world goes to hell in a hand basket, they're going to be right there on the front line."

"Mr. President," Brognola said solemnly, "when the time comes, those men wouldn't want to be anywhere else."

"STONY ONE to Stony Base. Over."

Barbara Price settled the cordless headset into place, then keyed the transmit button. "Go, Stony One. You have Stony Base. Over." She glanced at Aaron Kurtzman, who still manned the computer console. He nodded, letting her know he'd linked up to the incoming communication, too.

Bolan's words were fatigued and broken up by the road sounds and rumble of voices in the background. "What's the story with Phoenix One and Phoenix Two? Over."

"Both recoveries were successful," Price said. "How are you? Over."

"We lost two, Stony Base. They were gone before we got there."

She interrupted him. "We knew that was a possibility going in. Over."

"Doesn't make it any easier to accept. Over."

"I know. Over." Price could feel the pain in the big man's words. It wasn't a physical thing. Someone who didn't know him would never know it was there. Men like Mack Bolan and the other Stony Man warriors weren't demigods who marched off to face death and came back unscarred. They were men who felt pain and got scared and fought to deny the finality of death just like anyone else. But there was a driving force, a passion for life and freedom, that exceeded those mortal limitations just as it exceeded their own needs. It was that same force that carried them from battle to battle, conquering whatever defeats they faced within themselves.

"We picked up some hot readings on the Radiac Set at our previous twenty," Bolan said. "Can you provide intel? Over."

"That's a roger, Stony One. According to intel from our Wonderland connection, you've got the possibility of six SADMs within enemy hands. Over."

For a moment there was no answer. Then, "Our main target wasn't home when we went knocking. Any idea where he might have flown to? Over."

"No. *His* Wonderland connection is still operative, too, but Able is close to shutting him down. Over."

"Have they been informed about the SADMs? Over."

"Yes, but there's no reason to think one has been smuggled in-country. Over."

"Our target murdered people right before our eyes while he was miles away at the time," Bolan cut in. "Don't make the mistake of underrating him now. Over."

"Of course. You're right, Stony One. Over."

Bolan sighed. "I'm sorry. It didn't have to sound like that. I just—"

"No apologies accepted here, soldier. Your views are duly logged and noted, and entirely on the mark. I stand corrected. Over."

"As long as you're still standing," Bolan said softly. "Over."

Price smiled and let it show in her voice. "Stay hard, Stony One. All we have to do now is count down the numbers until this nightmare's run its course. Over."

"This is one nightmare that won't be over until our target is a confirmed fatality. Over."

Kurtzman shook his head and pointed at the screen at the other end of the room.

"That may not be possible, Stony One," Price said as she stepped toward the computer console. "Desert Lance comes to completion when we have those people out of there. If our target doesn't surface by then, it's a no-go operationally. Packrat and Skyhook have enough resources to pull you out of the area. They're in no position to refurbish another in-country trek. Over."

"If we don't take our quarry down," Bolan said, "then we've made a wasted trip. Everything we've worked to achieve could go up in nuclear smoke minutes after we've cleared the area. I'm not ready to settle for that, and I'm betting there are a few others over here who feel the same. Over."

"Think about it before you commit. You'll be going in alone. Over."

"It's been done before. Over."

"You'll get everything we've got to give from this end, Stony One. You know you can count on that. Over."

"I know. I don't like to countermand the program after we've hit it in full stride, and you're aware of that. But I couldn't sit idly by on something like this. Over."

"Understood. Over."

"I'll call again when we reach the rendezvous point. Stony One out."

CHAPTER THIRTY-FIVE

Washington, D.C.

Fifth Day—12:57 a.m.

Carl Lyons was impatient and growing more so. He shifted in the dark, grumbled beneath his breath and scanned the warehouse with his infrared binoculars. Nearly twenty-four hours had passed since the incident with Terranova. Able Team had followed a tortuous and nearly buried trail of movement and countermovement on the part of Hezbollah to the present location. If not for Terranova's information, they'd never have been able to pick up the trail as quickly. And the only thing they had working for them was the ticking clock Rihani had set into motion. Over sixteen hours remained before the deadline. Trying to cover AIPAC was a nightmare he didn't want to consider. The Jewish lobbying group had been hard at work in Washington since the whole situation had kicked off.

According to everything their combined efforts could turn up, Hezbollah was encamped in the Smiles Ice Cream warehouse across the street.

"Ironman," Pol Blancanales called softly.

"Go," Lyons answered into the headset.

"Gadgets says he just neutralized the perimeter security systems. Wanted you to know from the setup that it looked like we're going to be facing more sophisticated stuff once we're inside."

"By the time we're inside," Lyons said, "it's not going to really matter. They're going to know we're there. Leo?"

"Go."

"Got a readout on the available manpower?"

"I've counted eight guys so far. Sounds like too many for a night crew and not enough for an assault team waiting in the wings for the call to action. Probably there to keep the back door open just in case."

"I agree," Lyons muttered. He cursed again. Having to dodge the Mossad group that had been clinging to the shadows and their backtrail had cost them time, too. "Well, we're not going to find anything out until we open it up and see what squirms out from underneath. Any sign of our buddies, the Mossad?"

"No."

Running his hands over his equipment rig, Lyons moved out at a half crouch. He was clad in night black, his face darkened with combat cosmetics to blend in with the shadows. The Colt Python rode his right hip, a Colt Government Model was in shoulder leather and the Derringer Semmerling was tucked up the sleeve of his left forearm. A Gerber Mark II hung upside down on his chest rigging, and his CAR-15 was strapped across his back. He carried a flexible telescopic pole in his hands.

An eight-foot-high fence ran around the paved parking and work area of the warehouse. Y-shaped barbed wire strands flared out at the top, making the three-foot width a danger, as well. Even without the motion detectors Schwarz had taken out of commission, the fence was still a sizable risk.

And Lyons knew he was carrying too much weight to make it easy. He hit the transmit button on the headset. "Leo, I'm in position."

"Hold on," Turrin whispered. "I've got a guard breaking the routine."

Lyons knelt in the brush of the vacant lot across the street. They were east of the city now, almost down to the Virginia border. "Give me the go when you get it." He strained his eyes, trying to see the man the little Fed had spotted.

"It's okay," Gadgets called back. "The guy's just taking a leak against the side of the building. There he goes. He's trotting back up to rejoin the ranks."

"You're in the clear, Ironman," Turrin said.

Lyons stood and leaned into his footsteps, getting his forward momentum built up despite the curbs hugging the sides of the street. The telescopic pole bounced like a Marlin-attacked fishing rod at either end. He exhaled as he planted the pole at the edge of the sidewalk, feeling it go deep into the spongy ground. For a moment he thought it was going to slide through until it hit the fence. Then it caught, bending the pole.

He went with the spring of force, arcing his body over the razor-sharp strands of barbs as it propelled him forward. He flailed for balance, but couldn't find it with all of the weight strapped around him, and came down hard, landing on his side with enough impact to drive what little air remained from his lungs. Rolling at once, he stretched out full-length under the concealing cover of a row of trucks over ten feet away. Winded, he lay quietly for a moment and let the air come back into him.

"Ironman," Blancanales said.

"Here."

"In one piece?"

"Don't know about that yet," Lyons said as he forced himself into a crouch. "Still in the same package, though."

Lyons made his way to the gate house fronting the main street that ran at a ninety-degree angle to the one he'd crossed. The gate house was a small cinder-block structure with a wooden door and two windows on opposite sides of the building from the entrance. It wasn't air-conditioned. The windows were open.

The Able Team warrior fell into quiet repose in the shadows along the blank side of the wall. He slid the Gerber free as he sidled around the corner of the building and peered through the open window.

One man was inside, sitting on a metal folding chair, an M-16 within easy reach. Lyons grabbed the man's shirt-front and pulled, dragging him through the window and onto the rough pavement. His hand clamped over the guard's mouth while he slipped the keen edge of the Gerber between the third and fourth ribs. A few brief spasms later the man lay still. Lyons opened the door and carried the body back inside the gate house. He wiped his hands clean on the dead man's clothes, then keyed the small gate open beside the drive-through one.

"Olly, olly, oxen free," Lyons called softly into the mike.

Three black shadows tore free from the urban jungle across the street and sped through the man-size door one at a time. They were all dressed as he was, wearing tan scarves tied around their left arms.

They fanned out as they'd planned, deploying along separate routes, then converging on the huge warehouse. Lyons carried the CAR-15 at the ready as he got into place alongside one of the docks. He scrambled over the edge and rolled to the upper wall. A brief flick of the lockpick later and he'd bypassed the security door and was inside the lighted warehouse.

A pneumatic double-pump heartbeat filled the vastness of the warehouse storage section, issuing from the giant condensers and compressors. Lyons flowed into it, letting the noise—already a part of Hezbollah's sense of their world—be his defense against discovery.

Lines of freezers stood against the walls, and cardboard boxes and wooden pallets were scattered across the concrete floor, making Lyons think the last crew had been let off early. He kept a floor schematic in his head, plotting Blancanales's and Schwarz's paths. Turrin should already be in position on the roof to provide covering fire if they were repelled.

Despite the cool temperature surrounding him, his hands were sweaty from the exertions outside. He wiped them on his Nomex suit and felt the contoured hardness of the body armor beneath.

A Hezbollah guard stepped around the corner. Before the man could yell or reach his holstered weapon, the Stony Man warrior stroked his buttstock across the guy's face and dropped him to the floor. Then he slit the man's throat. No provisions had been made for dealing with prisoners. He ground out the compassion he felt for a helpless enemy and steeled his resolution. It didn't take much addition to realize where his loyalties and duty lay. If they didn't neutralize Hezbollah, a lot more American lives would be forfeited, as well as a certain amount of stability in the Middle East. He stored the body in a freezer and went on, closing in on the freight office located near the front of the building.

Politician waved from behind a stack of ice-cream-cone boxes. Lyons squatted beside him, looking up at the metal ribs of the roof for surprises. Schwarz stepped into place an instant later, finishing off the triangular assault pattern they'd decided to implement against whoever manned the freight office.

Large glass windows surrounded the freight office on three sides. The fourth side was a cinder-block wall. The office was big enough to comfortably hold the nine men inside. They were gathered in chairs and on desktops, watching CNN coverage of the hostage situation in Lebanon. A number of automatic weapons were in evidence.

Lyons didn't like it. Small numbers meant nothing or very little to protect—unless a lot more hardguys were waiting in the wings in the front quarter of the building.

Lyons stood up, remaining well within the shelter of the pallets at his side. He nodded at Blancanales and Schwarz, who both gave him a thumbs-up. Lyons tapped the transmit button on the headset.

"Go," Turrin said.

"It's going down, brother."

"I've got some questionable movement out here, guy."

"Mossad?"

"Maybe. I don't know."

"Have they made you?"

"If they had, I don't think I'd still be up here. This close in, they'd make me as one of the enemy."

"That's a big ten-four. Chalk it up, Leo, 'cause it's going down now. If it is the Mossad, I'd rather take my piece out of the middle than take what they'd leave behind."

"Understood. Good luck."

Lyons left the connection intact, signaling the others to do the same. Then he took a deep breath and bellowed, "FBI, assholes! Get your hands in the air!"

The reaction of the men inside the freight office was frozen for a moment, then skidded right onto the tracks of predictability.

When the first hand wrapped around the barrel of an M-16, Lyons cut loose on full-auto. Five-point-fifty-six millimeter rounds slammed into the glass windows and created even more devastating projectiles.

At least two slugs thundered into Lyons's Kevlar and bruised the flesh beneath. He gritted his teeth at the sudden pain and continued 3-round bursts until he emptied the magazine. Whirling around the corner of the pallets, he exchanged clips, moved the selector to single-fire and dropped the muzzle back into target acquisition.

Only two heads were moving above the wooden sheeting that surrounded the office below the windows. He squeezed the trigger and felt the CAR-15 buck slightly as the man went down. When he swiveled to track the other man, the target had already been dropped.

"Mine," Blancanales said.

"Hot potato going in to flush out anybody playing possum," Schwarz announced.

Lyons glimpsed the grenade as it was lobbed over the shredded front window, and he turned away from the explosion. There was a peal of thunder, then jagged glass splinters thunked solidly into the wooden pallets and cardboard boxes, standing out like quills from a crystal porcupine.

He rushed forward, drawing the Colt from shoulder leather. When he peered through the broken frame of the center window, it was plain that no life remained in any of the bodies. He kept the .45 in his hand as he moved around. "Pol, get that little black box into operation while I see if there are any rats left in the walls."

Blancanales knelt and took off the backpack he wore in addition to his counterterrorist gear. Unzipping it, he brought out the Radiac Set and switched it on.

"Yo, Leo," Lyons called over the headset.

"Go," Turrin said softly.

"Any movement?"

"They're definitely scouting us out, guy."

"Flip over to Channel Nine on the citizen's band and get a couple of troopers into the area. If it is Mossad, I want to lower the chances of a ballistic encounter."

"I'm on it."

"And keep me posted."

"After me, you'll be the first to know."

Lyons smelled the man lying in wait before he saw him. The odor was of cloves and pungent hair oil. He stood near the door leading to the front portion of the warehouse and thumbed back the hammer on the .45. "Gadgets," he whispered over the headset.

"Yeah?"

"I found a possum up here."

"That's me on your heels."

"Move it."

Schwarz moved silently and fell into position on the other side of the door. Ducking low, Lyons raced through the doorway. Enemy fire lanced through the darkness of the reception area in three places. Something hot flamed along the back of Lyons's neck as he lost skin on his elbows going into a prone firing position. He ignored the guy on the opposite wall, hearing the chatter of Schwarz's CAR-15 kick into play as he drew target acquisition on the man standing just inside the doorway.

Schwarz's target went down like a puppet whose strings had been cut, draping around an artificial elm tree and taking it to the floor with him in a flutter of plastic leaves. Punching two hollowpoint .45 ACPs into the chest of the man beside the door, Lyons started to roll, tracking onto the muzzle-flash of the man along the wall separating the reception area from the warehouse. An erratic line of 5.56 mm tumblers speared through the carpet in search of him. He fired as he rolled, centering on the target area until the Colt emptied. The terrorist was shoved back repeatedly into a filing cabinet until he went down in a dark pool of spilled papers and blood.

Lyons got to his feet, shoving a fresh clip into the butt of the .45. He nodded at Schwarz as the man stepped through the door.

"You about done in here?" Schwarz asked.

"Done as I'm going to get," Lyons replied. "Step lively. I make the body count at fourteen."

"Check." Schwarz grinned. "And to think you've got a reputation for losing track of little things like how many rounds you've fired in an engagement."

"Just keeping you older guys on your toes."

"Me and Politician, we're keeping the corn pad companies in business by hanging out with you."

Blancanales cut in before Lyons could think of anything that would pass as witty repartee. "Carl?"

"Go."

"I got readings in one of the freezers."

"A nuke?"

"Beats me. It's gone. There's a melted depression in the ice. Size looks about right, and the readings are on the money for the specs Kurtzman gave us."

"How the hell did that son of a bitch get a backpack nuke into this country?" Lyons asked.

Schwarz clipped a fresh magazine into the CAR-15. "This thing's been in the works for over ten years, guy. If Rihani had it pegged with one of those flesh-and-blood drones he took over years ago, chances are the players he was going to use haven't changed much. As long as you're not trying to waltz out into the public eye, a trained bureaucrat can stay around the business of government for generations. What we've got to deal with is the fact that it's *here*. Now."

"Only one place they'd go, Gadgets."

"I know."

"Going to be a solid gold-plated bitch finding it in time."

"We will. 'Cause we've got no choice. Try telling yourself anything else and you might as well pack it in now."

"I know."

"Me and Pol and Leo, we're in for the long haul."

"And you'll still be dragging ass when it comes to following in my footsteps."

Schwarz grinned. "Now that's what I wanted to hear."

"Fan out. Let's finish it."

Less than three minutes later the premises were secure and
Turrin was on the headset. "War council's broken up,
Carl," the little Fed said in a serious tone. "And the decision doesn't look good for the home team. I see movement
that I can almost define as hostile."

"Stick with it, Leo," Lyons said. "We're clearing out
now. Whatever was here is gone."

"Check. I already got that."

"What about the Washington blues?"

"En route."

"ETA?"

"Ten. Fifteen."

Lyons led the way back into the warehouse where Blancanales was putting away the Radiac Set. He kept the .45
ready in his fist. Working with Schwarz, he glanced through
the accumulation of bodies they'd collected. Faisel wasn't
among them.

"Ironman."

"Go, Leo."

"These guys are using standard two-by-two deployment
formation. Definitely military. Very hostile."

Lyons nodded at Blancanales and Schwarz, waving them
toward the doors. "We're outta here now. Shag ass, Leo."
He followed, dodging around the bulk of an orange forklift as he ran. "Get a fix on the heat and—"

"Incoming!" Turrin yelled.

Lyons flinched as the warning streaked through his eardrum. Then the rest of Turrin's transmission was lost as at least two explosions rattled the warehouse. The concussion threw him to the floor, and he covered his head as parts of the ceiling started to rain over him.

CHAPTER THIRTY-SIX

North of Damour, Lebanon

Fifth Day—9:23 a.m.

"Striker."

"Go, Phoenix One." Mack Bolan stood at the top of the high foothills off the Lebanon Mountains, looking back down the serpentine road the convoy had traveled. He used the communications gear stored in the rear of the jeep that he and Grimaldi were using as a command vehicle.

"We're coming in hot, Striker," Katz said.

The Executioner studied the changing patterns of smoke and dust dogging their backtrail. He keyed the mike. "We didn't make a clean break at this end, either. The enemy was more prepared than we'd given him credit for. And the Syrians appear to be on the verge of taking an active part."

A Land Rover loaded with equipment rocked to an unsure stop next to Bolan's jeep. McCarter and Manning got out, slinging the MP-5s they carried. Both men looked exhausted.

Bolan understood the feeling. It had been a long run. But no matter how bad they felt it, he knew the hostages were feeling even worse. "How are your people holding up?"

"We lost three more," the Phoenix Force leader said. "It couldn't be helped. Pursuit is too close. Iraqi jets have flown over our position five times."

"Understood. What about Rihani?"

"He wasn't in Sidon."

"He wasn't at either place in Beirut, either."

"That doesn't sound good."

"No."

"The hostage team was seriously undermanned at Sidon."

"It was the same in Beirut," Bolan said. "It suggests the hostages weren't the central focus of his strategy, after all."

"A delaying tactic?"

"I think so."

"He has a counterstrike planned. While the armies of the various countries are involved in the exfiltration of the hostages, and with the balance of power in the Middle East, he intends to move in for whatever kill is his final goal."

"Yeah, and they've got the firepower to pull it off." Bolan loosened his combat rigging. It was chafing him in the heat. The Nomex suit felt as if it were melting down around him.

Dust and smoke continued to roil along the backtrail. The warrior estimated that the armored cavalry hammering along in their tracks couldn't be much more than thirty miles behind the convoy. Hezbollah and other interested parties had organized quickly. Or perhaps they'd been expecting the rescue of the hostages.

A Syrian jet streaked by overhead. The Executioner tracked the fighter as it swept by. "How far are you from the rendezvous point, Yakov?"

"Perhaps as much as fifteen minutes."

Bolan glanced at his watch, then at the line of advancing vehicles. "Cut it. We'll meet you there. Deployment will be as we've discussed. This exodus is going to draw a lot of heat from the unfriendly nations surrounding us. Any misstep at this point might well put us under."

"Agreed. See you there."

The warrior hung up the mike and lifted his binoculars again. Below, climbing steadily in pursuit, were a mixed bag of Hezbollah and PLO forces, backed by a growing number of Syrian, Iraqi and Lebanese troops. The armament they had—jeeps, armored cars and tanks—told him they had the blessing and backing of at least one hostile nation. The hostages were prizes too valuable to release without at least a token play for them. American hostages in the Middle East had paralyzed American retaliation a number of times. Terrorists and terrorist governments knew that. He grimaced at the stark realization. Even a token bid for the hostages could result in dozens of innocent deaths.

He turned to the other Stony Man warriors. "Mount up," he said as he clambered into the passenger seat of the command jeep. He held on as Grimaldi released the clutch and caused all four tires to spin in the rocky soil. If Kissinger's teams made the airdrop as planned, they had a chance. No matter which way it went down, though, there were risks shared by everyone.

COWBOY JOHN KISSINGER sat in the cockpit of the Israeli transport plane. He glanced through the dirty windscreen and saw the swell of the Lebanon Mountains dead ahead. They flew well under radar detection, but there were so many ground and aerial troops deployed across the board that confrontation was inevitable.

"Five minutes, sir," the Israeli navigator said.

Kissinger dropped the clipboard onto his abandoned seat and made his way back to the payload area. Parachute-equipped packing crates filled the doorway, containing the matériel Bolan had requested. He listened to the pilot and copilot as they marked the area, counting down the numbers with the navigator. Then he nodded at the man at the door, who slid the hatch open.

Shrugging into a parachute, he strapped his weapons down around him, then—when the final numbers clicked through—he started shoving the crates into the slipstream. He paused to grab a crowbar, then hurled himself out, as well. Four men followed him, one for each of the crates.

The chute opened almost as soon as he was clear of the plane. He watched as all four crates floated down, working the shroud lines until he drifted in their wake.

He hit hard, rolling with the silk until he could cut free. Hiding the parachutes wasn't an option. The armies breathing down the necks of the hostage convoy weren't going to be taken by surprise at this point. Delayed maybe, hurt definitely, but not stopped. The aim here was to buy enough time for the exfiltration teams to connect with the shoreline pickup point eight miles away.

He hefted the crowbar and set to work on the nearest crate, yelling orders at the other members of the team. Boards splintered and fell aside as nails screeched and broke. Each man spread the equipment out in the prearranged manner so that the arriving teams would know where everything was.

The radio in Kissinger's ear crackled for attention. "Go, Wing," he said.

"Packrat, you've drawn the attention of an unfriendly down there," the pilot called out. "You've got an armored personnel carrier bearing down on your present position from the northeast. The crew must have seen your chutes. We'd love to help out, but we've got a couple of Syrian fighters streaking our way."

"Roger, Wing. Take care of yourself up there, and we'll tend to our own rat killing." Kissinger put his crowbar aside and reached into the crate for a LAW-80. "Ten minutes," he told the crew, "and that stuff had better be laid out." They returned to work as he ran toward the advancing APC. He tracked it by the dust it threw into the air, focusing a pair of Bausch & Lombs on it while he slung the rocket launcher over his shoulder.

Heat wavered between him and his target. Gradually the lines grew sharper, became more distinct, merged into the recognizable form of a Russian-made APC.

He went to ground as it continued to rumble toward him. He estimated it at twelve hundred yards out. The LAW-80's maximum effective range was a little over three hundred yards against an armored vehicle. He flipped up the reflex collinator sight with a thumb.

"That's right," he said softly to himself as the APC rolled steadily onward, "nobody out here but us sand pebbles. Come on, baby."

The crates had fallen into a small depression behind him and were partially obscured from the view of the APC team.

Kissinger watched as a man stepped up onto the viewing platform of the APC. Twin streamers of dust rose to Kissinger's right. The APC was four hundred yards away. He rolled slightly, using the binoculars briefly to bring the new vehicles into view. There was no mistaking the large transport trucks used by the hostage rescue efforts.

Shifting his attention back to the APC, he took up the LAW-80 and sighted in. The lookout had already spotted the hostage convoys and was pointing excitedly.

Kissinger squeezed the trigger. The 94 mm warhead burned free of the tube and slammed into the APC with devastating results. Discarding the useless weapon, the Stony Man munitions expert drew his H&K PSG-1. He palmed the pistol grip and raked it back into his shoulder.

The APC was on fire, with several pieces of it blown clear of the main wreckage and throwing thick black smoke skyward that would attract the aerial vultures in record time. With deliberate trigger strokes Kissinger dropped the two targets he found still moving, then got to his feet and flagged down the first of the approaching vehicles. He spotted McCarter behind the wheel of the Land Rover as he clambered in.

"Welcome aboard, mate," McCarter called over the grinding noise made by the transport truck.

Kissinger hugged the canopy-mounted luggage rack of the Rover and thumbed two loose rounds for the sniper rifle from a pocket in the Nomex jumpsuit. He dumped the magazine long enough to restock it, then clicked it back into place. Lifting his handkerchief, he tied it around his nose and mouth to keep out the dust. When he looked back up, he saw two triangular shapes diving from the sky like hungry gulls.

"SYRIAN," Jack Grimaldi said with conviction.

Bolan didn't question the pilot's judgment. Grimaldi had been born to fly, and when it came to things whose nature stemmed from the clouds, there wasn't a surer source. He peered up at the sky through a pair of aviator sunglasses.

The fighter jets streaked across the convoy, leaving gray contrails that evaporated slowly in their wake and sonic booms that closed fast.

"The supplies," Bolan said.

Grimaldi put his foot down hard on the accelerator. The jeep responded at once, bucking like a stallion as it cut across the uneven terrain.

The jets rolled over and came back around. Fifty-caliber chain guns blatted to life, gouging dirt and rock geysers from the rugged terrain. The truck drivers broke the loose formation they'd been maintaining, spreading out as they wheeled their vehicles in a frantic effort to avoid the devastating autofire. The thunder left in the wake of the jets washed away all other sound. Two of the transport trucks turned sideways, slewing down the incline in dust clouds that covered their tires and lower carriages.

Manning had the M-60 machine gun the Phoenix team had picked up during an earlier skirmish. He raked 7.62 mm fire after the rolling jets.

Bolan knew the fighter pilots would follow up with missiles and rockets on their next fly-by now that they had the ground range targeted. Absolute carnage would follow. Grimaldi braked the jeep and was out of the seat before the 4X4 had come to a stop.

He took a Stinger missile from the arms of a man who'd just unpacked it. "Set it up," the Stony Man warrior growled as he settled the Stinger over his shoulder. He narrowed his eyes as he tracked the returning jets, then tapped the transmit button as the man brought the missile launcher to life. "Yakov?"

"Go," Katz directed.

"Just as we discussed," Bolan said. "You're in charge of the hostages now. Get them out of the area while we buy you some time."

"Good luck," Katz said. There was no argument because there was no time. And the senior Phoenix Force member definitely knew the Israeli ground forces with their Mossad commanders better.

The line of transport trucks broke and flared around Bolan's position. He targeted the lower jet screaming out of the sky.

"Ready," the Israeli said, tapping him on the shoulder.

Bolan flicked a switch, signaling for an IR-lock, then launched the missile. The rocket roared from the tube, spitting out a solid pipeline of white smoke in its wake. It curved in the air as it locked onto its target, looking like a golfer's bad slice.

The Executioner dumped the useless tube, then reached for the next Stinger. His gunnery man held it at the ready. Before he could put it on his shoulder, though, he saw the first rocket lock onto pursuit path with the jet.

The pilot fought the stick, flipping the jet over in pancake glides across the sky. The Stinger missile tracked into the left jet, heat-seeker locked onto the target. Then the engine exploded, engulfing the aircraft in a cocoon of fire.

The second jet hesitated, as if waiting to see what happened to his partner, pulling up high into the sky. As the black cloud of smoke climbed free of the falling wreckage, the surviving fighter swooped from high altitude like an attacking falcon.

McCarter and Manning joined Grimaldi as the rest of the Spetznaz and SAS merged forces among the Care packages provided by Kissinger. Stony Man's arms specialist began deploying them at once, holding to the tactical actions Bolan had engineered hours earlier. Part of the team would remain mobile while the other became stationary to provide the wall of fire needed to halt ground pursuit.

The gunnery man tapped Bolan on the shoulder, signaling the second system had been readied. The fighter was staying higher on his latest run, pounding the ground with rockets. Holes gaped suddenly in the landscape. Solid downpours of debris fell across the hellground. A jeep containing three SAS soldiers was hit and spun end over end as the bodies spilled free.

Ignoring the trickle of perspiration running down his temples and pooling around his eye sockets, Bolan waited.

A sharpshooter never forced a shot. Range, the target's velocity, windage and the possibilities of other outside interference all had to be allowed for. To rush a shot was suicide, even if waiting meant the deaths of fellow warriors. A shot on target achieved an objective and saved lives. A premature one was chancy, with even more lives hanging in the balance to be lost if it was unsuccessful.

The line of rockets smashed into the terrain, and Bolan stood his ground as the onslaught marched toward him. A Volkswagen van that had been abandoned by the formation of the ground troops became a twisted metal hulk that only held the fireball in its belly in check for a moment.

Satisfied, feeling the rightness of the moment as only a combat-blooded sniper can, the Executioner took his shot, squeezing the launch trigger gently in midexhalation. The missile soared free, streaking the sky as it locked on target. There was no time for the pilot even to begin evasive action. The wing was blown off and gravity did the rest, sucking the jet from the sky and spreading it over the terrain in metal fragments.

The ragged line of shock troops became hard, fanning out the way Bolan had planned. The mobile troops became the outer arms of the attack, able to move quickly to shift the coming attack to the deception of a soft center where the ground troops waited to unleash sheer carnage.

Bolan dropped the empty Stinger and began calling orders, vectoring the outer troops as he monitored their progress through binoculars. He spread them out, curved them around, knowing the uneven terrain would help promote the effect he wanted to give. It was a suck, pure and classic, that had been used down through the ages.

Focusing on the line of vehicles cresting the gentle ridge of foothills, the Executioner lay in wait at the center of his trap. There was no denying many of the men standing with them now might die. There were no guarantees. A soldier who believed in his fight didn't ask for them. He asked only for a weapon and the room to use it. Whatever was made of the battle, he'd make it himself.

"Kick it off," Bolan ordered into the headset.

The outer perimeter of 4X4s fell into motion, driving toward the advancing line of tanks and armored cars scrounged up by the Hezbollah and PLO forces through Syrian and Libyan resources. The battlefield became freshly delineated as new scars were carved into the landscape. The roving 4X4s took an account of the troops, diving in with LAW-80s, M-79s and RPG-7s that ripped through the armament of the vehicles and left husks burning in their wakes.

A solid wave of smoke grenades fell into the mass of advancing terrorists. Thick black clouds roiled up into the air, confusing the drivers of the enemy vehicles, causing them to veer off course.

Bolan checked the battlefield. The vehicles were moving into the bottleneck situation he wanted. More confusion and damage would be generated as the terrorists fled into the fire lanes of their brother terrorists and were trapped in a cross fire.

Sounds carried across the land in rolling echoes. Big guns, assault rifles, flat cracks of pistols, all became a constant, punctuated by the sizzle of striking rockets.

McCarter's Land Rover dodged through the deadly fire being returned by the terrorist APC. Gaps opened up in the terrain, and the rescue vehicles staggered through.

"Station One," Bolan called out. "Open up."

Small-arms fire and M-203 grenade launchers from the two lines of SAS and Spetznaz commandos entered the fray, creating more confusion. Over fifty vehicles had gathered together under the Hezbollah pursuit. They were firmly entrenched within the loose confines of the closing jaws of the trap. The outside drivers responded to the attack from the sides, closing in on the middle vehicles.

"Comrade Belasko?" Kalinin called.

"Not now," Bolan said softly. He picked up the bandolier of grenades and magazines Kissinger had dropped at his side, shrugged into it, then lifted the M-16/M-203 over-and-under combo that had come with it.

The hostage rescue vehicles moved in closer as the waves of violence gained intensity. When the transport trucks were four hundred yards out, the Executioner shouted, ''Now! Station Two, clear the area!''

The dodging vehicles ahead of the Hezbollah and PLO forces cut to the sides and easily ran through the positions held on the closing perimeter.

''Station Three,'' Bolan ordered, ''lock and load! Take 'em down hard!''

A solid wall of death opened up around the Executioner as the Mark 19 MOD-3 launchers started propelling 40 mm loads. The front line of terrorist vehicles sagged. The vehicles behind them were caught with nowhere to go. The drivers had already been conditioned to believe only death waited at the sides. Now they were immersed in it. A sheet of flame seemed to erupt from the first of the downed vehicles and spread over the ones following.

Bolan added 40 mm grenades of his own to the assault, targeting vehicles that had broken free of the half-moon of destruction the special forces teams had erected. When those were gone, he triggered 5.56 mm rounds on selective fire that took out fleeing drivers.

As the last of the Mark 19s emptied its ammo box, he ordered his troops to fall back. The rescue vehicles in operation had already swept through the ranks of the wounded and disabled to pick up survivors. The gunners waiting at the pit of the trap were the last to load.

Bolan jogged to the jeep as Grimaldi keyed the ignition. He stood on the rear deck, making sure the teams were clear of the area. The Stony Man pilot raced the engine impatiently as the line of terrorist troops tried to reorganize themselves.

Tapping the transmit button, Bolan called out, ''Kalinin?''

''Here. We're confirmed in motion, Comrade.''

''McCarter?''

''Rolling high, wide and handsome, mate.''

At Bolan's signal Grimaldi fell into formation with the retreating vehicles.

The Executioner kept his position on the rear deck of the bouncing jeep. The barrel of the M-16 clicked against the roll bar. He surveyed the harsh countryside ahead of them. Less than four miles remained to the pickup site. Perhaps four minutes' worth of traveling. He checked over his shoulder. So far there was no sign of imminent ground pursuit. Then the sky darkened from the northeast as at least three dozen fighter aircraft dropped in from the cloud cover.

"Break left, break right," Bolan called. "I've got a visual on enemy aircraft."

"Syrians and Iraqis," Grimaldi said. He took evasive action, stuttering the jeep across the terrain.

A strafing run by the foremost jets was mostly wasted effort, but the second round started to pick up where the first left off.

"Stony One?" a voice with a West Texas twang rumbled.

"Go."

"You've got the pleasure of Mad Dog Terminator playing your guardian angel today, sir," the West Texas voice said, "and I got a whole bunch of merry madmen riding my coattails."

"Son of a bitch," Grimaldi said, pointing.

A wave of planes came in from the west.

"They're ours," Grimaldi exclaimed. He raised a fist in a salute. "Give 'em hell, you bunch of heroes!"

Bolan grinned and hit his transmitter button. "I thought this was restricted airspace even during the mission."

"Yes, sir. Well, you have a high hat in Washington to thank for this, sir. We figure he must like these terrorists about as much as he likes broccoli. Said he wanted us to clean the table for him."

The Syrian and Iraqi warbirds were already panicked and were struggling to break off the attack. The Harriers and Tomcats plunged in with a textbook attack that nailed the opposing jets down like swatted mosquitoes.

Two troop transport helicopters rode low over the water and the special forces teams rolled within sight. A half-dozen Russian Mi-24 Hinds held blocker positions around them.

Grimaldi drove out with the other vehicles, grinding as far into the surf of the Mediterranean as he could before the engine died. Bolan waited until the last man had boarded, helping with the wounded and the dead as they were winched up in nets from boom arms. The suck might have been successful, but cost had run high in lives among the special forces. They had eleven dead. Another eight were seriously wounded.

Wet and cold, shivering from the blasting winds created by the rotor blades, Bolan scanned the landscape as the helicopters lifted. The line of abandoned vehicles would gradually be absorbed by the sea. The smoke from the ground and aerial battlefields would fade. Hearing would return to normal, and the stink of cordite in their nostrils would disappear.

But it wasn't over. He knew that. It wouldn't be over until Rihani had been run to ground. As the helicopter lifted off, Bolan considered all of the Hezbollah leader's options, putting himself into the man's mental space.

By the time he touched down on the deck of the aircraft carrier, he was sure he knew where he could find Rihani. What he didn't know was if there was enough time left to stop the man.

CHAPTER THIRTY-SEVEN

South of Nahariyya, Israel

Fifth Day—10:05 a.m.

The train engine was lime-green, with *Israel Railways* painted on the side in white letters in three different languages. Apparently today was a slow day. It was only pulling twenty-seven cars. Like the engine, the caboose was lime-green.

Fahad Rihani wiped perspiration from his brow with a scented handkerchief. Despite the air-conditioning of the car, the burning rays of the sun were sucking the moisture from him.

Numair shifted behind the steering wheel. A MAC-10 hung in a customized rig under his left arm. Like Rihani, the young Iranian wore a business suit cut in a European fashion.

"Now," Rihani said as he opened the passenger door and got out. The train personnel were busy off-loading and taking on new passengers.

Numair followed. Three other men, all dressed in business suits, got out from the rear seat.

They didn't talk. Everything had been planned. The last groups to board would be the team bearing the backpack nukes and escorting the American and European prisoners. Their tickets had been purchased prior to boarding.

Rihani went unarmed. He was secure in the knowledge that he controlled all things. Every variable had been worked out to the last detail. Even with the border guards beefed up, with Israeli military personnel busy effecting the rescue of the hostages in Lebanon, it had been relatively simple to steal quietly into the country. After all, the Israelis weren't looking for any kind of invasion that didn't start with a bang—if the Israelis were thinking of a possible invasion at all. They'd been programmed to be the aggressors, as had the United States.

He strode through the heat, disregarding the handkerchief in his pocket as the perspiration cascaded down his bare scalp and funneled into his beard. He placed his foot on the steps leading up into the engine.

A man in coveralls confronted him. "You can't come in here," the man said quietly. He was round and soft, expecting no trouble at all.

Rihani looked at the man, holding him with his eyes while Numair reached past him. The silenced pistol in Numair's big hand coughed twice in quick succession.

Stepping over the dead man, Rihani moved into the control room of the engine. Three men dressed in coveralls similar to the first man stood at different banks of switches and dials. He spoke in Hebrew. "Which of you knows how to operate the train?"

The three men stared in disbelief at the corpse. Then the short man on the right raised his hand and said, "I do."

Numair raised his pistol and quickly shot the other two men through the head. They fell against the controls, then collapsed to the bloody floor.

"Good." Rihani stepped forward and wiped blood from one of the dual windows in front of the engine with the scented handkerchief. "You'll get to live a little longer." He checked his watch. "Are we ready to depart?"

"Yes."

Numair moved in close to the man, waving the pistol meaningfully.

"See that's it's done." Rihani moved through the engine toward the rest of the train—and this new batch of hostages.

THERE WERE four passenger cars. Altogether, counting the hostages they'd brought from Beirut, they had forty-three new hostages in waiting. Thirty of Rihani's handpicked men stood at his side, ready to assume total control of the train when it became necessary. The other twenty-two train cars transported a collection of goods ranging from citrus fruits and high-tech electronics to magnesium bromide.

The backpack nukes had been stored in the car following the last passenger car, guarded by six men carrying Uzis. He paused between cars, taking a moment to look at the dizzying landscape speeding by. Then he opened the door and stepped inside.

Rihani stopped beside the crates and considered the possibilities they represented. Less than one hundred miles separated them from the heart of Tel Aviv. The time to his destiny would pass as quickly as the steel rails beneath the charging wheels. His thoughts centered on Jamila and the contentment he'd found in her embrace. His life had been barren of politics when he first met her. Only later, through her death, had his life become tempered to that of a warrior.

Placing his hands on the wooden top of the nearest crate, he visualized it as his sword, shared with God. Together they'd hold it at the throats of the cursed Jews. Then, with a movement so sudden and so powerful that it couldn't be stopped, he would slit those throats.

The door opened behind him. Rihani came out of his reverie and nodded at Numair. "The engine section of the train?"

"It's under our control," Numair replied. "I came back to see if I could be of service to you."

"Not to me," Rihani corrected. "Our fates are sealed by our love for God and our duty to serve His wishes."

"As God wills," Numair intoned.

"The passenger cars?"

"They're secretly under our control, as well." Numair shrugged. "We only had to kill two more of the Jews, so there remains a number of them to use as hostages."

"Good. Even if the Israelis discover our capture of this train, they'll undoubtedly choose to attempt negotiations first. By that time we'll be in a position to destroy Haifa and Tel Aviv. There'll come a void upon this land, my brother, and our supporters can sweep in to fill that void. A new Arabian power base will be born in the inferno we bring in these boxes. The Jews will never recover from such destruction as we will visit upon them. Nuclear fire will bathe and burn out the Israeli roots that have prospered here wrongly.''

Rihani knelt for a crowbar they had packed with their equipment and began to open the first crate. The scabs at his wrists broke with his efforts. Blood streamed down his hands to mark the crates. He felt it only just and right that his life's blood stain the wood. Nothing of any value was achieved without shedding blood. He worked harder, never thinking of giving in to the pain.

CHAPTER THIRTY-EIGHT

Washington, D.C.

Fifth Day—1:17 a.m.

Carl Lyons screamed with the fury only a trapped animal could know. His body was battered and bruised and, in some places, bleeding. Buried facedown under a small mountain of acoustic tiles that had rained down from the ceiling, he could barely feel the gun still locked in his hand.

The echoes of the last explosion were beginning to die away. The smell of smoke and the heat of a raging fire was near.

He dragged his free arm under his body and forced himself to his knees. Tiles, two-by-fours and scattered bits of metal slid from his shoulders until he had his head clear of the debris. He fumbled for his headset, finding only broken metal and twisted wires. Dizzy and disoriented, he made himself stand.

"Pol!" he bellowed. "Gadgets! Goddamn it! Talk to me!"

A man groaned, and tiles shifted to the right. Limping over to the movement, Lyons plunged his hand into the pile of debris and found a shirt-covered Kevlar vest. He hooked his fingers into the collar of the bulletproof garment and pulled. Gadgets Schwarz came free of the wreckage, hacking and coughing.

"Pol?" Schwarz asked when he was standing.

"Don't know."

"Got to find him."

"Yeah."

Lyons unslung his CAR-15 and started sifting through the debris with the buttstock. "Does your headset work?"

"Beats me," Schwarz said as he bent to the task.

"Mine's toast," Ironman said. "Check yours. We need to know if Leo's still in operation."

"My God, Leo was up there when this shit came down." Schwarz hit the transmit button and began sending.

Lyons could hear the police sirens outside, but he knew with the fire raging through the building that it would be some time before any rescue workers tried to salvage anything.

"Hey, Ironman," a choked voice said. "How about a hand up out of this quagmire before something important catches fire?"

Unable to keep from grinning, Lyons reached out and helped Blancanales to his feet. "God, I hope I don't look as bad as you do."

"You look worse," Blancanales said with a wan smile. "But don't take it to heart. Hell, you started out that way this morning."

"Yeah, yeah, yeah. Wish I had time for all this brilliant repartee." Lyons glanced at Schwarz. "Leo?"

Schwarz shrugged. "Can't get anything."

Blancanales blew the action of his assault rifle clear. "Got any idea about how we're going to get out of here?"

A wall of fire seemed to be expanding in every direction. It sucked the oxygen from the air, making breathing uncomfortable, and the heat seemed to seep into Lyons's bones. Eyeing the orange forklift, he said, "I think we can manage that." He slung the CAR-15 and clambered over the loose piles of debris until he was in the metal seat of the forklift. The vehicle was nearly covered with tiles and boards, but the diesel engine caught smoothly when he turned the ignition over. "All aboard who's coming aboard."

Schwarz and Blancanales climbed on as Lyons maneuvered the forks to clear a space for the machine. The hydraulics whined and spit fluids as they struggled with the load. Grudgingly the rubble gave way before the long forks. Lyons put his foot on the accelerator and the front tires spun for a moment before finding purchase. Then the forklift rattled and shook as he drove it toward the nearest cinderblock wall. According to the mental map he had of the building, it would let him out onto the outside dock area, provided he could make it through the wall.

The forks impacted, one of them snapping off as the other sliced through. Lyons kept a grip of iron on the twisting wheel, forcing the machine to continue straight. A rending crash signaled the crumbling of the wall. The protective latticework of the cage overhead kept the cinder blocks from falling on their heads.

The forklift spun on through, driving hard to the end of a loading dock and tumbling over. Lyons kicked himself loose, rolling over the pavement and coming to his knees with the CAR-15 in his arms. He checked to make sure Schwarz and Blancanales were clear and found them already scrambling into position.

A police car pulled forward, then stopped, its red and blue lights spinning slowly. Almost a dozen others flanked it. A bulky figure got out on the passenger side and flipped a cigarette butt out into the parking area. "At ease, Lyons."

When he recognized Washington police detective Rollie Maurloe, Lyons lowered the assault rifle and stood up. "Damn sure took your time about getting here."

Maurloe shrugged. "Man tells me he wants to wipe his own nose, I let him wipe. And I didn't expect to run into a war zone. We're going to have to stop meeting like this." He stepped back and opened the rear door. Leo Turrin got out, looking rumpled and singed. "You know this guy?"

"He's one of us."

"Hey," Turrin said, "are you guys all right? When the building blew and I realized you weren't coming out, I tried to get inside."

"Feisty little guy," Maurloe said with a wink. He ignited a cigarette and pointed at Turrin. "Damn near broke an officer's jaw when we restrained him from going in after you. Figured you guys would make it out on your own or not at all.''

"I appreciate the vote of confidence," Lyons said.

"No prob," Maurloe replied. "It's my job."

"I hope you got here in time to nab the jokers who did this."

"Back of the wagon." Maurloe aimed a thumb over his shoulder.

Lyons slung his weapon and followed the detective's direction.

"I got a feeling," Maurloe said, "that you ain't gonna be happy about this." He nodded to the officers standing on either side of the door.

Lyons stepped forward after the door was opened. Six men sat inside with a collection of bruises and handcuffs. It was plain to see they weren't Hezbollah. "Who are they?"

"Oh, I got an assortment of names to call them," Maurloe replied. "Maybe they're real names, maybe not. But they're all Israeli citizens."

"Mossad," Lyons said.

Maurloe nodded in agreement. "What I figured. They lit up the warehouse with a couple of rocket launchers and were getting set to finish the job when we arrived on the scene to remind them they were on our turf."

"You can't hold us," one of the Israelis said.

"That's true." Maurloe blew out a lungful of smoke. "Every manjack among 'em comes blessed with diplomatic immunity."

"You guys fucked up," Lyons snarled, leaning into the back of the detention wagon. "Faisel was nowhere near that building when you hit it. All you succeeded in doing is letting him know we're burning up his backtrail."

"Faisel is *our* problem," the Israeli spokesman said.

"Wrong, partner. Faisel's *my* problem now. You guys had your chance to make this a joint effort and clean the slate once and for all. Instead, you had to worry about your own dirty linen catching fire and creating a stink. What your superiors have failed to realize is that this campaign isn't about what's gone on in the past and who screwed who last. This is about what's going to happen in the morning. If morning ever gets here.''

''We have diplomatic immunity. You can't—''

''Pal, all that diplomatic immunity's going to get you is a fast trip home. You're out of this race. And if I had the time, I'd hang around to drop you on your ass a few times just to see how high you could bounce.'' He moved away.

Maurloe nodded at the officers and the doors were closed. ''So what now?''

Lyons wiped at the crusted blood on his lip. He looked at Turrin, Blancanales and Schwarz, who were watching him. They looked as tired as he felt, but he knew they couldn't put it down any more than he was able to. ''I need you to buy me some time to put this together. I don't want their buddies to find out they're off the street for a while.''

''How much time? I can't keep these guys out of circulation forever. Somebody's going to be asking questions real soon.''

''A couple of hours,'' Lyons said. ''If that doesn't see the end of it, it's going to be too damn late, anyway, from the way things look.''

Maurloe grinned and extended his hand. ''No prob, guy. Me and the boys'll take the long way back. And it's about time to take a break, anyway. Set up a little defensive network around a doughnut shop on the outskirts of town. Only you're going to owe me. One of these days, after this is over, me and you are gonna hoist a few beers and talk off the record about what kind of shitstorm's going down in my city.''

Lyons took the man's hand. ''Done and done.''

THE CLOCK WAS TICKING. Lyons could hear its echo in every bone of his body. The doomsday numbers continued to fall while a madman and his army made their way through the city with possibly enough of an arsenal to level the metropolitan area.

''Flying Eye One to Ground One. Over.''

He unclipped the mike hanging above his head. "Flying Eye One, this is Ground One. Over." Without thinking he checked the night sky for some sign of the helicopters they'd requisitioned from Stony Man Farm for the chase. Flying Eye One was Schwarz. Flying Eye Two was Turrin. Ground Two was Blancanales.

"Ground One, we need to vector you in on a possible lead. Over."

"Ground One standing by," Lyons said, adding his twenty. "Over."

"Ground One, take a right on Q Street and haul ass toward the Naval Observatory. Over."

"Embassy Row? Over," Lyons asked as the directions clicked in his mind. He put his foot down harder on the accelerator, listening to the shrill scream of rubber as the tortured tires made the sharp swerve around the car in front of him.

"Sounds like a logical course of action to me," Schwarz said, abandoning all attempts at radio professionalism. "Those bastards can take out a lot of career diplomats with that little beaut of theirs and set a lot of negotiations back years. Policy-making in the Middle East between the superpowers could become a big joke."

"Ground Two," Blancanales said in a clipped voice. "I'm en route."

Lyons fisted the steering wheel as he whipped through the late-night traffic. All they had to go on was a quick inventory of Smiles Ice Cream trucks. One truck was missing that couldn't be accounted for in work orders and physical inventory. It wasn't much. Not enough to bet the life of a city on. Long shots sometimes paid off, but he made a practice of never taking them when the stakes were so high. But there had been nothing else to go with.

"Left," Schwarz called. "Onto Twenty-third Street."

Lyons powered the souped-up van into the turns as his fellow Able Team warrior called them out to him. He was in the thickest part of the line of embassies. The only two he knew for certain were the Japanese chancery, because of the ornate garden and the cherry trees, and the British embassy, a great mansion cloaked in shadows.

"Okay, Carl," Schwarz said, "you should have visual sighting of them...now."

Lyons spotted the Smiles Ice Cream truck in the circular parkway in front of the Mosque and Islamic Center. The 162-foot-high minaret was the centerpiece for the embassies of the Muslim countries. With the intelligence blackout over the hostage situation, Lyons had to admit it was the perfect hiding place.

"What are they doing?" Lyons asked.

"Attending the mosque," Schwarz answered. "Last rites or something, I guess."

Three hardguys stood by the ice-cream truck. Lyons drove on by, heading for Observatory Circle, thinking it would be better to come back up on them in the dark.

"Oh, shit, Ironman," Turrin called out.

Lyons grabbed the mike. "What?"

"Busted play, guy. The Mossad agents made the party after all. All hell just broke loose down there."

"Faisel and his crew are in motion," Schwarz said. "They lost men in the initial hit, but they're up and running."

"With that baby nuke," Blancanales said, "it's not going to matter if they're stationary or in motion. When it comes time to go kablooey, everything still goes kablooey."

Lyons took the steering wheel hand over hand, squealing the tires as he cut a one-eighty in the street that left three cars honking their horns furiously in his wake. His stomach tied in knots as he punched his watch, activating the five-minute timer he'd previously programmed in. Kurtzman told them it would take at least that long to detonate the SADM. He spoke into the mike. "Where are they?"

"Headed your way," Schwarz replied.

"Put a spotlight on that ice-cream truck and back me up," Lyons said.

"You gonna say when?" Schwarz asked.

Lyons grinned, staring into the glare of the oncoming traffic as he swerved out of his lane and sped back down

Massachusetts Avenue. "Trust me, Gadgets. You'll *know* when." He dropped the mike onto the floor and grabbed the CAR-15.

A spotlight lanced down from the dark sky and touched the ground. It whipped across pavement, cars and landscape, coming to rest on the wobbling Smiles Ice Cream truck with muzzle-flashes tracking after it.

Evidently the Mossad had expected no problems with the ground assault. Only one car appeared to be tailing the truck.

Lyons heard Turrin vectoring Blancanales in on the truck. He breathed out, snugging his shoulders into the heavy-duty seat restraints.

The hood of the pursuing car suddenly exploded upward as white clouds rolled from beneath it. The vehicle slowed immediately.

Fisting his CAR-15 like a knight of old getting set for a joust, Lyons yanked his steering wheel hard left, guiding the van into the truck's path from fifty yards away. His foot never left the accelerator. He fired the assault rifle's clip dry a heartbeat before impact, chewing glass out of the windshield in a solid stripe.

The driver tried to avoid him, but there was nowhere to go. Lyons cut the wheel, presenting the passenger-side corner as his battering ram. He felt the steering wheel collapse against his chest, leaving bruises under the Kevlar. His spine and neck seemed to come apart, then his skull bounced off the bullet-shaped glass of the Lumina's windshield. Blood sprayed down into his eyes from a scalp wound.

Unable to catch his breath, he forced himself to move as the heavy vehicle was shoved backward by the ice-cream truck's greater weight and momentum. He drew the Colt .45 as he kicked the door open. Metal screeched and gave way as his foot went numb.

Outside, Lyons fell to his knees and drew his first breath, wasting it on a curse. Something was broken. That was for damn sure. Ribs, maybe, but maybe something worse. Not giving himself any time to think about it, he wiped the blood from his eyes with his free palm and brought the .45 up into target acquisition. Three 230-grain bullets ripped into the surviving Hezbollah gunner's chest and blew him back against the locker area. Crimson stained the white wall behind him. The driver was slumped over the steering wheel. Lyons put a bullet through the man's head to make sure he stayed there. The corpse bounced but didn't seem to mind.

Making his legs work in spite of the trauma he was suffering, Lyons rounded the truck, intent on gaining the rear entrance. He kept his breathing shallow to keep the pain at a minimum. A glance at his watch showed him the broken LED crystal.

Movement out of the corner of his eye brought his head and gun arm up. Autofire shivered across the Kevlar vest, jarring the busted ribs. One round gouged out flesh from Lyons's left elbow, and he felt the rush of blood down his arm. He triggered the remaining three rounds of the Government Model's clip at the Hezbollah gunner, leathered the .45 and drew his .357 Magnum. Numbers were continuing to fall all around him and he'd lost count of where everything stood.

Blancanales was at the rear of the truck when he got there. The Able Team warrior was already in motion, racing to the bullet-scarred double doors.

Police sirens wailed, coming closer.

The doors were locked when Lyons pulled on them. Metal slivers ripped into his face as a triburst cored through the doors. He dipped a hand into his pocket and came out with a block of C-4. Leathering the .357 Magnum, he tore off a hunk of plastic explosive and quickly worked it into a slender worm, which he wrapped over the locking mechanism. Blancanales slapped on a timer and they stepped around opposite sides of the truck for protection from the blast.

Cars honked as they went around them, unmindful of the violence that had erupted out of the city night. Lyons laughed and couldn't stop, not believing the madness of the citizens who believed nothing out of the ordinary was going on. There was nothing like urban life, especially when it was viewed through a cop's eyes.

Lyons rolled back around the truck corner, catching sight of Schwarz's helicopter descending into the traffic and causing even more honking. The metal was hot. He ignored it, flipping the doors open and reaching inside. He raked out melted boxes of ice cream, spilling them across the street. Evidently the Hezbollah gunners had turned off the freezer section of the truck when they took it. The SADM was just inside the door, red lights blinking away as it cycled through its countdown.

Lyons reached for the strap, catching movement from one of the two lying on the floor of the truck, but it was too late to pull back. Faisel lifted his head, bleeding from his nose, ears and mouth from the concussive force of the C-4 charge. He yanked his M-16 into line, screaming in incoherent fury.

Twisting his wrist, Lyons felt the derringer .45 snap free of the forearm holster and slip into his waiting hand. He started squeezing off the double-action derringer, pumping through all five rounds as a stream of bullets exploded against his chest and blew him from the rear of the truck.

He landed hard, almost sucked under by the incredible amount of pain that hit him. He fought the encircling blackness with a force of will he didn't know he had. He tried to get back up, but Blancanales held him down.

"Easy, amigo," Blancanales said. "We have it now."

Lyons coughed. "Let me see."

Shifting him, Blancanales helped him roll over on his side as Turrin and Schwarz off-loaded the baby nuke.

"Faisel?" Lyons asked.

"Confirmed casualty. You rest easy. There's an ambulance on the way."

"If Gadgets doesn't get that little box stopped, there aren't even going to be any pieces for it to pick up."

Schwarz knelt and hooked up the device Kurtzman had given them to disarm the SADM. A sheen of perspiration covered Gadgets's face. A moment later the blinking red lights went out. Schwarz held up a thumb and smiled.

"Goddamn," Turrin said as he walked over. He lit a cigarette with shaking fingers. "That's as close as I want to come to getting a harp and a halo for a long time."

Lyons lay back, letting the blackness call to him. He grinned. "Leo, where you're going, they're going to give you horns and a spiked tail. Course, you may get to wear that monkey suit you were in the other day. That, and cloven Guccis."

Flicking ashes, Turrin smiled and said, "At least I'm not letting my age hold me back. I finished this run on my own two feet. Not like some other people I could name."

Lyons coughed and fought the pain. His head was swimming. "Pol?"

"Yeah?"

"Do me a favor."

"Name it."

"Make sure I've got clean underwear when I get to the hospital."

"Christ," Schwarz said as he came over, "after being this close to kablooey, who's got clean underwear?"

Lyons laughed, and the sudden pain that flared up from the effort pushed him over into unconsciousness.

CHAPTER THIRTY-NINE

Tel Aviv, Israel

Fifth Day—11:59 a.m.

Levi Leor, commander of the Mossad forces currently in and around Beirut searching for Fahad Rihani, gazed in tired fascination at the walls covered with Lebanese street maps. Somewhere out there the Hezbollah leader was still free, able to return yet again to haunt the dreams of the Israeli intelligence service.

Leor was rawboned and gaunt, feeling every one of his seventy-three years as he ran a wide palm down his face. He was still in the same uniform he'd worn three days ago. Showers were brief and far from relaxing when he could take them, and he'd spared none of his aides to see to his personal comforts.

Someone knocked at the door.

"Enter," Leor called. His shoulders automatically squared, and he clasped his hands at the base of his spine. He moved closer to inspect the street maps of east Beirut. It was unthinkable perhaps after so much military action had taken place in the city, but he was almost prepared to grasp at straws. The chase was maddening. The Mossad had nearly turned itself inside out in an effort to terminate Rihani. If it hadn't been for the interference of the Americans, Russians and Britons, perhaps the man could have begun rotting in an unmarked hole somewhere by now. The Mossad was notoriously efficient among espionage circles, but only if the field was clear. This time it hadn't been. Even without Rihani's own agenda to cloud things, the European and Russian goals of protecting the hostages had interfered with operations a number of times.

"Commander," the young, sallow-faced communications officer said, "I have news of the Washington-based teams."

Leor turned to look at the man. "Speak, Lieutenant, or must I pry the words from you?"

"No, sir. I mean, yes, sir." The officer came to sudden attention, eyes focused on the wall. "The Washington teams have been compromised, sir, and most of them are awaiting deportation as is due anyone with diplomatic immunity. However, the target has been neutralized. But there has been a—"

"What of Faisel?"

"Dead, sir. One of our teams was close on their heels when the American team took them out. It has also been confirmed that Hezbollah had possession of a Russian-made nuclear device that was recovered at the scene."

Leor felt his heart thud hollowly inside his chest. "Were the Americans surprised by this?"

"On the contrary, sir. Agent Tobias informs us that the American team was prepared for it and were successful in shutting it down after it was activated."

Snatching his hat from his cluttered but organized desk, Leor said, "Lieutenant, get me a jeep. Now. And get orders to the authorities at the airport to take the American team responsible for assembling the hostage rescue teams into custody. Then take your information to the prime minister's office. Dismissed!" He moved through the door, already making preparations for the operation in his mind.

COMMANDER LEOR'S JEEP skidded across the tarmac at Ben-Gurion Airport. The ten vehicles accompanying him slid into formation, sweeping across the lanes of air traffic. The airport had been shut down for the day to accommodate the American and Russian forces in the area transferring the hostages.

Leor couldn't believe the number of planes and helicopters that bore Russian markings. Especially not in accordance with the American planes and helicopters. The knowledge that more of them were on the aircraft carriers within Israel's territorial waters was mind-boggling.

Airport security vehicles closed in on his jeep, directed by his driver on the two-way radio. He breathed deeply, sucking the air into his lungs. The prime minister still hadn't gotten back to him concerning the nuclear devices the Americans had neglected to tell them about. No one was to be trusted. The politicians knew that. That was why Israeli alliances were so important.

The airport security vehicles trailed Leor's jeep to the American ground base in one of the hangars. A colonel, ramrod straight with training and youth, advanced on Leor as the Mossad commander stepped out of his vehicle. He hit the ground with his pistol in his hand.

"Listen, mister," the American colonel said in English, jabbing a forefinger toward Leor's chest, "I don't know what kind of shit you're trying to pull here, but you're fucking with the U.S. Army now."

"Shut up," Leor ordered.

The colonel's face purpled.

Leor flicked a hand. Two of his men stepped forward with Uzis at the ready. Immediately a half-dozen American infantrymen mirrored the move.

Unshaken, Leor looked the colonel square in the eyes. "Where is this Striker and his operatives?"

The American colonel crossed his arms over his chest. "Listen, dipshit, the last I heard Israel was a friendly country. We got an official invite from the Israeli government to be here."

"I want Striker," Leor said. Before anyone could move he aimed the muzzle of his pistol at the colonel's head.

The colonel returned his gaze full measure. "I don't know what put the burr up your butt, old man, but if you're looking for Striker and his wonder boys, they've already deployed out of here. If you take a glance over your left shoulder, you can wave bye-bye.''

Leor turned as the wash of the jet engines filled the hangar. Three planes—two fighter jets and a small Lear—climbed into the air. ''Where are they going?''

''Beats me. But wherever it is, those guys look like they're taking it mighty serious. I wouldn't want to be on the receiving end of anything they care to play. Most guys in their shape would've taken the first available Medevac and moved on toward some well-deserved R and R.''

Leor moved away, aware that his men covered his retreat before following. Once in the jeep he asked for a linkup to the prime minister's office, hoping there was still time for Israel to defend herself against the Americans and their disaster-minded brinkmanship. The Americans could never know the hatreds and motivations of the people who were part of Hezbollah. They'd been far removed from terrorism within their own country.

Striker and his men, if that had been truly them and they knew where Rihani was, would never be prepared for the all-or-nothing fires that fueled Hezbollah. Chilled at the thought that Striker would negotiate rather than act as the Americans were so wont to do, he prayed Israel would survive. Or that there would be enough time for the military to gear up and take matters into their own hands. And if the American team became a casualty, as well, so be it.

CHAPTER FORTY

Stony Man Farm, Virginia
Fifth Day—3:25 a.m.

"Mack's right, you know. The Israelis are covering Beirut. The Russians control the air traffic in conjunction with the American Navy, which has a total lock on the sea in that area. The train's the only way into the heart of Israel that hasn't been covered."

Barbara Price looked at Kurtzman. "You don't have to convince me, Aaron. If I hadn't believed him, we'd have scrubbed this part of the mission before it had the chance to get off the ground. Literally." Still, it didn't keep her from being any less edgy than him. She paced, feeling guilty that she had that physical outlet when Bear didn't.

Kurtzman tapped the keys of his computer console. Obediently the wall at the other end of the room flickered and changed, becoming an enhanced map of the Israel Railways route.

One of the white-suited computer techs raised his hand and waved. "That recon plane you ordered is on track, Aaron."

Kurtzman grunted and worked the keyboard. "Got physical reality coming on-line," he said in a distracted voice.

Stopping her pacing, Price checked the wall screen. The Israel Railways route disappeared, leaving aerial footage in its place. Disorientation chipped away at her senses. It seemed as if she were looking through the wall of the room down onto the train itself. The engine was lime-green. The distance, even with the magnification abilities, made it look like a child's toy.

"From where the observation plane's at," Kurtzman said, "we can see them, but they can't see us."

"We can't see much of them," Price replied.

"Yeah, but I can play with the radar figures a bit and get an exact location for our guys." He busied himself with the task.

Price almost breathed a sigh of relief when she heard the phone at her desk ring. She crossed the room and picked it up, turning to keep the wall screen in sight. The train continued on its way, curving as it wheeled slowly around a hill like a bloated caterpillar. "Price."

"Me," Hal Brognola said.

She could tell from the tone of his voice that the news wasn't good.

"Got a hot call from the Israeli prime minister," Brognola said. "Apparently Able Team's recovery of the nuke didn't go unnoticed. The Mossad had a team on the ground."

"Right," Price replied. "We'd already assumed that."

"Yeah, well, what we didn't assume was that they'd know for sure what the SADM was and be able to contact Mossad headquarters so damn quick. The President and I have had as much success ducking questions from the Israeli and British governments as a couple of goddamn amateurs. Needless to say, we and the Soviets are going to have egg on our faces for some time to come."

"If you still have faces."

Brognola grunted. "Yeah, there's that."

"I'm transmitting the cargo manifests and passenger lists now," Kurtzman said. Four of the printers at the other end of the horseshoe-shape table came to life and started spitting out sheets of paper.

Price said, "It's not going to matter that much when this is over, anyway, Hal. Whatever way this thing resolves itself, there's still going to be some changes in store for everyone involved in this, officially or unofficially. Anything that happens in the Middle East today affects the whole world. The important thing is to get Rihani and Hezbollah shut down before they cause any damage that isn't just ego-related.''

"In private conversation with the Man and me," Brognola said, "that's exactly what the British P.M. said."

"Smart cookie."

"I'm beginning to feel surrounded by them." Brognola cleared his throat. "The main reason I called is because the USS *Winkler* just confirmed the launch of at least eight Israeli warbirds less than sixty seconds ago."

"Their objective?"

"Striker and our guys. Call it a guess if you want, but I wouldn't want to bet against it."

Price raised her voice, directing it at Kurtzman. "Aaron, get me the widest range you can on radar in that sector. As soon as the Stony Man teams enter the target's airspace, I want to know about it."

"You got it. What am I looking for?"

"The eight Israeli jets burning air to get to them."

Kurtzman swiveled, talking into the headset that connected him privately with the rest of his team.

"The President and I are trying to get Israel to back down," Brognola said, "but they're stonewalling. By the time the dust and tempers settle on this, it's going to be too late to help our guys."

"Striker won't back away from this thing now. It's gone too far, cut too deep."

"I know. I just wanted to make him aware of what he was facing."

"I appreciate it, Hal," Price said. "So will he."

"Tell the man I said to stay hard when you talk to him."

"I will."

Brognola broke the connection.

"Damn," Price said as she cradled the receiver. The operations had been cut thin before, but she could see through the holes in this one.

"Got them," Kurtzman growled. He put the display up on the wall screen. Three red blips were followed by eight blue ones.

"How far apart are they?" Price asked.

"Ten, twelve minutes. It's hard to say. Maybe even a little more." Kurtzman put a hand to the headset he wore, then glanced at Price. "Striker's on the wire."

Price lifted her own headset and fitted it on. "Stony One, you have Stony Base. Over."

"Roger, Stony Base. How's Ironman?"

"Hanging in there. The man's made of stern stuff. The nurses will be lucky if they can keep him in bed after a good night's sleep. But it's not him I'm worried about right now. He's in safe hands. You're not. We've confirmed eight warbirds on your tail, Stony One. Over."

"Locals? Over."

"*Very* upset representation of the locals. That's a roger. Our smoke screen disappeared. They know all. Over."

"We're lucky it held as long as it did. Over."

"Maybe. We still haven't confirmed if your target is on board. It might be better if you—"

"He's there," the Executioner interrupted. "I'm locked into his mind-set now, Stony Base, and I'm not letting go of his shadow until he's down and out. Over."

"Stony One, your company's approximately ten minutes behind you. Over."

"Roger. We're touching down now. It just means we don't get a trial run. We didn't plan on one, anyway. This one's by the numbers, Stony Base, and they come from the heart. Stony One out."

Price listened to the radio static for a moment, then swept the headset off. She knew she'd just officially become one of the spectators for the next curtain going up on Operation Desert Lance. And she didn't like it one damn bit.

CHAPTER FORTY-ONE

Near Haifa, Israel

Fifth Day—11:33 a.m.

Mack Bolan ran, driving his booted feet hard into the packed earth of the hill. Sweat washed down his body thanks to the heavy weight of the body armor under the Nomex blacksuit. He ran uphill, breathing through his nose to keep the effort and oxygen flow under control. He ignored the stitch of pain in his right side. Katz, Encizo, Manning, James and Kissinger jogged after him, silent death at his heels.

The sunlight was blinding, making the sky almost impossibly blue on the other side of the rise. He could hear the train engine struggling with the grade, heard the wheels grinding against the track.

The Lear was a silver triangle over half a klick back, well out of view of the train's occupants. They'd run at full speed, holding together as a group, carrying full combat gear.

The Executioner flattened as he reached the apex of the ridge, clambering to the edge on elbows and knees with the H&K MP-5 cradled in his arms. Dirt stuck to his cheek, held there by a bond of perspiration and camouflage makeup. The blackface was painted in bold stripes now, not for its concealing abilities, but for the terror the darkness could strike into the hearts of their enemies.

He lifted his head slightly, keeping well behind the scrub brush that dotted the rocky ground. The train continued its ascent, slowing down to little more than thirty miles an hour. Getting aboard even at that reduced speed would still be a dangerous endeavor.

"Striker," McCarter's cool voice called from somewhere overhead.

"Go," Bolan whispered.

"It's confirmed, mate. They kicked off at least a couple of dozen passengers a few klicks back."

"Cutting down the amount of variables they must keep account of," Katz said.

Bolan nodded. It was a logical step once Hezbollah assumed direct control of the train and the passengers. That gave him some hope. If the terrorists were operating logically, their strategies could be planned against and countered. And sudden surprise was one of the greatest weapons in Stony Man's arsenal against them. He prayed it would be enough.

The warrior glanced south along the track. Haifa lay less than twenty miles in that direction. Even with that distance separating the city from the nuclear weapons, it wasn't enough to seriously reduce the danger involved. Thousands, perhaps millions, could still die. And that was a low estimate, considering that Kurtzman's last transmission had included information that Israel had aimed missiles in Russia's direction because the Mossad had learned the nukes were of Soviet make. A SADM going off here and now would only be the trigger heralding a conflagration that could level the Middle East and envelop the rest of the world. Too many fears surrounded the countries, creating a web of hostility that would only suck in everyone around them. Poised on the brink of disaster, Israel would fight to survive against anyone she perceived as a threat. In the current state of affairs, that might be everyone involved.

But to hesitate now in the face of what might be was the worst thing that could happen. The Executioner had been blooded in too many scenarios like the one challenging him now. All the Stony Man teams had: When confronting a foe in what Sun Tzu termed the death ground, hesitation could only get someone killed. If it didn't get them all killed.

Today success could be just as lethal.

The train chugged into position next to the hill and began to pass by twenty feet below and eight feet away. Marshaling his equipment, the Executioner nodded, then led the assault on the train. They ran in single file, angling alongside the train to gain forward momentum while remaining on the treacherous hillside above the top of the cars. Rocks twisted and shot away underfoot.

Bolan threw himself into the air and reached for the top of the eighth car. His breath whooshed out of him as he slammed into the rough metal, and he felt the vibrating echo of the other men hitting the car behind him. The sound was washed away by the turning wheels below.

Forcing away the pain, he rolled over on his knees, swaying with the motion of the train as he gauged the success of the Stony Man teams. Katz and Encizo had landed on the same boxcar he had. James, Manning and Kissinger were strung out on the next one.

The train's steep descent began almost immediately.

Wind ripping across his face, Bolan crawled along the top of the boxcar and lowered himself over the front, dropping onto the narrow coupling as he stretched for the door.

"Striker," Katz called.

"Go," Bolan said.

"We're in position."

"Hit it." Bolan unleathered his silenced SIG Sauer 9 mm pistol and aimed it at the lock as his hand closed around the release lever. He squeezed the trigger three times, feeling metal splinters and sparks drive into the exposed skin of his wrists. The door folded inward as he slammed a shoulder against it. Except for farm machinery, the boxcar was empty. He kept the MP-5 slung over his shoulder. Stepping back out onto the coupling, he tapped the headset's transmitter button. "Manning?"

"Home free, Striker."

"Good enough. Now hit your marks." Bolan moved, holstering his pistol as he stretched for the roof of the seventh car, closing in on the passenger cars. It stood to reason that the freight cars they'd landed on would be empty of terrorists, but they'd detailed the attack to avoid any unpleasant surprises coming back at them.

He hauled himself back up on top of the next boxcar, drew the SIG Sauer and kept it at his side as he jogged toward the front of the train. Keeping to the outside of the boxcar, he stayed where the roof would be most supported. The wind tore at him, driving invisible hooked talons into his skin and clothing, striving to tear him from the train. His footing became more sure as the train leveled off.

He leaped the gap separating the next pair of cars, landing softly on the other side. The doomsday numbers whisked silently through his mind, taking away whatever breathing space they had on the takedown. Discovery was imminent, couldn't be more than a few heartbeats away. And at any moment the Israeli air team could neutralize Grimaldi's and McCarter's striking abilities and leave the ground troops without aerial support.

Restructuring the train and its load from Kurtzman'a descriptions, he visualized the passenger cars in his mind. If at least two dozen passengers had been abandoned as the final assault on Haifa had begun, that left at least twenty plus the missing six from Beirut. The number was more than enough to ensure Rihani had a bargaining position if the train was stopped by someone willing to take the risk of interference.

The Executioner paused at the last of the passenger cars, waving to Calvin James. The Chicago badass nodded and ran on, hurdling the gap between the boxcar and passenger car with the skill of an expert athlete as he raced to the trio of diesel engines pulling the train. Manning had been assigned to the caboose. Katz, Encizo and Kissinger fanned out farther up the line, each choosing his own car to investigate.

Bolan lowered himself to the coupling, moving quickly into the metal embrace of the railed observation area at the end of the car. The wind was blocked away, leaving his balance more intact. Unslinging the H&K MP-5, he tried the door release lever and found it unlocked. He eased it open, peering inside.

The cushioned seats were filled with passengers. Four terrorists were inside with them. One stood directly in front of Bolan's door while the other three were spread out in a relaxed fashion, staring out the windows.

The guard near the door turned slowly, his peripheral vision blocked by his *ghutra*. The Executioner freed his fighting knife from his combat rigging with the flick of his wrist and buried it in the underside of the man's jaw as he stepped inside. Blood cascaded down his fist as he shoved the point toward the terrorist's brain. The man dropped like a stone, drawing the attention of the other people in the car.

Using 3-round bursts, Bolan aimed chest-high at the guards, managing to knock down the first two before they could put their weapons into action. The third man got off a long burst that chewed wooden splinters from the ceiling and drew frightened cries from the hostages. Dropping the submachine gun into target acquisition, the Executioner fired a stream of 9 mm parabellums through the Hezbollah gunner's screaming mouth.

He keyed the headset. "We're made," he said into the mouthpiece. "But this car's free of terrorists." He waved the passengers down to the floor. After making certain the four men were dead, he went on, checking the opposite door before going through.

The numbers were dead-on now and he knew it. Rihani had to know something had gone wrong. He couldn't assume otherwise.

RIHANI JERKED his head around, catching Numair's eyes. The young man gripped the M-16 tightly in his hands. "You heard?" Rihani asked. They were cloaked in the gray shadows of the empty boxcar. The sound of machine-gun fire wasn't repeated.

"Yes."

"Go quickly and check it out."

"Of course."

"And if it's our enemies come creeping out from under their rocks, may God Himself guide your bullets."

Numair let himself out.

Turning back to the row of SADMs spread across the scarred wooden floor, Rihani began setting the switches that would bring them into full, destructive life. For the first time since Jamila had been killed, prayers found their way past his lips. And they were prayers he meant to attend to himself.

THE FIRST BULLET creased Gary Manning's skull as he finished placing the C-4 charge and radio detonator. The next half dozen ricocheted from the metal planks of the stock car behind him. Two of the cows inside the car went down, covered over immediately by the other animals panicking inside the cage area.

The Phoenix Force warrior reacted instantly, rolling forward and grabbing the lip of the support structure under the stock car. His booted feet struck the railroad ties and rattled along until he could pull his weight up from them. He lost his MP-5 in the scramble. Blood ran warm and thick into his hair as he struggled to haul himself hand over hand under the train car along the struts toward the front end. He still hadn't seen the man who'd spotted him. Judging from the angle the shots had come from, someone in the caboose had fired at him.

He ignored the headache that bloomed to full life between his temples and forced away the screaming agony trapped in his shoulders as he held on with his feet and one hand while he unclipped the radio detonator from his combat rigging. Rocks spun free of the track bed and smashed into him with surprising force. The noise of the wheels hitting the rails was deafening, but the explosion of the shaped charge over the coupling holding the caboose to the train was still audible. It started up a new stampede above him as the cows bucked and stamped in renewed fear.

The frayed metal end of the coupling bent as it caught and held for a moment against the tracks before being ripped loose by the weight of the caboose. Dropping speed instantly, the caboose rapidly fell far behind. At least four terrorists were firing blindly from the railed area at the front of the car. The bullets smashed against the metal rails above. Then the caboose was gone, seemingly absorbed by the dust that separated them.

Smiling, tasting the blood from the head wound that trickled across his lips and reeling from the trauma-induced nausea in his stomach, Manning took a deep breath and climbed back toward the end of the freight car. He had to work hard to keep his fingers and boots from being jarred loose by the impacts of the cows' hooves above him. The ground rushed by in a dizzying blur, and he refused to look at it.

His fingers curled around the edge of the freight car's upper deck, and he pulled himself out into the glare of the bright sunlight. The sun was blotted out almost instantly by the thrusting muzzle of an M-16. The dark outline of the terrorist leaning down toward him loomed tall and unforgiving. A burst ripped free of the barrel, burning the Phoenix warrior's cheek as he dodged and tearing into the bottom of his neck where it joined his shoulder.

Reacting instinctively, Manning reached up and locked his hand around the barrel of the assault rifle. Ignoring the burning pain from the superheated metal, he pulled with all his strength. The terrorist pitched forward, following his weapon to the track bed below. His brief scream ended abruptly.

Manning's grip on the freight car was growing slippery with blood as he added his other hand and pulled himself up. "Stupid son of a bitch," he muttered weakly as he got to his feet. "You're supposed to shoot, not aim." He took a deep breath and drew his 9 mm pistol from his hip holster, then stepped up onto the rails along the side of the cattle car to make his way forward.

He hit the headset transmitter. "Striker, this is Manning. The rear guard's been neutralized."

"Confirmed, Gary," the Executioner replied. Autofire rattled in the background.

Manning knew somewhere up there a war was still going on. He hurried as fast as he could.

CALVIN JAMES TOOK a preliminary count of the men inside the engine room as he lay on top of the second engine drive unit. The three men were already in motion after hearing the unmistakable sound of an assault rifle cutting loose. There were no hostages up front, which made his end of things simpler.

A Hezbollah gunner clambered to the top of the second car as James drew his side arm. When the man's head cleared the top of the second engine, James squeezed the trigger and cored a 9 mm parabellum through his forehead. The man's face locked into a deathly expression of surprise, and he fell back down the short ladder onto his companions, causing them all to fall in a wild tangle of arms and legs.

Pushing himself to his feet, James sprinted toward the back of the train. The C-4 had already been placed. He tugged the radio control from his combat harness and thumbed the safety off as he made the leap onto the third engine.

Bullets cut through the air around him as he leaped to the front of the first passenger car. Some of the slugs smashed against the armor covering his back, knocking the wind out of him and spilling him off balance. He came down hard, rattling against the metal roof of the passenger car. The radio control squirted free from his hand and was caught in the slipstream of rushing wind as it skated toward the end of the car.

James lunged forward in pursuit as a ragged line of bullet holes blew through the top of the car only inches from his face. Evidently Encizo's part of the operation had soured, as well. Another bullet, this one from the two Hezbollah gunners pursuing him, slammed into his thigh and numbed his leg. He went down again, falling forward as he closed his fingers around the plastic case of the detonator.

His thumb jammed the button, and he felt the impact of the plastic explosive shiver through the passenger car. He grinned in spite of the pain as he swiveled on his stomach to view the results. As planned, the three driving engines had been blown free of the rest of the train, leaving it powerless to move any farther toward Haifa.

When he saw one of the terrorists lying prone while the other handed him a familiar-looking tube, James knew the kink in his part of the operation wasn't over. He hit the transmitter button on the headset as he began triggering rounds from the SIG Sauer in the general direction of the terrorists. "Grimaldi! McCarter! I got a serious problem here!"

"Go, mate," McCarter said.

"The guys in the engine room carried along a surprise. I'm looking down the barrel of a LAW-80 that's going to take out this first passenger car unless you guys can help out."

"On our way, mate."

James fired the pistol dry and rammed in another clip, hoping he could delay the terrorist's efforts at aiming the weapon long enough for McCarter and Grimaldi to climb down out of the heavens.

JACK GRIMALDI HEELED the F-14 Tomcat over, closing in on McCarter's fighter. The world spun blue and green around him as the cockpit did a full three-sixty and came out of it in a dive that brought them swooping down like hawks toward the train. From his altitude it looked like a narrow ribbon crossing the land.

His head was steady on the control stick, bringing the armament up to his specs. G-force shoved him back against the seat inside the flight suit, making his face feel flat and sluggish. "McCarter," he called.

"Yeah."

"You got the lead. I'm on your wing."

"Fair enough, mate. I'm taking out the front section. That'll leave you the rear."

"Roger."

McCarter thundered down in full-burn.

Grimaldi trailed less than fifty yards off his wing, respecting the Phoenix member's flying ability. The stick felt heavy in his hand. Sensor overlays flickered range readings and tracking cross hairs against his weapons system screen.

Rockets from McCarter's fighter thudded into the primary engine and generated a sudden sheet of orange flame that rose dozens of feet into the air. Grimaldi triggered his own pair of rockets and saw the resulting impact blow the rear diesel engine from the tracks. For a moment flames filled the view from the canopy, then he was through them, pointed once more toward the sky.

"Good shooting, mate," McCarter said.

"I had a hard act to follow." Grimaldi heeled over, spinning to lose altitude and speed as he came about for another pass. The three engines lay across the track in a scattering of burning debris. The forward car in the passenger lineup slammed into the flaming husks with enough force to derail some of the last cars. But it was better than trying to survive a direct hit from the LAW-80's 9 mm warhead.

"We've got company," McCarter said.

Grimaldi checked his own screen and confirmed the eight approaching blips. Seconds later the first of the Israeli jets became visible, streaking silver against the bright blue of the sky. He opened the frequency to Bolan's headset. "We're out of it, Striker, unless you're ready to declare war on Israel."

"Get clear," Bolan commanded.

"Roger." He didn't ask how things were going at ground zero. It would have only wasted time. He was professional enough to realize that, even though the human side of him screamed out to know because his friends were below. "McCarter?"

"Yeah, mate?"

"I feel like a chickenshit here."

"Yeah, but we did our job. Unless you intend to engage the Israeli air force, we got no choice."

"I know. Doesn't make me any happier about the situation." Grimaldi put the jets on full-burn, streaking for the border. He glanced over his shoulder out the canopy. Two Israeli jets followed them as an escort. The other six remained behind, spiraling over the wreckage of the train. He couldn't help thinking they looked just like vultures hanging there. The comparison sent a cold chill down his spine.

ENCIZO SIGHTED down the barrel of his pistol. At the other end of the passenger car the surviving terrorist guard held one of the American women in front of him as a shield. Even as he held the gun unwaveringly on his target, his mind cycled through the information Bolan had shared with them. He recognized the woman from the picture Kurtzman had forwarded from Stony Man Farm. Her name was Jessi Grafton and she was a reporter for a news magazine.

In the picture she had been pretty, confident in a quiet sort of way. Now she was dressed in clothes that didn't fit her, and her hair was a tangled mess. Still, she wasn't crying or struggling to escape, which gave him hope.

The Hezbollah gunner shouted something, screwing the muzzle of his gun more tightly into the woman's neck. Two other terrorists lay in crumpled heaps midway down the aisle. The passengers were down behind their seats, taking cover.

"Jessi," Encizo said quietly, "when I tell you to, I want you to turn to your left and drop as quickly as you can. To your left, away from the gun. Don't answer. Just blink your eyes if you understand."

The woman blinked twice.

The terrorist screamed another warning, shaking the woman as he made his threats.

"Now!"

Jessi wheeled instantly, biting into the fingers of the man's hand covering her mouth, striving to go to her knees.

Encizo's first shot went over the man's head.

The terrorist screamed in pain and anger, trying to bring the woman up and use his gun on her at the same time.

Firing continuously, Encizo stepped forward, watching his bullets strike home in the man's face, neck and chest. The corpse was blown backward, striking the dented wall where the engines had hit.

Encizo reached down for the woman, and she went into his arms slowly, crying mixed tears of fear and relief as he held her and soothed her. "Everything's going to be all right now. You did a very brave thing there." He held her a moment longer, knowing the seconds were disappearing like mist before a summer sun, then gently disengaged himself.

He left her sitting in a seat with another man he recognized from the Beirut list, then jogged hurriedly toward the rear door. James met him as he hit the observation area. Blood stained his teammate's leg. Wordlessly he reached up and helped James down. Together they moved back toward the rest of the train, ready to begin the compartment-by-compartment search while the last few seconds of the clock ticked through to signal the coming Armageddon.

YAKOV KATZENELENBOGEN slung the MP-5 he'd used to clear the terrorists in the passenger car, drew his 9 mm pistol and marched down the aisle. Moving on instinct, his conscious mind concentrating on the whereabouts of the missing SADMs, he put two bullets through each terrorist. Screaming confusion broke out around him. He spoke in Hebrew, trying to soothe the Israeli passengers, but he knew it would take more than words after everything they'd been through.

Reaching the other end of the car, he came out only a few seconds after Cowboy Kissinger had exited his own battleground. Bright spots of blood spotted the weaponsmith's sunglasses, letting Katz know the killing had been up close and personal.

"Your car?" Katz asked.

"Secured."

Katz hit the transmit button on his headset. "Striker?"

"Go."

"Kissinger's area and mine are secured."

"So is mine," Encizo cut in. "And I've got Calvin with me."

"Manning?" Bolan called out.

"Still with you, big guy, sweeping in on an end run."

Katz knew from the weakened tone of Manning's voice that the big Canadian was hurting.

"Spread out," Bolan ordered. "Those nukes have got to be here somewhere. Find them." He clicked out.

Katz stepped hurriedly down the stairs leading to the track bed, Kissinger at his heels. "Rafael, you and Calvin have the west side. Kissinger and I are covering the east."

"Roger, Yakov."

The scream of jet engines overhead drew Katz's attention. He shaded his eyes and watched the circling Israeli fighters above them. Satisfied they were going to do nothing at the moment, he pressed on, holding his submachine gun at the ready.

BOLAN JUMPED across the gap separating the two freight cars, a SIG Sauer in his hand. The MP-5 was strapped across his back, jarring into his spine with every movement. The sudden whine of autofire on either side of the train told him Kissinger and the members of Phoenix Force had their hands full.

His peripheral vision caught sight of a terrorist breaking cover in an attempt to heave a grenade. The Executioner wheeled instantly, firing from the hip, watching as the man fell to the ground and the grenade rolled loose, driving his fellow terrorists from hiding. They were caught in a deadly cross fire between Manning's gun and those of Encizo and James.

When Bolan turned back around to continue on, he had to use the barrel of his pistol to block the swing of the vicious sword aimed at his head. His hand went numb from the impact as he fell backward. The pistol spun out over the edge of the freight car and disappeared.

The loose grenade exploded, throwing shrapnel through the side of the freight car. Roaring with pain, the giant Iranian facing the Executioner swabbed with his free hand at the handful of wounds covering his upper body. The young man was stripped to the waist, wearing only his *ghutra,* pants and heavy black boots. A thin leather cord was looped across his chest, supporting the sheath for the sword. An M-16 lay at the edge of the car, telling the Executioner the man had chosen what the Iranian believed was the surest and fastest way to kill his adversary.

Bolan rolled to avoid the next swipe of the sword, and the keen edge bit into the metal roof of the freight car. He lifted a leg and jammed his boot full into the face of his opponent. The man screamed in pain and fury as blood covered his mouth and neck. He attacked with renewed force, striking with skill and anger.

The Executioner's hand groped for the pistol holstered at his hip only to find empty leather. He rolled backward as his opponent drew back the sword for another swing, coming to his feet with his hands before him.

Stepping inside the long reach of the charging terrorist, Bolan blocked the sword arm with his forearm and slammed the stiffened side of his hand into the man's throat. Corded muscle locked in rage met his hand, effectively blocking the warrior's move. He drew his hand back, holding on to the sword arm, and aimed a heel blow at the man's nose. It flattened and broke under the blow, and blood spread across the Executioner's hand and arm. Then a knotted fist seemed to come out of nowhere and explode against his temple.

Losing the sword arm, Bolan staggered backward, vision clouded momentarily with whirling black comets. He ducked, charging forward in an attempt to take the man off his feet. They crashed to the floor in a rolling pile of kicking legs and pummeling fists.

Bolan felt his lip split under a punishing blow and brought back a vicious right cross that felt as if it broke his numbed hand. Momentarily on top as they came to a halt near the edge of the freight car, he struck the terrorist's face again and again, seeking the tender spots, going for the kill. The sword had been lost somewhere in the struggle.

With a roar of anger the Iranian kicked him back, pinning him against the taller freight car behind him. Dazed from the sudden impact, the Executioner was slow to move as the young giant launched himself at him.

Gathered and lifted from his feet, Bolan felt the breath leave his body as the terrorist attempted to crush him in a bear hug. The Executioner denied the pain, denied the screaming need for oxygen to his bruised lungs, refused to scream with the agony as at least one rib gave way under the crushing force. He reached out, got hold of the man's jaw and skull in his hands and began to exert pressure of his own.

"Now," the man said in wheezing English, "now you will die and Allah will crush your soul as I crush your body."

Reaching into himself for the spirit and fighting heart that had driven him through so many encounters before, Bolan redoubled his efforts. The terrorist's neck broke with the sound of an oak branch cracking.

The Executioner fell with the corpse as the air rushed back into his battered chest. He forced himself to his feet, aware that the numbers on the operation had almost run out. Spotting his missing pistol against the lip of the freight car, he picked it up in his undamaged hand and moved for the next car.

Bolan was dimly aware that the gunfire had come to a stop. He heard Manning's voice over the headset.

"Striker!"

"Go."

"I found Rihani. The bastard's locked himself inside the car between us, and I got a peek through a rip in the wall. He's got the SADMs with him, and from the looks of things, they've been activated."

"Can we still shut them down?"

"If you can get me inside, guy. I'm about done in here."

The Executioner lifted a foot and rammed it into the door, splintering the lock. He stepped inside the gloom, the pistol leveled before him.

Rihani stood before him with the SADMs arranged at his feet like some kind of offering. He was ramrod straight, arms tucked neatly inside his bloodstained sleeves. His black gaze was magnetic, hypnotic, calling to a primitive side of the warrior's soul.

Crimson LED numbers flickered through a countdown on the arming device that linked them together: 57, 56, 55 . . .

"You're too late," Rihani said calmly. "It's over. You've lost."

Bolan raced to the other end of the car and let Manning inside. The Phoenix Force member was covered with blood, and the Executioner had to help him over to the trio of stacked SADMs.

"You can kill me now," Rihani said, "and rob me of the joy of being part of my revenge against the Jews and knowing the passage of the final seconds, but it won't matter."

"It's not over," Bolan replied, holding the pistol steady.

Manning punched buttons on the control box, working like a madman with a controlled precision that came from his years of experience handling explosives. Blood dripped from him and splotched the floor. "I'm in," he said excitedly.

Rihani's eyes wavered from Bolan's gaze, seeking the LED readout. Thirty seconds remained.

"Bypassing now," Manning whispered in a strained voice.

"No!" Rihani screamed, launching himself at Manning's back.

Bolan intercepted the man, using his body to block the Hezbollah leader's mad rush. Wiry strength powered the Iranian's blows, surprising in their ferocity, carrying him over on top of Bolan. Using leverage, the Executioner threw the man back.

Rihani flailed wildly, slammed into the wall, then grabbed for the M-16 lying on the floor.

"C'mon, baby," Manning coaxed in the background as the countdown reached fifteen seconds.

Rihani brought the muzzle of the M-16 up as Bolan tracked on target.

"That's it!" Manning shouted. "The program's been aborted!"

For an instant Rihani's concentration wavered as he looked at the linked SADMs and forgot about the weapon clenched in his hands.

Bolan squeezed the trigger and sent a sizzling round between the Hezbollah leader's eyes. "*Now* it's over."

THE MEDELLÍN TRILOGY
THE **EXECUTIONER**

Message to Medellín: The Executioner and his warriors are primed for the biggest showdown in the cocaine wars—and are determined to win!

Don't miss The Medellín Trilogy—a three-book action drama that pits THE EXECUTIONER, PHOENIX FORCE and ABLE TEAM against the biggest narco barons and cocaine cowboys in South America. The cocaine crackdown begins in May in THE EXECUTIONER #149: *Blood Rules*, continues in June in the longer 352-page Mack Bolan novel *Evil Kingdom* and concludes in July in THE EXECUTIONER #151: *Message to Medellín*.

Look for the special banner on each explosive book in The Medellín Trilogy and make sure you don't miss an episode of this awesome new battle in The Executioner's everlasting war!

AGENTS

The action-packed new series of the DEA.... Sudden death is a way of life at the drug-enforcement administration—in an endless full-frontal assault on America's toughest war: drugs. For Miami-based maverick Jack Fowler, it's a war he'll fight to the end.

TRIGGER PULL

PAUL MALONE

In TRIGGER PULL, a narc's murder puts Fowler on a one-man vengeance trail of Miami cops on the take and a Bahamian kingpin. Stalked by Colombian gunmen and a hit team of Metro-Dade's finest, Fowler brings the players together in a win-or-lose game where survival depends on the pull of a trigger.

**OKLAHOMA'S FINEST—THE MEANEST, TOUGHEST
BUNCH OF ROUGH RIDERS—HIT THE SOUTH OF
FRANCE....**

OKLAHOMA

COMPANY OF HEROES
William Reed

The action-packed, authentic account of America's National Guard
continues in BOOK 2 of SOLDIERS OF WAR.

This time, the focus is on Dog Company—the fiercest unit of the
Thunderbirds of Oklahoma. They are bound by blood and driven
by the fighting spirit that tamed a wild land—and facing tough odds
to save the Allied effort in this exciting World War II action.

Available in July at your favorite retail outlet, or order your copy by sending your name, address, zip or postal code along with a check or money order for $3.50, plus 75¢ postage and
handling ($1.00 in Canada), payable to Gold Eagle Books to:

In the U.S.	In Canada
Gold Eagle Books	Gold Eagle Books
3010 Walden Ave.	P.O. Box 609
P.O. Box 1325	Fort Erie, Ontario
Buffalo, NY 14269-1325	L2A 5X3

Please specify book title with your order.
Canadian residents add applicable federal and provincial taxes.

SOW2-1RR

A HARDWIRED COP
HOT ON THE PAYBACK TRAIL

HORN

ULTIMATE WEAPON

BEN SLOANE

Max Horn is up against a deadly plot. A renegade scientist with an eye for a profit is out to prove he's got what it takes—*maximum* killing power!

With the United Nation's building as a target for this madman's demonstration, Horn has to use all his masterful powers to eliminate the threat.
